Bloodwoven

Book One: The Binding Tenets Trilogy

G.J. Terral

Contents

Dedication — VI

Acknowledgements — VII

Left map — VIII

right map — IX

1. Chapter 1
   Bonds of Hope — 1

2. Chapter 2
   Bonds of Bone — 17

3. Chapter 3
   Bonds of Hate — 31

4. Chapter 4
   Bonds of Blood — 42

5. Chapter 5
   Brittle Hope — 52

6. Chapter 6
   Brittle Bone — 62

7. Chapter 7
   Brittle Hate — 72

8. Chapter 8
   Brittle Blood — 81

9. Chapter 9   92
    Boundless Hope

10. Chapter 10   104
    Boundless Bone

11. Chapter 11   114
    Boundless Hate

12. Chapter 12   123
    Boundless Blood

13. Chapter 13   130
    Burdened Hope

14. Chapter 14   144
    Burdened Bone

15. Chapter 15   155
    Burdened Hate

16. Chapter 16   165
    Burdened Blood

17. Chapter 17   178
    Bitter Hope

18. Chapter 18   184
    Bitter Bone

19. Chapter 19   193
    Bitter Hate

20. Chapter 20   204
    Bitter Blood

21. Chapter 21   217
    Blessings of Hope

22. Chapter 22   227
    Blessings of Bone

23. Chapter 23   236

    Blessings of Hate

24. Chapter 24   243

    Blessings of Blood

25. Chapter 25   251

    Burning Hope

26. Chapter 26   259

    Burning Bone

27. Chapter 27   267

    Burning Hate

28. Chapter 28   276

    Burning Blood

29. Chapter 29   284

    Broken Hope

30. Chapter 30   296

    Broken Bone

Epilogue   311

A Beautiful Tapestry

About the author   316

When you shine, I shine.

Acknowledgements

This novel and story within wouldn't have been made possible without the support of my closest friends, dearest family, and, of course, my supportive wife. MRT, as she requested to be called, did the header images for this novel, bringing unique elements from each chapter to life.

I want to express my deepest thanks to Cristiana "Cru" Leone for bringing my vision to life on the cover, to Dom for your attention to detail and fluidity in making me sound like a capable writer, and, of course, to Jack for taking my blotchy mess of a map and turning it into something really kick-ass.

A special shout-out to the awesome ARC readers who spotted formatting and comma issues prior to release. Thank you for your assistance and patience.

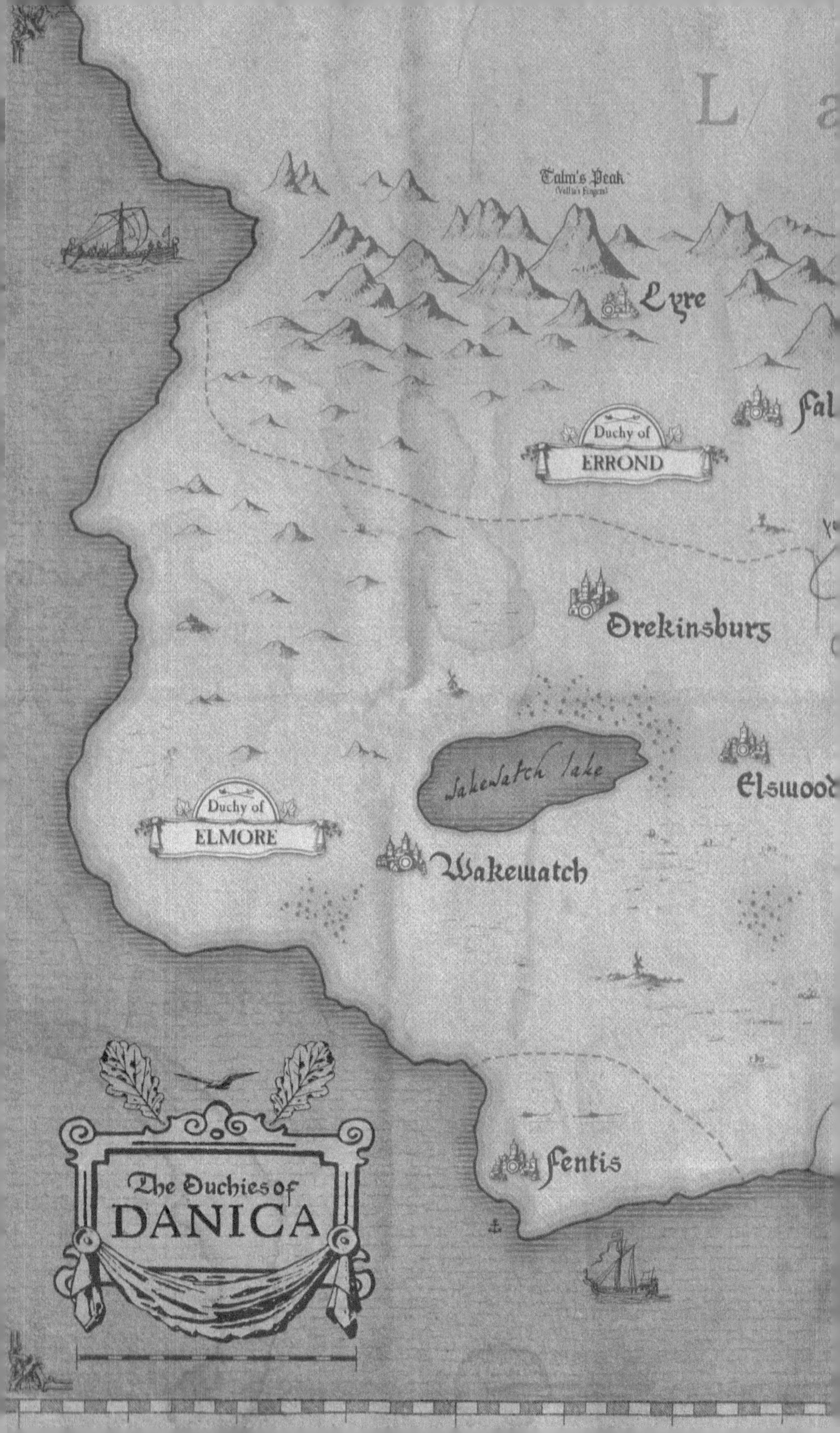

La
Talm's Peak
(Vella's Finger)
Lyre
Duchy of
ERROND
Fal
Orekinsburg
Wakewatch Lake
Duchy of
ELMORE
Elswood
Wakewatch
Fentis
The Duchies of
DANICA

rica
forest pass
Creekside
Hol's Land
Duchy of
HOLLANDER
iversbend
Wellgrove
Duchy of
WELLGROVE
Townsbridge
The
Ferrucium
Beholden to the
King in Ledrica

Chapter One

Bonds of Hope

Nothing good happens on moonless nights. Lin's mentor's words hung in his head, heavy as the crimson cloak on his shoulders. Words which, more often than not, tended to be true. Either Margaret was going to give birth before they made it to the village of Lyre, or Lin was going to murder her insufferable partner, Aemun. And here Lin and his two charges sat, riding through a black forest, a flickering, bouncing lantern's light the lone spark of safety for them. Not the least bit comforting.

Dark, clawing branches overhung the path, and each gnarled finger-like limb threatened to grab Lin from his saddle. And the roots were similarly troubling, protruding unevenly from the road, ready and able to lame a horse if not avoided. But Nebra, his horse, was Ferrucium-trained, just like Lin. Which meant she was good, any and all impurities hammered out long before they'd ever had their first ride.

And, as dangerous as it was, this was the path they'd been set on when Margaret and Aemun, the two he'd been assigned to escort, decided they just had to get to the small village of Lyre tonight. Tonight, of all nights. It didn't matter how vocal Lin had been about the lack of moon; the pair had insisted. Aemun called it foolish superstition, and Margaret, kind as she was, wouldn't take no for an answer. At the very least they should have made camp before sunset.

Lin dared a side glance at Margaret. The road was narrow and choked by the forest, so her and Aemun's shared mount was close enough that either mount tripping meant they'd all tumble. Margaret leaned forward in the saddle, her cheeks expanding and shrinking in forced breaths. Only the Six Gods and their One Shadow knew the pain she might be in. As if feeling Lin's gaze, she smiled at him.

"We can stop if you need to," Lin said, turning his attention back to the dirt road.

"She doesn't want to stop," Aemun said. "But if she squeezes my hands any tighter, I'm not sure I'll keep saddle."

Right. Lin had suggested a wagon. But no, too slow. Too costly. Aemun had seemed eager at the mention, but his opinion shifted at a whisper from Margaret, and before they set off, he'd made it exceedingly clear what Lin's fate would be if harm befell either him or his pregnant partner. Aemun was the grandson of a Ferrucium Weaver, after all. And Weavers held the fate of Binders, like Lin, in their outstretched hands. Appointing assignments. Issuing commands. Communing with the Ladrican King in the north and brokering peace across all of Danica. Not to mention casting judgment on those who broke the Binding Tenets. Weavers were the top, and Aemun's relationship meant his words were as good as spun threads of gold.

"We can make it." Margaret's voice was barely audible, like the whisper of a drowning woman fighting the waves for a single breath. Between the horses cantering, the wind whistling, and the beating of Lin's heart, he barely heard it.

Lin frowned. They *could* make it. That wasn't in question. But could they make it safely? Soundly? Lin wasn't sure. Even if he had been alone, he wouldn't have traveled much past the sun's setting, especially if the moon was hidden. Not even mentioning the increased rumors of untethered massacring some of the more remote villages.

Untethered. Lin shuddered. Even thinking about the magic-twisted once-human creatures sent a chill sinking down his spine.

Lin noticed something in the distance, past the twitching, dancing shadows caused by the orange glow of the lantern. Two specks of light, like eyes, stared at him. His heart pounded harder, and he squinted.

"I... I think I see lanterns ahead," Lin said.

"Do you, or don't you? One with the Sight should know the difference between lanterns and what else might shine in the dark," Aemun said.

Lin snorted and held his tongue. If this had been the first time the man had spoken to him that way, it might've caught Lin off guard. But despite the short time they'd been on the road together, three or four days now, Aemun often spoke in that tone, as if suggesting he was doing Lin a favor by letting *him* escort *them*.

Thank the Six. Without a doubt, the specks were lanterns.

Lin sniffed and frowned. A cloyingly sweet scent carried on the wind, like over-ripened fruit sitting in the sun for too long, but with an undercurrent of rusted iron. He urged Nebra forward, the seed of unease in his gut blooming.

"Just a little further. There are lanterns."

"What would we do without you?" Aemun asked. "You know, I'm still rather surprised they didn't send you with a partner." He pulled their shared mount closer to Lin's. "Aren't you, Margaret? Ehrm, surprised that is?"

Margaret winced and shook her head. Aemun shook his hands, arms still draped around her like he might protect her pregnant belly from view behind his cloak.

The two horses slowed as they came into the dim light shed by the two hanging lanterns marking the edge of the tiny village of Lyre. Worn posts were stamped into the ground, and a short stone wall, no more than knee high, went wide in either direction. As if a wall that low might keep out anything, let alone untethered or bandits.

"You should know how it is," Lin said, "Ferrucium Binders are spread thin as things are. One Escorter per pair is all that's needed to keep the peace." He shrugged. "But, if the last few days haven't proved my worth to you, I don't know that having a partner would change that."

Before Aemun could respond, Lin nodded toward the tightly packed homes. His orders had been simple—take Aemun and Margaret to the Ferrucium hold. But having a few days rest at Lyre would do all of them well. Especially Margaret.

"The baby. It's coming." Margaret alternated between word and breath, and even underneath the warm lantern glow, she looked pale and sickly. Sweat covered her skin, sticking strands of her dark hair across her brow and cheeks.

"Now?" Aemun asked.

"Yes, now!" Margaret hissed the words like a curse.

Lin scrunched his nose as they crossed into the village. Riding in as quickly as they did likely disturbed whatever peace the town had. Lyre, in a few words, was a collection of small, closely packed homes. Few had a porch, while others looked barely built well enough to be considered shacks. Each home bore a single lantern, though not all were lit. The dark forest swallowed the village, wrapping around it with greedy hands. He scanned the thatched roofs, straining his vision to the darker portions of the village where light met shadow and blurred.

"Physiker?" Aemun shouted.

Lin swept from Nebra and rushed to help Margaret from her position. When he reached for her hand, Aemun took hold of Lin's instead and gracefully left the saddle.

His grip was soft and gentle, but his tone was far from it. "Are you just going to stand there staring, *Escorter*, or do you plan to let the mother of my child give birth mounted on a horse?" Aemun frowned and straightened his cloak as he spoke.

Lin studied the way the man moved. Watching him, it was hard to believe Aemun was a Ferrucium Binder like Lin. Even if he wasn't an Escorter, he was still a soldier. Aemun moved like he hadn't had a single hard day in his whole life. And the way he bandied Lin's position around as if it were an insult made it hard not to strike the man, but that would be paramount to striking a Weaver, so far as Lin understood it. Without his help, Lin eased Margaret from her saddle.

"I've got you," Lin whispered.

Margaret nodded weakly, her breaths coming in and out in steady whooshes. "Please... please don't stray far."

Lin felt like he understood her meaning. Or perhaps it was wishful thinking that, despite Aemun's attitude, Lin and Margaret might've become friends on this short journey. They were both Ferrucium soldiers, and both had a love for watching people and describing them. Though Lin often focused on people's oddities, Margaret had, on many occasions, remarked only on the good qualities she noticed.

"We need a physiker, *please*," Lin shouted.

A wrinkle-faced man with a wiry gray beard waddled from beside a trough, a small goat following on a rope that looked a tad too tight around its throat. The man smelled like rancid meat and, when he was close enough to be clearly seen, looked like he'd recently rolled in a mud pit. His hair matted to his scalp in a greasy tangle, and Lin decided if this man were the physiker, he'd help Margaret give birth himself.

Lin approached him, blading his body so Margaret didn't have to be any nearer than necessary. He stared flatly at the man's thick fingers and nose. A nose that looked as if someone had stolen the meat of it, leaving behind sad cartilage and sadder nostrils, as deflated as they were. It was as if someone had, against their better judgment, stolen the piece of his nose that allowed him to smell himself.

Not that the Six Gods or Margaret would smile upon Lin for thinking such things. She'd likely point out that he looked well-loved by his goat and had jovial wrinkles around his eyes. But Lin noted the smell and the nose and knew he'd tell his friend and mentor, Denro, all about the man. The two of them would always trade descriptions of people when they saw each other after long stretches. Between this man and Aemun, he'd have stories for an entire night now.

Lin blinked as he realized the man had been speaking to him. "What?" he asked.

"Sorry sir, I esked iffin I could help yer."

Lin frowned at the man's dialect. "Are you Lyre's physiker?"

"That'd be Pyter Collier. Home 'cross th'way." The man waved, and Lin quickly wheeled Margaret around, rushing her to the larger-than-average building the man had waved at.

"Did you see his nose?" Lin asked.

Margaret clutched his arm tighter and gave a slight shake of her head. But she didn't speak and seemed entirely focused on her breathing.

In, out, in, out. In.

Lin's ass and legs ached, as hard as they'd been riding, and he couldn't help the pang of guilt he felt at thinking about it. If he was this sore, how much worse must Margaret feel?

"Almost there. Aemun, this home," Lin said, jerking his chin toward the wide home near the northern edge of the village.

"Obviously," Aemun said dryly. He'd pulled a wineskin from his saddlebags at some point and took a heavy pull on it as he jaunted over.

"Back here," a wisp of a man called. As frail as he looked, it was a marvel that his voice managed to carry with as much authority as it did. He stood at the back of the building and waved a hand overhead as he slid on a tawny apron. "Wounded?"

"With *my* child," Aemun replied. "I've got her. See to the horses."

Aemun elbowed his way under Margaret's side and sighed as he took the brunt of her weight from Lin.

"Wait. Please," Margaret whispered, hand clutching at the loose cloth of Lin's cloak. She stared at Lin, stared *into* him. She looked as if there was something else she wanted—needed—to say. Sweat covered her brow, sticking her dark hair to her temples and making her shine in the light of the lanterns.

"I won't be far," Lin said. He smiled and nodded reassuringly as he stepped away and toward the horses.

The physiker asked questions that Lin only caught the first clip of, and soon the group disappeared into the home.

Lin would care for the horses and then post sentry as he'd done many nights. Lyre was silent in the peaceful way of a village unbothered despite how they'd ridden in. Tucked into the dense forest as it was, it was one of the northernmost steads on the route southeast to the Ferrucium hold.

Lin rubbed his eyes and stifled a yawn. They really should've stopped at the last town, but Margaret had so vehemently insisted on getting to Lyre that Lin was afraid the pair might abandon him if he'd refused to push the way with them. And he didn't want to think about what the Weavers might do to an Escorter who failed to… well, escort.

'We'll be that much closer to the Ferrucium,' she'd insisted. While she wasn't wrong, it all felt so reckless. He'd heard enough horror stories of Binders struggling to give birth without pushing themselves hard for days on horseback beforehand.

By the time Lin was to the horses, he noticed the flat-nosed man who'd directed them to the physiker's home loitering mere steps away. Whether he was kicking rocks or admiring Nebra's flank was impossible to tell, but he kept far enough away not to be stomped on or bitten. The rope in his hand was slack, and the goat munched at the grass beside the man's feet.

"Second guest in so many days. I'd bet the wee ones are beside themselves," the man said. He scratched the goat's head idly as he spoke, then stared hard at Lin. His eyes were dull, dark beads tucked under thick brows.

But Lin couldn't stop glancing at the man's nose.

"I'm sure," Lin said. He pulled his eyes away, went to Nebra's saddlebags, and rummaged for the feed kept at the bottom.

"Ehrm. Sorry. Realized I didn't introduce myself proper. Alderman Pryor, at your service."

When Lin turned, the man wore a self-proud grin and extended his hand. Lin pursed his lips, held his breath, and shook the man's hand. "Lindel, of the Ferrucium."

The handshake lasted the span of three held breaths. When Alderman Pryor let go, Lin checked his palm to be sure he didn't need to wash it right away.

Villages like Lyre had Aldermen, coordinating efforts from whichever Duke ruled the duchy, who coordinated efforts for the people on behalf of King Lodram. Taxes and tithes and not at all anything that Lin cared about. Every Alderman Lin had ever met thought too highly of themselves for Lin's taste. But how *this* man had earned the title of Alderman was beyond Lin. Another point to share with Denro later. Perhaps he'd traded some of his nose meat for the title.

Lin choked back a chuckle and covered his mouth as if he'd coughed.

"Oh, no doubt. Knew by the red robes and bird on 'em, you lot were Binders. But I didn't expect three... Can't say I've ever seen more'n a pair pass through." Alderman Pryor touched the leather cord around his neck and pulled out a small unadorned metallic disk, a mark of his station, from under his collar. When he let it go, it settled against the crop of gray hair, like a headstone for a sad burial plot.

Lin gave a polite nod and returned to caring for the horses, loosening the first saddle strap. "Well, there are three of us," Lin said, then grunted as the strap came undone with a pull. "As you so keenly noted, because I'm an Escorter. Different role than most. Just here to help them get back home."

"Ehem," Alderman Pryor cleared his throat.

With Nebra's saddle off, Lin moved past the man to Margaret and Aemun's mount and began working the straps of that saddle. Alderman Pryor rotated with Lin, taking a small step as if he might follow him.

"Escorter? So... you aren't... aren't here to take any of the children. Are you?" the man asked, bushy brows knitting together.

The question pulled Lin from his thoughts, and paused his hands on the strap. Ferrucium soldiers didn't *all* have specialized roles, but most did. Escorters, Evaluators, Educators, Envoys, and Enforcers. Lin didn't evaluate children for Ferrucium recruitment. Neither did Aemun or Margaret, for that matter. But most people, even Aldermen, didn't understand the structure of the Ferrucium. And the more Lin had learned about it himself, the more he was sure it was deliberate obfuscation.

"Are there any here that need evaluation?" Lin asked. He kept his tone as flat as possible and didn't turn to face the man.

"Children, you mean?" Alderman Pryor asked.

"Yes."

"Here?"

Lin sighed and turned to face him. "Yes, I believe that is what *you* implied."

"Fair 'nough," the man replied, hand trembling as he touched his chain of office again. "No. No one here needs ter be 'valuated. Least of all children.

Though I think Lenpy here might have a knack for smelling the witchcraft you lot do."

Lin frowned and stared at the goat as Alderman Pryor touched its head. He'd make a note. Lyre needed an Evaluator, though odds were high it wouldn't be for a goat.

As if it had been stabbed or was indignant at Lin's thoughts, the goat let loose a blood-curdling scream. Nebra stomped, her ears flicking before swiveling around to listen to the north wind gusting.

Lin cursed under his breath. He'd let the man distract him, and the Alderman's stench had overtaken something he'd recognized on the wind when approaching Lyre—the tell-tale odor of saccharine rust. The thatched roofs were empty, and the trees at the edge of the village shifted with a fresh, cool wind that promised winter's impending arrival.

Alderman Pryor spoke. Something about the damned goat. *Lerny, Len?*

Lin frowned as the creature wailed again. He spun in a half-circle and noticed the flash of light. So swift, so subtle. Like the thinnest thread ever made had caught the sun and glowed with its warmth—a Binding.

The Alderman stared where Lin's eyes had landed, but he rubbed his eyes, squinted, and eventually shook his head. "What're ya starin' at?"

Lin had learned early on what a boon having the Sight was. A true gift from the Six to see the magic Binders were capable of. Generally known as Bindings, though the types were vast and many.

"Get inside and take that One-whispered goat."

If Alderman Pryor took offense to Lin's foul language, he didn't voice it. He hurried away, looking back after Lin more than he needed to, tugging the rotund goat by the lead around its neck.

Lin glanced toward the medicinary, and the field ahead exploded into thick bands of sun-kissed gold. It was like a swarm of fireflies flew into the air, twisting and spinning, deceptive in its lethality.

Drawing his blade was something Lin typically tried to avoid. As a Ferrucium soldier, he'd had combat training and *magic* training. And as an Escorter, he thought he was good at both. But combat always pressed thoughts into his head better left out. *Will this be the last fight? Will I not finally be able to start a family?*

Well-oiled, his sword was silent as he drew out the fine Ferrucium steel. It was one of the old weapons, forged with magic and given to every capable soldier once they'd completed training.

Lin extended his left arm in front of him. His sword, short and easily wielded one-handed, was in his right hand, hilt up. He'd been taught that forming a Binding, no matter the type, required a *focus*. Using his hollow-ringed pommel as one, he pushed his will and intention into the world like a thread through a needle's eye. At the same time, he pushed forward with his left hand. A simple Weave, like a thick, smooth rope, shimmered into existence and arced horizontally into the Binding flying at him.

They clashed with each other in a flash of light and dissipated into bronze-hued sparks. Lin searched for the source, keeping his arm extended and pivoting. The horses had moved further from him, and the goat shrieked in the distance.

Another flicker of light. Another forcing of his will into the world. Each Binding formed took a toll. They drew on a Binder's own energy, though the theories on why ranged far and wide. All Lin knew was what he'd been taught: Binding is a gift from the Six faceless, founding Weavers who created the Grand Tapestry of the world, and the drain was from their One Shadow. But there was a chance that drain was exactly what this assailant intended. Wear Lin down. It was impossible to know what sort of mental state an untethered might be in when it attacked.

Lin scanned the homes.

Again, a flash of bright, ethereal light arced toward him from his right.

Lin dodged around the magic, racing toward the home it had launched from. As he rushed, the cold air wet his eyes, but blinking the tears away could mean missing a Binding flying for his throat. So stinging as they might be, he willed his eyes to remain painfully alert.

There. He saw it standing in the shadow of a lantern-less shack.

Covered head to toe in stitched-in Bindings, blurred by tattered strings of cloth, was an untethered. There were flat, dull Bindings, Weaves. Sharp-edged ones, Wefts. Then there were the blasphemous Stitches that untethered laced into their flesh. Fell-Bindings, or Stitches, as most who possessed the Sight named them. It made untethered fast, strong, and even more inhuman. This one had wild eyes, Stitches shining in the colored portion. And it stared back at Lin.

Lin slowed his breathing and steadied his hands. It hadn't been guaranteed one of these One-loved abominations might attack, but that was why he was here escorting the pair.

Twin Wefts sliced toward him with a flick of the untethered's shining wrists. Binding without an apparent focus. It was unnatural, unholy. *Unfair.*

A blood-curdling wail tore from the medicinary, causing Lin to snap his attention to the building. Another softer moan followed.

Another untethered? Lin's stomach sank. Then, his right shoulder was warm and wet and screaming in pain. He shifted and avoided the second half of the pair of Wefts that hadn't stopped to wait for his attention to return to the fight.

I'm one half of a whole fool.

Lin rolled his right shoulder and spared a glance at the cut crimson cloth and bloody gash underneath.

The untethered sprinted across the field. Gangly limbs, intricate twisting lines of light just on the surface, like veins of gold, clawed at the earth as it ran on all fours.

It was to Lin in an instant.

The brightness of its Stitched flesh forced Lin to squint, but he straightened his blade and slashed at the creature. It snarled and, with each strike, sent out more Wefts. No dull-edged Biondings from this monster. It meant to kill him.

Lin stabbed, but the untethered caught the blade in its hands. Then, like a beautiful shining mold, Bindings spread from its palms across the blade's flat side.

What the fuck?

Separation was impossible once something was bound to another until the Binding broke, and while Ferrucium steel *could* break Bindings with its edge, excelled at it even, the steel was now stuck in the monster's magic. So Lin released his grip on his hilt and refocused his will, forming a circle with his empty left hand and threading his intention into the world. A flat Weave formed against the pommel of his blade and pushed it forward.

Lin knew better than to hope that would be enough, so he rushed forward and drew the short dagger at his hip.

With a push of Lin's hand, a second, sloppier Weave launched at the untethered's legs.

It growled, low and thrumming like its insides were hollow. Some untethered could speak broken words, remnants of their humanity, but this one seemed feral. Lin's sword bent in the untethered's hands, flexing, then sprung down with a spin and stabbed into the earth.

The untethered had broken its contact, likely to avoid having the same done to its wrists from the force.

With the barest twitch of its legs, the untethered jumped over the low Weave Lin had flung.

Lin blinked, sweat stinging his eyes. His cloak was heavy, his shoulder throbbed, and he couldn't help but look back to the medicinary. If there were a second untethered attack, it would imply intelligence. *Strategy.*

The untethered landed before him in a blur of gray-mottled skin and bright, twisting patterns.

Lin lunged at it. Swordplay hadn't worked. The unnatural, One-loved thing outclassed him in spell craft. So that left running or scrapping, and Lin had always been a scrapper.

Sharp-edged Wefts flew toward him through the air as he rushed to the untethered, but Lin ducked and dodged and got his arms around the creature and squeezed.

Holding onto the thing sent a reverberating hum through Lin's chest like the untethered was a wire strung too tight, and the wind itself strummed it. Partly because the untethered growled and partly because Lin could feel the magic of the Stitches humming against his own body.

The untethered kicked and pulled itself back, but Lin planted his feet. The sweat on the untethered's skin made it hard to keep hold of, but letting go meant dying. And dying meant those two he was sent to escort would do the same. The same would happen to the child being birthed and each and every villager here in Lyre. Dying meant he'd never have the chance to tell Denro about the places he'd visited and the people he'd seen. He wouldn't see what a good mother Margaret would be.

Lin squeezed and, moving his hands to angle it right, pushed the tip of his dagger into the untethered's side.

The untethered spoke nonsense. Its words were as knotted and unintelligible as the arcane light pierced into its flesh.

Sharp pain from the already wounded shoulder spiked as the thing sunk rotten teeth through Lin's cloak. The fabric stopped the worst, but the pressure was enough to bring spots dancing in Lin's vision.

Lin squeezed tighter. The untethered bit harder. The world spun, and then they were on the ground, Lin on top but struggling to remain there.

Lin moved his head away from the untethered's mouth and then headbutted the thing. Once, twice, three times. His sword rested in the grass too far away to reach, and the dagger was lodged in the monster's side.

The untethered's breath was hot and rancid, and between that and the head-butts, Lin verged on unconsciousness.

Lin screamed. Using the creature's neck as a focus, he threaded the needle of his will into the world once more and created a Weft so thin he was like to cut himself forming it.

The Weft sunk in slowly. Breath by breath. It looked like the untethered's flesh resisted it momentarily, sparking. Then the blood welled up, that same sickly sweet smell Lin had caught on the wind earlier rising with it.

The untethered kicked, flailed, hissed, spat, and writhed against the sharp magic, but with its hands pinned, all it did was let the Weft bite deeper into its neck. A final twitch, then it was still.

Lin slumped over. Heavy breaths puffed out like clouds in the cool air, disturbed by the steam from the untethered's blood. He looked around, but if there were more monsters hiding in the darkness, they didn't make themselves known. In the scattered islands of thatch and lanternlight, faces appeared, peering toward Lin. Children clutched tightly. Partners holding each other. Villagers who didn't know what the sounds of combat had been.

To those without the Sight, a fight had occurred, but they had no idea this... *thing* that looked so human was a monster driven by madness. Lin shifted his weight, rising unsteadily to his feet, and his shoulder throbbed.

They'd need to burn the corpse. Give the untethered a chance to plead its case to the Six above, but sure as Lin was a Ferrucium Binder, the One whispered this thing's forgotten name. *No doubt about that.*

Lin rolled the body to the side and pulled his dagger out, the metal blade flaking with specks of ruined metal. *Fuck.* He groaned and slid it into the leather at his waist. Then he found his Ferrucium steel blade, no worse for wear.

There was one positive thing about the village's size—it wasn't far to limp to the medicinary. Unfortunately, the short distance meant Lin didn't have time to plan for if there was another untethered within that had caused that terrible scream.

Lin rested his hand on the door, sucked in a breath, and leveled his sword.

The back door creaked open with a push, and Lin shuffled into the candle-lit hall.

Aemun stood in the center of the room, a dagger flashing in his hand and a look to his eyes just as dangerous.

A woman, pale and dark-haired, stood across from him. Her face was twisted in rage and fury, and tears streaked in a layer of dust on her face. *Second guest in so many days.* Wasn't that what the Alderman had said?

"Where were you?" Aemun spat the words at Lin. "*Escorter.*"

The woman shifted as if to run through the door. She didn't have any Stitches visible on her exposed flesh, and her mouth screwed like she planned to say something. But Aemun moved with her.

"She killed her. Attacked us right after Margaret gave birth."

"Killed her?" Lin whispered.

Shadows danced along the unadorned wall at the far end of the room. Cots lined the closest wall with cabinets resting overhead. Blood-soaked sheets were bundled at the foot of the nearest cot, draping onto the floor beside. Margaret lay amid it all, her face pale, eyes open and unfocused. A line across her throat like a grotesque necklace. She had an unmoving bundle in her arms, swaddled in the same blood-stained sheets.

Lin sucked in a breath.

"Help me kill her. *Kill her*," Aemun choked out.

"What?" Lin asked.

The physiker was nowhere to be seen.

"Are you suddenly deaf?" Aemun shouted.

Lin stumbled further into the room and leveled his blade.

The woman's hair was as dark as Margaret's, her skin just as pale, and she had streaks of blood along her forearms and face. She shook her head.

"I didn't—"

"Shut up!" Aemun hissed. He pulled his right hand up and started to form a slender, sharp Weft.

It didn't make sense. It couldn't make sense.

"I... An untethered outside attacked me," Lin said, looking back at Aemun. He blinked to stave off the tears that stung his eyes.

"She pretended to be wounded, lying in a cot, and attacked us. Killed Margaret." Aemun leaned over, pulled Margaret close, and breathed in deeply through his nose. Stifled sobs shook him.

"And the babe?" Lin whispered. His eyes felt heavy as they rested on the small, soundless bundle.

"*Kill* her."

"I will not die here for your crimes." The woman swallowed and adjusted her stance.

"She... she doesn't look untethered." Lin looked down at his sword and then at the woman. "Where is the physiker?"

"Did the monster knock the sense from you? I'm telling you, *she* attacked *us*! Do your duty!"

"I... I need to understand first. Where is—"

"You had *one* task. To safely escort us. My grandmother will be hearing of your *many* failings."

Aemun took a step towards the woman, her back against the opposite wall now.

Lin moved faster than he thought himself capable. In a blink, he broke Aemun's Weft and pushed the man back. He spun at the same time, sending out dull, flexible Weaves. Then he imagined, *envisioned*, the knot of the Weaves binding the woman's wrists and ankles together.

She didn't seem to possess the Sight and apparently felt the thrumming shift in the air too late to react. The Weaves caught her as Lin intended, knocking her to the ground.

Lin turned back to Aemun and leveled his sword at the man who had sprung back at him; dagger pointed at Lin's throat.

Then, the bundle in Margaret's arms cried, and the soft whimpers of a newborn carried through the room. Lin opened his mouth, closed it, and watched Aemun step back and look down at his child. *He had failed them, failed Margaret.*

"Move aside," Aemun whispered.

"No," Lin said. "Not yet."

Chapter Two

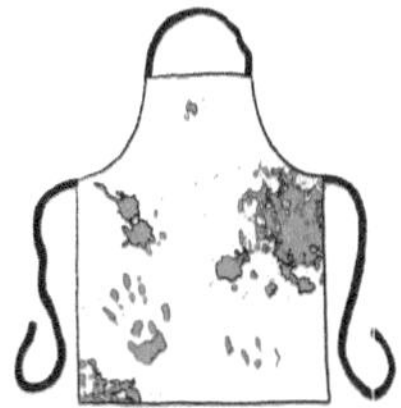

Bonds of Bone

Aemun jerked left and then stepped right, but Lin moved with him.

"Please take your child," Lin whispered. He wanted to look at the woman who'd slumped to the floor, but he didn't dare take his eyes off Aemun.

"Aemun," Lin said.

"Move." Aemun's word was shaped like the dagger he held.

Lin shifted so he could see the restrained woman. Her eyes were so full of hatred, brimming with tears so black in the dark room that they must've welled up from some wicked, bottomless pit. But Lin wasn't an executioner.

Steel flashed with Aemun's fist, and Lin pulled his chin back. But he couldn't step back, not without tripping on the woman. Aemun's breath was warm with wine on Lin's cheek, and the blacks of his eyes were as small as the fine tip of the man's dagger.

"I tell you to kill her, and you ask me why. I move to do so myself, and you stand in my way."

Lin swallowed and let his arms fall to his sides. Accidentally stabbing Aemun wasn't something he'd feel good about. Even if the man was a prick. "If she is guilty—"

"She is! I watched her do it!"

The child's whimpers had turned into full wails, and the woman on the floor struggled against her magical restraints. "It was *him*. I swear on my name, it wasn't me."

"Then the Weavers need to judge it so... Please. Let me see to this. Take care of your child. Please. If... When the Weavers find her guilty, you will have your vengeance. As Ferrucium soldiers, it isn't our place to kill indiscriminately."

"You act as if I didn't see her do it with my own eyes!" Aemun's hand shook, and his eyes danced. His mouth hung open as he looked down at the writhing bundle. His lips slowly formed a thin line, and he gently tapped the dagger's flat against Lin's chin. Once, twice, three times, pulling away on the final pat.

Lin exhaled, and the tension in his shoulders faded, replaced by the stinging throb of the bite wound.

"Judgment is right. Judgment *would* be fair. But what is right and fair about attacking a woman as she gives birth? You say an untethered attacked you? At least you saw the monster for what it was when it did. For me, it was too late! For Margie, it was *too late*!" Aemun hissed the final word and sheathed his dagger. He turned and scooped up the baby, blooded sheets and all. Pulling the sheets caused Margaret's corpse to slide, head lolling to the side and staring blank eyes toward Lin.

Lin had failed. He didn't need Aemun to remind him. His failure rested there, bundled in the man's arms. There had been a joy in his heart knowing that these three would have a family, *be* a family, even if Aemun was intolerable.

How often had Lin told Denro he'd thought about finding a partner and starting a family? *Too many to count.* Lin had been envious of what Aemun and Margaret might have. But with envy came the horrible pang, knowing that this child would be motherless or might never know how kind of a mother it'd had.

The restrained woman started weeping, hard, angry cries that made Lin pause.

"How?" Lin asked, breaking Aemun's gaze from his child. "How did she kill her so deftly only to be stopped moments after the deed?" Lin asked. It wasn't a fair question. Not now, but it was one that had to be asked. Aemun had been the only one of the two with a blade visible.

"For lack of other words, you call me a liar," Aemun whispered.

"I... I failed you. But mostly her." Lin pointed at the corpse. "I'm calling you nothing. But the Weavers will hear the words from the mouth of the accused. As is customary. And they will want to hear from the witnesses, no?"

Aemun frowned and nodded, eyes burning like fire straight at Lin.

"Physiker?" Lin called.

"Hiding. Hid when that *bitch* attacked us." Aemun sat on the cot's edge, trying unsuccessfully to stop his child's cries. He stared at Margaret's corpse like a man might while praying. He stared as if staring were the same as praying or that doing either could bring Margaret back.

The child cried louder. Maybe it cried for the loss it didn't even understand. Lin didn't know much about newborns. *Did they usually cry this much?*

Lin had never had someone like Margaret for himself. He couldn't imagine what Aemun was thinking or feeling.

Not that Lin made it a habit to attack Binders, but this woman had done a poor job, all things considered. If Lin had done this, he would've taken out the man first, as a woman just having given birth was defenseless when it came to wielding Bindings. But Aemun looked well enough, aside from the scrapes on his knuckles and the irritated scratch going from the bottom of his ear to the underside of his jaw. Lin stared at Margaret's corpse again, then looked away when he noticed Aemun looking up at him.

"Physiker!" Lin called, moving through the doorway. "The trouble is over for now. Please come out."

Whispers preceded two sets of steps, and then a heavyset young man with shoulders broad as a bear's rounded the corner. A lean graybeard shuffled behind him, the same wispy man from earlier, a tawny apron streaked with red over his torso and a cane helping him limp along in one steady hand.

"We want no trouble," the large one said. His curled, black hair was tied back to hide his face. Judging by his manner, he could likely give trouble better than he took it.

"I agree. I've had my fill and then some," Lin whispered, stripping out of his cloak and tunic and wincing as bits of fabric underneath caught in some of the caked blood of his wound.

"Oh. Nasty slice there," the old man said, thin lips drawing into a frown.

Lin nodded. "And a bite like to get infected if it isn't cared for. One of you stitch me up if you would, and the other... watch her." He nodded at the woman prone on the floor.

The big lad grunted and crossed the room. Lin couldn't have missed how the man's eyes drifted to Aemun. A side glance so sharp and cold it would be a mystery whether it cut or froze first, just under a layer of fear.

Aemun left the room without a word or glance. His head hung low, child tight in his arms.

"He gon' be alright?" the older man asked.

"I wouldn't be," the young man replied, sitting on the cot, the palm of his hand on the flat of his cheek.

"Dunno," Lin replied.

"More worried about the child. Without the mother, feeding and all," the old man said.

Lin nodded and winced as the first stab of many found roost in his shoulder. Stitches hurt almost as much as the initial slice since the physiker used no numbing agent. Odds were, he hadn't offered it because charging Binders for care was frowned upon and, in some duchies, wholly illegal. But that didn't mean you had to offer premium care.

"Surprised you lot don't just," the physiker said as he waved his hand and wiggled his fingers, "heal yourself up with the magic."

"Breaks old oaths. Binding Tenets, we call them."

"Seems like a waste," the younger one said. He kept his eyes low.

"It is to some." Lin exhaled through clenched teeth as the physiker snipped the final stitch and pressed a bandage firm onto the wound. "But madness, *untethering*, comes from doing that. Better to not tempt the One."

"Might've saved her if he had done it, no?"

"Herm," the physiker said.

"What?" Herm asked.

"Margaret wouldn't have wanted that," Lin said, glancing at the corpse. "We are taught early on that it is better to die tethered, tied to the Ferrucium and the Grand Tapestry than risk Stitching ourselves and untethering. On top of it being blasphemous. Bindings... most are temporary. But Stitches? They affect the *Six's* tapestry. Ruining it with permanent changes."

"It's like knowing how to mix poisons and not doing it to avoid breaking the Duke's laws."

Herm shook his head, curls bobbing at the motion. "He said healing his wound would break laws. How's that the same?"

"The concept is the same." The physiker stretched his back and looked towards the bloody cot where Margaret's corpse rested. He walked to a basin set against the wall and scrubbed his hands.

Lin sighed. They'd need to set a pyre. There was a chance Aemun was already about that task, but he'd need to double-check. "Physiker," Lin said.

"Please. Call me Pyter." Pyter stretched and pulled the apron over his head, folding it in his hands and seeming to weigh it as if keeping this specific one might not be something he wanted to do.

"Did you happen to see any of what occurred? Or hear it?"

Pyter frowned and looked down at the woman. "We really shouldn't say."

"Whatever you might've seen, I'll ensure neither she nor the other will raise voice or hand in response." Lin watched the restrained woman. Her head hung chin to chest, and her stare rested even lower.

Pyter nodded and breathed in deeply. "That one had been here, resting in a cot, complaining of a sore chest. Then you lot came in. The woman was ready to give birth, and the baby came quickly enough. Quicker than most, truth be told. Sickly looking and pale. Didn't cry... not a good sign. I went... Well, I went to mix a tincture to help the after-birthing pain and a separate one for the child to see if it might liven. I heard harsh whispers, but who was doing it? Hard to say. Next thing I know, two people were screaming, and when Herm rushed around the corner, the man you were with yelled at him. Screaming bloody murder. Real surprise seeing the baby pull through. Sad business either way."

"I'm truly sorry for any trouble we might've caused," Lin said.

Herm snorted and shook his head, straightening his back.

"What?" Lin asked.

"Can't say I've ever heard a Red apologize for the trouble they caused."

A Red. It had been some time since someone had called Lin that to his face. Even Ferrucium soldiers knew it was meant to insult them. Lin looked back down at the woman and clenched his jaw. There wasn't a chance he'd likely change the young man's views anytime soon, and he'd need to do something with her. "Can't say I've passed through Lyre before. Didn't notice a church." Lin pulled his shirt up and pressed the bandage harder underneath the cloth.

"Is there a question hidden somewhere in that statement?" Pyter asked, letting his apron fall to the floor and pushing it to the wall with the end of his cane.

"Is there a church I could go rest and pray at?" Lin clarified, slipping back into his cloak. "Maybe keep her there and out of your hair?"

"Not dressed up like some of the bigger towns, but I can take you to it." Herm rose from the cot and looked down at the bound woman.

Lyre couldn't have had more than forty spread homes and buildings, most of which rested close to the road. Simple buildings, all of them, and the same could be said of the church. From the outside, the building looked like it had been built before the village, and warm light leaked out from under the door. Three rows of pews, cut in half by the lane leading to the dais, marked six sections of seating. Stained glass windows made the candlelight look alive, each window depicting a separate member of the Six Founding Weavers. Though faceless, they each represented an aspect woven into the fabric of man. Cunning, wrath, wisdom, truthfulness, mournfulness, and dullness.

Lin settled into the empty front pew and set the bound woman beside him. Her Weaves held her arms tight to her sides, and they shimmered as he set her down.

"If it were up to me, there would have been more discussion," Lin whispered. "Aemun was acting odd. But things don't look good for you."

Sitting in a church beside a woman accused of murder hadn't been what he expected his night to turn into. As often as he referenced the Six, he wasn't a regular attendee of sermons due to his role as an Escorter, and based on some of the other more dubious traits the Six embodied, he wasn't sure if he *should* be.

"Why won't you speak in your defense?" Lin asked.

Her chin sank to rest above her chest, and she closed her eyes. "There is nothing more to say."

Lin exhaled. Her voice had sounded so brittle, like over-cooled iron. A flash of anger sparked in his chest.

"Margaret didn't deserve what you've given her. I doubt the Six will have mercy on you when telling the One of your crimes."

"I'm sure their voices will go raw, listing my crimes, if they have voices at all. But as long as the list is, her murder will not be written on it."

Lin tightened his knuckles and squeezed his eyes. "You claim innocence?"

"What do you think?" she snapped.

"I can't help you if you won't help me."

"The help you could give me was decided years ago. Decided when that crimson cloak was first rested on your shoulders, and you swore to the Six false Gods that you'd serve the Ferrucium."

Lin weighed her words. There was a chance she meant she didn't think he'd take her word over another Ferrucium Binder's. Or perhaps that she had, in some way, broken the Binding Tenets. Or that there was some shortcoming in what Lin could envision. What if this woman and Aemun knew each other, and she was a spurned lover?

"False Gods? So you are guilty?" Lin asked.

Like a waterskin spilling out entirely, she sunk deeper into herself and shrugged.

They sat in silence for a time. Long enough, when Lin turned at the sound of the opening door, his body ached more than it would have if he hadn't rested. His legs were tight, his back doubly so.

"Help me... please." Aemun dragged the last word out, and Lin wasn't confident the man hadn't been talking to the Six. His eyes were bloodshot, and dark bags had formed, made all the worse by his high cheekbones and fair skin.

Drifting on the wind was the familiar scent of smoke.

"You made the pyre?" Lin asked.

Aemun nodded, and his eyes locked on the woman. The entire time Lin had sat there, she hadn't moved. And even now, she sat motionless.

"Stay. If you try to run, you'll be caught. If you exit the safety of this haven as a funeral for the woman *you* killed is taking place, you'll be thrown onto the pyre." Lin spoke more for Aemun than he did for himself, but these things had to be made clear. "Nod, if you understand."

Her chin quivered, raised a hair's breadth, and fell back to her chest.

It was a terrible hour for a pyre. Clouds hung heavy in the sky, threatening rain. What had started as a cold breeze blowing from the north earlier in the night had turned into the sort of weather that would leave frosted dew on the grass come morning.

A field behind the medicinary, which appeared to have seen many pyres based on the circles where grass refused to grow, was lit by the warm glow of embers not kindled fully to flame yet.

"Where is she?" Lin asked.

Aemun jerked his chin, and together, they went into the medicinary. Margaret was off the floor and on the cot nearest the back door. Herm, the broad young man, sat on the cot beside the body and, when Aemun entered, nodded.

"Lin, please help him carry her," Aemun said. His voice was hoarse, and his hands trembled. He kept the small, tightly wrapped bundle in his arms and pulled the baby closer to his chest. It had stopped crying, but Aemun carried it like he worried the peace wouldn't last long.

"Gentle," Lin whispered. As much to himself as Herm.

"I'm a gentle fucking giant," Herm swore under his breath as he took the edges of the sheet near Margaret's head and pinched it up to form a carrier and shroud.

Lin exhaled sharply from his nose and moved to pinch the sheet near her boots. But he noticed a sheet of parchment no larger than half his hand width. It was stained red and stuck to the fold of her cloak. Lin pulled it away.

Wellgrove. It was the only legible word, the ink ruined by blood and smeared. He'd have to ask Aemun about it. Wellgrove was a sprawling city that housed Duke Wellgrove's estate and wasn't exactly on the way to the Ferrucium. But given Aemun's lineage, there was the chance that he had a meeting planned with the Duke, if the missive was even his.

"Going to grab it?" Herm asked, meaning Lin's end of the makeshift litter.

Lin looked up and nodded, placing the parchment in the inner pocket of his cloak. "I got it."

They carried the corpse, blanketed in a sheet stained as red-brown as her cloak, to the fire. Here, she would turn to ash and be worked into the tapestry of the sky, to be rewoven into her next life. Nobody seemed to watch him and Herm as they carried the body.

Pyter stood at the edge of the clearing, leaning on his cane, a folded scrap of cloth in his other hand. Aemun was at the edge of the pyre, watching the pulsing embers until Lin and Herm got close enough for him to watch them. The spectacle had drawn out some of the citizens of Lyre, and a young woman with dark skin and bright eyes had started singing the Mourning Ballad. Another villager at the edge of the clearing joined with a deep, bassy voice, and others took up the tune. It was an easy, sad song that even children learned early on.

Aemun nodded when Lin was close enough to walk onto the pyre, and Lin and Herm placed the makeshift cot down. Dried wood and leaves were stuffed under and around the body at random intervals. Aemun, clutching the newborn tight with one arm, placed most of the kindling. Each placement drew out another whisper from him, so low only he, the Six and One, and the corpse could hear what was said. Once the fire stoked to life, Aemun knelt near enough that he had to be hot despite the cold air.

When he finally rose, tears streaked his cheeks, but his expression was flat, and his eyes appeared unfocused. "Where is she?"

"Who?" Lin asked, knowing full well who Aemun meant.

"I don't mean my murdered partner, do I? Or the child I hold in my hands. So, who do I mean?"

Lin stared at the flames consuming Margaret's body and swallowed hard. "Where we left her." It wasn't Lin's grief to feel, not in the same way, but it ate at him from within. As if her spirit pressed on his chest, it was nearly impossible to take full breaths.

Aemun's eyes went from Lin's face to his hands to the space past Lin. "Bring her from the church. Please. Do this thing for me, seeing as you failed to protect Margaret. Do this, and I won't tell the Weavers of your failure."

Lin sniffed and ignored the comment. Hurt men say hurtful things. "I won't. If there were a motive behind this, the Weavers would want to know of it."

"Then look the other way as I drag her out." Aemun moved to step around Lin, but Lin followed.

"A Binder has been killed. Questions asked by those wiser than us are necessary!"

"Binder? My partner, my *bound* partner, has been killed. We should be beyond questions!"

Lin closed his eyes. The closest villagers had gone silent, the mournful song tattering and nearly coming undone until Herm picked it up from behind them, deep and gentle. If Lin knew Aemun better or had been with the pair escorting them for more than a few days, he might consider it. The One knew how badly he'd treat someone if they hurt Denro.

"I understand..." Lin started.

"How could you? I know of men like you, Lindel. You're *unbound*. You've no partner. No one would mourn you if it had been you who died and not her!"

Aemun's left fist looked clenched as tight as his jaw, the space between him and Lin as narrow as his eyes. Lin kept letting his eyes drift to the scratch running down the man's jaw, red and bright in the dancing firelight.

"Tonight, I've lost a woman I might've soon considered a friend. And I won't meet her again until I take my place in the Tapestry. I don't want to lose you too. And as Ferrucium soldiers we have duties that transcend personal grievances. One of our own has been murdered, and questions will need to be answered. But you still have your child. See to its needs."

"Go fuck yourself," Aemun snarled, turning away from Lin and approaching the fire. "Let us go to the Weavers and let them judge the both of you."

***

The pyre burned long enough that it was like the embers and ash floating up had painted the heavens in streaks of orange and red. Most of the villagers had returned to their homes in the early hours of daylight, and now only Alderman Pryor remained near the pyre's remains.

"Sad state of things," Alderman Pryor whispered. Behind him, munching away on a dry leaf, was the goat. "But, knowing you two were busy mourning and dealing with all this, we had that other fellow you killed buried. Our woodsman handled it."

Lin blinked and licked his lips. He hadn't forgotten about the fight; his shoulder wouldn't allow that. But he had forgotten to take care of the corpse. "The Weavers will hear about the help given to us today."

The Alderman gave a yellow-toothed grin and scratched his chin. "That woman in the church, she really killed that other gal you two had with you?"

"Seems like it," Lin whispered, looking over his shoulder at the ramshackle church. The three windows on this side of the building showed the representations of dullness, mournfulness, and wrathfulness. Each was a lone, dark figure with limbs in various positions.

"Baaa," the goat bleated.

"And we saw to your horses. Well-trained things," Alderman Pryor mused.

"They are." Lin stretched and watched the Alderman rub his hands together and blow clouded breath into them.

Lin sighed, fished into the purse at his waist without a preamble, and brought out two marks. "We appreciate that you didn't have to do much of what you did. Now, related to our first conversation."

Alderman Pryor's grin fell from his face, leaving only the awful flat nose and a spark of suspicion in his wet eyes.

"I'll ask again. Are there any children here who the Ferrucium needs to send an evaluator for?"

"Baaaa."

"None," the Alderman said.

"And if I escort this woman and Binder and get back within the fortnight, when I have proper time to check your words against the truth, the same will be true?"

"The Six know it will be."

Lin flicked the two coins gently into the air, and the Alderman had a hand on one but fumbled them both in his attempt to catch the second.

True to the man's words, the horses were both grazing on the opposite side of the church, barely glancing at Lin as he approached the building. Inside, a woman dressed in various colored sheets of silk and velvet, six different specific colors—seven if counting the black thread stitching it all together—moved from candle to candle, lighting them. Red like berries crushed under the heel, blue like the midday sky, purple like a healing bruise, green like ancient moss, yellow like wildflowers, and orange like honey.

The accused, wrapped in glowing Weaves, was right where Lin had left her. She glanced up as Lin approached. Imagining her praying through the night for some sort of salvation was too easy, and she had ruddy tear streaks down her cheeks as if she'd spent most of the night weeping.

"We'll leave and take you to face the Weavers' judgment. Nod if you understand."

She nodded.

"If you try to flee, Aemun will be in his rights to take your life. Nod if you understand."

She nodded.

"You will ride with me, and if you killed a Binder, as you are accused of doing, that means you yourself are likely capable of Binding or have some small talent for it. Assuming this is true, you should know I have the Binding Sight. No Binding will be woven into existence before me without my eyes seeing it. Nod."

Her nod was slower, warier, but eventually came as her eyes burned into his.

"And if it is found that you are innocent, in some way, I will fight to see justice."

Lin lifted her and walked her out of the building. She smelled like travel and sweat, and where his hand rested below her elbow, he felt taut muscle.

Aemun was waiting by the horses as they exited the church.

"Think they have any horses here?" Lin asked as much to test the man's temperament this morning as it was to say hello.

"Not likely. And even if they did, I wouldn't waste coins on a horse for someone who won't be alive to ride it for much longer."

"She'll ride Nebra then."

Aemun shook his head. "Make her *walk*."

"Up you go," Lin whispered.

She stared at him for a moment. "No. I'd rather walk."

"I'll help you up, but I won't argue this."

Getting her into the saddle proved harder than Lin initially expected. Between her unwillingness to actually ride the horse to the way she squirmed and fought any time his hands drifted too close to her back, it became a task that seemed less and less worth the effort. Eventually, she was atop Nebra, glowering, but bound hands clasped to the reins.

"And what's to keep me from fleeing?" she asked.

"Nebra won't listen to you. And honestly? You don't seem like the type." Lin whispered the last part and glanced around to make sure Aemun wasn't within earshot.

As if his worries over whether the man could hear him voice his doubts made Aemun manifest, his voice carried back to Lin. It dripped with condescension. "Since you won't make her walk, do me a favor, *Escorter*." Aemun stalked over and pressed the bundle containing his baby toward Lin. "Can't ride and carry her. So hold her with more care than you did my deceased lover. Don't let *her* die."

Lin pulled the bundle close to his chest. Her eyes were closed, and she looked asleep, wispy light blonde hair frizzing from underneath the wrap Aemun had her in. He'd seen Ferrucium women strapped with carriers for their babies before, but he doubted Lyre, of all places, would have any craftsman or weavers dedicated. And he didn't have time to ask as Aemun mounted his horse and urged it forward.

In the early morning hours, Lyre looked smaller than it had the night before. Especially as fewer people were afraid to venture from their homes. But not a child was in sight. Lin chewed on the inside of his mouth and led Nebra with one hand, cradling the child with the other.

"How did you feed her?"

Aemun looked back and frowned. "Goat milk."

The accused killer groaned, but when Lin looked up at her, she was looking away into the distance. Surely, milk was milk. Wasn't it?

Lin stared at the baby's face. "Maybe we find a wet nurse."

"I tried. Claimed not to have any here." Aemun shook his head. "Filthy lowborn liars, the lot of them."

"Next town, then," Lin whispered. The baby wriggled, and Lin pulled her tighter to his chest. "What name have the Faceless Six blessed you with?" he said, even softer.

"Keep up. The sooner we get to the Ferrucium, the sooner we get rid of our burdens." Aemun said it so harshly that Lin was sure *he* counted as a burden to the man.

Chapter Three

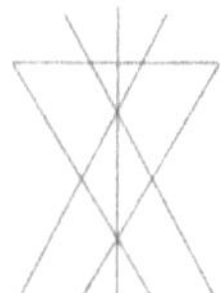

Bonds of Hate

"Hurry yourself," Lin called back to the prisoner. She'd been allowed to step into the brush to relieve herself and had been aside far longer than any previous stops.

The path they were on was a main road, upkept by one of many dukes beholden to King Lodram, but Lin couldn't recall which particular duke was to blame for the current rutted, uneven stretch. Aemun, atop his horse, was strides ahead. In the two days since they'd departed Lyre, the man hadn't spoken. Not to Lin, the woman, or even soft mutterings to his child.

Lin turned at the rustling of foliage as the bound woman emerged onto the path. Her hair was a tangled mess with leaves and sticks emerging, and dirt lined her cheeks.

On the first night, Lin had decided that having both her hands and arms held by Weaves was unnecessary and dangerous if she somehow fell off Nebra. So he'd broken the soft Bindings around her arms so that if she *did* fall, she might break it with more than her face. But she hadn't thanked him, and it had earned a literal growl from Aemun.

Lin yawned. He hadn't slept since departing Lyre, not fully. Not with Aemun's demand for vengeance and the chance that Margaret's accused killer might only be waiting for them to let their guard down. Though Lin doubted that.

The woman cleared the brush, using her elbows to cover her face from the sharp-pointed leaves.

"Have you been to Fallo before?" Lin asked, guessing none would respond except the newborn slung across his chest in a wrap carefully made from his cloak. She cried soft, sad whimpers that made Lin regret not stuffing scraps of cloth into his ears when making the sling. Aemun had refused to use his own cloak for the project, insisting his cloak was a non-standard issue and of a quality imported from some eastern island.

"I have," Lin whispered to the baby as if her cries had been in response to his question. "But it's been a while."

The baby squirmed.

"We'll find you some food."

She squirmed more, whined lower, and seemed all around unhappy. Lin couldn't help but think how different it would be if Maragert were still around.

Nebra nickered off to the side, her large eyes and sensitive ears swiveling towards him. At least he had her firm presence if nothing else. Lin couldn't recall another time he'd been less comfortable on an escort—not a single one.

Lin looked down at the woman's worn, mud-covered shoes and sighed. "Up you go," he said with a jerk of his chin toward Nebra. There was no comfort in harassing a person soon to be judged for execution by forcing her to march.

She shook her head.

He jerked his head again. It was the sort of dance they'd done several times in the past two days, and both seemed tired of it.

"He'll leave us if you don't hurry up," Lin whispered.

She stared at him. No. She stared at the weeping bundle strapped to his chest and licked her lips.

"Go on now," Lin urged.

"Fine." Her voice was harsh and grated for lack of use. Once one foot was in Nebra's stirrup, Lin helped her up the rest of the way. He made sure to avoid her back as she squirmed and kicked at him if she deemed him too handsy. Not that Lin tried to be.

"Why are you so kind?" she asked.

Lin froze. He hadn't thought he was being kind. They'd barely fed her, and she was being escorted for execution. *Judgment*, Lin corrected his thoughts.

There was a chance she'd be found innocent, even if Aemun was adamant about her guilt.

"We aren't monsters," Lin said.

"Are you sure?" she asked. He looked up into her face, bands of hair, the same shade as Margaret's, shielding her eyes. She was lean, and the dirt coating her cheeks made it hard to tell exactly how old she was. Lin's age, maybe, if not a few years older.

"Of course."

Lin briskly walked alongside Nebra until Aemun's back was visible again and slowed his pace. His shoulder ached stiffer than anything else, and his stomach growled. He had some salted meat and stale bread when they first woke, but now the sun was near the horizon, and they hadn't stopped for anything else since the last stop to relieve themselves. He looked up at the woman. If the fingers of hunger had begun poking his insides, they must be scraping at hers. Starved people struggled to work Bindings into existence, and unless a person was untethered, they couldn't even Bind without full use of their hands, even if they had the energy.

Lin shook his head. Taking both the use of her hands and sustenance from her seemed excessive, but if she was indeed guilty, Lin could *almost* understand why Aemun demanded it. But if she wasn't guilty, there was only one other option. He stared at Aemun's shoulder blades, then looked up at the woman's expressionless face. He couldn't put his finger on it, but something felt off. *Wrong* somehow.

Lin blinked and realized he'd been staring at her, staring at the way her dirty and stringy hair fell across her face like frayed curtains. And between her hair, she stared back. Eyes dark, glassy, and heavy-lidded.

The baby continued crying, but he'd already checked to see that she was clean, another thing Aemun deemed Lin's duty. They'd given her what milk they'd pressed from the nuts Aemun had on hand. What they needed was a wet nurse, not juice from nuts, but the nearest town was still a ways off. *And there's no guarantee they'd have one.*

By the time the sun had fully surrendered the sky, Lin's feet felt as sore as his shoulder, and he'd eaten the rest of the acorns he'd been saving since before he first met with Aemun and Margaret.

"I thought you said we'd be to Fallo by nightfall?" Aemun looked down at Lin. Lips pressed into a thin line. Hair wind-tousled and dark auburn without the sun showing the brighter blonde streaks within. That was the first *real* thing the man had said since leaving Lyre, and it was edged with a tone not fit to use with a stray dog lest you wanted to get bit.

Lin surveyed the area. They'd passed the split in the road a ways back, which meant they should be near Fallo and the river bend that cut back on itself afterward. They *should* have passed several of the furthest farms, but Lin hadn't seen any lanternlight, and the thin moon only peeked out from behind the thick clouds occasionally, so seeing anything further ahead than them was a struggle. Fallo should've been similar in size to Lyre, aside from the extra pastures and homesteads and...

"What?" Aemun asked. He followed Lin's gaze.

Against the deep blue sky stood darker shapes like hills, but this part of Danica was mostly flat compared to the west. So that implied buildings.

"I think I see a two-story, likely the inn. Against the sky, there. Other shorter buildings, too."

"Why is it so dark?" Aemun asked as if Lin would know.

Lin strained his eyes. It wasn't uncommon for the deepest parts of winter to see the oil running low or the wood spent, but this was far too early for that. "Draw your blade and prepare for the worst," he said, unsheathing his.

"Come down and take your child," Lin whispered once they'd gotten close enough to see the buildings clearly. All was dark and quiet, save for the faint glow of gold-hued Bindings cut into the distant slanted, thatch-covered roofs.

"I'd rather not be caught on foot if I should prepare for the worst," Aemun hissed.

"Shit," Lin cursed under his breath. "Here." Lin stabbed his blade into the earth and undid the knots holding the cloth sling together. With shaking hands and held breath, he cradled the baby and raised her to Aemun. She began to cry again, and her wails increased as Lin pulled his hands away. As if she'd gotten as used to his touch as he had her warmth.

Aemun glared at Lin. Then he urged his horse forward. Painfully slow. The steed's big eyes seemed to search everywhere. Its ears went flat, and its tail swished back and forth so much it could start a breeze.

Lin grabbed his sword and followed, leading Nebra but stopping at the short wall of stone that most would consider the true edge of Fallo. His chest felt cold, bitter cold, without the child's warmth near his heart.

Now that Lin was closer, he could make out the exact shapes stitched to the roofs. Velkath's Sigil. A heretical, One-loved symbol, so far as the Ferrucium's teachings were concerned.

"What do you see?" Aemun asked. His horse stomped the earth.

"Velkath's Sigil. Stitched into the roofs."

Aemun spat. "A noseless dog could smell the blood. A whole river of it."

Lin sniffed the air, and his stomach turned. A door slammed, the sound carried on the wind, and corpse birds cried and flew into the air. Lin spun at the sound of flapping wings, searching the rooftops and dark corners for any sign of movement.

"Stay here," Lin said, looking up at the woman but speaking to her and Aemun.

"We could just leave!" Aemun urged. "We only planned to stop for a wet nurse. What's the harm in leaving?"

"There could be survivors. This is likely the work of an untethered which means it's *our* duty to investigate."

Aemun snorted but stayed saddled and stared into the darkness. "If it was a massacre, someone might need to report it."

"Someone might," Lin replied as he stalked into Fallo, or the corpse of it, listening, wishing his breaths weren't coming so hard or his shirt didn't feel so tight around his throat. His vision pulsed purple at the edges, and he tried to slow his breaths. The smell of death, like this had been a battlefield, overwhelmed him. Worse than the Alderman of Lyre or the rancid, metallic scent of the untethered he'd fought.

Lin moved against the side of a low building with loose boards, more a shack than anything else, and listened. Or he tried to. The baby wouldn't stop crying in the distance, wailing like something actively attacked it.

Sparing a glance over his shoulder toward Aemun and the woman, he saw them sitting there, unmoving. Aemun leaned forward in his saddle with his child strapped around him in Lin's cloak, and the woman slumped in her saddle with rounded shoulders. It would be his luck that he'd find Aemun with another corpse when he returned.

The wind whistled as if competing against the baby's wails, and another slam came from some door, not smart enough to realize now was *not* the time to be slamming. But in the wind, the scent of blood hung heavy. Blood and shit and death.

Steeling himself, he turned the corner of the shack and stepped deeper into Fallo.

The layout resembled Lyre's. But Lin stared at the difference, his stomach turning into knots, and bile climbed burningly up his throat.

Each of Velkath's Sigils was formed of Bindings. That he'd already known, but each Binding stitched a torn, bloody limb in place. *Bindings and blood.* Was there even a name for the sort of Bindings holding those limbs to the roofs? Stitches, he supposed, but that would mean that in death, each of the poor people afflicted had unintentionally blasphemed. Lin wasn't sure they'd find their place in the Grand Tapestry, and that made the sickness rising in him quicken.

There had to be thirty homes, and nearly every roof had a sigil: three connected triangles, all made of limbs, stabbed through and accented by glowing lines like bright needles. All Lin knew was that Velkath's symbol was a twisted version of the Six and One's holy mark.

Slam. Thud. "Cawww." A carrion eater's cry echoed through the night, and the sound of heavy, hurried wings took flight from Lin's left.

Lin gripped his hilt tighter, knuckles aching at the force.

Thatch shifted above him to his right, and the thudding slap of limbs tumbling to the ground came from behind. The baby wailed over and over. Undulating cries like an alarm. As if that was all the disparate body parts had been waiting for, the sigils shattered out of existence, Stitches exploding into shoots of ethereal sparks. Like hail made of bones and flesh, they crashed into the earth.

More birds broke away, merely dark shrieking shapes against the sky.

Wefts flashed into view, slicing from Lin's left and right. He tried to move out of the trajectory, but his boots refused to budge, and when he glanced down, he saw Weaves tethering him in place.

Lin fell backward, crashing down as the Wefts cut the air where he'd been. "Untethered!" he screamed.

From his back, he watched a lone figure blur into existence. It landed as if it had crashed from far above and glowed head-to-toe like a falling star, kicking up debris in a cloud.

Lin focused his will, threading the needle, and willed the Weaves undone from his boots. But they stayed fast in place. It felt like he was trying to peel away strips of bolted iron with raw fingertips. Destroying a Binding had never felt *so* painful.

"What?" Lin gasped.

As if rising from the darkest shadows, more forms appeared—five, no, six figures. They weren't covered like the first, but they were all Stitched—each and every One-whispered one of them.

Lin pulled himself back, ankles straining, slipping, burning against the leathers of his boots.

A trap. Untethered had laid a trap. And not just Fallo in general, but the way they'd bound his boots. Lin was to his bare feet in a breath and stood with his sword up, blocking the first of several fast Wefts that launched his way. He felt two more flying at his sides before he saw them, and once the Binding pressing into his blade exploded into sparks, he slashed at the other two, barely catching and destroying them before they bit flesh instead of steel.

Ferrucium steel was just as deadly as any other metal sword, but it was so much more in the hands of a Binder with the Sight. It was a shield, a blade, and a tool for channeling his will into the world. But that didn't mean he could face six untethered alone. *He'd barely survived the one.* Lin sprinted barefoot, struggling not to slip as he made his way to where he'd left the other two.

"Did you say untethered? How many?" Aemun shouted as Lin approached.

"Too many. And some seem to move like the wind itself."

"Get on your horse. Let's go." Aemun turned his mount.

Lin hesitated. Running seemed right. But between Aemun and himself, they might be able to stop the monsters. "No," Lin snapped. "If we leave these monsters here, Lyre or another village might be next."

"We can't save others *there* if we die *here*! And you'd have my child die here alongside us? What do you think you're doing?"

Lin stroked Nebra's neck and focused his will. With a push of his free hand, he snapped the Weaves that held the woman's hands in place.

"Have you lost what little mind you had left?" Aemun snarled.

"She will aid us or die alongside us." Lin turned his back on the two, heart pounding in his ears.

"She hasn't eaten in days. She is a killer! You..."

Aemun's voice trailed off as Lin rushed forward. Odds were, based on what he saw, all three of them would die. But he had to tilt the odds any bit he could. And something about that woman being a killer hadn't sat right with him. Not the way her eyes had lingered on Margaret's corpse. The pain oozed from her expression that night as if it were a festering wound that might *never* heal. But more than any of that, he didn't think running was an option because the creatures here were fast and seemed intelligent. They'd already laid one, if not two, traps. There could be more.

Lin watched the group of untethered stalking toward him. Of the handful of times he'd encountered untethered, true madness-twisted monsters with Stitches in their flesh, he'd never seen so many. Lin blinked. One was missing. He double-counted, stepping back, bare feet sliding in the mud and damp grass. Muck squished up between his toes, and given the slaughter here, he fought to keep its composition at the back of his mind.

Falling from the heavens, the same glowing untethered exploded into the earth in front of Lin. It had no visible eyes and wide-banded layers of Stitches across the top of its face, like bandages made from the magic that broke the Binding Tenets. Its hair was in stringy clumps, and it raised its hands, showing long, brittle-looking, cracked nails and a toothless smile.

A razor-sharp Weft exploded outward from its hand without warning.

Something knocked into Lin, and he was jolted away, legs dragging through mud. He realized Aemun hung half from his saddle, gripping Lin under his arm. The steed crashed away, the child wailing full tilt.

Lin struggled to lift his feet, his heels and toes paying the price against the unkind earth. The only thing that had kept his flesh from peeling and splitting was the slick mud that coated Fallo's lanes in a sheet.

"What the fuck!" Aemun screamed, wheeling his mount around. Aemun's jaw was set, and he stared at the town center from where the untethered stalked toward them.

"We have to fight," Lin gasped, struggling to his feet and pulling away from Aemun.

Aemun let go, eyes wide. "We can't stay and fight *this*. There is no one here left to rescue." He gripped his child tight to his chest as it wailed.

Maybe the baby had known what they were heading into? Knew what sort of darkness waited for them at Fallo, and that was why it had screamed so much. Each wail a mourning keel for the loss Fallo faced.

"What... about the woman?" Lin asked. "And Nebra. You left them back there?"

"You freed her. If she's fled and stolen your horse, you can't blame me," Aemun growled.

The earth beside them erupted into a shower of debris, and the untethered stepped from the shallow crater of mud it made. The Stitches lacing the top of its legs were thin and intricate but became thick and crude near its feet.

It kicked up in a flash, its foot sparking against the edge of Lin's sword—Ferrucium steel sparking against *flesh*. It shouldn't be possible. It shouldn't exist.

Lin squinted at the intensity of light from the contact. Like small, ethereal flowers blooming and wilting over and over again.

Aemun flung several wide, flat, arcing Weaves to restrain the monster's movements, but the untethered avoided them each time by the barest margin. All while kicking upward at Lin.

Each strike rattled Lin's bones and sent him sliding back, heel digging deeper into the thick, sucking mud.

"Run, warn the Weavers," Lin said, clenched jaw biting back the words.

A kick aimed at his knee found its mark, something popped and crunched, and Lin collapsed onto his side.

From the ground, Lin watched Aemun turn and flee. Watched the man's red cloak trailing behind him even as the gangly untethered raised its Stitched leg into the sky.

Lin raised his sword and blocked the crashing heel, but his blade wrenched from his hands, and he fell to his back.

The untethered stalked towards him, tattered cloth fluttering around its waist. A Binding Lin couldn't name formed without focus, like a simple glowing thread blinking into existence between its claw-like hands. *Thread?*

With each step it took, Lin dragged himself back. The bottoms of his feet stung but were soothed by the cool, damp soil. His knee ached and didn't help with leverage. The untethered knelt, nearly mounting Lin, and Lin raised his left hand and formed a focus. A Weft. He'd make a Weft and break the Thread the untethered—

The untethered's hand jolted out, catching and squeezing Lin's left hand, its skin dry and scratchy. Its long nails pressed into the back of Lin's hand. A red Binding, twisted and contorted like a living thing on its ring finger. But Lin's focus was ripped from that as the untethered tightened its grip.

Lin's Weft hummed in his left hand as he tried to release it.

Bindings, no matter the type, never *felt* warm, but the one he had woven started burning his palm, and in seconds, it twisted and warped around his fingers. The untethered cocked its head to the side, eyeless face devoid of emotion. It opened its mouth, a guttural groan escaping its toothless maw.

The Binding, no longer sharp-edged like a Weft should be, twisted around Lin's fingers, tightening again and again until his fingers ached and swelled. Lin yanked and pulled and tried to free his arm, but the untethered held him firm. Lin jostled, kicked, screamed, and reached for his sword, feet away now. More untethered pressed in around them.

The untethered released Lin's hand.

Lin shuddered and drew the knife sheathed at his waist. It was flecked in orange dots, metal eaten away by the untethered's blood. It wasn't wholly covered, but the edge was lost. His left arm twitched, and the jolt that ran through him caused him to drop the useless knife. The strange Binding around his fingers had lengthened, expanding from joint to joint and connecting like a glowing tattoo.

His thumb jerked back first, bending back over itself. The other fingers followed simultaneously, each making a wet, sick pop. The Binding spread lower, gliding across his skin down to his wrist, and Lin was sure it traveled up his arm, based on the hum, but his sleeves covered it. Lin squeezed his wrist, willing the Binding to break and snap, but it refused. *Refused.*

His wrist crunched backward on itself next, and Lin couldn't contain the howl that tore through him.

Between spots of pain flashing in his vision, he saw a tattered cloth scrap as dark red as spilled blood floating on the air, swirling like the golden sparks of a Binding breaking.

The last thing he saw was the earth shifting into the horizon, the mud and muck sucking at his face and clothes. Darkness swallowed him entirely as the magic continued past his wrist, and his elbow twisted out of the socket.

Chapter Four

Bonds of Blood

Lin drifted, each step lighter than the next. It was the lightness that only came with dreaming, where one's body wasn't truly their own. He walked through countless thick forests, over hundreds of burbling streams, and between buildings taller than any he'd ever seen, and still, he wasn't any closer to home. But worse than the weightlessness, than the searching, was the overwhelming intensity emanating from his left arm. Looking down at it hurt. It *hurt*. He was no better than his rusted dagger, speckled. Pieces of himself eaten away. Fire kissed him from within and without, burning him as it grew brighter, centered on his left arm.

Lin jolted awake, but heavy blankets stifled his movement, the weight pinning his torso and right arm. For a moment, he thought it was the baby's pressure against his chest. But no, he was soaked in sweat and underneath a layer of folded, tucked blankets. Slowly, painfully, Lin forced his right arm free. His left looked like a torch. And if not for the heaviness he felt, he thought he might still be dreaming. Lines of Stitches ran along his arm, marking his flesh. Marked *him* like an untethered.

A real fire, small and smoldering, was alight beside him. His head pounded a dull throb that resonated in his aching arm. Judging by the fact that he was alive and not in the strip of the field he last remembered, perhaps it was fairer to say he'd been set next to the makeshift fire pit. But who'd moved him? *Aemun?*

Lin tried to sit up, but a firm hand pushed his right shoulder back down from behind him.

"If I don't finish this, it won't set right," a raspy voice said.

Shifting his head to get a look wasn't easy, but Lin managed. The prisoner he'd been escorting the last few days looked forward, eyes unfocused, sweat beading her pale brow. Her hands moved deftly through patterns Lin didn't understand. The air between her hands and his flesh seemed to hum, and her fingers glowed faintly. She was forming a Binding, but it didn't look like a Weave or Weft, and... Six, she was making Stitches.

Each motion of her hand sent another thin, intricate glowing line across his flesh, then into it. She had already fixed his elbow and worked to repair his snapped wrist and broken fingers. The skin, torn and tattered as it had been, was mended. But in doing these things, she'd broken the Binding Tenets. She'd marked him as one of the untethered.

"S-stop!" Lin croaked. He winced and blinked back tears as he tried to jerk his arm away.

The magic tracing onto his flesh slowed and then stopped, leaving his wrist and fingers unmarked. But they were still unnaturally bent. Broken. "If I stop here, you will be left with no less than three broken fingers and a sprained wrist. Is that what you want?"

"Undo the Stitches you've already worked. Before they set fully into my flesh."

She sighed, and her hands lowered a margin towards his chest. Lin realized his head was resting on her lap, her crossed legs functioning as a pillow for Lin while she worked on his wounds. Her eyes narrowed, and she shook her head.

"That isn't how it works." Her whisper was like stone dragging on metal.

"Why didn't you ask? Why didn't you ask if this was what I wanted?" Between the weight of the blanket and the constriction he felt as his world was shattering, he couldn't pull himself away. Each breath fought to come after the next.

"I'm sorry I didn't ask if you wanted me to save your life, but it had to be done," she said.

Lin blinked. "Had to be? I could have lived with a broken arm, let it set, let it recover. I'm a Ferrucium soldier. Wounds are expected, and they *will* heal!"

The woman reached across him, causing him to flinch as she pulled the edge of the heavy blanket from underneath him and revealed his torso. Like snake bones, Stitches ran from his clavicle to his navel. The flesh puckered and irritated, but the wound closed. Lin stared at it.

"The blood loss would've ended you. I acted as quickly as I could."

The woman's voice was calm, but there was no sorrow or regret in her words. She held her chin high as she looked at him, eyes drifting down past his navel.

Lin looked back down at the Stitches. He felt their subtle hum and let his right hand drift to the glowing magic. He dug a nail into his flesh, but aside from the pain, nothing came from it. They could call the magic anything they wanted, but that didn't mean it was a literal stitch that could be pried free.

"You washed me?"

"Best I could," she said.

"You... you didn't ask if this, any of this, is what I wanted!" Lin tried to yell, but his voice cracked, and his lips did the same. Each word was a rusted dagger.

"I told you. I didn't have the chance. It was either heal you or let the carrion take you along with the other corpses. Now, may I finish your hand?"

Lin hadn't noticed exactly how much his fingers ached until she brought his attention back to them. Each digit screamed. Each joint was a painful reminder of the defeat given to him and a defeat of a different sort still to come.

"Can it be undone?" Lin whispered. And he hated himself for asking. Having your flesh Stitched broke the very *first* Binding Tenet. There was no clause or occlusion for undoing it, but it would keep him from being labeled untethered to others like him who had the Sight. *Wouldn't it?*

"I've heard rumors. Magic older than the old magic. But you won't find me swearing on that."

She gestured to Lin's hand with hers and stared at him.

Lin nodded and squeezed his eyes shut, but the tears came all the same. Somehow, it hurt more and more as the pain faded. It didn't go away entirely, but it seemed that the injuries and aches nearest the Stitches dulled to background noise.

How much time passed, Lin wasn't sure. But when the woman finished, the sky was a shade lighter, and the fire was no more than embers and ash. She had worked silently, and Lin had nothing to say. He was an oath breaker. The One *would* whisper his name for each marking on his flesh. Every time he considered speaking, a sickness in his gut threatened to climb up from his throat. But perhaps he'd be able to redeem himself. Or remove them before his eventual death. The Ferrucium Weavers might not see Lin's unwillingness to be Stitched as a reason for forgiveness, but perhaps the Six would.

The woman was right, of course. Without her aid, he'd have been dead. The wound along his torso felt as deep as it was long. He *knew* that. Could feel it in every closed wound. In his bones even.

But *the Binding Tenets.*

Anyone with the Sight would know him for what he was. A lawbreaker. One step closer to being *untethered*. If not an untethered already.

"W-what's your name?" Lin asked.

"Hmm. Is there some list I should expect whatever name I utter to appear on?" she asked as she pulled herself away.

Lin's head dropped to wood planks, then lifted and settled onto a makeshift pillow. "No," he whispered.

"Then why do you need to know it?"

"I'd like to know the name of the person who saved me. Even if... even if it isn't the way I would've gone about it."

She sighed and looked at him, shoulders slumping and eyes rolling. "What *else* was I meant to do? *You* freed *me*."

"I don't know. I don't. But you said there might be a way to remove it. To fix it. So thank you for saving me. Truly."

She snorted. "Thanks from the man who wanted me to face judgment not days ago?"

"Better judgment than immediate steel. But we both need one of the two now. Can't get away from that."

She stared hard at him. Her lips were thin, and her cheeks gaunt, making her dark eyes look large. It was unnerving the way she seemed to study him.

"Tylle," she whispered.

"Until what?" Lin asked.

"Til-leh," she accented the syllables as she rose, then walked toward the door.

"Tylle. How did you save me?"

"Magic," Tylle said as if he were a fool for asking an obviously answered question.

"No... I mean those untethered, they were monsters."

"I saved you by being more of a monster than my enemy and more of a savior than the man who thought to save me."

"Why didn't you run? You could've."

"I considered it. By the time I had a real chance, it would've been hard to get away. But really, I'd hoped to get taken into the Ferrucium so that I might cut the threads of the Weavers at the source." Tylle left the room, her clothes baggy on her lithe frame.

Lin lay still, considering her words. Had she truly thought herself capable of killing the Weavers? His mouth opened, then shut, and his eyes fluttered and did the same. He had more terrible dreams: drowning in a pool of glowing, white-hot iron, like a weapon waiting to be smelted. But every time he was tempered, he broke. Then he melted again, cooled again, and shattered again.

When he next woke, the sky had turned a clear, bright blue free of clouds. The fire was all ash now, and chills racked his body. He tensed, and his wounds ached at the motion.

Tylle was nowhere to be seen. But a slow, earth-churning sound carried from outside. Lin rolled to his right, careful of his arm, and stared through the narrow slats in the wall. She was out there, in the middle of Fallo, building a pyre. The logs and kindling she must've assembled earlier, but now she dragged bodies. All the bodies. Not at once. But she finished one and moved to the next quickly enough. Like it was simply a thing that had to be done.

Lin struggled to his feet. Each movement made it feel like the wound across his torso would pull open, but the glowing Stitches held. A wave of shame washed over him. He only needed one hand to count the number of untethered he'd helped condemn in his life. And now he was one of them. His name might as well have been One-whispered. *It will be.*

Cold air greeted him when he stumbled out of the shack shirtless. His trousers were caked in dried mud and he was still barefoot, but the sun worked into him, warming against the wind.

"Lie back down," Tylle called once she noticed him. She was picking up stray limbs like kindling, her pale face expressionless. Her black hair was braided over her shoulder in pleats, neatly done compared to how she'd worn it the last few days.

Fallo smelled rotten. Decayed. *Sick.*

"You're sending them to the Six?" Lin asked, hopeful.

She shook her head and went back to her task, moving from the pyre to a body, or whatever was left of it, and back again.

Lin shambled to a wall where a foot was sticking out of a bucket, flies buzzing and dancing on the meat of it. Bile rose in his throat, and he turned away.

Tylle was to him in a breath, taking the foot and shaking her head. "*Go.*"

"But—"

Her jaw set, and she sighed, turning hard eyes onto him.

"I want to help. Sitting still was never something most would claim I'm good at."

"Dragging bodies is done. Not many were whole. And I think this was the last limb." Tylle raised the foot into the air as if she were brandishing something interesting and not wholly macabre. "At least the last one not taken by wolves or those damned birds."

Lin followed her gaze up and noticed the large, circling black specks.

"Let me pray with you at least. Sing the Mourning Ballad to help send the deceased to the tapestry above." Lin stepped forward, and Tylle raised her hand, palm flat out toward him. "What?" he asked.

"You can pray to your *false* gods if you want. But I will pray for these nameless souls as *I* see fit. And you will not disturb me until I finish." Tylle turned away from Lin and stalked to the unlit pyre, placing the foot near the bottom and stepping back.

"T-they aren't false gods," Lin said, stumbling after her. His feet sunk into the churned earth, and under the sun's light, he saw how brown the grass was.

"The Six? Nameless, faceless imitations of Velkath and his brothers and sisters."

"The Six are representations and reflections of the aspects of men. Or we are their reflections. They aren't imitations. Maybe you would've hesitated more to mark me untethered if you had faith in the Six and One."

Tylle wiped the sweat from her brow and shook her head. "They are the carcass of Danica's true Gods. They are bones left where bodies should still be."

"Who are you to make such claims?" Lin asked. It was one thing to break the Binding Tenets to save his life—an act that, on the surface, was fueled by good intentions. But to say the Six were corpses? That was blasphemous.

"A priestess of Vellyr, brother to Velkath. Only *one* of Velkath's *six* brothers and sisters." Tylle raised her thin brows and shrugged as if her statement had just proven some law of the world irrefutable.

Velkath.

Lin frowned. "The untethered stuck people to their roofs in that crossed triangle of Velkath's. What sort of God allows that?"

"A cruel one," Tylle replied. "But if the Six are watching over them as you say, aren't they also cruel for allowing it to happen?"

She moved slowly, as if she measured each step, and pulled a flower from a satchel at her waist. Then another and another until she held nine flowers, each with petals whiter than any Lin had seen before. Pristine petals. She laid out all nine at separate points on the pyre.

"But," she whispered, "untethered worship nothing but themselves. Whatever compelled the untethered to attack this village, kill its people, and weave their body parts to the roofs is to blame."

Tylle pulled flint from her pack and struck it. Shick-shick-shick. She hammered an iron bar across the stone until smoke tendrils curled from the stacked wood and bodies in front of her.

"And he is known as Cunning Velkath, not cruel," she added.

Lin frowned and moved to a spot mostly unsoiled by muck and blood. He sat, keeping his eyes on Tylle as she worked.

Separately, they prayed. Tylle to her hedonistic *gods*, him to the Six, and their One shadow. Whether the deceased would be woven into the tapestry of the world or not, Lin couldn't know. The Sight allowed him to see Bindings. Both, Bindings and the Sight to see them were gifts from the Six and One, but the souls of the dead and damned weren't ever anything Lin could see. So, all he could do was hope and pray.

He liked to imagine souls were pulled and plucked like loose threads. That way, when they snapped, there was a reason for it. To make the Tapestry better and more beautiful. If not, then why did a soul like Margaret's have to be plucked?

Eventually, Tylle rose, face flushed from the heat of the pyre. Dark smoke funneled into the air, and she watched it for a moment before adjusting her pack and walking back to the shack Lin had woken up in.

Lin waited. He let the warmth of the grim fire settle into his bones and stared down at his left hand and arm. There seemed to be only two options set before him. Run from the Ferrucium and his duties—his oaths—and live a simple life as far from their reach as he could. But a reach that shadowed all of Danica was hard to avoid. Impossible even. Or, he could turn himself in. Plea for mercy to the Weavers and explain that his escort failed. At least Margaret had been burned and sent to the heavens. Lin hadn't seen Aemun's corpse, but that scrap of floating cloth before he passed out could only have come from Aemun's cloak.

"Mercy is the best course. My wounds were bound without my consent." The words sounded false even as they came from his lips. The Ferrucium was many things, but known for mercy wasn't one of them. Perhaps the Weavers knew of a way to remove the Stitches. Knowledge they kept secret to prevent people from Stitching into themselves in the first place.

Lin chewed on the inside of his mouth, and his stomach growled. He pulled his knees to his chest and hung his head. A pang of guilt rushed through him as he wondered if Tylle had moved Aemun's and the baby's bodies onto the pyre, praying to her false gods for their afterlife. Aemun might've been unbearable, but even he deserved to join the Tapestry. Lin touched his chest and shut his eyes tight, remembering the feel of the child against his heart. Warm. *Whole.*

When the heat finally became unbearable, Lin rose and shuffled to the shack.

Tylle sat against the far wall, legs crossed, left arm held in front of her. Her right hand was flat and held inches above her left. There was a hum and scent of magic in the air. Her face was expressionless, and her eyes were half closed.

"What're you doing?" Lin asked.

Her eyes darted up, but then she looked back at her hand. A scarlet-colored Binding twined around her ring finger. It was an unusual Binding, like what the untethered had borne.

Lin's brow furrowed, and he took a step forward. "Stop that." But it was too late. He'd come too late, and the red ring was already formed, twisting and writhing even once her right hand dropped to her side.

"You're no better than an *untethered*! And every time I turn and ignore one thing, you throw another in my face. I should never have unbound your hands!"

Tylle slumped, sliding her legs out from under her, and rested her elbows on her knees, hands dangling between them.

"Nothing to say?" Lin asked, stepping forward.

She sighed. "I owe you no explanations. But from our little conversations, I know you won't aid me. And I don't plan to wait for you to rest and heal, only for you to bind me in my sleep and drag me to your prison for judgment."

"Aid you? In becoming a monster? For every Stitch you work into your body, another is worked on your mind, and madness is sure to follow. The leg-kicking fuck of an untethered had a red Binding like that."

"An exaggeration told to keep the truth locked behind Ferrucium steel. And I don't want help in becoming a monster. I don't *plan* to become a monster. I meant my revenge. I didn't kill Margie. That fled bastard did. He slit her throat and kept me from Stitching it to save her. Not to mention stole away the last piece of her."

Lin stared at her. "Why didn't you speak up sooner?"

"I did and was ignored. But really, who would you have believed?" Tylle asked.

It was true. She had claimed innocence. But even so, Lin wasn't sure. Aemun was an ally, a Ferrucium Binder like him. That didn't mean they were a monolith, incapable of having bad actors. But why would Aemun have killed his partner, the mother of his child? He shook his head. "I don't know."

Chapter Five

Brittle Hope

Margaret. *The child.* Lin's back itched against the wall he'd slumped against. He'd thought Aemun had acted odd about the whole thing. And if her words were true, if Aemun had killed Margaret, then he was as much a traitor as Lin. Moreso, since Lin hadn't made a choice to break the Tenets. Still, this woman *was* a heretic, clearly against what the Ferrucium stood for, and now bore the same red Binding he'd only ever seen on untethered. His eyes had drifted to it at every opportunity, not a Weave or Stitch, but something else entirely. Now, she'd left long enough ago that Lin thought she might not return, and his eyes drifted to where she'd been seated. How was he meant to trust anything from her mouth?

But she saved me without need. Obviously, she hadn't needed Lin's help to survive those monsters.

Lin's shoulders slumped, and he hung his head, staring down at his hands. Hands that couldn't save anyone, even himself. He shifted as the sound of wings and the cries of carrion eaters carried across Fallo.

Steps approached from outside, and then the door slammed open. Tylle stalked in with the same frown she'd worn when she left. A look that seemed etched into her face and made her look older than she likely was.

"Still here?" she asked.

"Where else would I go in my current state?" Lin asked, a dull, aching edge to his words. "Where else would you *like* me to go?"

She shrugged and shivered. With one booted foot, she closed the door. It didn't stop the occasional gust of wind, but it cut the cold air enough to keep Lin's teeth from chattering.

Lin watched the black smoke pillar climbing to the stars through the slats.

Tylle sighed and shook her head. "Have you considered what I said?"

Lin nodded, eyes landing on the red Binding around her finger.

She followed his stare and busied her hands, pulling out nuts and mushrooms from the pack at her waist. Honeycaps, acorns, and a thick, dark-shelled nut Lin hadn't seen before. Bulbous and sectioned, it looked swollen and strange. He knew the other two were suitable for a Binder's diet. Gifts from the Six that helped replenish the magic energy within. But that third thing smelled sour and decayed as she cracked its shell.

"So we go our separate ways." Tylle leaned forward and handed Lin half of the acorns and honeycaps, keeping the unfamiliar third nut to herself. It was a statement, but her eyes asked a question that her lips didn't.

Lin pursed his lips and ran a hand across the stubble of his cheek. "What is that?"

Tylle rotated the foul-smelling nut. "Food. Good to replenish the spul."

"Spul? Soul, you mean?"

"No. Spul. The energy we draw on when weaving our intention into the world. It is our thread and has an end to its length. This and some of that—" Tylle waved at the honeycaps and acorns "—help keep the fatigue at bay. Nothing beats meat, of course, but this is the next best thing."

Tylle grabbed the nut at both ends, digging her fingers into the fleshy bits. Juices leaked down her wrists. It ripped apart easily, but the odor caused Lin to gag and cover his face with his arm.

"Surely you don't mean to eat that?" Lin asked from behind his elbow crease.

A grin broke across her face, and she tossed a smaller half of the thing to Lin.

Lin caught it and blinked as juices splattered from its flesh. His nose burned from the aroma. The exterior was softer than he expected, and the fleshy bit *looked* almost like well-seasoned meat. If Lin squinted. But that smell rivaled

Lyre's Alderman for potency. He'd have to add this odd food to the list of things to tell Denro.

A wave of fresh pain washed across him at the thought. Denro had the Sight. He'd see Lin for what he was immediately. Lin stared at his left hand, wet from juice, Stitches damply glistening.

"Try it," Tylle said, licking the juice from her fingertips.

Lin sighed. Then poked a finger into it and tasted the juice. It was sweeter than the honeycap mushrooms or even honey-dipped nuts, with the texture of a fleshy fruit and a metallic aftertaste.

"Corpse-seed. Grows in the shade of dead trees."

Lin wiped the back of his hand across his mouth. "Never knew."

"You were Ferrucium born? Or picked up as a child?"

The question was like an arrow shot from his blind spot. Lin shrugged and leaned back against the wall. His side ached, fingers tingled, and for the life of him, he couldn't decide what Tylle's game was.

Tylle wriggled where she sat and rolled another corpse-seed to Lin, the fruity nut bouncing against Lin's ankle and spinning to a stop. "Your horse—"

"Nebra? What about her?" Lin blurted. He'd been so busy thinking about himself and Tylle's story that he hadn't considered how Nebra had fared against the untethered.

"... is grazing in the field straight west of here. Not too far. I was going to say when you go to leave, you can find her there."

"I..." Lin didn't know what he meant to say, and the words fell from his tongue as quickly as his mind.

Tylle scrunched her nose, and her chin dipped. "Take care, Lin. Thank you for releasing me when those monsters attacked." She rose and looked around, checking to be sure she hadn't left anything.

"Wait," Lin whispered. He stared at her. At the bright crimson that danced on her ring finger. "You said Aemun killed Margaret."

"Margie," Tylle corrected.

"Margie? Margaret, you mean," Lin said softly. "But either way, swear it on your gods and mine."

"What?" She frowned.

"Swear to me that you saw him do that. Swear that if I help you bring him to justice, you'll help me find a way to remove the Stitches marking me as untethered."

"It isn't the markings that make a person untethered."

"You know what I mean. To any with the Sight, I am untethered. I've broken the Binding Tenets."

Tylle looked like she might spit the way her mouth puckered. "By that logic, I, too, am untethered, no?"

Lin looked down at his muddy feet, then met her eyes. "Yes."

"I swear by Cunning Velkath and Wrathful Verbanth. I swear it on Wise Vellia and all the other siblings that I witnessed Aemun murder my *sister* when she begged him to flee the Ferrucium with her. If I lie, the Six can whisper my name to the One." The last bit sounded spoken in spite, the words hollow.

"Sister?" Lin studied her face. She was leaner than Margaret had been, her eyes shades darker. But Tylle had the same hair and the same shaped nose. And that half smile she'd given earlier... "You two planned to leave Lyre together..." Lin trailed, mind racing to understand it all.

"*Three*. My sister hoped Aemun, the man she claimed and swore oaths with as a partner, would choose her, but instead..."

Lin watched as her voice died and her eyes dropped. She looked like a pale flower wilting.

"Why... why would anyone abandon the Ferrucium?" Lin asked, using the wall to help him rise.

"Why?" She asked. "True. I'd relish staying with a force that abducts children. I'm sure you are glad you don't know whether you were taken in from some remote village or born behind walls that blot the sky."

Lin's eye twitched. "Families are compensated. Villages with children who get taken are given a further reduction on their tithes!"

"Yes. A handful of coins for a lifetime of service."

Lin flinched at the venom in her voice, and he steadied himself against the wall.

But she didn't stop. "Not to mention they hoard knowledge of magic, so the self-named *weavers* not only steal our people's children but also our history and future, all in one swoop."

"K-knowledge is protected to prevent people from learning independently and untethering! It is to keep Danica and its people safe!"

"And that plan has worked well for the Ferrucium, has it?" Tylle booted the door open. It slammed so hard against the wall that the hinge broke, rattling without swinging back. She jerked her head and pointed at the column of smoke.

"And then when they find a *loose thread*, they indiscriminately kill them. Zero tolerance for those who fit outside of their 'tapestry,' another term they've stolen from our faith. *My* faith."

Lin failed to find a response at first. Every point she made was biased. But that didn't make it wrong. Some of them were thoughts that he'd heard expressed by Denro before, though not so blatantly rebellious or heretical. "Untethered are a danger to themselves and others," he finally said.

"Actual untethered are. I know that well enough. But if you think they're only unlearned men and women practicing independently, then you're a larger fool than I thought!" She shook her head and squeezed her fists into balls. "This... this is why I didn't bother saying more earlier. Redrobes are killers, soldiers, and people last. You are not an exception."

"I am my own person, and I'm not a killer. I could've ended you back in Lyre. Or let Aemun do it. But instead, you were taken for judgment. *Spared*."

"How big of you. To spare an innocent woman."

Lin frowned and took an unsteady step toward her. "I did what I thought was right. And I'll continue to do so."

"So when our differences are cast in a light that makes it so you can't ignore my shadows, what will you do?" Tylle hissed. It was unnerving how calm she kept her expression.

"What I feel is right," Lin whispered. "And I hope you will do the same, like helping me remove the magic from my flesh."

"I swore on my Gods, and I don't take oaths lightly."

Lin studied her face. A sliver-thin scar ran across her right cheek. The purplish circles underneath made her dark eyes darker, and she stood tense like she was ready for a fight. If he went with her to find Aemun, who had likely fled to the Ferrucium, they could all go before the Weavers and unknot this tale, assuming they found a way to clear Lin's flesh. *And if Aemun's the monster, as Tylle claims, save the child.*

"You've made many... points on the failures of the Ferrucium," Lin whispered. "Let me... let us go together and get the truth from Aemun. One more night of rest, and I'll be ready. Please."

It was her turn to study him, and her dark eyes searched his expression, likely reading his body language like he'd done to her.

"Make an oath on it to *my* gods. They don't take oath breakers lightly," Tylle said, splaying her fingers in the air between them and wiggling her ring finger.

"Is that what those are? Binding Oaths?" Lin asked. If it was, that made sense. He'd heard of them before but hadn't seen one, and seeing the red twining Binding on an untethered of all things had kept it from recall.

Tylle spat on the floor beside them and stared at him with a curled lip. "No. You want to go with me. You will learn again, as a toddler would. Repeat after me... Bludwieve."

"Bloodweave," Lin replied.

"No, not quite," Tylle shook her head. "But it's good enough. Now make an oath."

"I don't want a Bludwieve."

"It is fortunate, then, that I'm not asking that of you."

Lin sucked in the smoky air. "I'll swear on your gods." And he did. He named the ones he could recall and swore. "I'll aid you in finding Aemun, but more importantly, the truth. I'll do everything I can to save the part of your sister that remains in this world." *Margaret deserves at least that.*

A flapping of several wings sounded from a nearby roof.

Let the Six aid me in this and whisper my name to the One if I fail.

Confliction wasn't the right word for the splitting indecision in his gut.

"He is likely headed straight to the Ferrucium," Lin said. "But I did find a parchment with Margaret. All it had written on it was the name Wellgrove."

Tylle's nostrils flared.

"Perhaps a meeting point?" Lin asked.

"Not part of our plans," Tylle said, gaze drifting out to the horizon.

"So maybe somewhere Aemun was planning to go? I was only with them for a few days and hadn't had the route discussed beyond Lyre."

"Wellgrove is a ways from here. If he intends to keep the child alive, he'll still be searching for a wet nurse."

"On horseback," Lin replied.

"On horseback." Tylle nodded.

"With two days head start."

"Three, since you want to rest one more night," Tylle said.

Wanted wasn't the right word there, either. Lin *needed* one more night of rest. Stitching his wounds had stopped the bleeding and had healed the bits that were broken, but the pain and soreness hadn't entirely faded. His wrist and fingers were numb, and the large scar down his torso itched like mad. But they were set into his flesh now, sure as his hair was to his scalp. *For now.*

"What large towns are on the way?"

"Townsbridge if he cut south. And Riversbend if he didn't," Lin said. "Biggest two I can think of."

"He could stop at any of them. Do you know if he would make a stronger effort towards either one?"

Lin shrugged. "He didn't speak openly about his plans."

"Guilt can turn the tongue into iron," Tylle said, face turning and cutting a harsh silhouette against the pyre remains. Her gaze lingered on the horizon, past the buildings and fields that made the now ruin of Fallo, past the trees that cropped up in various pockets, so far was her stare that there could only be one thing she was straining and undoubtedly failing to see. *The Ferrucium.*

"I would guess..." Lin chewed on the inside of his mouth and stared at his mud-covered toes. "I don't know. He complained about the roads more than any other Binder I've traveled with. If he had it his way, they would've stayed holed up exactly where they had been before I was sent to them. He didn't want to move before the birth, but Margaret insisted on making it to Lyre."

"It was where we decided to meet beforehand," Tylle whispered.

"Oh." Lin shivered.

"Also, you keep using the name Binder. You, me, those of us with knowledge of our spul, we are the children of the First Weavers."

Lin nodded. So it seemed she did know the truth of the Six, even if she didn't prescribe to the faith.

Tylle's brow raised, and she shook her head. "Not your Six. I can see it in your eyes. Velkath and his siblings were the First Weavers. And they are far older than the pale copies the Ferrucium and the foreign king they submit to crafted. But even the terms they created and teach are shackles to keep our people chained. You're a Binder? You work *Bindings*? Terms of bondage meant to keep your dreams narrow and restrained. Those you call Weavers? The three who rule the Ferrucium? An unearned title. We are all *Wievers*. Each and every one of us who access our spuls."

***

Lin stared up at the ceiling, unable to sleep despite needing rest like a drowning man who needed dry land. Tylle's soft breaths were in the even pattern of her sleep, sounds he'd adjusted to over the two days on the road before Fallo. He'd found Nebra earlier in the day, and she rested beside the shack, snoring.

Of all the One-loved things Tylle had said, the one thing that kept running through his thoughts was whether he'd been Ferrucium born or picked up as a child. Soldiers like Lin didn't get to meet their parents, even if they were Ferrucium soldiers themselves. Not the way Aemun knew his lineage. And amid all that, there was a weight of guilt, knowing Margaret's child might never know who her mother was, pressed into his chest. *Pressed right where the babe had been swaddled for those few days.*

Lin rolled onto his side and stared at the Stitches wrapping his fingers and wrist. Each knuckle looked like a star, the way the glowing lines distorted through his tears. And his wrist appeared adorned by a brilliant golden bracelet made of silken thread.

A tear welled in his right eye and became too large. It rolled down his cheek. He'd made an oath; even if he hadn't made it directly to *his Gods*, he'd thought of them when he said it. He had to find the truth.

But... would an oath from someone who had already broken the Binding Tenets even be valid to the Six and One? Or would it be like spitting into the wind and calling it rain? Or, worse of all, would it be an oath spoken into the void with no one to hear it?

As he stared at the Stitches that laced into his flesh, he considered how beautiful he thought they were. And that made a surge of disgust well up within him.

He curled his hand into a fist and considered punching the floor. Nebra didn't deserve the disturbance any more than Tylle did. But Tylle *had* done this to him. *Without* asking. All her stories, admonishments, and confidence surrounding her knowledge being correct were *infuriating*.

Motionless, floating in his own dark mind like a lost man at sea, one option kept finding its way to the front of his mind. One singular way to end his embarrassment— end the haunting questions that insisted on repeating. End the doubt. He could take his own life. A part of his mind seemed to whisper that it was the only honorable thing to do as far as upholding the Binding Tenets went. But the only thing keeping the Weft from his throat was the knowledge that the Ferrucium would decree it themselves if he presented himself to them. Therefore, his hands would be clean in the sight of the Six. If the Six even had eyes to notice how his hands glowed.

The thought was so confident, so insistent.

When Lin finally fell asleep, he was greeted by a nightmare of drowning, a lake of murky water surrounding him. He was a blade finally formed, but his edge was chipped and rusted, his steel dotted with imperfections. But he didn't break when dipped in, and red Bindings, like Tylle's Bludwieve, bound him to the depths, and try as he might, he couldn't swim up. Countless bodies floated around him. The last he could recall seeing before he awoke, all sweat-covered and disoriented, was Margaret's pained face.

Chapter Six

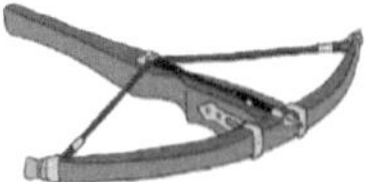

Brittle Bone

When they left Fallo, they did so under a blanket of bloated gray clouds. Rain sprinkled intermittently, pitter-pattering on the road and leaves, washing away the hovering stench of smoke and death. Tylle took the lead, walking ahead. She had a large pack strapped across her back that she must've scavenged from one of the homes, and fresh, tight-fitting trousers, a loose blouse, and a thin cloak had replaced her tattered clothes.

Lin slumped in Nebra's saddle and yawned, stifling a shudder as the rain's soft, cool kisses touched his skin. He had a fresh set of clothes in Nebra's pack, but when he first saw the clouds, he figured it would be best to keep on what he had already worn.

"We need to find you a horse," Lin called, squinting against the random droplets.

Tylle nodded but thumbed the straps of her pack. "The first big town should be Riversbend. Odds are we'll find one there."

They traveled for the better part of the day in silence after that. The skies didn't clear, but eventually, the rain stopped entirely. The wind did the opposite, howling through the pockets of trees at the sides of the road as if to blow more rain from the clouds above. Pockets that turned into an entire forest of trees like bones, bare of leaves save for the piles that rested at their roots.

Lin stared at his left hand, the strip of leather rein he held obscuring some of the Stitches that ran along his flesh.

"Trade with me," Lin said.

Tylle looked up at Lin. "You sure?"

Lin nodded. "If I don't stretch my legs soon, they might stop working."

A grunt escaped her, and she shrugged her pack off. The cloak she'd found was sheer compared to the thick one Lin had wrapped the baby in, and he thought it was odd she hadn't tried to find a thicker one for herself.

Lin slid from Nebra, stroking her neck as he found his footing. He walked around her side and pulled a handful of nuts from the pack at her flank.

He touched his waist with his other hand and remembered he hadn't replaced his knife yet. "Happen to have a knife?"

Tylle, one foot in the stirrup, nodded towards the scavenged pack she'd taken from Fallo.

It felt rude to go through another's belongings, considering Tylle had taken everything from people who couldn't argue ownership. Lin looked at it and weighed how badly he needed the blade. With a sigh and a glance down at his left hand, he opened the pack.

He rifled through it and found a sheathed knife among extra clothes, rations, and coins.

"What do you need it for?" she asked.

Lin drew the thin, sharp blade and tested its weight. A paring knife by the feel of it. He answered her question through action, pulling up the hem of one of the tunics in the pack and stabbing the tip into it before dragging the knife horizontally across the fabric. The ripping sound startled Nebra, whose tail swished aggressively, and her ears pivoted towards the noise. He did it two more times, making the tunic unwearable.

With a shake of his head, he sheathed the knife and moved to put it back into her pack.

"Why don't you keep it on you? Never know when another cloak or top that needs slicing might come around."

"Hmph," Lin snorted. He put the knife back into the pack.

She stared down at him, her head cocking to the side. "After all you've been through these last few days, you're worried about…"

Lin wrapped the first strip of cloth in a crisscrossing pattern around his fingers, hiding the Stitches marking his flesh. He wove it around the front of one finger to the back of the other and finally tied the end around his wrist. He squeezed his fingers shut several times as far as they could go to get a feel for it.

"Gloves would have worked well. Get used to wearing long sleeves, which shouldn't be an issue with winter around the corner. Did you have to ruin that top?" Tylle asked. Her eyes were on the road ahead.

Lin smirked and grabbed the pack. Having the Sight meant seeing all forms of Bindings. But that was all. It didn't allow you to see through things like clothing or armor. A person could be Stitched head to toe, and no one would know the difference. Not that a slip of cloth would keep him from a Weaver's judgment, but more that he could go unmolested if they crossed another person with the Sight. At least unless they got close enough to feel the hum of energy, but a piece of him knew it was to hide the failure from himself more than anyone else. He'd caught himself staring at them more and more. *They were beautiful.*

Tylle's pack felt light enough as Lin lifted it to his shoulders. "You should put a cloth band or something around your finger," he said.

"Why?" Tylle asked. When Lin didn't answer, she shook her head and looked at him, expression incredulous. "That can't *really* be what you stole precious moments of our time for or why you ruined a perfectly fine top. To hide magic that most people can't see."

Lin flushed. "*I* can see them."

"That is where we are different. I *wish* I could see my Bludwieve. I've heard few types of Bindings match their intricacies or beauty."

Lin frowned and made a fist of his left hand. His palm and wrist itched where the fabric was loose. "We differ more than just there," he said.

"You know... in the old days when more of our people knew about Velkath and his family, more people *also* had the Sight. And wearing your Stitches, as you call them, on open flesh was a mark of a true warrior. And then there would be wise men and women made wiser by, how you say, Binding their minds." She tapped the side of her head and, noticing a stray strand, pushed her hair back behind her ear.

"Blasphemy." Lin gasped, staring up at the woman. "They'd have gone mad!"

"Possible. Maybe more so now than back then, but the risk was worth the reward."

Lin studied her while he worked on the nuts in his hand. She *could* have Stitches lining her legs, arms, and torso. Hidden as she was under the thin cloak and baggy long-sleeved shirt she wore. But he'd have felt them humming when they'd touched. And he'd had his head resting in her lap. "I saw no Stitches lining your flesh."

"I've not claimed to be a warrior."

"Yet you slew a handful of untethered? One of them the truest thing to a monster I've ever seen."

She shrugged. "It was weak by the time I was upon it. And the rest were more walking corpses than threats. I told you before, I'm a priestess of Vellyr."

Lin had finished deshelling the small, gritty nuts and eagerly crunched into them. "Let's pretend that the Six and One are... similar to your gods. What does Vellyr represent?"

"None of them... *represent* any one thing, not the way the false six embody men's virtues. Verbanth *earned* the description wrathful. It is the same as Velkath earning the title of cunning. Truthful Vellyr."

"Truthful?" Lin narrowed his eyes. A convenient aspect to represent if you are attempting to earn someone's trust. "Really?"

Tylle nodded. "For every lie Vellyr spoke, he added another 'Stitch' to his flesh."

"And this is where you tell me, to his death, his flesh was pristine?"

"Oh no." Tylle grinned. There in that smile, the way her cheek dimpled and lip curled, Lin could see the resemblance to Margaret. "He would have been as bright as the sun to you. But marking his flesh as such was him accepting *his* truth and showing his true nature to anyone who knew him and had the Sight. Which, as I said, back then were many."

Lin sighed and rubbed his temple. "You are a priestess, aren't you?"

She laughed fully, clutching tight to the reins. "Why do you say it like that?"

Her smile, though her lips were thin, was infectious. Perhaps because she so often *didn't* smile. Lin joined her despite the throb that had started behind his eyes. "You speak like one. I expected some tale manufactured to convince me of *your* trustworthiness. Instead, you somehow made it into a story I'm meant to self-reflect on."

"You believe so?"

"Seemed like it."

"If it did, it was not by design. Simply the story of how Vellyr earned his title." Tylle seemed to sober, but there was still a light in her eyes that Lin was sure hadn't been there before.

"Are the others also titled so ironically?"

"No. Which surely makes Vellyr smile, I would think."

Lin grunted. "What lie did you tell to earn the Bludwieve you've marked yourself with?"

Whatever joviality had spread between the two of them dissipated before the question entirely left Lin's lips. He looked up at her, noting her silence and her jaw tightening.

"I'm so—"

"I told Margie... I told her she'd be safe if she returned to me. I couldn't keep that promise. So now it stands for something else."

"I'm sorry," Lin finished what he'd started to say.

If she had a reply, she kept it to herself.

Silence swallowed them like a starving mouth and chewed on them well into the night when they made camp, digesting them in the morning once they broke it.

By midday, they had crossed the first proper intersection. Old weatherworn signposts stood sentry at the opposite corners. Riversbend, written in common script and faded, lay in the direction they were heading. Lin turned and read the northern post.

Fallo. Not that he'd expected anything else.

The sound of a horse and accompanying wagon wheels creaking from the westward path caught his ear. Tylle held a hand out to Lin, motioning for him to stop. She craned her neck, leaning forward on Nebra's back as if she could see past the prickly leafed brush around the bend in the path.

"Let's just cross," Lin said, stepping forward.

"No." Tylle shot him a glance that seemed to imply he was the biggest fool she'd ever met.

"Why not?"

"To see if they have news, or goods, or any number of things. Wagons mean wares most of the time."

Lin frowned. That was true enough, but what did it mean the rest of the time? Prisoners, likely. Children being taken to the Ferrucium, possibly. He clicked his tongue. There were only a few ways Lin could imagine this going, and none were necessarily good. He spared another glance at his wrapped hand as the wagon and its riders cleared the bend and bush.

It looked like a prison wagon, wide enough on the front for two people to sit side by side on the bench. It was pulled by a single, strong-looking horse.

The riders were both wrapped in cloaks of varying red shades. Likely little more than a sign that one had been in the sun more than the other, the way Lin's had been sun faded compared to Aemun's. A woman held the reins, her face gaunt. Her skin was pale but red and blotchy. The man on the bench beside her had a stocky build, dark skin, and stubble. He leaned back in his seat, a wide-brimmed hat covering the top half of his face.

Like a saw, his snore carried over the creaking wood of the wagon, heavy and ragged. No matter how Lin tried to interpret the solid-topped wagon or the pair operating it, they were Ferrucium soldiers. If they had children, they were likely Evaluators like Denro. The woman holding the reins hit the man's knee once, and when he didn't immediately wake, again with the back of her hand.

Lin smiled as politely as he could and then glanced at Tylle. Her expression was flat, but her knuckles were pale on Nebra's bridle.

Slowly, the man pulled his hat from his eyes and rubbed the bridge of his nose. The wagon slowed, and the driver looked both ways across the road, stare coming to a rest on Tylle and Lin.

"Waiting for something?" she called over the wheels as they crunched to a stop in the stone-riddled dirt.

"Was hoping you might be traveling merchants," Tylle replied.

Lin kept a smile on his face. Perhaps Tylle *actually* hoped it was a merchant's wagon, but he was sure she didn't *want* it. Not really. Not the way she so vehemently disavowed the Ferrucium and the control it had over potential Binders. No matter what Tylle said, they were Binders. Magic was Binding. It felt blasphemous somehow to consider it Weaving, even if she pronounced it oddly. *Wieving.*

"Sorry to disappoint," the man replied groggily, eyes scanning Tylle, then locking onto Lin at her side. "But now that you've seen us not to be merchants, no need to wait at the intersection like bandits." The man chuckled at his own words. Looking at them, it was apparent Lin and Tylle weren't bandits any more than they were merchants.

The woman let the reins fall from her grip, and the wagon came to a complete stop. The single horse, a tall chestnut, snorted and swished its tail.

"If you aren't bandits, good. If you are, that's fine, too. Times are hard. But the Ferrucium takes all kinds, one way or another. If you're looking for work to earn some honest coins, we can help. If you want to try us, well, like I said, that's fine too. But it'll end badly—for you, I mean."

Lin stepped forward, clicking his tongue at Nebra. She followed for a step before snorting and stamping her front leg. Tylle held the reins and shook her head.

"We don't have time for this," Lin whispered to Tylle.

"You two are the ones who stopped in the middle of the road. You could go, and it wouldn't hurt anything," Tylle said.

"Six watch over us. You're *trying* to pick a fight," Lin hissed.

Her lips parted to speak, but the cracking of wood siding exploding into shrapnel splintered her voice.

An untethered stood on top of the wagon as if it were the most natural thing it could do. It was swathed in a tattered cloak stained a mold-laced brown, its hair stringy and clumped. Face gray, ashen even. Its limbs were free of obvious Stitches, but it had a plethora of crude, rough bands of light across the flesh of its torso, visible through the tattered cloth.

Children's screams erupted from the wagon simultaneously as the wood exploded, but they were sharper, higher pitched, and more painful to hear. The soldiers at the head of the wagon moved instantly. The man, short and thick, drew a Ferrucium steel blade. His partner shifted her cloak and pulled out a bolt shooter, standing and turning at once.

Lin blanched. She'd had it pointed right at them.

"Untethered!" the woman screamed.

Lin moved. His ribs were sore, his limbs still heavier than they'd ever been. He heard Tylle shout something as she sprung from the saddle. If her concern had been the possible children being transported, then there was no way she'd let the wagon and its contents be eviscerated by the untethered.

He didn't have time to think about *why* an untethered was attacking a random caravan or *why* he'd seen more of the One-whispered monsters in the last few days than he had the better part of the year.

Bolts arched overhead, and the untethered slammed its fist into the top of the wagon three times before the wood fully caved, rotten-looking blood staining the falling debris. Lin and the other man were upon it before it could look into the hole it had made. The man used his pommel as a focus for his will like every Ferrucium soldier had been trained.

Lin formed a circle with the fingers of his left hand, threading his intention into the world and lancing several Wefts at the monster. There was no hesitation in the assault, no trying to limit its movements with Weaves. This monster looked even more far gone than the one in Lyre. The soldier beside Lin stumbled as the wagon shook, his Weave forming dull and flaccid. *Malnourished.*

Without turning its attention from the wagon top, the untethered crafted and unleashed a swathe of Wefts and Weaves without apparent pattern or focus. Vast threads of ethereal light flew toward Lin and the unbalanced Binder beside him. Lin drew his sword and swung at the Weft heading toward him. He parried it, and it bit into his blade before cracking and dissolving into light particles. But past the fading light, he saw his Weft cut into the untethered's flesh. It sliced vertically down its abdomen. Where there were no Stitches, it bled streaks of brown down its side. But where it had the Stitches along its torso, Lin's Weft shattered.

Lin's hands trembled. A nick the size of a person's tooth had chipped from his sword's edge.

How did you defeat it? 'By being more of a monster than my enemy.' Tylle's words echoed as Lin gawked at the grotesque monster. This was the first time he could recall seeing one lit by the sun, even if the clouds made the day a bright gray.

The other soldier wasn't so lucky. He seemed not to have the Sight, based on the blood pouring from his arm. But despite the wound, he had found his footing and was making another Binding.

Lin refocused on the untethered. These fights, standing against untethered, were what made Ferrucium soldiers. These moments where life and death were on the line. If only Tylle could see it the way *he* did. They weren't monsters for taking and training children. *These* were the monsters.

Tylle had somehow gotten behind the creature. Lin focused and sent two more Wefts at it: one high and one low.

The woman had given up on the bolt shooter, the angle too bad or the shots too slow, given the intensity of the situation. She had circled around on the ground and threw fast, sloppy Weaves at the untethered.

Tylle was a blur. She struck high with the back of her hand, smacking the untethered's head. Then, she swept low with her leg, knocking the monster to the ground. It rolled preternaturally fast, and Bindings Lin couldn't identify manifested around it like a cocoon. They looked like a strange mix of flexible Weaves and sharp, dangerous Wefts. Tylle didn't have the Sight. She'd made that clear, but somehow, she reacted as if a Binding had formed before her. The increased tang of rust on the air or the intense pulsing energy might have alerted her.

"Bindings!" Lin shouted, working his own. Sweat stung his eyes, and his heart throbbed painfully in his chest. Inside the wagon, the children screamed again. Most were crying for their parents, one clearly trying to console the smaller ones.

Tylle nodded and picked up a sharp plank of broken wood.

The untethered rose to its full height, obscured by the distortion of swirling Bindings in the air.

The cocoon of Bindings shrunk inward until it fit into the untethered's palm. It twisted into an orb of spiraling ochre light.

"Get down!" Lin yelled, diving to the side as the world exploded in a flash of light so intense that it seared the back of his eyelids even with them closed. He landed hard, and something popped, reverberating in his bones.

Chapter Seven

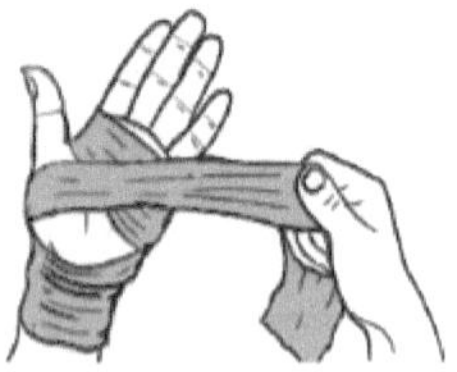

Brittle Hate

Lin's left arm lanced with pain. He opened his eyes, but it was like a blanket of bright golden light had been draped over his face. Or worse, as if the explosion had seared into his pupils. He blinked over and over, but nothing changed.

"Lin!" The force of the words was a shout, but it came through like it had been screamed from down a long hall. He rolled, regretting it immediately as fresh pain stung his arm. Jaw clenched, he rose. With his right hand, he wiped at his eyes, the skin sensitive but not wet with blood or humming from magic.

He blinked several more times. The world faded into a bleak grayness, and there were washed-out silhouettes where he thought people might be.

Two figures stood over a third, with a corpse-shaped mound near them.

Lin stumbled toward them, each step jolting his arm, each jolt tearing another grunt from him. He was sick of being broken. Sick of feeling so frail. He was a *Ferrucium* fucking soldier. A *Binder.* Not a twig meant to be snapped at the slightest breeze.

By the time he was to the silhouettes, they had clarified into people. Tylle was forced onto her knees, hands bound by Weaves, a short sword pressed to her throat.

The pair of soldiers looked as rough as Lin felt, but to the side lay the untethered, dead in a pool of oily, brown blood. "Not another step, or she takes it through her throat."

Lin started to stumble but caught himself and froze.

"Who are you two?" the man asked.

"Lindel of the Ferrucium, main assignment escort."

If the revelation he was with the Ferrucium surprised the duo, they didn't act like it. "And her?" the woman asked.

"Tylle..."

"Of the Ferrucium or not?" The man spat the question like he'd already formed his expected answer.

Lin licked his lips and stared into Tylle's cold, hate-filled eyes. "I have the Sight. She is no untethered."

"That's not what we asked," the woman snapped. "She isn't one of us, is she? A woman Binding at her age, untrained or instructed by the Ferrucium, it is only a matter of time before she *becomes* untethered."

Lin winced as he let go of his left arm and held his palm out placatingly. "I know. I know. But she has saved me several times, and we are heading to the Ferrucium. *Together.*" Lin jerked his chin at the untethered. "She did that, no? This is the second untethered of that caliber that has attacked us in so many days."

"Hmph." The man spat a pink-tinged wad of snot into the dirt.

Lin leaned to the left and caught his footing. He looked around and saw the wagon on its side, its top destroyed, entirely detached from the horse, which had better sense than to stay. Inside, three children huddled against the far wall, barely visible.

"Let us... Let us be on our way, friends."

"No," the woman spat. "We *tried*. But she refused. Do you not recall?"

Lin nodded. "Nothing makes a person see reason like the tip of a blade at the base of their throat."

"It's too late for that." Her voice piqued.

"Then let us all go to the Ferrucium and have her be judged. She could be an asset!"

"She is too dangerous! Suppose she is not Ferrucium, which you have all but guaranteed now. In that case, she is a threat to the Ferrucium and doesn't deserve judgment." The man spoke, his eyes locked onto Lin's.

"People deserve chances. If we don't give them, we are no better than untethered."

The man shook his head. "Greta, detain him."

Lin watched the woman turn to him, a knife in her left hand, the other free for forming Bindings.

Greta jerked her pointed chin at him. "Come on," she said. "We'll get you to the Ferrucium, and Weavers can decide what to do with you."

"And her?" Lin asked.

Greta shook her head. "Drew will do what needs to be done. Simple as that."

But it wasn't *simple*. Lin nodded and staggered forward, breathing heavier than he needed to and stepping more awkwardly than necessary. He held out his arm and nodded, "For the Ferrucium. For the Six watching me and so that my name need not be whispered to the One."

Tylle shook her head and looked down.

The fact that his left arm had popped when he landed wasn't something he was faking or exaggerating. As Greta grabbed it, rougher than necessary, he fell to his knees and tumbled.

Lin screamed louder than needed, but if Tylle knew anything about him, it was how he handled pain. And he hadn't screamed nearly so loud when the untethered had first broken his fingers or snapped his elbow back. He needed Tylle to trust him, to look at him.

"It's broken," Lin howled.

Greta shifted and shook her head. "Get up! We don't know if there are more of those One-whispered untethered lurking, and you screaming like a stuck pig doesn't help!"

Lin nodded. Not at her words but at the moment Tylle looked up at him.

Tylle blinked and narrowed her eyes.

Using the man's hilt as a focus, Lin jerked his right arm back, threading his intention into the world and slamming a Weave into the man's torso. Greta yanked Lin back with so much force his shoulder roared in waves of rippling flame.

Greta snarled and stabbed down.

"Hide them all you want. I feel them under this cloth! You've bound your flesh, and the One will know your name, oath breaker!"

Before her blade could find purchase, Lin punched her. He swung up and hit her pointed jaw as hard as possible. He didn't feel good about it. Somehow, Binding made everything a little less personal, and the look on her face as she staggered back proved that she felt as insulted as she was injured. Her nails had dug into the cloth wrapped around his hand and wrist and loosened it, the bright Stitches shining in the corner of Lin's eyes.

Feet away, Tylle had somehow tripped the off-balanced Drew and had risen to her feet. But her hands were still Bound tight in front of her.

Lin focused on the gap of *her* hands and imagined her bonds snapping. That small thought seemed enough as the Bindings wrapping her wrists broke away in a spray of golden sparks.

Tylle moved like her body was made for violence, each movement bleeding into the next. She disarmed Drew, took the weapon as her own, and ended his life before Lin could argue that she shouldn't.

Greta charged at Lin, forming a Weft with one hand and slashing with the other. But she stopped before her magic materialized, and her arms fell limp to her sides. Her knife fell to the ground beside her. Lin wheeled around, confusion seeping over him.

A Needle, a type of Binding hard to make and harder to control, stuck out from the base of her neck. Her lips moved, but only a soft groan escaped her. He'd heard of Executioners using them before but had only ever seen it demonstrated once on a pig during training. Greta twitched, legs and arms spasming.

Lin fell to the ground, exhausted.

"No condemnation for killing them?" Tylle asked. She adjusted her tunic and stepped toward the wagon.

Inside, the children were quiet and still.

"I think... I think this time, there was no choice to be made. They didn't want to see reason. Planned to kill both of us by the end."

But was that the case? They didn't want to work with *Tylle,* who clearly felt the same as they did, but they were willing to at least let Lin be judged by a Weaver. Something he'd already determined was correct. Doubt burdened him as much as the discomfort of his wounds, and he stared at the corpses for a long moment.

"It's alright now, young ones. It's alright." Tylle's voice was low and as close to gentle as it could be, like how she had spoken when tending to Lin's wounds.

Wounds. Lin looked at his arm. The bone wasn't protruding, but something *felt* broken. He rotated his shoulder slowly. It wasn't there. Clenching his fist told him it was something in his forearm, so while Tylle cajoled the children from the wagon, Lin undid the makeshift wrapping around his arm.

His mouth had gone dry, and his right hand trembled.

"Lin, come meet the children. They're from a small village no more than a day back west."

Lin shuffled over, wrapping the scraps of cloth around his right arm as he tried to keep his left arm as still as possible.

A boy older than the others had scratches along his forearms and a mop of greasy brown hair. His skin was dark, like he had lived most of his life under the sun, and his eyes were the color of clay. He couldn't have been more than seven years old, and the other two were easily half his age. Two girls, one as dark as the boy and the other as pale as Tylle, stared up from behind his legs.

"This is Lin. He's a friend."

Lin shot a glance at that. Likely, it was something she was saying to ease the children. He *knew* that. But could they ever be friends? *If she was telling the truth about Aemun?* No. Their fate was decided when Lin had first earned his crimson cloak. She'd said as much.

The girls' fingers tightened into the boy's trousers, and they tried to hide further behind his legs.

Lin looked at his arm and frowned. If they were scared of Lin, perhaps they all had the Sight and saw him like the untethered? It was the only thing that made sense...

"It's okay..." Lin stared, shifting so that his Stitched arm was hidden.

"You're another Redrobe, yeah? Heard you call it out," the boy said.

Tylle started to speak, then stopped, eyes finding Lin's and searching for the answer.

"Yes," Lin replied. "I'm a Binder, something those two thought the three of you were fit to become. And there's nothing *wrong* with that."

"Then why'd you attack them?" the boy asked.

"We didn't. Not at first. But it seems maybe they weren't nice people," Lin whispered.

"And you are?"

"Yes," Tylle answered for Lin. "He is a *good*, nice person."

"Are we taking them back to their home?" Lin asked.

At the mention of home, the children, even the oldest, began to cry.

Something about the tears, the snotty sobbing, made Lin cringe. They hadn't thought he was a monster because of his Stitches but because of his words. And that, more than their reaction, was a spur underfoot to him.

"Tylle. I think my arm is broken."

Tylle frowned and pulled away from the children. "Let me take a look."

He did, and she held his arm, running her hand over the flesh, goose prickles rising at the unexpected tenderness of her touch.

He expected some sort of Binding. A sense of guilt and anticipation warred within him. With a twist, Tylle jerked his arm, and it made a grinding pop. As intense as the pain had been in a burst, it faded, still there but dull.

"Dislocated was all. Don't lift anything heavy for a few days, and you'll be alright."

Lin rolled his wrist and frowned.

Was he disappointed? *No, that couldn't be it.* But there was no denying he had expected her to somehow use magic to fix his break, and he hadn't wholly been against the idea. He'd... looked forward to it, hadn't he?

"Thank you," Lin said. He straightened his back and began to rewrap his fingers and wrist with his cloth scraps.

"W-why are you doing that?" the darker girl asked, voice high, shaky and squeaky. She continued to hide behind the boy but stared at Lin with the same clay-colored eyes as her makeshift protector. Tears left streaks of dust down her round cheeks.

"It makes me feel better about the decisions I made. About myself." Lin tried to smile, but there was a reason he'd always been on escort assignments and wasn't an Evaluator like Denro. He had never been good with children. That's why he'd been doubly surprised when Aemun foisted the baby-carrying duties onto him. But the warmth had been unexpectedly pleasant. And he thought he'd done well enough.

The girl didn't seem to notice how forced his smile was. Her eyes were on his wraps, on the Stitched flesh underneath them.

"Can you see the lights?" Lin asked, raising his arm and letting the scratchy cloth slide down a bit from his wrist.

Her eyes were big, filled with a blend of fear and curiosity that only children ever seemed to truly have. She nodded.

The older boy shook his head, and the other girl whispered something under her breath, but Tylle had grown still.

"She says she sees things, but my little sister likes to make up stories. We know there really isn't anything there." The boy had stopped crying the soonest, but he still fought to keep his voice from quivering.

Lin smiled. It had been the same for him. Even during training, other kids thought Lin had lied when he described what Bindings looked like. Some were bright and beautiful, most actually, but others were dull and weak, speckled like a bar of iron left out in the rain. Everyone could *feel* the hum of magic if they were close enough. But feeling and seeing were two very different things. At least the Educators had supported him and corrected the other children regarding the Sight.

"She isn't lying," Tylle said. "Tell us your names, and we'll get you home."

"P-promise?" the oldest asked.

"I swear it on my god Vellyr."

"Micha." The boy put a hand on the pale girl's head. "Jules." He tapped the one who looked blood-related to him. "And I'm Roge."

"Tylle and my companion, Lin. Have you eaten?" Tylle checked the children over. There were a few scrapes and bruises from when the wagon toppled over, but nothing serious. She kept their attention from the bodies as best she could.

Lin was happy to leave her to that task. His breath fogged before him, and his whistle for Nebra seemed to stretch out, lasting far longer than it had any right to. The horse that had fled the wagon grazed down the side of the road and perked up at Lin's whistle.

"Come on then," Lin whispered, the horse easing toward him.

Nebra, short and stout compared to the wagon-pulling chestnut, came trotting up shortly after, and a genuine smile found its way onto Lin's face. She nuzzled up against him, snorting through his pockets, looking for treats he didn't have.

"I'll get you something soon, girl." His eyes stung as he buried his face into her neck and breathed in her scent. She smelled like the road, the wind, and everything he loved about traveling for the Ferrucium. Lin swallowed and pulled himself away, wiping a hand over the wet spots his tears had left in her coat. He'd drawn a line today by choosing Tylle over fellow soldiers. It felt like a betrayal, even if Lin didn't know those two personally. But if he didn't know how to remove Stitches, then they'd likely not either, and there was still the issue of the Binding Tenets being broken in the first place. He was a traitor in the Ferrucium's eyes long before he raised a hand to save Tylle's life. He knew that.

Lin closed his eyes and pushed it down, tamping and pressing it like tobacco into a pipe. But he'd been doing that for so long that he wasn't sure how much more he could fit before the pipe would need to be lit.

Nebra snorted near his ear, and Lin opened his eyes. He could still make things right. Speak to the Weavers, beg for absolution of the Six. Even if his name did get whispered to the One, he could... Lin watched Tylle moving with the children. Graceful, strong. Her expression was soft despite the hard lines on her face. She hunted Aemun and wanted revenge and to take back the baby. Would she want to raise the child once this was all done? *Would she want his help?* Lin shook his head and pushed the thought aside. Tamping it down, just waiting to burn like all the rest.

They needed to get these lost children back home. Lin sighed, wishing he wasn't as torn as the cloth scraps wrapped around his left hand.

Chapter Eight

Brittle Blood

It took less than a day to arrive at Creekside, the small collection of homes the children called their village. It had to be the smallest village Lin had ever visited, but it was quaint. Seven houses spread between a wilderness pocket to their east and a low-running silt bed to the west. A small stone bridge carried the path over the creek, though when Lin looked over the side, he was sure the moss-covered stones weren't necessary. Perhaps it had been a river once, but that time had long passed, and either way, Lin doubted it. The village might've had the name Riverside if that were the case.

"Micha, be still," Roge said. Out of the children, he was the only one not trying to clamber off the horse before it stopped.

Lin steeled himself.

"Greet the families with an expression like that, and they might think you bear terrible news," Tylle said, brushing a loose strand of hair back. Her braid had devolved over the last few days into a disparate number of strands, and the one she pushed back was added to the collection behind her ear.

"I may yet," Lin replied, sliding from Nebra's saddle.

Tylle pursed her lips, shifting her gaze to the children.

Chickens squawked as Micha and Jules raced down the village's well-worn paths. The children cried out, and confused calls responded. In moments, more people than homes had gathered.

A woman, belly swollen, cried as she saw Micha and pulled the pale little girl into her arms. Roge and Jules were swept up into a separate embrace. Lin shifted his weight then turned his back on the scene, checking Nebra's straps and, once he exhausted that, looking at the wrappings on his arm.

"We should speak what the children can't or don't know how to explain," Tylle said.

Lin licked his lips and glanced over his shoulder at the families reuniting. "You can."

"You trust me to that? I could just throw the Ferrucium to the wolves in my explanation."

Despite her admonishments of the Ferrucium, he had no doubts that she'd at least be honest about what had really happened. *Another* untethered attack. "You could, but I don't think you would."

"Does seeing happy families really make you so uncomfortable?" Tylle asked.

Lin raised a brow and crossed his arms. "No."

Tylle shook her head and stalked forward like a wolf, heading to the heart of the village in search of lambs.

Voices were carried, but the words were lost over the snorting of pigs from the nearest home and the clamoring of chickens. Lin stopped trying to listen and made his way to the creek. It had been a little while since he'd had the chance to forage, and honeycaps could often be found near water sources. What water was in the creek didn't move fast enough to burble, only trickling down onto a few patches of pebbles before running off into a narrow silt bed that lasted as far as Lin could see. But along the older trees, the soft orange glow of unpicked honeycaps shone like faint Bindings. Careful not to slip on thick moss or damp stones, Lin stepped across the creek.

"You the man that brought back my children?"

Lin's shoulders tensed, and he turned to face the person approaching him. The man was slim, with a shirt that hung off his slender limbs like a sheet. He raised his hands to show they were empty as if he thought Lin might run when confronted. It wouldn't have been a surprise if Tylle had sent the man his way and said something to that effect.

"I happened to be there. But the real hero was that priestess," Lin said, hoping that would nip the conversation before it had to go further.

"I ain't worried about her. Son told me you're a Redrobe. She ain't."

Lin nodded and narrowed his eyes.

The man stood at the opposite edge of the creek, which meant he wasn't more than a hop away, and the frown on his face was plain under the unshaved patches of wiry hair. His brows were thicker than his spotty beard, and his haircut was militant. He had the same clayish brown eyes as Roge and Jules but seemingly without the sharp alertness that both the children shared. And from where he stood, the stinging scent of ale wafted from him.

"So, you brought them back on whose authority? Cause we ain't giving the coins back." The man crossed his arms. He didn't speak with the righteous anger of a furious parent. It was like he was *ashamed* to be confronting Lin.

As he should be.

"The Six seemed to decide that it was best. No worries about the coins. Now, if you'll—"

"But what if it wasn't?" the man asked, softer.

"Excuse me?" Lin stopped attempting to climb the steep bank and turned to face the man entirely.

"What if them leaving was the best that might ever happen to them? And now you say the Six decided my kids ain't worth better?"

Lin looked the man up and down again, the village a poor backdrop in the dusky evening light. "Jules has the same gift I do. She could find a life within the Ferrucium, but there is no guarantee it'll be easy, good, or..." Lin trailed off, seeing the doubt in the man's eyes. "Until she is old enough to have her blood, she'll be trained in physical and magical combat. After her first blood, she is taught how to manage that alongside Binding, which could be fatal if done incorrectly. Then, she will be evaluated and paired with a partner. We are all soldiers, and then there are specializations. Escorters, Evaluators, Educators, and other positions, but she would likely fall into one of the first three. They will expect her to bear children, who you will never meet, and they, too, will become soldiers. Roge would experience much of the same, but he doesn't have the Sight and will likely be seen as... less valuable."

"But what... what if that's still better than this." The man seemed intent not to cry, but his clay-colored eyes looked as wet as the creek bed, and his chin quivered. He spread his arms as if to encompass all of Creekside, and as small as the village was, it nearly felt like he could have.

"If you think that's the case, let them decide. If they want, take them to a larger town and find a Ferrucium Evaluator." The words fell from his mouth before he realized he'd spilled them.

"Was that your path?" the man asked, arms now hanging limp at his sides.

Lin stared into the father's eyes. He'd first assumed the man was purely greed-motivated, but it was more than that. "Yes," Lin lied.

Thick brows furrowing, the man nodded, his chin nearing the top of his bony chest. "And you've lived a good life?"

Lin sniffed and sighed. "Better than most. Worse than others."

They shared a look, and then the man turned away, moving as quickly as he had approached, baggy sleeves and trousers billowing behind him.

A chuckle bounced from Lin's chest as he returned to the honeycaps on the higher bank. Roots and small stones stuck out from the bank's wall, and the damp earth smell comforted Lin. As an Escorter, he didn't often have to deal with direct questions from the parents. Sure, people occasionally pressed him on issues like Lyre's Alderman had, but he hadn't dealt with a fallout like this before.

Overhead, a twig cracked, and Lin looked up to see Tylle staring down at him from where the honeycaps sprouted. She frowned and, for a moment, looked as if she planned to kick leaves and sod over the edge at him.

"What?" Lin asked.

"You."

"What about me?"

"You were not evaluated as a child, taken, let free, and returned of your own choice to be evaluated later. You don't know how you came to be a soldier."

Lin pinched the bridge of his nose and blinked up at Tylle. "Fair."

"So, telling that man—"

"What he wanted to hear was a kindness," Lin finished for her. "I've no doubt that going to the Ferrucium would offer them a better life than out here."

"*You* don't get to make that decision for *them*. That is the entire problem with the evaluation!" Her voice cracked. She scowled, and Lin was sure he'd never seen her look older or as fierce. "They don't get to say no. Refuse the coins, and you're stolen away in the dead of night."

Lin shook his head. "No. And I'm not good with children. You got to see that firsthand. But the pain in his eyes—well, it was what he wanted to hear. Telling him otherwise wouldn't have done any good."

Tylle sighed and looked down, glancing at the honeycaps near her worn boots. "I sometimes forget that just because we've traveled together these few days doesn't mean you see things the way I do or know what I know. It's easy to forget when it's just you, me, and the road."

Lin nodded. "I get that. I do. But your refusal to understand where I'm coming from is just as frustrating. Now... would you mind getting those for me? I didn't realize there was an easier way up and around."

Tylle seemed to ignore him and crouched so that she was closer to eye level. "You know... the lie you told the father, it's not far from the truth of how things had once been. When Wievers braided their hair for tradition, when each pattern woven through hair and fabric *meant* something, parents would show their children Wieves. And when they were old enough to journey from home, seeking their *Uethes*, they would learn from masters."

She pronounced the strange words in the same throaty voice she'd used to say Bludwieve, and Lin knew it was meant to be an ancient thing. "Oath?" Lin asked.

"Close enough." Tylle nodded. "A personal thing to them. And each formed a story in the tapestry of the heavens. When the foreign kingdom of the north pushed in, they overwhelmed our people and then tricked them into policing their own. The Accords."

Heat ran up Lin's back, and he crossed his arms. The steady drip, drip, drip of water on stone nearby was like a child pulling at his ear, begging to be heard when adults were conversing.

"Am I just meant to take your word? That what you say is the truth? *Wieves* and *Uethes* and Danica not originally being part of the kingdom?" Lin snapped.

Tylle frowned and picked the honeycaps one by one. After a long pause, she said, "No. I don't tell you hoping you'll believe me or demand retribution for our peoples' stolen history." She shifted and held out the sweet-smelling mushrooms. "It is so that I can say I tried to open your eyes, with everything in me, when the time comes, and we part."

Lin reached up and grabbed her hand, holding it gently. "I-I can admit that my world is narrow. In the Ferrucium, we are taught the importance of *why* we patrol and why things are done the way they are. We aren't mindless, like ants, to crawl around purposelessly. But you—" Lin tightened his grip "—should admit the same. You don't know what or why we are taught, just that it interferes with *your* view."

She looked down on him. Her lids were half closed, and she looked at him with *pity*.

Drip, drip, drip.

"Lies you've been told from such an early age you can't recall when you first heard them aren't *views*. I've heard the spoken tales told around fires. I have seen texts that barely survived flame. I've felt—"

"Prove it. Show me the truth then!"

"I can't show you what you don't want to see," Tylle said, reminding Lin that she was still a priestess with words like those.

"Bullshit," Lin snapped, releasing her hand. The honeycaps fell and landed in the layer of pebbled, slow-going water. He huffed and turned away before he said something he might regret.

"Lin." It was only the second time she'd called him by his name since they'd met, but turning back to face her wasn't an option. He clenched and relaxed his hands repeatedly as he stalked away, following the creek's bend northward as it sloped uphill and widened.

The trees eventually thinned into a glade, and the breeze cut harder for it. Smoke snaked into the sky where Creekside should be, and he could see farther tendrils doing the same. These were signs of scattered villages with too few reasons between them to consolidate or fight each other for land.

Lin stared up at the stars that blinked into existence. Even as a child, he liked to think they were stitched into the sky by some powerful Binder of old. He shook his head. Tylle likely had a twisted story for that, too. He ran his hand over his head as he stared up, trying to understand how he was meant to travel with her without them fighting at every disagreement.

But that was precisely his issue with *her* logic. All her little notes on Danica's "true" history were stories to him. Unsubstantiated claims. Of course, he'd seen things on the road that could be better, like the state of Danica as a whole. But the Ferrucium was the light standing against the darkness. The only thing keeping the untethered controlled. Fallo flashed in his mind. The attack on the wagon and at Lyre. Since getting into Tylle's proximity, he'd had The One's own luck.

Wind rattled the broad leaves that clung to the skeleton-thin trees like strips of cloth that hadn't sloughed away yet.

"Achoo. Choo." Two muffled sneezes, back-to-back, came from the direction of Creekside.

Three times, he'd gone to be alone, and three times, Creekside had offered an interruption to his seclusion.

"Come out," Lin called. His hand went to where his dagger would be, and he remembered it had rusted. His mind went to the knife sitting nestled in the pack with Nebra. He made a circle with his index finger and thumb of his left hand and threaded his intention through it. A Weave blurred then focused in his hand like captured starlight.

The high-pitched squeal indicated two things: it was a child, and they could see his magic.

"Jules, I know it's you," Lin called. He looked around.

"P-please don't hurt me," she called back from behind a tree that rested on the slope next to a thicket of brambles and a ravine cut that didn't look too deep.

"Why'd you follow me?" Lin asked, walking forward and leaning around the tree to see the small child huddled there. Her knees were dirt-stained and pressed close to her chest, and she clutched something tightly in her hands, looking up at him with tear-filled eyes.

A pang of guilt stung him at the pathetic sight.

"Don't... don't be scared. It's alright." Lin let the Weave dissolve into motes of golden-orange dust.

Her eyes reflected the light like veins of gold in clay soil, and her clenched hands loosened. She held a collection of honeycaps tight enough that some stalks looked crushed.

Lin tensed against the breeze. "Did you bring those for me?"

Jules's eyes fell to her hands, and she nodded.

"Why?" He frowned. She wasn't even wearing a coat. "Here, I'll trade you." Lin plucked a bright purple flower and handed it to Jules.

Lin took the honeycaps and tucked two of the eight or so into his cheek. The sweet, acidic notes were balanced by the earthy bitterness of the stems. They were no substitute for meat, but they did more for a Binder than to ease hunger. Honeycaps were one of the best sources for recovering exhausted magic. Not nearly as potent as the corpse-seed Tylle had shown Lin, but enough that any tingling numbness he'd felt at his extremities was washed away in a flood of warmth. He couldn't help but wonder if Tylle had a tale for why they rejuvenated Binders. *Wievers*, Lin thought mockingly.

"So, why'd you follow me?" Lin asked, his words hindered only slightly by the bulge of sweet mushrooms in his mouth.

Jules shrugged and swung her arms, long sleeves rising a hair, then falling and brushing stray leaves and dirt as she lowered her shoulders.

"If it was just to bring me a snack, I appreciate it." Lin swallowed and ran his tongue against his cheeks to alleviate the grit. "But it makes me think you were watching me and Tylle speak."

Jules didn't reply.

"Were you?"

She slowed her tiny steps and, without looking at him, nodded.

Lin shook his head. This was why he hated dealing with children. They were difficult, obstinate enigmas. "If you don't talk to me, I won't know what you want."

Jules's lip quivered, and they were close enough to Creekside proper that Lin could see her mentally debating running for whichever sad shack was her home.

"I thought I'd see your arm," she whispered. The threat of tears glistened in her eyes, and her dragging sleeves shook like drapes caught in the wind.

Without looking, Lin touched the scraps of cloth he'd loosely rewrapped around his wrist. "Why?" he pressed.

"It's so pretty," Jules said, directly looking up at him. Her big, sad eyes seemed to rest on his face and constantly flickered to his left arm.

Of course, he agreed. He'd always thought Bindings were beautiful. But *Stitches*? Jules didn't know how *wrong* it was to feel that way, what sort of path that thought might lead a person down.

Lin knelt and hunched to be at eye level with the child. "You shouldn't follow strangers, and you really shouldn't tell people you think Stitched flesh looks *pretty*." He squeezed the wrap between his fingers and undid the knot.

Like the sun's light climbing the horizon at the first break, his arm glowed as the layers of wrapping came undone.

"Why hide it?" Her voice squeaked, and she reached a tiny hand out, fingers not reaching past the billowing ends of her sleeves.

Lin fought the urge to pull away as she touched the magic, humming lines. "Because not everyone who sees them… thinks they're as pretty as you and I do."

Her grin was mischievous, and her eyes lit anew.

"It is our secret. A secret between friends. We can be friends, can't we? You can't tell anyone how pretty I think they are, especially my other friend. Understand?"

He let the small child play with his hand, moving the joints so the Stitches moved with them as they walked. As old as he was, he hadn't been assigned a partner, hadn't found someone to make a binding vow with, and, in turn, have a child with. Aemun had named him true that night in Lyre. Lin was *unbound*.

But that didn't mean he hadn't thought of it. Hadn't enjoyed the warmth of Magaret's child swaddled to his chest.

Before he knew it, they were at the tiny home Jules lived in. While he still considered it more of a shack, he noticed the care put into the exterior. A flower bed with tiny seasonal wildflowers of various shades of pink. A well-used broom. A line of laundry, empty. And lines etched into the doorframe at multiple heights, one of which Jules's head aligned with perfectly. He knocked on the door, and a woman, paler than both children and their father, with sharply angled features and a frown that could turn an untethered away, answered.

"Jules! Ain't right of you to go wandering. Ain't proper."

Despite the thin-lipped frown, the woman embraced her daughter, and Roge's face appeared in the space behind her.

"She brought me some food, and I appreciate that. I wouldn't want her getting into trouble because of it," Lin said, stomach grousing at the fragrance of spiced meat. A wave of warmth came from inside. The press of bodies and conversation seen and heard within made it seem as if the entire village had gathered inside the tight quarters. As the woman moved aside to let Jules in, it looked like they had. Even Tylle and an older gray-haired woman were visible whispering in the corner.

"That's well and good, but she knows better," the mother said once Jules was led away by Roge. "Appreciate you bringing her back. You're welcome in if you'd like." She looked him up and down as she straightened her shoulders.

Lin shook his head. He cleared his throat, unsure where or when the tightness had snuck upon him. "The offer is appreciated, but I'll see to my horse. Thank you." He walked away without looking back. Looking back meant he might see Jules staring after him with hurt on her face, or he might regret not pressing into the cramped space and enjoying the warmth of company. He *wouldn't* sit beside Tylle and hear her tell tales of the old ways lost to the people. Lin hadn't come to Creekside for any of that. An Escorter of the Ferrucium didn't engage in that sort of thing, and he couldn't bring himself to think otherwise.

Lin checked on Nebra and the other horse, then walked to the stone bridge, finding a patch where the wind wasn't cutting and the ground less damp. He slumped against the stone, trembling at the coldness of it, and stared at his left arm he hadn't rewrapped.

His right hand held the cloth scraps, ready to be re-tied. The Stitches ready to be hidden. Deftly, he brought his right hand to his left wrist and traced his fingertips across his flesh, feeling the warm hum of magic thrum through his fingertips. He rested his head back and stared at the stars, neck at an odd angle just to see the sky, while he went from joint to joint with his index finger.

Drip, drip, drip.

Chapter Nine

Boundless Hope

Lin yawned and stretched, his eyes tearing up from the intensity of both actions.

"You wouldn't be yawning so much if you'd slept on an actual bed," Tylle said.

"I doubt they had an *actual* bed between the whole village."

Tylle snorted, "As rude as that sounds, you're not entirely wrong." She stretched her arms, and her neck made a soft pop as she turned it one way and then the other.

They had run Nebra and the horse they'd gotten from the wagon hard for the first half of the day and now ate at a good stretch of road past the broken wagon they'd pulled the children from. Lin had slowed to look at the carnage when they'd passed it. Wild animals seemed to have already made work of the bodies, and flies pestered them as they passed.

Once they were well down the road and the destruction was a memory they wouldn't likely have a chance to return to, Lin chewed on the last bit of dried meat Tylle had handed him that morning. Scraps the denizens of Creekside had apparently gifted her for a night of stories and prayers.

They stopped shortly after at a creek that seemed like the older brother of Creekside's sad, shallow thing.

Lin found a shaded tree and slid to rest at its roots, shutting his eyes and losing himself in the warm rays that snuck through the branches. As cold as it had been the last few days, the fresh breeze was a comforting difference that wrapped around him like a familiar cloak.

"We need to keep going," Tylle said. "The longer we take, the further away Aemun and the child get from us."

"I'm only resting my eyes."

"Vellyr knows you aren't *only* resting them. But again…"

"I should've slept indoors on whatever those people thought would pass for an actual bed."

"Why have you been doing that?" Tylle asked, her voice growing closer.

Lin blinked open his eyes and squinted at her. "Resting my eyes? Because I'm *tired*!" His voice snapped more than intended, but she didn't react, instead bending over and resting her hands on her knees to stare down at him. Her face was half-obscured by shadow, but her eyes caught a sunbeam and lit a brilliant shade of light brown with patterns he hadn't noticed before. They were the color of young bark with lines extending through the colored portion that looked like branches or roots.

She shook her head, lone braid rewoven and tighter than the night before, dancing at the motion. "Touching your fingers and wrist. Are the injuries bothering you? They shouldn't be."

Lin looked down and saw that he was, in fact, running his fingertips over the Stitches. *Feeling the hum they produced.* "No." To prove his point, he splayed his fingers and bent all of them at once, then one at a time as he rolled his wrist. "It's relaxing, is all."

"The feeling can—I've heard the feeling… can be intoxicating. One Stitch can often lead to the next in weaker-willed people. In anyone, really," Tylle said, eyes locked on his.

Lin frowned at that. He *had* thought she might Stitch him again. But he hadn't wanted it like a drunkard would want a draft, had he? "I'm fine. But the sooner we get to someone who can show me how to undo it, the happier I'll be."

Tylle nodded and exhaled. "After the way you stormed off, I was surprised to see you waiting by the horses this morning."

Lin struggled to remove a stringy piece of meat from between his back teeth with his tongue. He shook his head. "I regret the way I ended our conversation. And I've traveled with enough hard-headed cocksuckers to know the escort doesn't end just because of a disagreement."

Tylle cocked her head to the side and braced against a breeze that shook the leaves overhead. As if the tree above was applauding Lin's apology. "Are you calling me a hard-headed cocksucker?" Her brow arched, and she looked like she was holding back a smile, but her delivery had been as dry and chill as the gust.

"Half of that, at least, but it'd be improper to tell a lady *which* half," Lin said. Six, was he flirting with her? And more than that, was it working? A smile played on his lips as he stared at her.

Tylle stared back, the wind making the shadow on her face move to block her eyes. "Ugh."

And Tylle walked away.

Lin watched the blade of a woman and shook his head, eyes closing to rest, the last thing he saw being her braid swinging with her steps. Maybe he had imagined the half smile.

"We really don't have time for you to *rest* your eyes," Tylle called beside the horses. "Up."

Lin blinked several times and slowly, as slow as he could while making actual progress, rose to his feet.

As he approached the horses, Nebra gave him a sniff and nuzzled against his palm. "If I offended you, I'm sorry."

"I don't take quick words of apology any easier than I do quick words of anger," Tylle said. She climbed onto the chestnut mare's back and continued working a braid she'd started in its mane that she'd left half-finished when they stopped. Tying knots and looping hair seemed to come naturally to her, her fingers slender and deft.

Tylle caught him staring and nodded toward Nebra. "I could do her next if you'd like?"

Lin pulled himself into the saddle and shook his head. "When we find Aemun and get the truth *and* remove these Stitches, I'll likely return to the Ferrucium. No Ferrucium steed has those… braids. Nebra wouldn't need to stand out."

"What good would returning do?" Tylle asked. Her voice was flat, matter-of-fact sounding as if it weren't a question. As if he should *know* it wouldn't do any good.

"More truths, perhaps. While not as extensive as say the Fentian scholars' collection, the library there is vast. I could learn about some of these traditions you keep mentioning."

"I've heard of the records kept with the Ferrucium. They put the *lie* in the word library."

Lin frowned. "It isn't spelled the same. And really, we call them the archives."

"You know what I mean." Tylle gave him one of her half smiles, a dimple forming on the same side of her face as her scar.

"I just meant I could compare the stories you've told me against the information there."

"You roll your eyes whenever I try to teach you about Danica's past."

Lin flicked his tongue against his tooth and shook his head.

"Yes, you genuinely do. Or you cry like a baby bird fallen from the nest, but the gods didn't see fit to dash your skull against the stone on the way down."

"If I'm a bird fell from a nest, are you the wolf stalking the tree?"

"Wolves don't stalk trees," Tylle corrected. "But yes, I am like a fox in that sense. The most helpful fox you've met, though, and not one like to snap fangs around the throat."

"Then tell me a story. Tell me why braiding is important to you."

Tylle nodded and stopped moving her fingers momentarily, staring at the horse hair in her hands. "In the days before the Ferrucium took control, different braids represented different sects of our people, their roles within those sects, and even their prowess at Wieving.

"But it also became a way for the traitors, those who allied with the kingdom to the north, to determine who to seek out—for good or ill. And then, learning this, many who would resist stopped using the patterns that marked them. They stopped wearing the braids of our mothers and fathers and their mothers and fathers."

"Your braid is simple," Lin said.

"These days, those who know and remember and fight keep a single, simple braid—tight enough to be a reminder but plain enough not to draw unwanted attention."

Lin narrowed his eyes. "The Weavers, they have highly stylized braids."

"Traditions that they kept, having no fear of being betrayed since they themselves have lineage to traitors. It is a sad truth that to keep Wievers and our power from becoming a threat, we were shackled by the very people meant to lead us. They feared Danicans so much, they chained us to ourselves."

"What if it was for the best?" Lin asked.

Tylle shot a dark look his way. "There is no world where taking an entire people's history and feeding them a shallow facade is for the best. It is like holding a candle to your eyes and telling you it is the sun. Or spitting on you and calling it rain. *That* is what it is like when you compare the Six to Velkath and his kin."

"A simple story," Lin said. "About the braids, I mean." He'd always thought that the Weavers' high rank within the Ferrucium was why they didn't shave the sides of their heads. They didn't have to. Though, that was still partly true. And just because Tylle voiced it didn't make the story *wholly* accurate.

"In my experience, the more complicated a story, the more lies are there to fill in the gaps."

"Your god teach you that?" Lin asked.

"Vellyr has taught me much." Tylle's dimple returned, and she turned her focus back to the horse's mane she twined between her fingers. "If you insist on being a baby bird, be one that flies again once it has fallen."

Lin took in her words and shifted in his saddle, suddenly uncomfortable. He ran his fingers through Nebra's coarse mane and considered what she was saying. The image Tylle was painting made unease fill his gut, least of all because the Ferrucium's sigil was the double-headed eagle with wide-spread wings and outstretched talons. He spared a glance at the deft movements of Tylle's fingers as she plaited the horse's hair, twisted and looped the ends, then ran the bits through each other, making a sort of hanging net from the mane.

"I could show you. If you don't want me to be the one to do Nebra's mane," Tylle said, not raising her eyes from her task.

Lin looked away and settled deeper into his saddle without a word.

They rode in silence after that, with the passersby increasing as the day went on. One friendly farmer let them know they weren't more than a short trek to Riversbend, but they'd likely miss the market unless they pushed their pace. Whether the man meant it as a way to offload some of the produce he hadn't sold or not, he succeeded. Tylle got a stained sack of beets, roots still attached, and a bundle of the saddest-looking carrots Lin had ever seen. Lin got the *second* saddest bundle of carrots and a bushel of greenery that the farmer swore would've sold out if any more Reds had been in town since they'd bought them all up on account of 'how good it is for the magic.'

Once they were out of earshot of the man, Tylle shook her head. "Good for the magic. Couldn't pass on it?"

Lin ignored her. The man had just seemed so earnest. And Lin had never heard of the corpse-seed either, so the chance that there were bushy, tough greens that also helped with making Bindings wouldn't be impossible. The Six had gifted the Binders of the world with magic. It made sense that they'd created a variety of ways to sustain it.

"But he did say if there were *any more* Reds," Tylle mused.

Lin turned and looked at her now, Nebra stepping closer and closer to the chestnut mare as the road narrowed between a patch of trees with low, forehead-knocking branches overhead. "Which means there might be some there."

"Which means *Aemun* and the child might be there. It is the largest town since Fallo."

Tylle had a point, but it still seemed unlikely. The man, if he had survived and was uninjured, had two to three days' lead on them. Even with a newborn, it seemed likely he'd set a pace hard to match. They'd also turned back to take the children to Creekside, a detour that felt more and more unnecessary when Lin thought back on it, even if speaking with Jules was a bright spot on a cloud-filled experience.

Lin pulled his right hand away from his left, realizing he'd been retracing the Stitches. For a moment, his heart stalled, and he shuddered. He needed to cover it again if they'd be around other Binders. Or maybe…

The thought and decision tore him all the way to Riversbend, which they made before nightfall. If Creekside was an ironic name, Riversbend earned its name and then some. The Telms River bent in no less than two places, but it looked like more might be up the way. Tucked between the two notched bends in the vast, slow river, the town was as tall as it was wide. The homes and shops closest to the river were on stilts and painted in hues of bright red, burnt orange, and blistered yellow, like performers at a traveling fair. Laundry, just as colorful, hung across alleys like flapping flags.

Lin had only been to Riversbend once, years ago, and he hadn't expected it to be quite so gaudy. The streets smelled of overly sharp perfume, and music carried over the cries of a rowdy crowd. It was a far cry from the tiny villages sheltered and separated by the deep northwestern woods of Danica, where he often felt the most at home.

"You look like you ate something sour," Tylle said.

Lin relaxed his jaw and squinted at the sun's light bleeding over the river's surface as if it had died just below the horizon.

"Big towns make you nervous?" she asked.

"No."

"Worried that we won't find Aemun?"

"No."

"Worried we will?" Her tone had grown more tense with each question, and she nearly snapped the last one out as she dismounted and led her horse into town on foot.

Lin snorted and shook his head. There'd been too much to think about lately. Too many things he didn't have answers for. Finding Aemun had been a simple goal to keep in mind, but the closer they got to finding him, the larger the knot within Lin became. What if Tylle *wasn't* telling the truth? About Aemun or even knowing someone who might have a way to remove the Stitches. It was easy enough to imagine her using him to get to where she wanted to go. But she didn't need him. Sure, he'd saved her life, but well after she'd first done the same for him.

Stables were easy enough to find as Lin followed Tylle into Riversbend proper. True to the traveling farmer's earlier words, the market area had been cleared for the night, stalls and shops broken down or shuttered with padlocks in place. It reminded Lin a little of the Ferrucium's outer square, where vendors and suppliers filled the space like crops in fields. Lanterns hung intermittently on shop faces, and as they entered the square itself, music from three different buildings competed to drown out the sound of the slow river.

"By foot or river?" Tylle asked.

"What?" Lin turned and looked at what she meant. The stretch of stilted buildings was interrupted by a sizable, cobbled path that led to a dock. It looked like an old, worn splinter stuck into the side of the sunset-soaked river.

"The Ferrucium is days from the closest river, and the one it is near isn't the Telms. A sailing vessel, maybe, but we wouldn't find one this far upriver. All the legal ports are Ferrucium managed anyways. And I'd imagine Aemun would have come to the same conclusion."

"By road, then." Tylle shrugged and adjusted the straps of her pack, beets hanging from the side like tumorous growths. She turned and walked along the right of the main path through the square.

The revelry spilling into the night air sounded sweet to the ears and made Lin think back to the few and far-between chances he'd had to visit the markets housed within the Ferrucium walls after nightfall in his youth. The taverns there never seemed to get quite so rowdy as what he saw elsewhere in the wide world, but those had been fond memories. Lin licked his lips, thought of his first kiss, and inhaled the scent of wine and sweat that quickly faded.

The buildings that housed the music and laughter were all two-story complexes, and the closer they got to them, the more muddied the belted songs became.

"I'd rather find somewhere quiet to stay if you don't want to continue on," Lin said, raising his voice to be heard over the jovial crowd.

"I want to ask if they've seen Aemun."

"I doubt he'd have stayed somewhere like this with a newborn." While he hadn't known Aemun all that well, Lin was pressed to think of any Ferrucium soldier wanting to stay somewhere as obnoxiously loud as the riverside taverns. Especially one with a newborn. "You ask around at these three. I'll check the... less loud areas of town."

Tylle frowned but nodded. Lin lost sight of her braid in the press of partying people and sighed. A deep drum beat competed against unharmonized voices and the sound of a skilled person playing a stringed instrument somewhere in the middle of the press.

While the town itself was lively, there were noticeable pockets of calm silence, much like what Lin had expected when he learned they were approaching Riversbend. It was traditionally a fishing village, and a way down from the square, there was a stretch of dock roped off from the river and three people sitting on crates staring off across the water. Lin ignored them, noting the bitter-scented smoke that hung in the air around them. A bottle clinked across the wooden planks and rolled until it fell over the side and splashed. "Any word?"

Lin turned to see a man stepping from under a shadowed overhang where small dinghies rocked against the dock. He looked lean and haggard and clutched a dark cap like it alone might possess salvation for him from something terrible.

"What?" Lin made a circle with the thumb and finger of his left hand and placed his right on the hilt at his waist.

"Any word... any word?" The man's cheeks were gaunt, his skin dirt-stained and clammy, like he'd been pulled from the muck of the river and only recently put on land.

"Word on what?" Lin stepped to the side to keep from joining the twisted cap in his grasping hands.

"Dar, better leave him alone, or you'll get worse than the last man gave you!" a woman with brushed-back, tangled auburn hair called. Her back was turned, but she craned to watch as the man, Dar, lumbered towards Lin.

"Word on the monsters. The stitchers. The ones who come after and the ones who walked before. The—" His hat quivered in his left hand, and he raked his right hand across his chest over and over, long, dirty nails digging thin gouges.

"Calm down," Lin said. He turned to the trio, and at the same time, the sleeve of his tunic was yanked hard.

"Oh, by the One, Dar." The woman screamed. "Please, please don't hurt him." It wasn't clear if she meant that last bit for Dar or Lin, but Lin didn't plan to hurt the man. Far from it. On his travels, he'd seen people broken by the world, trounced and trampled by events out of their control, and this man seemed to be speaking about untethered. *The stitched ones.*

Lin tried to pull away gently, but Dar's grip was firm. Lin's tunic dug in at the seams, pulling tight under his arms and neck. Pulling away didn't do anything, and the man pressed in, smelling every bit of filth and sickness.

"P-please tell me, is there any word?" Dar howled. Both his arms trembled, muscles strained as he yanked and clenched Lin's tunic.

Lin pulled away and pushed the man simultaneously, stiff-arming him squarely in the chest. The sound of tearing fabric preceded the riverside breeze that brushed his underarm.

"Please!" the woman who'd been calling this entire time was at their side, and Lin started to create a Weave.

"Everyone, stop!" Lin yelled. The Weave threaded into existence, inches from wrapping the trio and Dar to each other. It would have rooted them in place, but the pain in the woman's voice and the agony in Dar's eyes had stilled his hand from finishing the motion. Everyone stopped. Dar, the woman, and the two men who had risen were all motionless as if time itself had frozen.

"I do have word," Lin said, heart thrumming in his ears. The last thing he wanted or needed was to get into an altercation with innocent townsfolk. "Release me, and I'll tell you."

Dar looked down at his hand and nodded, taking his left hand to his cheek, scratching in tandem with his right.

"He ain't been right since getting here. Says he came from Drekinburg. The only survivor from what he says."

Lin nodded, thoughts unwantedly flashing to Fallo and the horrific scene he'd encountered. He wasn't sure he'd been by Drekinburg.

"The Ferrucium is doing everything it can to stem the... stitched ones. We've made several strong pushes, and I'm confident soon there will be no more monsters haunting our peace of mind," Lin lied. There had been no pushes that he knew of, no progress towards curbing the soaring number of Binders going mad—*untethering*. But the Ferrucium had been collecting children for as long as it had existed, specifically to stop the chance of untrained turning into untethered.

"Good, good, good, good." Dar nodded, smiled, and scratched, his eyes wet and distant.

"You made it sound like he accosted someone else recently?" Lin asked.

"What? Oh yeah, sure did. Shorter fellow, blonde mop, sides not shaved like yours." The woman replied, spitting some dark stain to the path beside them and clearing her throat as she did. "Dar asked him his usual string, and the prick threw him into the Telms. Took time to fish him out."

"Happen to catch a name?"

"Fuck no," the woman spat. "Sorry," she added, looking down at her boots and holding her hand to Dar.

The man took it, stepping forward unsteadily, and without a word, she led him over to the crates and sat him down alongside the other two men. Lin frowned. Dar didn't need to sit on crates; he needed a physiker's attention. A whole handful of their attention.

"You recall which way the prick headed?" Lin asked.

"Riversquare, days ago now," one of the other men, who'd been silent until now, said.

"Did he have a newborn with him?"

"Dunno. Not on him if he did. The man smelled like a week's worth of ale," the woman said.

Lin stared into the darker parts of Riversbend, where he had thought to find refuge, and then turned back to the louder, brighter part of town.

It wasn't where Lin would have wanted to stay, but he could see Aemun throwing the man into the river if he had crossed this way. The Six knew he could see Aemun doing far worse if it came to it.

"Anywhere else to stay besides Riversquare?" Lin asked.

"With us, if you liked the company enough," the woman cackled. "But no, no inns other than there."

Lin nodded and headed back to the sounds of a city that seemed not to understand that night was meant for sleep.

Chapter Ten

Boundless Bone

"He stayed here for the last three days if who you mean is who I mean." The innkeeper shrugged. She had broad shoulders atop a frame set on wider hips and seemed to frown at the memory.

"Doing what exactly for three days?" Lin asked. It wasn't like a Ferrucium soldier to rest in a town for no reason. He could have been wounded or taken ill. Perhaps he'd found a wetnurse. Lin blanched. Had something happened to the newborn?

This particular inn, The River's Bender, was the largest of the three in the festive town and where Lin had eventually found Tylle the night prior. It also had an available room. Staying feet from each other out in the wilderness had become the norm, but somehow, sharing a room felt more personal, and Lin didn't sleep well on the floor across from the bed. The fitful night's rest had left Lin grouchy and sore well before they'd found the innkeeper tending to the hearth. The wood wasn't stoked yet, and the chill creeping off the river had found free room and boarding within the inn.

The innkeeper scratched her chin. "Whoring and drinking, best I could tell. Nothing unusual. Had a little thing with him. Came alone, save the child." The innkeeper arched a brow, and a grin split her wide jaw. "He owes you any coin?"

Tylle shook her head.

"We were separated from him on our trek. Thought he might've been waiting for us."

The woman nodded, eyes dancing around Lin's face appraisingly. "He acted like he was waiting for not more than the next bottle but set out with a group not long after they arrived. Ferrucium by the cut of cloth. And the way they didn't seem keen to pay for lodging. A day or two ago. More Reds than I'd ever seen in one place."

Lin chewed on the inside of his lip and sighed. "Did he or they happen to hint at where they might be heading?"

She sucked at her teeth and shook her head.

"Well, I appreciate you taking the time to speak with us."

With a sniff and a cough, the innkeeper nodded and returned to stoking the wood in the hearth. It was early, but Lin didn't think it'd be long until the revelers from the night before joined the living once more and shuffled from their rooms in droves. A festival celebrating the autumnal had apparently fallen a few days before their arrival and, from what Lin had heard, would last a few days after as well. It wasn't something Ferrucium soldiers celebrated. At least, not that Lin knew of.

"Let's go before a crowd stirs," Tylle said.

Leaving Riversbend felt like walking out of a dream.

"Another night of terrible sleep," Lin finally said, turning and looking at the stretched buildings of the town reflected across the river. Visible only where the fog wasn't thick and rolling.

"And this time, I can't blame your own foolishness for it," Tylle said, a slip of a smile gracing her face.

Lin grunted and climbed into his saddle. "The good news, if there was any to be had, is that we might have a chance to catch up. If he's moving with several soldiers at once."

"We need dull Virt to smile some of his luck on us. Opposed to the constant piss I've been tasting on the wind."

Lin ignored Tylle's reference at first. He didn't know Virt anymore than he knew Vellyr. Although Lin wouldn't spit at good luck from any source since Fallo. After a breath of contemplation, he decided it best not to dismiss the chance at good fortune so easily. He caved and gently replied, "The Six know the truth you speak." Just in case her words reached the ears of *someone* that mattered. For all he knew, mentioning both the Six and her Gods might give them better luck than just the seemingly random name of one of hers.

Lin snuck a glance. By the set of Tylle's jaw, she disapproved.

"Why are you so angry when I mention the Six? You don't see me snarling when you mention yours." Lin pulled the reins and slowed Nebra.

"There are many religions. Most of which do not offend me."

"Then why—"

"But most of them aren't... aren't propaganda spread to a people to keep them from the truth. Most aren't pale imitations, shadows of Velkath and his kin. It is offensive because it is familiar. It is angering because it, like *Wieving* being known as Binding, is a spit in the face of Danica's history. What better way to make people malleable than to give them faceless, nameless Gods? To take away both the good and ill of what the First Wievers went through?"

"If it is as you say, and the Six and their One shadow *are* Velkath and his, then isn't it enough to know that we pray and honor the same Gods?"

"You pray to shadows!" Tylle said.

Pain and sincerity coupled in her voice. Anger and sorrow danced in her eyes. And she stared at Lin until the silence had stretched too long. Lin had no reply. The Six, well, that was something he'd find all across Danica. But Velkath? All he knew of that name was that the "god" seemed to be revered by untethered.

"You know, last night I met a survivor from another town destroyed by the untethered," Lin said. It was all he could think of to fill the silence, even if it wasn't the best choice. He hadn't meant to start a fight with Tylle. So, this was what he came up with? For fear of another long day without discussion. Lin grimaced, waiting for her response.

"Really?" Tylle asked.

"Yeah."

"Which town?"

"D-dre-something," Lin replied. The full name was lost on him.

Tylle shook her head and looked forward.

"If I remembered, I'd say," Lin said sharply before she could stab at him for his failure.

"It's not that," she said softly.

"Then what is it?"

"Do you know how often I encountered, as you name them, untethered before we met?"

"How would I know that?" Lin asked.

"One time before I met Margie in Lyre. One. *Single*. Time."

"Sounds like good fortune," Lin said. But the truth was close to the same for him. Not *only* once, but few enough times that he'd seen more untethered since Lyre than he had his whole life before. Well, at least *real* untethered and not just those fools who'd broken the Binding Tenets.

"To truth, I am blessed. But not in this," Tylle shook her head and stopped her mare entirely. The horse stomped, nickered, and all around seemed to represent how Lin felt. *Uncomfortable*.

"But there have been plenty of tales. So, until now, you'd only seen one, and I'd only encountered a few, but there were numerous reports," Lin said. He exhaled into his hands and watched the warmth of his breath slip between his fingers like the control he had over this conversation.

"Reports of whole villages being massacred?" Tylle asked.

"Not to Fallo's extent, but—"

"Entire towns." Tylle snapped her fingers. "Gone like that!"

"It is possible that in the Ferrucium's efforts to train the young and keep them from going mad, untethering themselves from the Tapestry, many of this last generation were missed?"

"You should know better than that how long the Ferrucium's fingers are. Children don't get *missed*. They don't go overlooked. Even that tiny, insignificant ring of huts had been visited by Evaluators. You think enough children have been missed to cause what we saw at Fallo?"

"It could be possible," Lin said.

"And the Tapestry isn't something you can *untether* yourself from. You can add to it. You can take from it. But as long as you breathe, you are part of it!" Tylle's voice grew louder and louder as she spoke.

"The Binding Tenets tell us that Binding is like taking a paintbrush dipped only in water across the Grand Tapestry. The mark will fade, leaving it as it was. Unless you untether. Unless you Stitch your flesh, which dips your brush in blood and *ruins* the Grand Tapestry."

"You really believe that? Tell me, do you *feel* untethered? From this small, simple act? Isn't the Grand Tapestry—" Tylle looked as if she bit and chewed at the word before deciding it wasn't to her taste "—Isn't the Tapestry better for having you alive to experience it?"

Lin didn't know what to say. He struggled to admit that he'd rather have died than ruin the Grand Tapestry. At least, that was how he first felt, but over the last few days, something had changed. Perhaps it was speaking with Jules, or maybe it was the effect of seeing the Stitches in his flesh each time he awoke—unless it was the cruel machinations of the One warping his mind.

"No. T-the Grand Tapestry was perfect at its inception, and if that means I should have died, then so be it."

"Horseshit. You can sit there and lie to yourself, hedging responses so that your loving Ferrucium will kill you *after* interrogating you instead of before, but don't lie to me. Vellyr will never love you if you can't be honest."

"I don't give two shits about Vellyr's love! I don't want it. I don't want anything other than to keep people safe. That's why I'm a damned good Escorter." Lin stared at the knuckles of his left hand, the Stitches across them fuzzing in the early morning light. "I feel this discussion has gotten out of hand. All I meant to say was that things are worse all around... and... and..."

Lin swallowed. He'd lost the thread entirely. Whatever point he'd hoped to make sent sailing on the wind out of his thoughts.

"And?" Tylle questioned, expectation and irritation on her sharp face.

"I don't know," Lin whispered, then said louder, "I don't know why things have worsened, but they clearly have. But what you're insinuating and asking me to believe goes against *everything* I've been taught. And I'm a rational man.

Or at least try to be. So, taking your words at face value isn't possible. I need evidence, not empty accusations and finger-pointing."

Lin used the reins to steady his trembling hands.

"You are willing to consider harsher truths than most," Tylle said, her voice lowering like a dying breeze. "It could be argued I've been trying to peel open your eyes with a dagger edge instead of flower petals."

"What?" Lin jerked his head around. Tension was building a headache centered above his eyes, and he realized he'd been furrowing his brow.

"I've been too cruel in going about these conversations. Believe me, Lin, I haven't meant to imply that I think you are a stand-in for where you've come from."

The path widened, but the chaos of wilderness pushed in closer around them. Greedy, strong-armed branches waited to catch them off guard and knock them from their mounts. Some still wore braceleted leaves, fruit hanging like baubles.

Lin ducked and shook his head. "But I *do* think I represent the Ferrucium in some way. You shouldn't divide me from it so easily. I can name others who've mentored me and, like myself, would allow you to speak."

"Before finding me guilty."

Lin's shoulders twitched, and he nodded, but she had taken to the left of the road and was now well ahead of him, so he doubted she saw. That was the unfortunate truth, the one that hung heavy around his shoulders like a cloak made of iron. No matter what truth they fished from Aemun, the hook was in Tylle and Lin the same. Lin for being Stitched, Tylle for Stitching him. But judgment was the right path. If Lin was left to his own—he ran his fingers over the softly buzzing Stitches across his hand—there was a chance he'd feel forced to add more to his flesh. And all the hope in his heart wouldn't stop him from sliding down that slope once he slipped.

There'd been a point where he'd thought Stitches couldn't possibly be addictive, but now that he had them, he understood it. It was like a hunger deep within that wasn't sated from eating, an itch under his skin that begged to be scratched with more Stitches, and the thought of how his other arms might look emblazoned with the magic.

Lin yanked his right hand away and stared ahead, feeling guilt for even considering having the audacity to alter the Grand Tapestry further.

By the time they'd made camp, the silent tension had lessened. They'd passed broad fields already harvested, seemingly in preparation for the chill that chased down from the north. The trees had thinned and given way to more organized groves.

The camp itself was just a sneeze away from the road. If Lin rolled the wrong way, he would likely touch it or Tylle. But as spread and organized as the surrounding trees were, the chances of making a camp that travelers wouldn't see were slim.

Tylle laid out a tiny, tight ring of stones, and soon, a fire tickled the air.

"Can I tell you," Tylle started, looking toward him, "how our views on the Tapestry differ?"

Her face was painted in dancing shadows, but her expression couldn't have seemed more sincere even if lit by the sun itself.

"How?" Lin whispered.

"Vellia, Velkath's eldest sister, was the first Wiever. But she only ever added to the Tapestry—for good and ill. She taught her brothers and sisters, who in turn taught their children and villages until most of Danica knew the ways of Wieving."

The fire crackled, and Lin turned his attention to the flames. Tylle spoke softly, her words as dangerous feeling as an uncontrolled flame.

"But Tel'Myr, The Shadow, also learned. Wicked Tel'Myr. Vellia discovered the workings of Wievings. Many of the different forms you're familiar with, many more lost to most now. She found that all Wievings left the Tapestry as it was, but some were capable of changing how it was perceived for a short time—a short time on the scale of the Tapestry."

When Tylle grew silent, Lin looked up at her face. "And?"

"And?" She asked back.

"I don't see the moral in this tale."

Tylle shrugged and pulled her knees to her chest. "I didn't say there was one."

Lin huddled closer to the small campfire, torso itching as he moved. It had been days since he'd considered the Stitches crossing his chest, and he ran a hand under his shirt, feeling the soft hum. Tylle's story didn't make sense. Of course, Stitches altered the Tapestry. They were the only permanent type of Binding Lin had ever seen.

He pulled an apple from the pack at his side and crunched into it, stretching his sore legs. He loved riding, but he knew from years on the road the soreness never disappeared.

"If we rest for half a night instead of the full night, we might catch up. I just can't believe he spent three whole days drinking and fucking," Tylle said, more anger at the end of her words than the start.

Lin shook his head. "Maybe that's the time it took to ensure the child was in good health? If it's even him. Might not be."

"It's him," Tylle whispered.

"What's your plan?" Lin asked. "I mean, if we get there, and he's got a whole squad of innocent soldiers with him?"

Tylle scoffed. "I've thought a lot about what I might do. Slit his throat as he did Margie's. Find out if he has a family like Margie was to me. Make him watch as I kill them."

Lin shuddered. "Family other than Margie's child? Six, you mean that, don't you?"

She didn't reply at first, eyes on the flames, shadows still dancing across her face.

"I've told you. I want Aemun to get the judgment he deserves. But do you really think doing such things to *innocent* people would make you feel better?"

"You keep saying innocent as if you're the one who decides such things." Her braid was laid across her shoulder, and she twisted the end in her hands.

"You know what I mean," Lin replied.

"Are they innocent if they could have stopped him from being the man he became? Are any Ferrucium soldiers *innocent* if they uphold the atrocities the Ferrucium committed? If they take children, whether through malice or ignorance?"

Am I innocent? The thought stabbed Lin like a needle prick into his mind, and he tossed the apple's core to where Nebra and the chestnut grazed.

"What did you do before all this?" Lin waved a hand as if that might encapsulate what he meant.

"You mean before my sister was killed before me, and I began to travel with a man who more and more seems to not care for my vengeance?"

Lin swallowed. "That's not fair. It seems you've decided again to use a dagger's edge."

Tylle sunk into herself, her shoulders slumping, chin lowering. Was he glad that his words had such an impact? No, they were just her own thrown back at her. Was he sorry that she seemed a held breath away from sobbing? No, that wasn't it, either. Despite their disagreements, in their time together, he'd come to respect her, if not for her mind, then for her prowess. Watching her fight back the exhaustion and sadness. He'd come to look up to her.

Lin pulled his knees to his chest and wrapped his arms around them.

"As a priestess, I've traveled more than most. Some, too few, remember the old ways, and I would go to the villages offering prayers of protection and more."

Most of the time, her countenance was like Denro's—older and wiser. But here, as vulnerable as she looked, she really couldn't have been much older than Lin. "You traveled like the Evaluators, then?"

Tylle shrugged, dropped her braid, and found a wide, brittle leaf that she rotated in her hands. It crinkled as she crushed it. "I've never ripped a child from their parents. Never had my boot on the neck of those I claimed to protect. *That* is the difference."

"But if you traveled, teaching the old ways, that leads me to believe there are those with ears to hear it."

"I just said as much, didn't I?" Tylle scratched up another dead leaf and played with it.

"So, there is a faction that would resist the Ferrucium? Or pockets of people?" Lin narrowed his eyes.

"I never said that."

Lin dug a nail under the nail of his thumb and raked dirt from it. "But you said you knew of people who might know a way to remove Stitches?"

"I did."

"But they aren't rebel Binders, like you?" Lin snapped. He knew he sounded suspicious, but if there was even a chance that she was keeping this from him, any trust they'd built up until this point would be crushed as easily as the leaf in her hand.

"You can stare at me like that all you want. I *never* said such a thing."

"But you implied it. After everything we've been through, would you not tell me of this? Really?" Lin asked.

Tylle stared at him. Either her lip curled, or the dancing shadows made it seem such, but there was no mistaking the soft shake of her head. "Lin—"

"You still don't trust me?"

"How can I... when it seems you don't trust yourself? No. I don't trust you enough to tell you anything that might put more people I care about at risk. I know someday these threads I'm clinging to might unravel, and when they do... when they do, I hope you're the man you seem to think you are."

"And what kind of man is that?" Lin asked, wincing at the pain from stabbing harder into his nail than he intended.

"A just one," Tylle whispered, crushing the leaf she held the same as she had the first.

I am.

/ Chapter Eleven

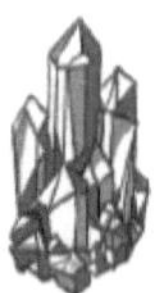

Boundless Hate

It seemed that falling asleep in contemplation had become a habit of Lin's. When he awoke in the cool morning air, Tylle was gone, and the fire was out, but both horses grazed nearby. His tunic stuck to him despite the biting air, and he smelled of sweat and fear. He didn't recall having any more nightmares, but he didn't feel well-rested, and his bones seemed to ache as much as his muscles.

Lin rose, stretched, and shambled to relieve himself. The trees, while looking well-plotted at night, were clearly organized in rows and stretching columns. They had to be close to Duke Wellgrove's own city. It had been the largest town on their path south, and as hard as they'd been riding between terse conversations, it made sense that they'd be close.

Between the rows of fruit-bearing trees, Lin caught a glimpse of Tylle. She brought her arms up, held them outstretched for a long moment, then lowered them. Either meditation or fighting forms. Or perhaps both, seeing as she claimed to be a priestess. Lin leaned against the closest tree and watched her long enough to become embarrassed that he hadn't called out to her when he noticed her glance at him.

"Morning," she called. "Care to join? I'm almost done."

"You do this every morning?"

"I should." She swept her arms up and held them angled to the sky above her head while bending at her knees. "But sleep didn't come easy to me after our conversation last night."

A sign of guilt?

"Maybe after Riversbend, the open air wasn't so sweet as an actual bed."

"Perhaps. But I think it has more to do with what you asked before. About people who'd be willing to fight the Ferrucium. I do know of a group. And I'm sorry I tried to imply otherwise. I decided I do trust you. You saved me when you didn't have to."

Six, she couldn't have looked more earnest as the morning light cast a halo around her head, and her cheeks flushed pink.

"I understand. I think I'd have done the same if I were in your position." Not that he knew exactly what the extent of her group went to. But for all Tylle knew, Lin was the type of man who would turn her and hers over to the Ferrucium Weavers once he'd removed the Stitches from his flesh or as a way to broker clemency for his transgressions.

Tylle lowered her arms and stretched her neck back and forth, a sound like a mix of moan and groan escaping her thin lips. "Good. Because I feel I must be honest with you about what we may find in Wellgrove."

Lin's thoughts immediately went to the blood-stained note he'd found tucked underneath Margaret's corpse. "The missive? You and your sister were meant to get here afterall? So, we will encounter a pocket of people here, right under Duke Wellgrove's nose?"

Tylle shook her head and closed the distance between them, looking up into his eyes. She smelled like sweat and a dash of honey. "Yes. But no. That note you claim to have found wasn't ours. Which means it was either a coincidence or Aemun's. If it was his, he planned to come here all along. Leaving me far from feeling secure. And yes, I have allies here. Which makes Aemun's presence sicken my gut all the more. *That* is why sleep was elusive."

"Are these allies... Are they the ones who might know how to remove the Stitches?" Lin asked.

Tylle narrowed her eyes and nodded. "I have reason to believe they would. But do you know why Aemun would want to go to Wellgrove?"

"Not a clue. Perhaps he's meant to meet the duke?"

She continued staring up at him, studying his expression.

If the note belonged to Aemun, it had been from before Margaret's death, which meant whatever he wanted in Wellgrove had little to do with the newborn. Wellgrove wasn't exactly out of the way en route to the Ferrucium, but if Aemun was rushing to return home, Wellgrove was a detour—a detour he'd possibly planned to take all along.

"Perhaps," Tylle eventually said.

Wellgrove was surrounded by farmlands, which were dotted with stretches of orchards. The roads were straight and seemed well maintained, especially compared to the forest-choked paths that northern Danica had. Of course, the trade-off was fewer villages like Lyre and Creekside. Sure, they passed an occasional home, but those likely belonged to tenders and not owners. They pushed through the day, slowing only once Wellgrove's exterior stone walls broke the horizon.

On the road, it wasn't often that Lin would spend time in the larger cities. Most of his escort missions were through the parts of Danica that were less developed. He'd learned early on that the closer he worked to the Ferrucium Hold, the easier the jobs had seemed. The stretches of Danica towards the north and west offered him more freedom. More adventure. He'd report to one of the Ferrucium outposts and get his next assignment. Often sticking to the same areas, helping to fill in the gaps to get soldiers safely from point to point.

That was why when he entered Wellgrove, the smell of the large city overwhelmed him. The cries of vendors, accents varied and harsh, broke across the main thoroughfare. They'd missed the vendors at Riversbend, but that would have been a poor man's market compared to the bustling streets of Wellgrove.

"How are we meant to find anyone in all this?" Lin asked.

Tylle dismounted and nodded in the direction of the largest building.

Wellgrove was a city with buildings that looked as planned and lined as the groves for which it had been named. Square-angled alleys and paths cut off from the main road as if architects had guided the growth of the sprawling city from above. A trellised place. But to be so orderly, so neat, meant that spurs were cut, and sections of the town prevented from growing. In the time since Lin had last visited, many, many years ago, it hadn't grown at all. Dead on the vine, stagnated. That was how Wellgrove appeared.

"The duke's manor?" Lin asked, following her gaze.

"Not exactly." Tylle led the way to a stable and fished marks from her pack to pay the young, foul-smelling stable hand.

"We can separate. Waste time going through the taverns and inns and maybe ask the town's guard, and ultimately let him slip through our fingers. Or…"

"Or?" Lin asked, taking the bait. He wasn't sure why Tylle was acting so strange, but her demeanor had shifted since setting eyes on Wellgrove's tall, imposing walls.

"Or we go to the individual who would know all the comings and goings to and from Wellgrove."

Lin pulled Nebra's pack from her side and let the stable hand take Nebra's reins. "One person couldn't possibly track all that," he said incredulously.

Tylle turned around and pulled him close, her hand resting on his arm. "Not them alone. But they have a network. If Aemun is here, they'd know."

Lin couldn't shake the feeling that this was some trap or trick. Out on the road, if things had taken a worse turn, he could've run. But here? The walls loomed overhead, the two-story buildings blocking as much sky as land. "Lead the way." If they found Aemun, it would be worth the unease. Lin could get the truth from the bastard's own lips. *And what if Tylle was the liar?* What if, after all of this, it is revealed that she killed Margaret as Aemun claimed, and he'd helped her survive? Well, the Six would have his name whispered to the One for that.

Tylle walked with her shoulders back, chin held high, and moved through the shifting crowds fluidly. She walked along the paths, avoiding hawkers and beggars as if they were the same, without a look back to ensure Lin was still behind her. But he was, if barely. She led him down piss-smelling alleys, cutting and crossing in such a way that Lin was sure she meant to confuse him.

"Tylle," Lin called.

"We're not far."

Whatever light had been left to die on the horizon was obscured by the tall buildings and taller outer walls. As if mourning the sun's presumed death, the wind bellowed and whipped between the walls on either side of them. Lin shuddered. The stench of closely packed life mirrored the horrible odor of Fallo in a way, and Lin looked up, expecting to see untethered markings along the walls. But no limbs or people were stuck to the buildings. In fact, Lin hadn't seen even a blink of any sort of Binding since entering Wellgrove.

They'd come to a sloped section, walking up a damp, cobbled path intersected by narrow alleys every fourth stride or so. More than a few times, Lin had been accosted by bandits out on the roads, and he couldn't rid his gut of the familiar unease welling within it. A person didn't travel through areas like this unless they wanted trouble. Unless they *invited* it. The sound of boot heels skittered from the right. Lin saw a flash of a black cloak and a sliver of a pale metallic mask. But it wasn't *just* a mask. It was a nightmare from his youth at the Ferrucium made real. Tylle didn't slow, and Lin rushed to get ahead. If the side street continued parallel to this one, they'd get intercepted.

"Tylle!"

She seemed to ignore him, and Lin ran alongside her now, watching the alley openings. Nothing. Nothing. Nothing. Something grabbed his left arm, yanking him hard. He spun, his momentum carrying him against a stone wall that looked as old as Wellgrove itself. And then they were in a small, cramped room.

"Have you lost all sense?" Tylle snapped. Her forearm was pressed to Lin's chest, pinning him against the cold wall.

Lin blinked. Her nose almost touched his. He pulled his right hand away from his hilt and raised it slowly. "Have you? We were being tracked."

Tylle shook her head and took a step back. "I doubt that."

"I saw…" Lin struggled to explain it. He hadn't seen those flat, inhuman masks since he'd been a child. It wasn't the sort of mask you'd forget. But he'd never been told who they were other than emissaries to the King. "A northern emissary?" he said weakly.

"And that compels you to almost crash into a wall?"

He hadn't noticed the wall. Lin took a deep breath and forced himself to examine the room. Crates, deflated sacks, and empty bottles littered the tight space. The stench of mold hung in the air, mingling with the smell of their sweat and making Lin feel even more uneasy. Light seemed afraid to paint the room in total relief and didn't come past the opposite door more than a step inward, casting everything in a flat orange-gray.

"I'm sorry," Lin said weakly.

"Focus. Please. But what makes you think you saw a Ladrican? It's not unheard of for them to visit a duke, but that doesn't mean they travel the back alleys."

"The mask. Flat, with only thin slits for the eyes and mouth. They'd visit the Ferrucium. Trainees would end up missing once they did. It was only later I learned they were from the North and not a branch of Ferrucium soldiers."

"King's Noose." Her words were hushed as if she whispered a curse.

"What?"

"A Nooseman. That is what they are known as among... among my people. As wicked and deadly as *true* untethered. Let us hope that is not what you saw." Tylle pulled her arm away and held a finger up to her lip, eyes narrowing towards the door they'd just slammed through.

A shadow passed under the doorway, and Lin froze. He hadn't heard the name King's Noose before, but it implied all it needed to. The beginning of a Weft formed at his fingertips. Tylle, apparently feeling the hum of energy as close as they were, shot him a glance and shook her head. The shadow passed away after a moment, but the absence of sound didn't ease Lin's nerves.

The Weft dissolved into motes of light, and Tylle pulled Lin towards the opposite door. "Silence is our friend. Don't speak until I do. You trust me?"

Lin knew what answer she wanted. But he wasn't sure. If he did trust her, his doubt wouldn't be thrumming in his ears, begging him to flee the dank cellar. "I want to."

Tylle's frown deepened. The room's shadows made her age in moments through that one motion. "I can't promise that the person I want you to meet can remove the Stitches. I can't promise that if he can, he *will*. I can't promise that, if you still want, you can return to your old life. But if things go poorly, it will be both of us who suffer, that I can promise. You know these things?"

He knew them without her speaking them into existence, but the fact that she did salved his turmoil, if only slightly. "Lead the way," Lin whispered.

What Lin had thought to be a small interior opened through a hall into a long expanse of damp stone that looked cut straight from the earth itself. The hall was lined with Wanderer's Ore, a relatively inexpensive material that glowed faintly. Orange was the most common light shed, but there were rarer azure stones sprinkled in the mix further down the hall that hurt Lin's eyes.

"Isn't Wanderer's Ore dangerous?" Lin asked.

Tylle slowed her pace and looked over her shoulder. "It can ignite when submerged in water, but it takes more than a damp room to ignite it."

Lin had heard horror stories of infants sucking on the bright stones, flames erupting from them moments later. He almost kicked a fist-sized chunk before thinking better of it. "I was also told the light corrupts a person's vision."

Tylle shrugged and continued down the long hall. Eventually, once it became clear that this wasn't a typical building, stairs leading up came into view.

"Remember. Don't speak. Let me do any talking."

"Why wouldn't you want him to talk?" A voice, scratchy and raw, sounded from the top of the steps. The man peeled from the wall as if made of shadow. He was short with a beard as scratchy looking as his voice sounded and a wide-brimmed hat that seemed a size too large for him. "Is he dull? Or foreign? Or... worse?"

Lin had taken a step back, touched and moved his hand from his hilt several times as he gauged the narrow hall was a poor place for sword work, and started to form a Binding. But Tylle stood still—motionless, silent—until she crashed into the man with the force of a taut thread snapping. The man was eye-level with Tylle only because of the steps he rested on, but his hands slowly wrapped around her, and they embraced.

"Little Tylle, look how tall you've grown," the man's whisper did nothing to ease the dragging of words from his throat.

"And how old you've gotten!" Tylle said. There had been moments on their journey together where a spark of light and laughter could be seen burning within the woman. But if this spark had been a visible thing, a *real* thing, it would have lit the hall far beyond what the Wanderer's Ore was capable of.

The man pushed her to arm's length and studied her. He peered around her shoulder and rested his dark eyes on Lin. "Come on. Grovetender sent me to meet you. Strange things happening in the city. It's best we move quick. Figured I'd never see you and Margie again once you two left. Where…"

Lin hadn't known what to think of the man, but in the time it took him to ask about Margaret to the harsh inhaled breath Tylle took, his hat was off, and he'd pulled Tylle back in for another hug. "Not here. Not now. Let's move. I'm sorry. I'm so sorry, little one." And he pulled her up the stairs, supporting her, barely looking back to ensure Lin followed.

When they reached the top of the steps, the man, face dark and wrinkled, stopped and turned to face Lin. In an instant, far faster than his short, stocky build implied, he had a knife under Lin's nose and a hand gripping the back of his head.

"Pael!" Tylle reprimanded. Her voice echoed through the stairwell.

"Name?" Pael asked.

Lin went cross-eyed, staring at the tip of the sharp blade. "Lindel. Friends call me Lin."

"*Friends*. Fucking Reds, you mean. You know he's a Red?"

Lin licked his lips and studied the man. His hand didn't tremble, and his eyes were as hard and sharp as the weapon pressing into Lin's nose.

"I wouldn't bring someone in I didn't trust," Tylle said.

Pael's face shifted through a range of emotions. His brows narrowed, and his nostrils flared. Then his lip quivered, and a waggle of fat just under his chin did the same. He blinked away the beginnings of tears, and a rueful smile so slight it might be missed in the dark of the landing crept onto his face.

"I don't know what happened to little Margie. Yet." Pael dug the edge deeper into the bottom of Lin's nose, the blade flat cold against his lip. "But I'm sure she trusted the fuck she was with. Didn't she?"

"She did," Lin said before Tylle could reply. "I knew her for a short time before her death, and she was... she was a good person. Genuinely so. A trusting person. But... but I couldn't protect her. And now, I'm trying to find justice for her death. I swear."

"You still one of them?" Pael asked, his hand relaxing the hold on Lin's head. "After all that?"

That question stung as much as the knife's edge when Lin didn't immediately answer. Not a cut, not yet, but a painful reminder that it *could* be.

"I'm not sure," Lin whispered. And he wasn't. Which hurt to admit. He swallowed. Maybe if he could remove the Stitches, maybe if he could prove his worth, he'd be accepted back. "But I know that I want to help Tylle."

"Fairest answer I think I could expect at the moment. Things considered." Pael lowered the dagger tip, letting it run lightly across Lin's torso to tap against the humming Stitches on his left hand. "I won't press you again, but next time, if something feels off, I'll cut first and ask questions later. Fair?"

"Fair."

Chapter Twelve

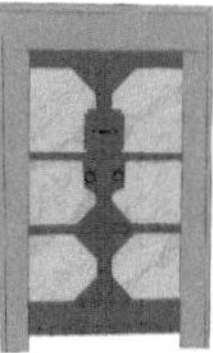

Boundless Blood

Pael moved like an oil-slick shadow, Tylle easily keeping pace behind him. Not the fastest person Lin had ever trailed, but Lin was breathing heavily as he matched pace. The landing had led down another long hall, though this one had been worked stone, and the air warmed enough to imply they'd made it above ground.

"Manage your breathing. Won't make a good first impression to have you gasping like a drowned man come to shore," Pael said breezily. Tylle shook her head but hadn't looked at Lin since they'd started moving.

"Wouldn't think," Lin sucked in a breath, "You cared that much about *first* impressions."

Pael slowed, bare feet slapping the stone. His thick beard was split by a smile that showed surprisingly nice teeth despite the rest of his appearance. "Never said I did. And I've met Grovetender more times than most. So far from my first impression."

Hairs rose on the back of Lin's neck, and he stared down at the man. "Who is it? Grovetender, you've said that name several times now."

Pael looked to Tylle, who gave the slightest shake of her head. "Our benefactor," he said with a shrug. "Now, can we continue? Or do you wish to try again at something witty?"

Lin nodded, rubbing his right hand along his Binding-covered wrist. "Let's go. I'm good."

"I've got several witticisms for that... but for now, keep up. Not much further."

True to his word, the hall zagged on itself, but at the far end, they came to a grayish, green door. Pael dug into a satchel at his waist and pulled out a key that looked as old as he was. The door opened into a storage room of sorts. Old pieces of armor and weaponry sat dust-covered on racks, and the only light came from a large chunk of Wanderer's Ore that Pael produced from the same satchel.

"Shut it behind you," the older man said, nodding at the door.

Lin stared into the musty room ahead. In all his travels doing escort missions, he could easily say this was the most unease he'd ever felt. More and more, it seemed he was getting into a position that he wouldn't easily be able to remove himself from. It felt as far from the open roads as one could get, without being jailed or stuffed into a dungeon.

The door slammed shut as Lin pulled it toward him.

"I said shut it, not slam it." Pael snapped, face lit only by the blue glow of the ore he held.

Lin had never seen a piece quite so large. Especially not a blue one, as rare as they were.

"You aren't afraid to hold it?" Lin frowned at the man and stone.

"Not everyone can afford oil."

"Not everyone can afford to lose their vision," Lin rebutted. "Or have it explode!"

"Have you ever seen it happen?" Tylle asked.

Lin's cheeks grew warm. "No."

"Bah, all of that is just tales they tell to keep honest men and women buying oil."

"They?" Lin asked.

Pael didn't respond but continued forward, the ore in hand emitting a soft glow that painted everything a sickly pale blue, closer to gray. It was clear they'd entered a large building, but as looming as the exterior complexes had been and as winding as the halls were, he was lost with where in Wellgrove they might be. If not for the general sense of upkeep, they could've been in any long-abandoned warehouse, or even a crypt. Not that crypts were common in Danica. But the dukes and their cities were odd compared to the numerous villages that dotted the countryside.

As they walked in shuffling silence, any semblance of time was lost. Lin's stomach growled, and an emptiness had taken root above his navel. As if even his unease had abandoned him. The dim light hurt his eyes, but his left hand functioned as a torch of sorts, or at least like a torch that had once burned brightly and now was only a glowing ember within charred wood.

Pael stopped and shook his head. "Close now. I need to be clear about what follows. And you need to be clear about your understanding."

Lin squinted as Pael turned the Wanderer's Ore towards him. "What?"

"Grovetender might decide you're not worth keeping around. Understand?"

"Then why would I want to meet them?" Lin opened his eyes fully but raised his hand to shield them.

Tylle started to speak, but Pael turned the ore's light to her and shook his head. "Way I see it, he's your best bet if justice is really your main goal. And he's meeting with another visitor who might be able to help answer if someone matching the man you two hunt has come through."

"And he knows how to remove Stitches?"

Pael barked out a laugh, his grin stretching wide as he cupped his hand tighter around the stone to keep the light from shining as aggressively as it had. "Stitches?" he chuckled out. "If anyone knows, it's him."

Lin stared at the man and lowered his hand. "And this... Grovetender. He's a man of his word?"

"If he isn't, I'm not a man well-loved by Venya."

"Are you?" Lin asked.

"I like to think so, but being liked and loved are two different things, and neither guarantees either of us will see tomorrow," Pael said, voice trailing to a whisper as his words bounced off the walls. "Ain't that right, little Tylle?" His voice softened as he asked.

"Right," she whispered.

"Venya is one of Verbanth's kin?" Lin asked.

Pael let more light slide through his fingers and cocked his head. His mouth slipped into an appraising frown, and he leaned in. "I can't think of a single Red who'd be caught dead talking 'bout them."

"He's not a Red," Tylle said, tapping the back of Pael's hand that held the ore. "Now go. I'm interested in meeting this visitor. When did they get in?"

Pael shrugged and tightened his fingers around the ore, shielding the light. "Grovetender has been... well, let's say they've been reclusive since arrival."

Lin glanced over his shoulder. Since entering the cramped, echoing halls, he'd felt trapped. And the further they got from where they entered, the heavier the sensation felt—oppressive. He was sure neither of them would kill him if he ran. But Lin would still have the Ferrucium to deal with and the Stitches that marked him as untethered.

The hall opened into a wider room with benches that lined the walls, like a communal rest area. Sounds of hushed conversation carried from the leftmost doorway, and Pael clung to the rightmost wall, sucking his teeth as he glanced around.

"You look lost," Lin whispered.

"I'm not," he sighed and jerked his head to the right when they approached a sconce-lit intersection. Three tapestries hung on the opposite wall, different images displayed on each, but a story played out in thread from left to right of a man breaking chains of light and destroying the shadows that clung to the prisoners.

"What—"

"Shhh," Pael interrupted, raising a lone, knobby finger to his lips to accent his point.

The deeper they went into the building, the more it felt like none of them were meant to be there in the first place. Whenever steps sounded, Pael would press flat against the wall and stare bug-eyed at Lin until he did the same. Tylle moved with her typical grace of a honed-edge blade. Pael tightened the strap of his satchel so that it was snuggled closer to his armpit than near his waist, and he placed the key and chunk of ore back in it.

"Let me do the talking if there's any to be done," Pael said.

Lin nodded.

"Let *me* do the talking," Tylle corrected, staring hard into Pael's eyes.

"And..." Pael pressed the tip of his pinky finger into his right ear and twisted it several times. "If things go bad, I'm the worst sort of bartering chip. Taking me or my life won't do you a spit of good. And the same goes for her. Except she'll likely call the bluff and kill you 'fore you can kill her."

"I wouldn't do something like that," Lin protested.

"Shh," Tylle and Pael said simultaneously.

Voices carried with the sound of soft steps from the adjacent hall. Three or more people were crossing the hall that intersected the strip they stood at. Pael flattened further, sucking his gut in.

"—taking the time to let us inspect the manor in a civilized... manner."

"Of course. As we've communicated numerous times to the envoys, we have nothing to hide and fully back—"

Lin and Pael were stacked so tight that the man's pungent aroma brought tears to Lin's eyes, slightly blurring the passing forms. A man dressed in a sleek coat trimmed with gold against a green material so dark it could have passed for black under less light was trailed by two other individuals. He'd been the last to speak and did so with a leisurely tone. The other speaker, accent thickly powdered with northern inflection, was a woman. She walked a step behind the well-dressed man, matching his stride effortlessly.

Lin froze, breath catching. The third individual was a Nooseman. Tall and lean, a flat mask obscuring their face, dark cloak with red stitching, a nod to Ferrucium ties despite reporting directly to the Ladrican King.

Pael shook his head and leaned to watch the trio depart. "*Come on,*" he mouthed, breath not pushing the actual words into existence. Slinking across the hall, like a forest cat stalking prey, Pael moved. His steps had been soft, but now they were somehow perfectly silent. His dark, dirty feet left no mark as he pushed aside a random floor-length tapestry to reveal a door. In vivid hues of orange and red, it depicted a table surrounded by six shadows. Faceless, the shadows seemed to stare at him as he approached, boots scuffing stone as he followed Pael through the hidden doorway.

"Another hall?" Lin asked.

"You expect each room to attach itself to the other?" Pael snapped. "Door is just ahead." His tone was impish, a cruel glee that seemed unnatural for the man. Not that Lin had known him that long.

The door was a slab of mostly smooth metal, with veins of silver becoming more apparent the closer they stepped to it. But as clear as the veins became, the rest of the door fuzzed, the Stitches on his wrist and fingers humming *tighter*.

"What sort of..." Lin trailed off, touching his right hand to his temple, failing to assuage the pain throbbing through his head.

"Easy," Tylle said. "It will get worse before it gets better. But it *will* get better."

Pael clicked his tongue and nodded. "Don't always get better."

Standing feet away, Lin felt drawn to the strange, dark door. But even as he swayed closer to it, it felt like his skin wanted to crawl off. Whatever Pael did to open the thing was lost to Lin. The movements were unclear, and his focus was so disjointed that Lin couldn't have known, even if the man had simply pulled a handle.

Pael slid under Lin's right arm as easily as a tailored crutch and carried him through the doorway. The room beyond was softly lit, and the air felt and tasted fresher. But it could have been a damp, shit-covered cellar for all Lin cared as he fell against the closest wall and dry heaved. One breath retching, the next sucking in as much air as he could before his stomach convulsed and the cycle repeated.

When Lin blinked the tears from his eyes and refocused his vision, he noticed Pael had moved further into the sizable room. He stood, looking much like a weed among flowers, near a desk, where two others stood speaking with him.

Lin rose, wiped his mouth, and approached the desk, each step from the doorway mercifully lighter than the last. Tylle was beside him, seemingly better off than he was, but staring into the distance like she'd seen a ghost.

"If I'd known it'd get you that bad, I might've given you a bit more warning," Pael whispered. He held his hat in both hands and stressed at the edges of the brim. Pale stubble ringed the crown of his scalp.

Lin swallowed and nodded, looking around at the room—an office filled with cabinets, trinkets, and shelf upon shelf of books.

"An eye for books?" the man seated at the desk asked, rising and cupping his left hand into his right. He was as tall, if not a hair taller, than Lin, with short-cropped black hair and a neatly trimmed beard. Tailored clothes with fine, gold-colored stitching made him look regal, much like the man he'd seen walking in the halls. His sharp eyes made Lin think of the Nooseman, and Lin scanned the room, suddenly wary of the darker corners.

The man cleared his throat. A single silver ring on his right hand caught what little light the room offered.

"I... Yes. I've always dreamed of visiting the Fentian scholars and seeing their trove," Lin said, rubbing his eyes.

"Escorter?"

Lin took a double-take. He hadn't been able to focus much since entering the room. Certainly not on the diminutive pair that stood beside the desk while the other man had captivated his attention.

Aemun.

"You two know—"

Tylle blurred past Lin like a shot arrow.

Pael moved far slower than Tylle, perhaps in an effort to intercept. Lin was rooted in place, the moment unreal. And then the man cleared his throat for a second time, louder, somehow *heavier*, and Tylle slowed to a stop, tears in her eyes.

Chapter Thirteen

Burdened Hope

"Grovetender. You would let a snake coil itself into the flowerbed?" Tylle's voice was frigid compared to the flame in her eyes.

"You're mixing metaphors," Aemun said drolly.

"Please, no need for such a grandiose title in front of guests. Erias will suffice." If the man had any concern for Tylle's outburst, he didn't show it. He held his lone-ringed hand out towards the center of the room and pointed at the unoccupied space between Aemun and Tylle. A woman bearing a small bundle stood beside Aemun. Her eyes were large, and she'd paled at Tylle's question.

"Guests," Tylle snarled.

"Guests," Erias said, firmer. "Escorter? So, you are also Ferrucium?"

"He—" Pael started to speak, then silenced at a wave from Erias's hand. The squat man shifted so that he stood closer to Lin but didn't try to speak again.

"Speak," Erias said, eyes narrowing at Lin.

"I am. I was. I..." Lin stumbled over his words, looking from Aemun's near-expressionless face to Tylle's twisted mask of rage. This could be a moment to ensure his future, to free himself from the Stitches that haunted him. "I was abandoned by the man you claim as a guest. Though, I'm not sure it was his fault. And I was saved by Tylle here, though the methods broke doctrines I held... hold dear." Lin raised his hand, giving anyone in the room with the Sight a view of the Stitches marking his flesh.

Aemun tsked, but Erias continued looking on impassively.

"I was led to believe that if anyone knew of a way to remove Stitches... it would be the Grovetender." Lin continued. "And Tylle told me if I traveled with her and helped her find vengeance against the man who killed her sister, she'd help me remove the Stitches."

"Margie is truly dead then?" Erias asked.

Tylle exhaled and nodded. She hadn't taken her eyes off Aemun since entering the room. It clicked now that as Lin was recovering from the strange effect of the door, she'd already spotted the man.

"Tylle, openly speak your grievances." Erias's tone was calming on the ears. His voice was strong and deep, with an inflection that spoke of a formal upbringing.

Aemun folded his arms across his chest and kept glancing at Lin's hand. His lips were a thin line of disgust and disbelief, and his eyes were narrowed and disapproving. Apparently, the man had the Sight all along, something he'd kept to himself. Typical soldiers like Lin had to share that information to prove their worth, but knowing Aemun's lineage, it made sense he'd not disclosed something so valuable.

Tylle's glare was as fierce as a raging flame, the heat of it making Lin avert his glances for fear of burning.

"I'd been informed by Margie she was ready for extraction, so I went to Lyre to retrieve Margie from the mission she'd been on. In her innocence, she confessed secrets to the coward who stands before you now. And he killed her once she bore his child. Lin found us before I could confront Aemun and took me into custody but insisted I have a trial. Shortly after, we were ambushed by a swarm of untethered. Aemun fled. I was able to save Lin's life. He speaks the truth; I told him you might know how to remove what he calls *Stitches.*"

Erias was silent for a time. His silence seemed to swallow everything in the room, not even the newborn making a sound to disrupt it. "Aemun here came to me specifically seeking asylum. There are pieces moving on a board that have been stagnant until now. He is a guest under my protection and has shared valuable information about the inner machinations of the Ferrucium. A coup, once only a distant hope, is entirely possible now, thanks to him. We could wrest control of Danica back from Lodram's filthy fingers. And we've both made promises over the last two days to ensure this."

Lin shuddered, the earnest passion in the man's voice pulling at strings Lin hadn't thought he had within him.

"Erias," Pael whispered. "Sir, all due respect."

"Hold your tongue or find it held for you. I respect your brother and recognize you as a good and true Duke's man. But this is far beyond your *limited* understanding. Do you comprehend?"

Pael sucked his teeth and nodded, eyes digging holes into the floor between his feet.

"Lin," the man continued, "a soldier who, through no fault of your own, has broken the Ferrucium's *Binding Tenets*."

Lin shifted and, for lack of anywhere better to look, stared down at his boots, Pael's wiggling toes beside him drawing his attention. The man's blackened feet dug into the raised carpet, toes splayed and writhing like worms coming up from mud after a rain.

"An oath breaker, of a sort." Erias sighed and pinched the bridge of his nose. "I've felt Margie's loss deeply. And we will have our blood for it. But it won't be now. It won't be at the expense of my guests or ambitions. Tylle, I know how much you and your family have given for this cause. I know. Do you still trust me?"

Tylle blinked back tears. Her knuckles were white, and her jaw clenched before she whispered. "I can't. Erias, I can't let him get away with this."

Lin's stomach dropped. If he'd had any doubt about Tylle's version of events, watching her struggle to obey a person she clearly owed some sort of fealty to dispelled it. Margie's killer was in the room, and he stood there untouchable. Unreproachable. All because he'd given this man, this *Grovetender*, Ferrucium secrets?

Why had his breaths become so hard to form? Tylle deserved better. Margie deserved better. This wasn't justice.

Lin conjured the Weft, flatter and faster than he'd ever done before. He wasn't sure if he even used a focus. And it shattered just as fast as if the air itself resisted the Weft's formation. A solid knee crunched into his thigh, buckling him to the ground.

Erias held a lone hand out towards Lin, the ring on his finger glittering with thin silver strands of light. It looked so similar to the veins in the door's material, like a spider web wet with dew— gossamer. In his mind, he felt like he'd walked back through the door. His bones turned to jelly, his skin wishing to flee his useless muscles.

Pael pressed into Lin, smothering him with more force than Lin thought the man was capable of.

"*Asylum*. Do you think someone would come to me for protection, and I'd be unable to provide it? Take him to a cell."

For a moment, Lin thought only Pael was holding him. Then he realized Tylle had been one of the two bodies pressing him to the ground.

"Tylle... I... I'm sorry," Lin whispered.

Set into one of the darker sections of the room was a heavy door, dissimilar to the intoxicating, nausea-inducing door they'd first stepped through. Lin watched, head spinning, as he was dragged through it and down a set of steps that showed no care for his jellied legs. Then, in a moment, he was in a cell, the bars closed gentler than he expected.

"I told you it might go bad," Pael whispered.

Lin grabbed the rough iron bars and pressed his brow to them. "I... I don't know why I did that," he said.

"Because you were the only one of us in there brave enough. Or the only one without the sense to know better," Pael said. "I... it might not seem like it, but he is a fair man. A good one and I think my sense of people ain't bad. Compared to most, that is. You didn't hurt no-one. You should be alright if you keep your senses when speaking with him next it happens. Alright?"

Lin nodded. The cold press of iron on his palms and forehead was a balm against the headache that resounded within his skull.

Tylle leaned against the adjacent wall outside the cell, then sunk to the floor. Her position seemed the same as the one she'd taken in Fallo, leaning against a wall as the world collapsed around her.

Pael looked like he planned to say something else, fumbling for the words, then shook his head. "I'm gonna make scarce for a bit. Those other guests in the duke's home. Didn't like the look of them, did you?"

Lin jolted his head up and regretted it as the world pulsed in waves of purple and silver. He'd forgotten about the Nooseman. "Tylle called them King's Noose. And I've seen them at the Ferrucium hold before when I was younger."

"Ah. Nooseman." Pael shuddered and nodded. "I'll see if there's any word on the why of them being here." He scratched his chin and dug into the satchel, pulling out and setting down the fist-sized chunk of Wanderer's Ore he'd carried earlier on a small slip of a table against the far wall.

Pael left up the stairs, the soles of his bare feet silent on the stone.

"Who is he to you?" Lin asked.

"Pael? An old friend. A Duke's man. Duke Hollander's man, to be specific. Grovetender works closely with several other duchies." Tylle's voice sounded jagged like shattered iron, and when she looked up at Lin, tears streaked her face, lit by the pale blue glow of the ore.

"I'm sorry, Tylle. That we didn't get here sooner."

"I'll kill him. Even if it kills me. I swear on Vellyr." Tylle choked out the words and held up her ring finger where the crimson Bludwieve twisted softly.

"I know," Lin said. He swallowed, his body slowly coming back under his control. He rolled his wrists and stretched his legs. The cell was small and one of several that lined this section of the wall. Water dripped periodically onto the musty straw that coated the stones underfoot.

Tracking time in a cell with no windows was impossible, and sleep took him in waves, though the rest was fitful. When he finally awoke to the sound of banging on the iron bars, he was sorer than when he'd first sat down. A vague memory of a dream hung with him, of hot iron being struck over and over with a fierce hammer. But whether the dream had come first or the striking on the bars had, Lin wasn't sure.

"Lindel." Erias tapped his palm against one of the bars, his ring band clanging and echoing.

Lin rose slowly and noticed Tylle's absence immediately. "Erias."

A smile touched Erias's face, and he tapped the bar again, softer this time. "I regret the footing we found ourselves meeting on. Tylle has since spoken highly of you. Aemun less so. But I understand why you lashed out as you did. Aemun claims you're untethering. Are you?"

Lin blinked at that. Of course, by Ferrucium standards, Lin was. But... Lin felt he knew Erias meant it the way Tylle might. "No."

"I am in the business of freeing Danica from Ladrican rule. And in that pursuit, a pursuit passed down to me from my mother and her father, there have been terrible losses. Margie, Margaret, as she would have called herself lately, is only one of many but a fresh one.

"And while I can't imagine feeling it as poignantly as Tylle does, it does hurt me. Every loss does." Erias paced and ran his hand across each bar as he passed it. "Aemun claims to be related to one of the self-titled Weavers. Is this true?"

Lin swallowed the lump in his throat and nodded. Erias spoke sweet words, but it didn't mean anything if he planned to let Aemun get away with murder.

"He claims that Ferrucium forces are spread thin. Is that true?"

Lin shifted. "Am I a prisoner?"

Erias turned back to him and frowned. "What do you think?"

"Why are there Noosemen here?"

"Investigating the rumors of untethered and rebels."

"What are that door and your ring made of?" Lin asked, feeling that, for once, answering the questions haunting him was within his reach.

Erias held his hand up, and Lin flinched. But there was no strange effect, no odd silver silken threads blowing in the breeze. "Old Magic. Bound Metal. No. You aren't a prisoner. But I can't let your attempted attack within my study go unaddressed. I want Tylle to have her vengeance. I do. But my agreement with Aemun transcends a single life. And I have an offer for you."

Lin licked his lips and pressed closer to the bars. "What?"

"You are an Escorter, no? Escort Aemun and his child to the Ferrucium. I have a special force that will join you closer to the hold, and they will infiltrate and seize control of the Ferrucium, installing Aemun as a leader. Peacefully, if possible. Once there, you don't have to fight, only protect that man. I think most Ferrucium soldiers are like you. Willing to listen, willing to still dream. You could help be part of something larger than yourself, truly make an impact in the welfare of all Danica."

Lin's stomach twisted. "Overthrow the Ferrucium?"

"Aemun claims to have a faction that will side with him based on his name alone. And if not, he claims he can at least get my people to the heads of power."

"The Weavers?" Lin asked.

"Yes, the moniker taken by families of traitors that betrayed Danica to Ladrica so long ago that people seem to have forgotten we were ever free." Listening to the passion in the man's voice was like listening to Tylle speak about her Gods.

"And you believe all his claims?" Lin asked.

"No," Erias whispered. "I'd be a fool. But I believe in my people. Tylle and Pael will go with you."

"She agreed to do so?" Lin asked, eyes coming up to take in the full of Erias's expression.

"She is a true daughter of Danica. And she will do what she must to ensure her sister hasn't died for nothing. It is possible, if one believes in the fates, that Margie had to tell Aemun about our pocket of rebellion so that he might enable this dream. But we have contingencies. And if Aemun has only been spinning a yarn, then Tylle will end his life."

"And you aren't worried that we all know who you are? How easy it would be to send the whole of the Ferrucium's might crashing in on Wellgrove."

"Not now. Years ago, perhaps. But now? I feel it in my soul that the tapestry is falling together, and it will be beautiful. And if that is what must happen, so be it."

"What do I get in exchange for escorting Aemun?" Lin asked. If Tylle truly was on board, then it made his decision easier.

"Exactly what you came to me seeking. The key to removing your Inlay."

"Inlay?"

"Stitches, as you called them. Wievings put to the flesh."

Lin met Erias's eyes. "I don't trust you."

"Only a fool would at first meeting." Erias sighed and lowered his gaze to stare down at Lin's boots. "Danica has been through a lot. Most don't see the Ferrucium for what it is. Sure, they understand their children are taken, and that plants a seed of pain. Then, the children with potential who may have been missed during "evaluations" are hunted and called untethered. But they don't understand their taxes are raised to fuel a hungry Kingdom that tightens its noose around our throats, pushing ever closer into Danica itself. Scout parties raid our northern borders, protected by the Ferrucium. I know the self-named Weavers think they are the wall holding back a worse evil. But why should we tolerate evil at all? King Lodram has trained our fighting force for us. The Northern Kingdom, Ladrica, doesn't have its own Wievers. Binders. Whatever you wish to call them. We take control of the Ferrucium; we take back Danica."

"You'd start a war," Lin whispered.

"We've been at war. Fighting a losing battle in silence. But I was not the one to start it. They were. Think about my offer. Set the ideas of pride and justice aside to truly consider what I say."

Erias rubbed his chin, his neatly trimmed beard making Lin touch his own outgrown scruff. It tickled his palm.

"All I need is an oath from you. One more… material than the Binding Tenets. Those awful beliefs used to shackle our people. Don't work Bindings into your flesh. A form of keeping us weak. Don't worship any Gods other than the Faceless Six and their One Shadow. A form of keeping us close-minded. Don't Bind without a focus. Another shackle to prevent Wievers from reaching their true potential." For the first time since they'd spoken, Erias looked truly disgusted. His lip curled, and in the pale blue light of the Wanderer's Ore, he looked sickly.

"What sort of oath would I be making?" Lin asked. He needed answers. He *wanted* to do what was right. If the Ferrucium had hidden the truth of their people's past, that was terrible. And something Lin couldn't live with. Lin's stomach knotted just thinking about it. He couldn't count the lives taken to ensure Danica stayed beholden to King Lodram through the Ferrucium's control.

"Fealty, to me. But more importantly, you swear to protect Aemun."

"And if he betrays you?" Lin asked. "Or rather, *when* he betrays you."

Erias tapped a bar with his ring again, harder this time. "As I said, there are contingencies in place. So yes. If it becomes clear that he has betrayed us, your command to protect him dies just before he does."

"I could say no," Lin said. And he could. As much as it might pain him to be so close to having a way to undo the Stitches, he could tell this man, this self-righteous man, to go fuck himself. But where would that leave Tylle? Traveling with a man she wants to kill but is forced to stall her vengeance? It made Lin's heart ache.

"You could. I wonder how the dukes, my brother, and his contemporaries might react to the Ferrucium sending an untethered assassin into the heart of Wellgrove. Caught only by happenstance and luck, it would be war —a full, messy, unnecessary war amongst our own people. But if we can cut off the Ferrucium's head peacefully, we will be in a better place as a whole when King Lodram makes his move. And trust me, he plans to move."

"And you swear you'll tell me how to remove the Stitches?" Lin asked.

"I swear, once it is done, I will tell you all I know." Erias looked into Lin's eyes. "Tylle will aid you in making your *Uethe*."

***

Tylle sat beside him inside the cell, legs crossed. Her pale cheeks made the dark circles under her eyes more pronounced. Erias had left them alone, heading out to undoubtedly speak with Aemun.

"You really think this is for the best?" Lin asked.

Tylle sounded like she was trying to clear her throat and then sighed. "Yes. I do."

"I'm sorry. When you weren't acting, I couldn't help myself. It was obvious you had been telling the truth, and it seemed like Aemun would get away with it. And he is somehow. And I'm sorry." Lin reached a hand out towards hers, but she pulled her own back.

"Stop speaking and focus."

"No. I mean it. I acted… out of the fear of losing you."

Tylle shifted, knees pulled to her chest before settling into a crisscrossed position. "Focus. We can discuss what we both have lost and stand to lose later."

With the two of them in a single cell, there was hardly any room to adjust himself. His rear was near the damp stone, and a creeping cold had begun numbing his right leg. Drip, drip, drip. The water falling from who knows what seemed to mock him, interrupting what little peace he'd find in his mind and making him have to focus all over again.

"Keep your hand flat."

Lin extended his fingers, flattening his hand as much as he could. The skin at his knuckles paled at the stress.

"He said you'd help me with an oath."

"Uethe. Bludwieve."

Lin frowned but didn't pull his hand away. "They can be removed like Stitches, right?"

Tylle sighed and rolled her neck. "Older magic than simple Inlays. But yes, if you can remove one, you can remove the other. Breaking an Uethe and removing it are two different things. Now *focus*."

"Am I meant to—"

"Focus," Tylle cut him off. "In this moment, the space above your hand is the *focus*, your heart is the iron *will*, your mind the *weaver*. This is true Wieving. You need no sign, sigil, or outward focus. Just your heart, hand, and mind. A Bludwieve is nothing more than a Wieving made with an Uethe of the heart."

Lin formed a fist with his right hand, picturing the Bludwieve threading into existence.

"Tch." Tylle slapped the back of Lin's right hand and shook her head. "In the room with Aemun, you did a true Wieving. Do it without the excess like you did then."

That confirmed it. Lin had thought he might've, but in the commotion and confusion afterward, he hadn't considered it again. "I'm not an untethered." Though he wasn't sure if the words were more for her sake or his.

Tylle stared at him. "After all we've been through, do you consider me an untethered?"

Lin shook his head and stared at the back of his hand.

"Patterns *can* help guide our will. But sometimes, our will, faith, and hearts know what shape to take in the world around us without those guides. The Ferrucium doesn't teach that, for it empowers the individual to dream."

"You're saying that untethered have stronger... wills or faith than us?"

"I'm saying their hearts know what shape to take without the guidance. Their hearts are violent, volatile things, reflected by their Wievings."

Lin stared at the air around his left hand. No shimmer, no tell-tale red strands twining.

"It's not working," Lin whispered.

"Draw it up from within. Picture your finger. Consider the Uethe you wish to make."

Lin did. That was the one aspect of it he'd understood immediately, even if he didn't like it: "To protect Aemun and help serve Erias."

The fingers of Lin's left hand ached, but he kept them stretched as far apart as possible and exhaled. He closed his eyes and imagined the Binding twisting and twining into existence. His goal was to help Tylle find revenge and to remove the Stitches from his flesh. But could he even manage that and serve Erias? He peeked through his pressed-shut lids at Tylle. More than any of that, he had a feeling that he wanted to see this blade of a woman smile.

"Whatever you're thinking of, let your heart press it into this world. Sear it into your flesh and mind."

Her words were so soft, the movement of her lips so slight, Lin wasn't sure she had spoken at all. But he nodded and tensed as if straining his muscles might somehow help.

Before it became visible, it hummed into existence like a plucked cord. As red as the cloak he'd worn for most of his life. Redder, brighter. It wrapped around the heart finger of his left hand, twice, three times, looping under and around itself. Seamless, no knots or loose bits with which one might undo it. Binding, Wieving, as Tylle called it, *was* magic. Lin had always known that, but there was something *magical* about the moment. Lin shifted, his tunic sticking to him, and sweat dripped from his nose.

"How do you feel?" Tylle asked.

"Light. Focused. Nervous," Lin rasped.

"Nervous?"

Lin nodded. "Can you blame me?"

Her expression said she was considering whether she should or shouldn't fault him for feeling that way. But her head shook, the lone braid sliding over her right shoulder.

"I was aware of what it meant when I formed mine. Truly aware, with the knowledge of our peoples' stolen past. I was just as nervous. You were asked to swear an Uethe with doubt about the truth in your heart, yet you did so anyway."

"Sounds foolish when you put it like that," Lin whispered. But was that what his Uethe had formed from? He stared at the slight curve of her lips. Had he pressed Erias's will into himself, or had his last thoughts of Tylle been what made the blood-colored band finally form?

"Faith is never something I'd call foolish."

"Even after everything, I sometimes forget you're a priestess." Lin flexed his left hand and stared at the Bludwieve, expecting it to have stilled despite knowing the few he'd seen never stopped.

"Would it be a better reminder if I wore ostentatious garbs, like those devoted to the Six and One?" Tylle smiled softly.

"If it is as you constantly remind me, and The Six are merely... poor copies of Verbanth and his family, I would expect your faith to have certain garments of office."

Tylle nodded. "There are vestments, even baubles. But such things don't belong on the sort of travels I set out on."

Lin paused, any reply falling short of leaving his dry lips. She'd set out to save her sister. Of course, she hadn't dressed in the raiment of a priestess.

"Erias should be back soon. He'll fill you in on what's to come. I hope..." she sighed and leaned back onto her palms, stretching one leg out from underneath her as she did and nudging Lin's leg with her heel. "I hope you find solace once this is all done. Once the Inlay is removed from your flesh."

Lin raised his brows.

"What?" she asked.

"If Aemun still breathes, I think solace will be a thing long lost to me."

Her gentle smile lifted at the corner, adding extra lines and a hint of youth through the mischief touching her eyes. She tapped the back of Lin's hand once, then a second time gentler. "All we can hope for is that he proves himself to be the man we think he is."

"A leader?" Lin asked.

Tylle sneered and shook her head. "A snake. Coiling and biting to survive. He will betray Erias; it is in his nature. And when he does, I will have my vengeance."

Tylle rose and exited the cell. A basin of water had been set out beside the glowing blue ore beforehand, and she scooped two cups through the water and filled them.

"I'm sure after swearing an Uethe, he'd want something a bit stronger than water." Erias's rich voice carried from the steps as he descended. His hands were lost in the folds of his sleeves.

"Want and need are two different things," Tylle said before gulping down her cup's contents and taking the few steps necessary to hand Lin the second cup.

Lin hadn't realized how thirsty he was until he watched the water trickle out the corner of her mouth. He rose on shaky legs, stumbling forward and catching his full weight against the iron bars.

"Thank you." Lin straightened his back. Tylle touched his shoulder, letting his shaky hand fully grasp the cup.

With a hand on his shoulder, Tylle helped direct Lin to where the basin rested at the desk. It wasn't that she hadn't been kind in spurts when they'd traveled together, but after everything, he hadn't expected to see this softer side of her. This Tylle was undoubtedly the person who would, and did, risk everything to attempt to rescue her sister. He was sure of it. The cold and merciless killer was the mask she'd slipped on to get through it all. Or she was playing him. But if that was the case, she was a better actress than a priestess.

Erias allowed Lin to gulp down his cup, refill it, and splash the front of his tunic with most of a second cupful before speaking. "Lindel, this is our chance. The one that has been years in the making, and I'm confident that my people, the true children of Danica, can cut the threads that the Ferrucium try to bind us in. You have made a Bludwieve. Tell me, what Uethe did you make?"

"To aid you. To protect Aemun." Lin wiped his mouth with the back of his hand.

"May I approach?" Erias asked.

Lin looked to Tylle, whose expression was smooth, and back to Erias with a hesitant nod. The man who acted like he had as much authority as a king *asking* to approach had filled Lin with as much concern as the basin had been with cool water. Both worried his stomach all the same.

Erias's steps landed softly, the heels of his boots striking the stone in rhythmic taps. As he approached, the scent of citrus and fresh-cut pine rolled from his clothes in intense, pleasant sheets. "This may hurt, but know that I bear no ill will or intention to harm you. But a true Uethe takes two parties, and while the Bludwieve is your burden to bear, what comes next is mine."

Lin didn't have a chance to agree or decline before the man's ringed hand shot out. He might've fought back against the man's palm on reflex if he hadn't been so tired, but instead, Erias's hand swallowed his face. Despite starting cold against Lin's flesh, the ring's band pressing into his brow began stinging and burning.

"Though he was lost, this child of Danica has been found. Let Cunning Velkath watch over his mind, Wise Vellia guide his heart, and Wrathful Verbanth stoke his ire. May Mournful Venduur never whisper his true name, nor Wicked Tel'Myr find him lost in his travels. Truthful Vellyr, aid him in fulfilling his oath."

White-hot intensity pressed into his brow, and Lin's eyes rolled back. His arms and legs tensed and relaxed in waves, and his muscles cramped.

"And may he have better luck than Dull Virt," Erias whispered as he pulled his hand away. A single, moonlight-colored thread trailing the motion.

Chapter Fourteen

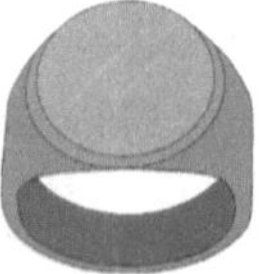

Burdened Bone

Lin sat across from Aemun, hands flat on the table in front of him. Aemun held a knife and fork and hungrily tore into what looked like a seared lamb chop with crushed leaves of sage. The seat adjacent to Aemun was occupied by the woman who'd been beside him earlier. She was a slight, young-looking thing with a shaved head and tired-looking eyes who held Margie's child to her breast underneath what Lin assumed was his old cloak.

Erias sat in a chair with a high back and dipped a bread end into a small ramekin of spiced oil. "Eat," the man said before taking a polite bite of his bread.

Lin's stomach complained at his lack of urgency, even as the warm bread and meat of his own plate tantalized him. "Where is Tylle?"

"Dogs don't usually eat at the table," Aemun muttered. "Usually."

Erias tsked. "She is gathering supplies and caring for herself, Aemun."

"Apologies. Like to never get along, her and I."

"You blamed her for killing Margie and tried to get me to kill her in your stead. You don't think she has reason to hate you?" Lin asked, stabbing a fork down into his own lamb, mouth watering at the juices coming from the meat. It had been days, longer even, since he'd had fresh food. And try as he might to have his anger subdue his hunger, it wasn't working. Plus, he knew having his strength if push came to shove would be more beneficial.

"Did I?" Aemun asked, shrugging it away. "Hmm." A grin played across his face as if he found immeasurable pleasure with each working of his jaw.

The newborn cooed from underneath their cover, pulling at invisible strings attached to Lin's heart. He hadn't thought he'd be so happy to see the child safe and sound after everything. But it was safe to say that by the time they reached Fallo, he'd been closer to the newborn than he had been to Margie.

Erias scratched his chin, the Bound Metal ring shining when the dancing flame of a lamp came into the room.

Pael appeared silently beside Erias. He looked the same as when he'd left the cells, wide hat looking unnecessary atop his head indoors, drawn low over his eyes so that even the lantern light barely lit him. He nodded at Lin, then leaned in and whispered softly into Erias's ear. His voice didn't carry. "If you'd excuse me, I must attend to my brother. I'll return shortly." Erias rapped a knuckle against the tabletop and rose, towering over them as he made and held eye contact with everyone before departing. Pael followed behind him, silent as a shadow.

Aemun licked his lips before wiping the grease around his mouth with the tablecloth. "Wouldn't have expected Duke Wellgrove's brother to be so imperious."

"I never did find out," Lin started as he tore a chunk of bread away, "what role you had in the Ferrucium. Envoy?"

"Many things, *Escorter*. But yes, Envoy to the various ducal houses, given my rank within the Ferrucium. Envoy to the Ladricans, at times." Aemun smiled, eyes drifting to Lin's left hand and lingering on his ring finger. "For the record, I am sorry you were left behind in Fallo. Those monsters... It really couldn't be helped."

Lin frowned and pulled his left hand under the table, using his right to dip his piece of bread into oil. "What's done is done. Now, we are both oath breakers of a sort."

Aemun laughed, deep and hard, and even wiped a tear from his eye. He continued until even the woman beside him, after staring for long enough to make Lin uncomfortable, began giggling. He took a long pull from the goblet beside him. His lips stained red from the wine within. "I am not an oath breaker. What I will do alongside Erias is strengthen the Ferrucium. Strengthen Danica. He and I and his people disagree on a few things, of course, but there will be mediation. There *can* be compromise. As we are now, there is no compromise. Not with a king who views all our people as untethered. Yes, you heard me; all of us are unsavable *monsters* to Good King Lodram. No longer will we have to listen to the commands of a cruel king, treated as dogs to get scraps from under the table. I am no oath breaker."

Lin tried to find the lie in the man's words but couldn't. It matched with most of what Tylle and Erias had said about the north. But then he saw Margie. Pictured her sitting there in that seat where the girl, who'd only stopped giggling once Aemun had slammed his goblet beside her, sat.

"Why did she have to die?" Lin asked.

"Why did who have to die?" Aemun asked.

"You know who I mean," Lin growled.

"Oh," Aemun said. Either he was too deep in the goblet, or he really hadn't considered the answer to that because he stared into the cup for a while. He looked up to speak, but the door opened, and Erias breezed in with all the solemnity of a man attending a funeral. His face was drawn, and any bit of the charm he'd left the room with originally had fled like ash blown away on the wind.

"What've you done?" Erias's words dripped with barely-held fury.

Lin flinched, and the breast-feeding woman did the same. Aemun gulped from his goblet and looked up over its lip, eyes like a wolf's.

"Many things. Clarity, Erias, please." Aemun met the man's hard stare and didn't blink away.

Lin pushed his chair back and exhaled. With a shift, he moved closer to the woman, nodding at her in an effort to calm her. Her large, nearly bugged-out eyes took him in, and she nodded back.

"I can take the child if you need to make yourself decent," Lin whispered.

She nodded again, more uneasily this time, as her head swiveled over to Aemun. The man waved a hand at her dismissively. In a blink, the child was out from under the covering, eyes not open, impossibly small hands clutching for something, anything really if Lin had to guess. The woman moved to stand, but Erias snapped his fingers and stared violently towards her, jaw working.

"Sit down," Erias commanded. "Why is Wellgrove suddenly inundated with several Noosemen? One I understood as a possible coincidence, but three?"

"Oh." Aemun nodded. "Likely because I sent a messenger bird to the Ferrucium and my Ladrican contacts asking for aid. Of course, I would never have done something after our agreement, but this particular safety net I had threaded *before* we came to terms."

"And you didn't think to mention it to me?" Erias asked.

"I imagined the Grovetender I'd heard so much about would be able to deal with a few inquiring sets of eyes. And if you're now saying you aren't up to the task, I'm left wondering if this partnership is really as integral to my future as you've made it sound. And I never thought they'd send any of those masked monsters since they aren't Ferrucium soldiers. Perhaps an attempt to maintain appearances of peace?"

Lin stared at the two men, feeling suddenly like a fly caught in a web between two spiders, his wings ripping with each struggling jerk to free himself. Then, he looked down as the baby shifted in his arms. His old cloak, tattered and torn, hung across the woman beside him. Six, she looked miserable. Sweat dotted her brow, and she shivered every other breath.

"Of course, I can handle this. But we are beyond the point of little tests of each other's mettle. You will need to leave immediately under the cover of night. Pael will guide the two of you out, and Tylle will meet you at the western edge of town."

A look of disappointment found its way onto Aemun's face, and he pouted out his lower lip. "We will never be beyond that point, Erias. Not as long as I breathe."

"Get out," Erias spat.

Lin chewed at his lip and rose, baby clutched tight to his chest. "Erias, this proves he can't be trusted."

"This proves he considers the path ahead," Erias replied, rolling his eyes to rest on the baby Lin held.

Aemun sighed and gestured at the girl to take the baby, and she did. She swaddled it, shivering the whole time, and pulled the wrap tight across her chest. Muttering unintelligible things to the child as she worked.

"Why didn't you have him make an Uethe?" Lin demanded.

"Because you don't shackle your partners," Aemun said.

"No, you just kill them!" Lin hissed.

"Enough." Erias clapped his hands and shook his head. "He's given me something more valuable than his sworn word to prove his loyalty. Even if this recent revelation makes me doubt my own sense."

Aemun rose in that same lazy, fluid motion he possessed and stretched his limbs. "I've given Erias keys to the kingdom, so to speak."

"You've given him enough rope to hang himself with," Lin said. There was something about Aemun's face, perhaps the arrogance of a life easily lived. The way he looked down on everyone. Since he'd been back in the man's presence, his once rude quirks had seemed to shift into a whole persona. Maybe Margaret had balanced him, somehow. Maybe—

Erias was on him in a moment, the back of his hand catching Lin across the cheek. The notch of the ring struck the bone of his eye, and he immediately felt it swell, but beyond that, the metal, that strange *old magic* Bound Metal, burned.

"I said enough. Doubt this man all you want, but you will not impugn *my* intelligence. Understood?"

Lin nodded and stared at his boots, just noticing Pael standing behind the man. It made sense that he'd been there the whole time. His eyes weren't visible below the brim of his hat, but Lin was sure he was avoiding looking him in the eye.

"Pael, lead them out. Take the back alleys. If you're caught, do what you do best." Erias straightened his thick top, smoothing out the lapel. "Lin. See him safely to the Ferrucium, and you will have your prize. I swear it on Verbanth and all his kin."

Lin didn't miss Aemun's snort as he strolled over to where Pael waited or the fact that Erias mentioned the one name associated with wrath. What had he gotten himself into?

"Ready?" Pael asked.

Lin nodded and clutched the child tighter. "And if we get split up?"

"Don't fall behind. Any of you." Pael cocked his head and made a face at the woman. "And if I say quiet, it means all of you." And then Pael was moving. They passed through the awful metal doors, not nearly as debilitating as they'd been previously, though the woman trembled and gasped once they were more than ten feet from it.

"Gather yourself," Aemun said, grasping her by the arm and pulling her along.

Lin wasn't positive, but it seemed like the first words he'd seen the man speak to her. When she sidled beside him and took the child, Lin fought the urge to clutch the babe and not let her be taken.

Pael slowed and peered around the corner ahead of them. They weren't walking back through the tapestry; instead, they had taken a right turn that felt the air grow even colder than the initially damp and chill tunnel they'd first walked through. "Clear," he whispered.

After years on the road, walking through pristine halls where suits of antiquated armor, metal, polished, and bulbous, lined the furthest walls made his hair stand on end. And where there weren't suits of armor, it seemed someone had the nerve to hang banner after banner interspersed in the gaps. It would have been better if they'd just knocked all the walls down and let nature take the town. Carefully organized groves looked pretty enough, but Lin had always loved the wilderness.

Pael rushed, then paused to let Aemun's woman catch up—just to rush again. Lin's legs threatened to cramp from the stop-and-go of it. Whatever time he'd spent resting, if anyone would call it that, in the small cell hadn't been enough.

Eventually, through the winding halls that turned into a short tunnel by the end, they made it to an exterior door. Slick, mossy bits hung to the wall, and the damp earth smelled like it hadn't been disturbed in ages. Lin scrunched his nose and hunched to avoid hitting the lower-than-average ceiling.

"It would help if you ditched the cloaks," Pael said. The man didn't look like he'd just been slinking through what Lin had to imagine was Wellgrove Manor. He certainly didn't look any worse for wear from when he'd first met the man.

"And let my child freeze?"

Margie's child.

"And let your child get out of the city away from the King's Noose you've thought to bring to our throats. And the few Reds that have been spotted watching the city gates. Odd behavior, no?"

Aemun shrugged. "If Erias can have contingencies, so can I."

Lin cleared his throat. "The time for bickering is past us. Tylle should be at the eastern gate, no? Which means she's waiting, likely with horses. And the longer she waits, the more danger she puts herself in. Let's move."

Pael squinted one eye up at Lin, cocking his head and scratching the tuft of gray-white hair that sprouted from his tunic. "Those cloaks are gonna get us spotted. But—" he waved his hands like a pauper magician pretending at magic "—that'll be your problem, and I'll be a shadow."

The section of Wellgrove they moved through didn't seem patrolled. Not that Aemun seemed to care. The man practically strutted as he walked, not once looking back at the woman he entrusted his child to.

"Are you alright?" Lin fell back and slowed his pace to match hers. It's not that he hadn't noticed her before, but she'd seemed dressed to fit in with Erias's chambers, like any other decoration piece. But here, out on the dark streets, he saw her dress had been torn near the hem, and her slippers were caked in grime, making her constantly slip. Six, she hadn't been prepared for this. Hadn't been made to be prepared more like it.

"Fine," she whispered. Even her voice sounded weathered and worn.

"If the child is too heavy—"

"Escorter, perhaps leave my child and her carer to me and do your job? It's odd to have an Escorter at the *back* of the procession." Aemun had stalled underneath an overhang and rolled his wrist impatiently.

Pael—barely visible where he stood—started to move again. This section of town, there was likely a reason he'd led them through here. Entire buildings looked dilapidated, ancient in construction, with rotted beams and broken tiles.

"Not much further. Almost out of this fucking mess." Pael's gruff voice carried back as Lin passed Aemun to follow closer behind the stout man.

"I've got a feeling it'll be a long night before we're out of this mess," Lin whispered.

Pael slowed, matching his gait with Lin's. "How's your cheek?"

"Oh." Lin touched where his flesh had split. The wound was tender, the blood drying, and the reminder of how far above Lin Erias seemed to think he was fresh. "Not worse than anything else I've gone through the past few days. He ever strike you?"

Pael cleared his throat and looked over his shoulder at Aemun. "Never gave him a reason. And he knows it wouldn't go his way. I'm not *his* man. He can stick all his groves up his pompous ass for all I care. But he's good at what he does. Leading the people. Pulling the strings."

"And yet it seems he was outsmarted."

Pael snorted. "Outsmarted by that... fop? I doubt it. Outplayed maybe. Put in a situation he'd rather not be in? Certainly."

The gate came into view like a dark maw rising from between buildings, lit by two torches set too wide to be the gate's eyes. Guards, clothed in the deep verdant hues of Wellgrove's livery, stood at attention. Both guards looked as tired as Lin felt, judging by how their shoulders slumped and the posture of the leftmost guard as he leaned against the wall.

"Little late to be traveling, no?" the younger of the two said, eyes perking up at noticing the approaching group. His gaze lingered on the woman behind Aemun.

"On a damn-near moonless night, no doubt," Pael muttered. "But some business can't be kept away by the dark any more than some fools can't be drawn to the light." With a deft hand, he tossed something to the guard, a small coin purse by the sound of it landing in his palm. "If you see some Reds, like this prick, asking questions. Tell 'em you didn't see anyone. Fair?"

"I haven't seen a thing all night," the older guard said. Her eyes were sharp, and she carried the weight of someone who might bully others simply by her size. She smiled big and winked at Pael.

They went through the gate as a group, and true to Erias's claims, Tylle stood at the outskirts of the eastern gate with three horses—Nebra and the chestnut she'd gotten from the wagon earlier and a third, lamer-looking mount. Tylle's expression was flat, placid as they approached.

Aemun approached Nebra, stifling a yawn with the back of his hand. "What are the rest of you expected to ride on?" He placed a hand on Nebra's saddle, taking the reins and almost getting his foot into the stirrup before Lin was on him, pushing him to the ground.

Tylle and Pael moved simultaneously, each taking up space between Lin and Aemun. The woman cowered to the side.

Aemun stared up from the ground, fingers splayed and ripping at the sod at his palms. "Protection," he scoffed. "Tell me, do you think there will be a place for you in the Ferrucium ranks once this is all done? Even if you can remove the Stitches, I know you're untethering in the truest sense, and I can promise you there won't be a place for someone like you in Danica's future."

Lin pressed forward, and Tylle's hands touched his chest. Gentler than he expected. Pressed there and held as her eyes looked into his face. Lin knew tears stung his own eyes, knew that his hands trembled, and that he'd formed a Weft in the space between him and Aemun. Formed it without a focus. And it hurt. Six knew it hurt as a blistering pain started at his ring finger and seared its way up his arm. Breathing became harder, impossibly hard, as a tension built at the sides of his neck as if someone the size of the guard who'd winked at Pael had him in a headlock.

"You can't." Tylle's lips seemed to say, but he couldn't hear her over the sound of blood pulsing in his ears.

Pael walked over to Aemun and helped the man up, dusting dirt and dried grass from his back.

"Release it," Tylle mouthed.

Lin did—barely. The Weft felt impossible to let go of, like holding onto a hot ember. He'd wanted to let it go and release it as soon as he made it, but it wouldn't move.

"Each time you raise a hand or blade at me, it will be worse for you. You swore an Uethe, as he calls it. You made a Binding Oath. Fucking idiot," Aemun said. Then he spat at the ground by Lin's boots and stalked over to the chestnut mare, saddled and ready to go. "Gwen, come."

The woman, Gwen, paused and then rushed over.

"You look ridiculous. Cover yourself," Aemun spat. He rummaged through the saddlebag and pulled a scratchy cloth from within. "I hope you ride a horse better than you care for my child."

"Yessir." Her voice was soft and shaky.

"Little Tylle, now that we've had enough excitement for a night, care to share a horse with me?"

Tylle frowned at the third horse, not nearly as fit looking as the two Ferrucium steeds. "Perhaps we can alternate."

Pael shrugged. "Or you could run alongside. I'm sure you could keep up."

Lin, only half-listening to the conversations, shook his swimming head. He'd hoped that the Uethe he made had somehow been subverted. That his desire of wanting to see Tylle truly happy would've taken priority over protecting Aemun. He hadn't thought it would result in blinding hot pain if he raised his hand at the man. A person couldn't keep up with a horse hitting a full stride, let alone a Ferrucium-bred one. He looked down at his left hand and the writhing crimson ring that encircled his finger. Tylle truly had taught Lin something when they formed his Bludwieve. A focus didn't have to be tangible. That *was* a lie fabricated by the Ferrucium. One of many, possibly. A construct allegedly made to keep all Binders, all Wievers, yoked to the Binding Tenets.

Untethered.

The more Lin struggled away from that title, the more it seemed to fit. It slid around his throat, choking him every chance it got. But if he was untethered, was that so bad? The Ferrucium claimed it was wrong, but if anything that Tylle and Erias said proved true, then perhaps it wasn't such a wicked thing.

Lin shook his head, attempting to clear his thoughts. Erias and Aemun were alike. Men like that got off on control, perceived or not, justified or not. "Pael, get on behind me. And don't squeeze too tight. I'm sore."

Chapter Fifteen

Burdened Hate

L in shifted in the saddle, stretching his legs as much as possible without pushing backward into Pael. The stout man took up more than his share of the saddle and clutched onto Lin like a child learning to ride for the first time. His hands tickled Lin's stomach occasionally, and Lin could feel his cheeks burn at the indignation of it. At least the older man smelled better than he looked, almost like stale rosewater.

Tears blinked from Lin's eyes, the wind's hard kiss like a demanding lover not taking no for an answer. But more than that, his mind had slipped to when he'd first been taught to ride. He'd never be able to count how many times he fell from the back of Denro's horse. To this day, Denro didn't let Lin forget that he was the sole reason he gave up on educating trainees and instead became an Evaluator.

"If you were selected, we need keener eyes making those judgments."

Lin's grip on the reins loosened, and he leaned forward.

Nebra's breaths came out in heavy snorts, and sweat shone on her coat, a light lather on her sides.

Denro's words haunted Lin. The man, his *mentor*, had been right. Lin, a betrayer, a breaker of Tenets, a... And now look at him. What would Denro think, seeing Lin? That he was two halves of a whole fool, likely.

Aemun and Gwen rode ahead, her clutching to him as tightly as Pael had to Lin. But every so often, Lin had watched him try to pry her grip free. Whatever their agreement was, it seemed the further from Wellgrove they got, the more disdain he showed for her.

Lin craned his neck and stared behind at Tylle. Her expression was still, passionless, flat. As if she'd slipped on another mask, separate from the gentle priestess and cold killer. It was an odd wish, but the desire to ride with her swelled inside him until he looked away. He should've killed Aemun twice over by now.

"Are my old eyes playing tricks, or is there the light of a camp up ahead?" Pael pointed with a shaky hand, and sure enough, over the ridge was a squared building with a flag fluttering in the dark, impossible to see clearly.

Lin squinted. "What road are we on?"

"Eastern path, towards a lake," Pael said.

"And the Ferrucium Hold."

"And that, yeh."

"Probably a Ferrucium outpost. Manned if the torches are any indicator. Best we avoid it."

"How can we when he's already on the path for it?"

Pael was right. The path they were on was wide and forked a ways back, likely from travelers not wishing to pass so close to an outpost. Most citizens, at least most Lin had met, didn't outwardly show hate for Ferrucium soldiers, but that didn't mean they wanted to go out of their way to approach them.

"Let's hope he doesn't have any more *contingencies*," Pael spoke the last word in a high-pitched whine.

They followed Aemun, the path narrowing enough that it ran through the outpost like a toll gate. Either side of the road and building were surrounded by uneven hills that made Lin imagine archers and Binders hiding in every dark dip. He should've recognized the area sooner, but most of his escort missions had been in the far north, well away from the hill lands southeast of Wellgrove.

"Shit," Pael whispered. His thin fingers dug into Lin's side.

Aemun had already slowed and was speaking up at a sentry who leaned over the parapet lining the walkway above.

"They say the gate is closed until morning." Aemun didn't try to hide the contempt in his voice.

The stars were already dimming, though the sky past the outpost didn't look any lighter.

"So, we wait?" Pael said.

"We can't wait," Tylle called from behind.

"So, we turn and take the other path," Lin said, shifting so his Stitched left hand wasn't visible. In all the talk of removing the magic markings, he'd somehow grown used to seeing the beautiful glow against his skin. He'd gotten too comfortable staring at the twining crimson band.

"I refuse to ride all the way back there. I didn't come on this path just to get turned around by some no-name, no-role foot soldier. By the time we got back there and progressed past this point, the gate would've opened. On whose orders is this outpost closed?" It was hard to tell if Aemun's cheeks reddened or if the color was due to the torches, but the more he spoke, the wilder his hand movements became.

"Captain Lazara."

"And is that name meant to mean anything to me? Hmm?" Aemun struggled to dismount, finally slapping Gwen's hands from his waist. It looked like she had the good sense to try to keep him saddled.

The soldier shook his head and cleared his throat, but a hand grabbed his shoulder from behind, and a tall, lean woman peered over the side of the parapet beside him.

"My name might not mean anything to you. But it means a whole deal to the Ferrucium."

"If it did, I'm sure I'd have heard it by now."

"Oh, no worries, Envoy Aemun. Your reputation proceeds you, and there are things that even *you* don't hear."

There was a silence, and Lin moved to dismount, noticing Tylle already had.

"But this order to shut the gate doesn't come from me exactly. It comes from Dennick."

"And who the fuck is that?"

Lin had moved to stand beside Aemun, the man either too arrogant or too—then he smelled it. "By the Six man, you're drunk!"

Aemun whirled, his hand almost catching Lin in the exact spot as Erias had. But Lin caught it and held it. Staring into the hateful man's eyes.

"Take that look from your eyes. You don't get to look down on me," Aemun spat, yanking his hand free.

While they'd been talking, Pael had moved to the front of the saddle and seemed to sink lower into it than Lin thought possible. Tylle had slipped from view, and five more soldiers had lined the parapet beside Captain Lazara.

"Dennick is a Nooseman, and you know how it goes with them. They said they wanted all outposts coming and going to Wellgrove closed unless they came personally and said otherwise."

"Weaver Azhura—"

"With all due respect to *all* the Weavers and their high station in the Ferrucium, it doesn't matter," Captain Lazara said. One of the soldiers had brought a lamp up beside the captain, and Lin saw her in full detail. A pretty woman with full lips and cold, hard eyes. Her hair was short and tied back out of her face into a small knot at the top of her head. Her cloak was the same as most Ferrucium soldiers, but her rank meant black fur lined the collar, and a single golden X was stitched into either side of her shoulders.

"Aemun, let's go," Lin said.

"No!" Aemun shouted. "Either let us pass, or we will force our way through."

Lin's stomach sank. He didn't understand why Aemun was being so belligerent, other than proving himself to be an insufferable prick, even more so than he already was. He also didn't like that a Nooseman was involved in this.

"Aemun. Force your way through and kill us, or we let you through and find ourselves facing the King's Noose for breaking their order. Either way, we're at an impasse." Captain Lazara sounded level and prepared.

The road along either side was quiet, the hills blocking the wind and causing a funneling effect towards the outpost.

"You're right. Morning isn't so far away," Aemun touched a hand to his brow and yawned, turning, and staggering to the horse Gwen still sat atop. Then he spun. His Ferrucium steel sword was out, and he formed a Weave, launching an attack at the gatehouse. "You will respect me!"

The counterassault was immediate and unrelenting.

Pael and Gwen seemed unable to see the sharp, sickle-like Wefts as they sliced the air toward them. Captain Lazara moved efficiently. Weft after Weft after Weft, flying like she was a one-woman army. The other six or so soldiers seemed to be focusing on defense, and soon, the outpost was lit by flashes of light as Aemun's Weaves and Wefts were shattered one after another.

Lin knew Tylle was more than capable of defending and attacking on her own, and still, a large part of him didn't want to fight Ferrucium soldiers at all, so he defended Pael and Gwen. Lin made a quick focus with his hand and destroyed the closest Weft. Remembering that he didn't necessarily have to do that would take some time. Precious time that could save his life in a fight. The act of Binding used to feel like threading a needle. Now, without slowing the power through a focus, it was more like pouring water through a needle's eye.

"Lin?" Tylle came into view, one hand holding a wicked dagger.

Aemun, drunk as he smelled, cut each Weave and Weft flying at him with precision. His sharp-angled face lighted with each explosion of golden light.

"What?" he called.

"Fight back!"

Lin stared up at the outpost, at the faces of the soldiers who'd only been defending themselves. He continued breaking their magic, unraveling it like loosely knotted threads. Weaves were easier to break, Wefts less so. But he did it, pushing past the urge to use a focus as the hail of magic assaults continued. He'd drawn his own steel but hadn't swung it.

"Fight back!" Tylle spat again.

"They haven't done anything!" Lin finally snapped.

"If you don't kill them, they'll kill all of us. You, me, the child, Pael. And those two. All dead."

Lin gulped down that particular truth. He couldn't care less about Aemun, but Margaret's child was as innocent as the soldiers, if not more so. "I... I'll try," he whispered.

"You have to do more than try. Quit pretending like they aren't the enemies. *Please.*"

"I wasn't." Was he? Lin shook his head. "I wasn't. But enemies, friends, either way, they're people like us, fighting for what they think is right and good."

Tylle shrugged.

Lin stared. He was tired. Tired of running and chasing shadows he once might've considered allies. Tired of doubting himself and his beliefs. But she was right. Lin might not have attacked first, but until he removed the Stitches in his flesh, and possibly even after that, if Aemun's threats were true, he couldn't consider Ferrucium soldiers allies.

Lin ducked under a Weft from Aemun's direction and, pushing his will into the world, formed three Wefts, each thinner than the last. Two caught a soldier apiece, poor sods not blessed with the Sight or able to avoid the fast-moving Bindings. One went over the third target's head as they cowered down.

Pael seemed to have the sense to retreat with Nebra, guiding her and Tylle's mount back away from the conflict, but with the uneven hills surrounding them, a true retreat seemed impractical. Gwen screamed as dirt erupted around her and the horse's feet, but the mount being Ferrucium-trained meant it didn't startle or stamp the way Tylle's had begun doing down the road.

Lin had never been in a battle. Not like this. Not against other people. *Aside from those soldiers whom Tylle had confronted back before Riverside. Aside from bandits and robbers.* But those hadn't been *battles.* He ducked a stray Weft—it seemed the soldiers that remained above had begun forming and sending Weft after Weft blindly, a poor imitation of their captain who seemed to be a skilled Binder and fighter. She'd jumped down at some point, moving as fluid as water, striking at Aemun with Binding and blade.

Aemun snarled, backfoot giving more and more ground. It seemed they both possessed the Sight and while they seemed matched in Binding skill, Captain Lazara overpowered him with her blade. Strike after clashing strike.

Lin rushed in, siding up alongside Aemun and swinging his sword horizontally at the captain's overextended calf. But she spun, blade clanging, pushing both of them as she sped up. Each strike felt exploratory. Each hit tested something unseen that made Lin jerk back at the last moment. As he pulled away, she pushed in, and Aemun, failing to seize the opportunity to take advantage of the flank, retreated. He threw one or two dull-orange Bindings, more like limp threads than proper Weaves, and fled to Gwen.

Fuck. Lin hadn't meant to take her on his own. But, of course, Aemun had run.

Captain Lazara nodded at his left hand, hanging in the air like a torch against the darkness. "Are you the reason the Noose has us all in arms? A single untethered?"

Lin formed a fist and leveled his blade. "I'm not untethered."

"I've heard that before." And by the narrowing of her eyes and clenching of her jaw, he believed her. She was ready to take his life. Though, to be fair, she seemed ready to kill all of them if it meant keeping from disobeying the Nooseman.

"I mean it."

"I'd believe it about those Fell-Bindings. Seen that done to people against their will. That red one, though. That was a choice."

"Shut up," Lin snapped.

She lunged, sword tip sweeping up in an arc meant to open his torso. Lin barely blocked the blow and tried to counter-swing but took a punch to his nose for his efforts. He pulled his face away as a Binding, a Needle, formed where he'd just been. She didn't stop attacking, each movement so precise and practiced as to give him no room to truly counter.

Lin sliced wide, anticipating her to deftly avoid it. She did, veering left with ease. Watching her move was like watching echoes of Denro's training from Lin's youth before he became an Escorter. Fast as a Binding forming, she pressed her attack. Lin blocked her overhead swing, her blade edge catching in the nick along Lin's edge. From the Weft that bit Ferrucium steel. An idea sparked like a Binding exploding. If there was one thing that had kept Lin alive despite the few untethered he'd encountered before Lyre or the bandits and robbers that lay traps in the thick of woods far off from the Ferrucium, it was his ability to adapt. To watch his enemies and allies alike and *learn*.

Lin dodged left, his flank uncomfortably close to a sloping hill. He only needed to avoid her enough times and make it to enough separate points to plant the seeds of his plan. Captain Lazara pressed in, keeping enough distance that her sword couldn't be disadvantaged in hand-to-hand combat. Once she committed, Lin spun, rushing the other way, wary of her range.

"You fight like a child," she said.

Lin made broad, sweeping Weaves at various heights, and she broke them instantly, showering both of them in golden motes of dying light. Having the Sight was a blessing, and Lin watched the beautiful trap he'd been setting spring. Like snakes vining to climb a trellis, the Bindings he'd placed near her feet slid around her ankles, anchoring her in place. Surprise flashed across her face, and then rage as she went to shatter them as she had all the rest.

In Fallo, Lin had been unable to break the trap laid by the untethered. The why or how of it was lost on him, and he didn't put any faith that his own might resist the captain's power. So, he charged her and shoved her with all his force. She tripped, tumbled, and rolled to a stop, her weapon two arm-spans from her as dust kicked up.

"Skillless coward," she hissed.

Aemun seemed to come from the shadows himself. "My Escorter is many things. But one thing he doesn't seem to lack is the ability to *survive*."

"He is untethered!"

"We are all tools with different purposes," Aemun said, then leaned in close to her and whispered something that Lin couldn't hear.

Captain Lazara lashed out, attempting to stab a Needle into Aemun's face, but missed at the angle, and Aemun's boot crunched into her shoulder. With a downward thrust, his sword caused a gash across her throat. Blood pooled and mixed with the rocky dirt, her Needle snapping like a twig and fading like dying embers. The captain's steel reflected the outpost, and Lin saw himself momentarily. Stitches in his arm, sweat and blood streaking his face. Lin's stomach twisted, and a sour taste filled his mouth. *Untethered.*

"What did you say to her?" Lin asked.

"I told her if someone bars her way to the Grand Tapestry, to fight like a cornered animal to earn her place," Aemun said. A smile touched his face, and he ran a hand through his hair. "Let's move before the King's Noose arrives. Interesting technique you used there. Does it have a name?"

"Snare," Lin whispered. At least, that's what he'd thought of when caught in it back in Fallo.

The outpost gate was open, and three dead soldiers were slumped against the lower portion of the wall like forlorn sentries.

One soldier groaned as Lin neared. Their flesh looked ashen, their hair and eyes dark against pale gray flesh. "B-bastards," he groaned, spit and blood clinging to the edge of his mouth, forming a string of red saliva that stretched to the dirt but didn't break. His right arm was missing at the elbow, a smooth cut. The outcome of a stable-enough Weft biting flesh.

"I'm sorry," Lin whispered. He leveled his sword at the man's throat, preparing to drive it in to end the man's suffering.

"Bullshit."

"No, really. I'm sorry."

"You think I'll let you take me and stick me to the walls?" the soldier asked with so much pained conviction that it hurt to hear it. They hadn't done that to anyone. They *wouldn't* do that to anyone. This wasn't Fallo, and they weren't monsters.

"What?" Lin asked, blade trembling. "What did you say?"

The soldier clutched his wound but made a circular focus with his fingers, and his magic spurted in unstable, sputtering orange sparks. It was impossible to tell if he meant to try to Stitch the wound closed, but even Lin knew a missing limb wasn't fixable.

Lin hesitated, and the dying man finished the Binding. What Lin expected to be another weak Weft or Weave aimed at his knees launched into the sky like a shooting star. It streaked into the air and then bloomed like a budding flower. Intensely bright. Painfully bright. He'd never seen anything like it. Hadn't thought Bindings were capable of something so... abstract.

The soldier was dead. Blood soaked his remaining hand and clothes and the dirt under him. There would be no answers from his lips, only the slight snarl he'd worn on death. No explanation of what that magic had just done.

Tylle's steps pulled Lin from his stupor. Her expression was grim as she looked over the area they had fought.

"He..." Lin started.

"Never felt a hum quite so strong."

Lin nodded and swallowed hard against the lump in his throat. "Like a flaming arrow that blossomed." Lin mimicked the explosion with his hands.

"A signal, maybe?" Tylle asked.

"A signal for whom?"

Tylle frowned and stared toward where Aemun rested with the woman and child. "Take a guess."

"You think so?" Lin shivered. Neither of them said it. *Noosemen.*

Chapter Sixteen

Burdened Blood

Lin stared at the space between Tylle's shoulder blades as if he might see the tension resting there. They'd met back with Pael, the balding man apparently clever enough to read both Lin and Tylle's expressions and recognize that any questions he might ask would yield few answers. They'd taken two horses stabled at the side of the outpost and set the others loose, though being Ferrucium-trained, they likely wouldn't stray far.

Aemun and Gwen, now on separate horses, rode ahead. Gwen kept her head down. She sat saddle awkwardly, confirming the suspicion that perhaps she hadn't ridden much, if at all, and she had the child strapped to her chest.

"I don't like that he forced his way through. Felt like he expected it, no?" Pael kept his voice low, and if the question was intended for Tylle, she didn't answer.

"We seemed stuck. Odds were, they'd had a way to summon the Noose the whole time. Right?" Lin chewed on the inside of his mouth and played it all back in his head. The burst of light had been like a sun appearing for a split second. How far would that light stretch to those able to see it? Certainly to Wellgrove.

The scene played back through Lin's head. The captain dying brutally, and Lin failing to stop Aemun. Not even failing when he really thought about it. To fail, he would've had to make an attempt. He loosened his grip on Nebra's reins and blinked, pulling his stare from Tylle. He blamed her. In his gut and heart, he *blamed* her. It hadn't been her fault. None of it had. But still, none of it would've happened if she hadn't Stitched him. Hadn't introduced him to

Erias as if the man was capable of great feats, only to learn he'd choose to work with a monster like Aemun. If Tylle hadn't broken the Binding Tenets, if she and her sister weren't involved in a *rebellion*, none of this would have happened.

As if she could hear his thoughts, Tylle slowed her horse. "Did you hear that?"

Lin hadn't heard anything. Even the wind seemed still.

"Aemun," Tylle called.

Tylle set her jaw and shifted in her saddle when he didn't slow or call back. The hills that had courted the outpost had given way to wild forests cut through by merchant routes and well-worn paths. A tangled mess of foliage overhead and thick brush made it an opportune place for an ambush.

"I, for one, have had enough of his surprises. Like to burn the next town we cross down, fiery as his temper is." Pael's hat was scrunched in one hand as he ran another over his stubbled pate. "And if that happens, I'm gone. Like as not, I wanted to see you to Carine and her lot, but I'm no fighter, and that last scrap took about everything from me."

"Not that I'm one to judge, but didn't see much fight from you."

"Bah. Didn't say I did. I said it took a lot out of me. I'm more of a... eh." He waved a hand, face twisting as he tried to think of the correct phrase.

"Duke's man. You'll knife, fuck, or talk your way through all of Danica if Duke Hollander needed it," Tylle said flatly.

"Right. Scrapping with those who could kill me paces out with magic I can barely feel, let alone see? No, thank you."

Living with the Sight, it was easy, so easy, to forget that some people never focused their will. Some never shaped thought into intention and formed a Binding of any kind. And most of those who did *never* saw it. He stared down at the Stitches in his hand, wondering if the Sight was perhaps a double-edged sword. If the blessing didn't exist, no one would know he'd even broken the Tenets.

"Well, he wasn't like this before. His temper, I mean. Not that I knew him aside from the days before Lyre. Though he was always a bit of a prick," Lin said. "But maybe now that he's working with Erias, his intentions have changed."

"I think he was testing us." Tylle had slowed enough so that she was side by side on the narrow path, and despite the feelings he'd had a moment ago, he was glad to have her so close again. Traveling alone together along the roads to Riversbend and then Wellgrove, those were moments he missed now that they were with Pael and Aemun.

"How so?" Pael asked.

"Loyalty and strength, if I had to guess," Lin said. Maybe he'd wanted to see if Lin and Tylle would kill for him. Or he'd wanted to force a fight out of pettiness for Lin's initial assault when they'd first departed Wellgrove.

Tylle's chin wavered, then she shook her head, rubbing a knuckle into her right ear and cocking her head to the side. "You really don't hear that?"

Then Lin heard it, a whistle so low that Lin thought he'd imagined it under the beating of hooves and wind that rushed past his ears. A shiver took Lin, and he clenched the reins, leaning lower into Nebra. "Go, girl."

Pael followed his lead, and Tylle wasn't far behind. In moments, they were upon Aemun and Gwen. The path was too narrow, so they slowed to match Aemun's pace before the man called his mount to a stop. He craned his head momentarily before spitting to the side, almost hitting Nebra.

"What is that One-loved smell and sound?" Aemun asked.

"Don't know," Lin said. He'd planned to elaborate further, but a pungent aroma of decay and rust crashed into him like a wave. Gwen gagged and almost lost her saddle as the horse whinnied and stamped.

"Don't know?" Aemun snapped.

Before Lin could respond, Tylle raised a hand. "Is that a camp ahead?" she asked.

Lin strained his vision. All he could see ahead was the hungry, swallowing darkness of thick-branched trees. Even the main road they'd been on for the better part of the night fought to keep the forest from falling into the path.

Pael's horse trotted towards Lin from behind, gaining ground. "Smells like the south end of a northbound ass," he called. No one replied, and Tylle's eyes had grown wide.

Lin's throat was dry, and he couldn't form words, so he nodded.

"You know," Pael whispered, "and it's not a single bit my business, but perhaps we go another way. Haven't had a good feeling about this since we left Wellgrove."

"This is the quickest path," Aemun whispered.

"There are three other routes just as quick—or they would've been if you hadn't rushed off this way in the first place. We might lose a day or two once all is said and done. But I've got a nose for this, boy, and trust me when I say this doesn't smell right."

"Shut up, old fool. Erias might value your lip service, but I need very little of that from you. Now, let's go. The longer we dawdle, the tighter the Noose gets around our throats."

Lin watched in shock as Tylle slid from her saddle and crouched before disappearing into the thick, rustling brush. He cleared his throat and said, "I'm not leaving her."

The whistling grew louder, higher pitched.

"All this time, and you haven't changed. Even if you're untethering."

"You know, you might not understand, but she saved me—my life, that is. She also took it from me, in a way. But she *saved* me when you ran like the coward you are."

"And how do you think she managed that? By being brave? No. Better a coward than a monster," Aemun hissed. "But that is fine with me now. Meeting Erias was the best thing that could've happened. And don't kid yourself. You are a monster. You just haven't learned to use your fangs yet." Aemun urged his horse forward, a grin on his narrow face making him look prouder than normal.

Lin rubbed the bridge of his nose. "I'll show him a monster." He struggled out of his saddle, his right leg aching and cramping near the calf.

Pael was beside him, hat in hand, satchel tucked under his arm.

"Sounds like... you're having the same issues with yourself that you are with her."

"What?" Lin looked sideways at the man. He'd had many impressions of Pael but, for some reason, hadn't thought the man particularly perceptive.

"I mean, it sounds like you're blaming yourself for something, maybe *many* somethings, but you know, in your heart, you shouldn't." Pael cleared his throat. "And what you said to Aemun about her saving you. Listen. She's a hard one to love. Harder one to get real love back from. If that's what you think of when you stare at her the way you do. I've been in plenty of positions where the person I love detests me." The man didn't seem to plan to stop rambling until a sound of crashing through brush and foliage to the side drew all their attention.

"Twelve of them. Some robed, others not." Tylle's voice came out flat and hard.

"Twelve of what?" Aemun called, hand going to his hilt.

"Reds if we're lucky. But I think untethered. Like what attacked Fallo."

Lin's stomach sank. Six knew he was tired—too tired for another fight. "How could you know?" he asked, his voice sounding weak even to his own ears.

"I can't be sure. But there was one small campfire and a force by the looks and sound of it."

"Getting where we're going quick won't do us any good if we get there and half of us are dead. We turn back." Pael put on his hat and shook his head.

"No," Tylle said. "We can't leave if it's more untethered."

"And if it's not," Aemun asked. "If it's soldiers, you'd cut through them?"

"Stop. We all know that everyone here would do what must be done to survive. You proved that this very night. Tylle, how confident are you that—"

Lin's words were lost as the whistling sound peaked, and he covered his ears. Like the Bloom the dying soldier had formed, light erupted in the sky. Lin blinked, trying to recover his ruined night vision. Gwen screamed and tumbled off her horse. *Six, the child.* Tylle moved too quick for Lin's poor vision to track, and Aemun was a blur of blade and Binding made manifest as he cut through several untethered swarming them. Fallo's fall had been horrible. The bodies, the stench. But seeing the untethered move en masse through the forest, Stitches glowing like unearthly fireflies as they rushed past, terrified him. There seemed to be so many in the dark that he'd easily be overwhelmed if he were alone.

Like lightning breaking across a cloudless sky, a series of quick Wefts snapped into existence, slicing away in all directions from where Tylle stood. They cut bark and flesh alike, leaving deep gouges in the surrounding trees and dropping two of the closest attackers.

A second whistle, opposite from and lower than the first, sounded from the west and was followed by a third, closer one. It was like they'd stumbled into the middle of a hunting party, unaware they were the prey. *And the untethered were the hounds.*

"If we get separated," Tylle shouted, "regroup at Farmer's Ridge."

Lin didn't know the town, and he wasn't as familiar with this area as he'd like. Now that his vision had partly returned, he saw Pael crouched beside a large rocky outcropping. He held a dagger in one hand that caught the light from the various Bindings so well that it wouldn't be a surprise to learn it had been crafted for just that.

Lin crashed into the closest untethered, favoring steel over Bindings that might give his position away. The monster had been rushing to Pael's hiding spot. Lin ran it through from behind. Their blood glowed like the magic lacing their flesh, luminous in the dark night. These untethered bore Stitches more like the one that had attacked in Lyre, crude designs haphazardly placed across the flesh, marring the muscles and distorting their features. This one's lips had been Stitched shut.

As the untethered died at his blade, Lin spun. He counted nine. Nine more monsters and that was after Tylle and Aemun had already slain several. He hadn't made his way ten steps from Pael's hiding spot when something like the weight of a boulder slammed into his side, taking his air and footing from him. Lin rolled, but the force pressing down on him kept his hips pinned, and his heels slipped on the loose, leafy earth. It shouldn't have taken a mountain of a man, intent on killing him, to make him realize he hadn't been paying enough attention to his surroundings.

Short, rasping breaths, then a high and sharp whistle. "Got you now." His accent was off-putting. It was familiar, but in the moment, as the man crushed him, Lin couldn't bring himself to place it. Aside from his voice, the only feature that stood out in the dark was the man's armor. It was polished with an oily sheen that matched the Ferrucium-forged blades.

Lin's heart thrummed in his ears, and his vision pulsed purple. The armored man kept his weight pushing down, one hand on Lin's right wrist, the other clumsily pressed into Lin's throat. Clumsy or not, it hurt and pinned Lin.

Between purple pulses, Lin forced his will into existence. Three Wefts scratched against the armor, sparking ineffectually.

The armored man shifted and exhaled, then chuckled. "Ferrucium steel, you untethered fuck—"

Lin gasped at the cracking noise and spray of blood. The pressure on his neck ended as the man's hand fell to the side, and his weight crashed entirely onto Lin. A wicked bolt stuck out from the back of the man's head.

"P-Pael?"

Pael's hands shook as he labored to reload the crossbow, the mechanism clacking.

"W-where did you get that?"

"I've had it hidden in the farthest reaches of my tight, pretty ass. Does it matter right now?"

"No," Lin gasped. He pulled himself out from under the armored man and sucked in greedy breaths, but by the time he was on his feet, Pael had finished reloading the crossbow and had taken a half step toward the forest's edge. Aemun, Gwen, and Tylle were all missing, but a break in the brush made it clear that a large group had rushed through. "That man spoke. Not untethered."

Pael nodded and raised his weapon.

Lin couldn't study the man or take more meaning from his stare. Tylle had pushed in, expecting Lin's aide, and was likely outnumbered.

"There could be more like him. I'm not sure," Lin said.

"I think I should tell you, I'm not planning on running. Not now that we've kicked the ant pile. Go help her, and I'll see you don't get taken down from the side again." Pael's jaw trembled, and he planted his feet. "Go."

Screams sounded from the camp, overtaking the gruff, barking orders that had just reached Lin's ears. Tylle, knowing they were outnumbered, must have retaliated hard and then led the attackers away. Not that numbers had ever dissuaded her from action.

Lin rushed through the thicket. His ankle throbbed in time with his heart, and the cramp from earlier reared its head again as his calf spasmed. *How does Tylle do it?* The answer was likely Bindings, maybe her Uethe, but he expected her to say it was related to her faith. Lin frowned. If Aemun got out of this unscathed, he wasn't sure he'd hear Tylle mention her faith again. It wouldn't be fair. He'd thought the man might be able to clear his name, vouch for him if he returned to the Weavers Stitched and begged for mercy, but as Tylle said, that hope of a bird died falling from the nest. Aemun had no love for Lin, and the feeling was mutual.

Three tents remained upright around the small fire pit; a fourth and fifth were collapsed. Several bodies were hidden under the tarp, and even in the pitiful lighting, the blood stains glistened. Further away, fifteen strides, a caravan's back jutted out next to a massive tree with gnarled, low-hanging boughs. The sort of tree honeycaps were likely to be found under.

Lin tightened his grip on his hilt, examining the blade. The chip of its edge looked worse, but he hadn't the foresight to take any of the other blades they'd encountered.

Clanging of steel and grunts of exertion carried from near the wagon's front, and Weaves flew west to east and east to west. A stray Weft exploded into the wagon's side, sending chunks of wood and cloth flying like shrapnel.

Lin approached slowly, hoping to catch an enemy off guard. Another two untethered corpses, fronts stained from their wounds, slumped against trees.

Tylle blurred into view, landing atop the wagon and causing it to shift from the force. Her hair frayed and eyes wild, she looked nothing short of untethered as she formed focus-less Bindings. No, there was a focus. It was just in her mind like she'd taught Lin.

One of those armored individuals circled the wagon front, their own broad Wefts chipping the wagon wood and branches above in a flurry.

Leaves rustled overhead, and in a blink, two shadows dropped on either side of Lin. One punched at Lin's throat, the other swept into a low kick aimed at Lin's ankles. Their limbs glowed a dirty orange.

Avoiding either attack would take time Lin didn't have. He'd been too focused on watching Tylle's opponent for an opening. Lin lowered his blade, catching the flat of it against the low sweeping blow, and blocked the punch with his left arm.

Lin's blade reverberated from the blow, and his forearm screamed from the pure force traveling up it. But his right arm drew his attention as a line seared its way along his bicep, and blood trickled from the slash he'd taken.

Thin, string-like Wefts lashed out from both sides in a blur, tens of sharp, muddy orange lines whipping in consecutive strands. The edges gouged the earth under them, and they split his flesh when the attacks found purchase. He'd be flayed alive at this rate, stuck between two untethered. Each biting attack took a piece of him, physically and mentally. It tore into him, tore into everything he knew about Binding. These attacks had the flexibility of Weaves with the killing power of Wefts.

Lin broke Binding after Binding. Having the Sight had always aided Lin, but now, amid the trees, each stray lash was a distraction, his eyes struggling to track them all. They were discordant, unaimed, a flurry of attacks, not all slicing toward him. For every two Bindings broken, another would slip through, and a new, thin cut would be carved into his flesh. He *was* breaking apart the attacks, but he was outnumbered, and his opponents didn't slow.

Even as sharp as the Bindings seemed, they weren't the razor-edged sort that could sever limb from body. And there was a delay, slight as it was. Not a wide margin, but enough time to form a plan.

Three more slices licked his injured left arm. They stung, cutting deeper than he expected, but he'd wanted them to land. More whip-like Bindings would come from the right as the left attacker refocused. The downtime passed in a gasp, but Lin launched himself leftward, blade scraping through the dirt and leaves underfoot. He slashed up, grunting and clenching his teeth as the other untethered sent a barrage across his back. Following through with the blow hurt tremendously. His back screamed, but his blade caught the untethered from their lower left rib up to the bottom of the opposite collar bone. His sword jolted from his grip as the nick caught on bone and wrenched away as the body crumpled backward.

Lin spun, vision pulsing, as he sent Wefts as quick as the pair had, ignoring the lightness that flooded his head. He couldn't feel his toes, but his heart *burned*.

In moments, the untethered stared up at the stars with blank eyes, body riddled with slashes from Wefts so sharp it was a wonder Lin hadn't cut himself forming them.

How many left?

Lin stumbled toward the wagon. Blood trickled warmly down his back, the material of his shirt sticking to sections where the flesh had split widest. Tylle and the other armored enemy were nowhere to be seen or heard, and even the crackling fire seemed to grow softer with each of Lin's steps.

A low whistle preceded a thunk from behind.

Lin spun and watched a young girl, Stitches along her limbs and face, fall to her knees five paces behind him. A bolt stuck through her neck, and the light of a Binding sparkling at her fingertips faded. Lin saw two Paels standing near where he'd pushed through the brush until he blinked, and his vision clarified into one man. He hadn't made himself go this far since he was much younger, training in the Ferrucium halls where they'd taught the danger of overdrawing. He'd never had his vision blurred nearly so badly. Binding was a balancing act, and he paid the price for overdoing it. *And the blood loss didn't help.*

Roots and chunks of wood threatened to trip Lin, but he staggered between covers, moving from tree to tree as he made his way to the back of the wagon. His mouth was dry, and his left arm hung at his side, shoulder throbbing. If anyone hid behind or in the wagon, they didn't make a sound.

Lin inched forward, preparing for whatever might lie before him. As skilled as the untethered were, odds were Tylle was in danger. *Aemun* was in danger. It sickened him to consider that he might have to save the man. He wasn't giving either of them enough credit.

Limbs were strewn around the front of the wagon, red cloth tatters fluttering in the wind. Lin might've lost his stomach if battlefields like this weren't becoming the norm. This level of carnage was expected when Tylle fought—or when dealing with untethered at all. The line between the two seemed to narrow with each passing day. A chill ran across Lin's neck, and he passed the limbs, innards, and bits and pieces of the enemies who'd thought they might stand against Tylle and Aemun.

"Lin!" Tylle's voice was hoarse like a fire burned through her throat. "Up ahead, around that bend. He's run into the bushes like the snake he is!"

"What?" Lin froze.

Tylle appeared beside him; skin stained dark from blood and sweat. Her eyes were wide, and their whites seemed too large. She moved like she hadn't fought through enough untethered to raze a countryside.

Lin blinked as a blinding light filled his vision through the trees.

Tylle tensed and put a hand on Lin's shoulder. "What?"

"Another Bloom," Lin struggled to say. He cleared his throat. "Where is Aemun and the child?"

"I told you he ran. Wouldn't say why. Wouldn't stop smiling. I think this was him. I think this was *all* him."

"Tylle... even if I find him and this is all his doing... my Uethe."

She touched his face, her trembling hands wiping sweat and blood from his cheek. "If he has broken his allegiance to Erias, you can. I'll be there in a moment. I just need to catch my breath. These armored ones are tough."

Lin noticed the body she stared at, the armor plating glistening like oil. There were other metals out in the wide world, but there was no mistaking the way Bindings barely scratched the surface. Ferrucium steel armor.

"I... I think the enemies are Enforcers. Ferrucium. The circumstance caught me off guard, but I'm sure of it. Why they're working with untethered? *Actual* untethered, I couldn't say. Why they attacked us unprovoked... I don't know."

"We can puzzle out the why later. Chew this," Tylle pressed half a corpse-seed into his hand. Her jaw started working furiously as she bit into her own.

The juices were a salve, the sweet taste pulling his attention back to the world in sharp focus. Where the sounds had been muffled before, Lin now heard each leaf crunch underfoot, each thud of their boots, and each heavy, tired breath.

"Go. I'll be right there."

But Lin hesitated. *Why* was she so confident? If Aemun had been planning something all along, why wait until now? And hadn't Aemun proven time and time again that he matched prowess at least with swordplay if not Binding skill? Aemun had *begged* Lin to kill her, but he'd been the one to put her back against the wall. In everything he'd seen Tylle do, he had grown to respect her battle prowess and believe she could take vengeance on Aemun. The stone's pressure settling onto his gut forced him to rethink. People ran for two reasons. To flee out of fear or to put themselves in a better position.

"Tylle," Lin whispered.

Like streaking shadows, two cloaked figures flashed into Lin's field of view, flanking the area Tylle was sure Aemun hid near. Tattered black robes flared out, and intricate, thick Stitches lined the flesh underneath.

"Untethered!" Lin screamed. He was sure Tylle didn't have the Sight, positive of it, but she'd moved before the scream had even torn its way out of his throat. With corpse-seed renewed energy, Lin pushed towards them, four paces behind Tylle and gaining.

"Get to Aemun. I'll handle them!" Lin said.

"No, I'll have a better chance holding them off. You go deal with him." Tylle didn't wait for confirmation. Her right hand tensed, and she sent out arcing Wefts. A dagger flashed into her left hand.

Lin rushed ahead, the two enemies moving in unison to intercept him, faces coming clear as the distance between them closed. Or what would have been faces if not for the thin, flat metallic masks covering them.

Lin stumbled to a stop. *Noosemen.* Not one, but two of them against *him.* He doubted he stood a chance against the King's personal Binders, even if he'd been fresh and uninjured.

As the pair shifted, so did Tylle. A wide, low Weave lashed out from her like an extension of her arm.

"Go!" Tylle screamed.

Lin could hear in her voice what she wasn't saying. *Go, and Vellyr help you if he gets away after this mess.*

But *going* was easier said than done. Tylle proved she was a one-woman army, but the enemies before them moved in tandem. The leftmost one sent out a flurry of focus-less Wefts that cut and churned the earth like the claw marks of a tremendous beast. Tylle attempted to unweave them, and when that didn't work, she sent her own Wefts. It was like daggers clashing against broadswords. Their wills exploded into a stream of golden-orange sparks.

Lin ducked then darted right, zipping past the rightmost one and hurtling to the ground into a roll. Dirt sprayed up as a Weft ate into the earth where Lin had just stood. If he hadn't rolled, his neck would've sprayed more than the dirt kicked up behind him. His feet came under him in a sweep, and he was past the Nooseman.

Tylle grunted from behind, but Lin pressed forward as fast as he could. Paces ahead, a figure clambered over a sizeable flat log, a red cloak flaring out from the motion.

"Aemun!" Lin screamed.

The figure froze and then turned to face him slowly, sword held limply and pointed down in the stance of the Ferrucium.

Chapter Seventeen

Bitter Hope

Lin was upon the person in a flash, shifting his weight to avoid the sword, wishing he'd the sense to keep hold of his.

But it wasn't Aemun. It wasn't even a soldier. Gwen screamed and dropped the blade, throwing herself into Lin. The cloak that had been around her shoulders crumpled to the forest floor. She clutched his bloody tunic, hands raking the wounds across his back as she sobbed.

"Where is Aemun? Where's the child?" Lin asked. He wanted to pull away, but she held him achingly tight. They'd barely spoken to each other, but Six knew he didn't think he could leave her alone as she was.

Her words were incoherent as if her snot and spittle made them stick in her throat.

"I... I don't have time for this!" Lin tried easing her shoulders back, but she pushed forward harder, grip tightening.

"P-please," she whispered. "I-I-I don't know where he went. H-he t-took little Azhalia." The last word stretched into a whine. Whatever her background had been before all this, she clearly wasn't built for the stresses of battle. *Azhalia?*

Lin ripped himself away, her fingers dragging across his back in sharp focus. "Hide and be quiet. I'll find him. Both of them," he added when she moved to grab him again.

A seeping sort of silence blanketed the darker parts of the forest. A choking, smothering darkness that gave nothing. No fauna, no combat, nothing. Then, like web glistening with dew, the faintest trail of Bindings caught Lin's eye. He would've mistaken it for starlight if he hadn't seen how dark the night sky was earlier in the evening, obscured by thick clouds.

Lin struggled to slow his heaving chest. The whole thing *felt* wrong. Noosemen. Untethered under the direction of what appeared to be Ferrucium Enforcers. Aemun working with a man intent on ripping control of Danica from the Ferrucium and, by extension, King Lodram. Ever since Fallo, the only moments that had felt even remotely right or normal were the few quiet ones he'd had with Tylle on the roadside. And he'd left her facing two Noosemen to track Aemun.

"I'll kill him," Lin whispered. What Lin had thought was a trail of Bindings ended up proving to be gouges sliced into various trunks and branches of the thick-pocketed trees. And blood. Thin glowing smears of it that Lin had thought only untethered could make.

Lin crept into a clearing cut through the center by a quiet, slow-moving creek.

Two people, Aemun and a Nooseman, had weapons in hand. They seemed to be speaking, but Lin couldn't hear them. Then the baby, bundled to Aemun's back, wailed. Low and mournful.

"Aemun. You snake!" Lin shouted. If he was conversing with the Noosemen, the very people he'd summoned to Wellgrove, he'd betrayed Erias.

The other person turned their head, the flat brushed-metal mask a slab devoid of emotion. The darker robes they wore fluttered as they spread their arms out, Stitches lining their visible flesh in bright, nearly white, circular patterns.

Lin steadied himself and pushed into the clearing, scanning, hoping that there were no hidden enemies. Lin blinked; he couldn't help himself with the stinging sweat, and the Nooseman was gone.

"Shit." Lin spun. Nothing behind him, nothing around him but trees and wind. He turned to face Aemun and spat. "You!"

"Me?" Aemun replied. He'd shifted his stance, sheathed his blade, and pulled the baby, Azhalia, into both arms.

"Don't take that tone with me. I have eyes. I saw you!" Lin looked at him and the way he'd angled the child. Walking forward felt like stepping into a trap, and echoes of Fallo wouldn't shake from Lin as he swiveled to look at the trees.

"But do you have ears? Or a thinking brain, somewhere under all those Fell-Bindings?"

Lin paused, then shook his head. He wouldn't let this conniving man trick him. He'd seen Aemun conversing with the Nooseman. Tylle had watched him flee from the fight. And now he'd placed the child between Lin and himself in case Lin attacked. "I do. And at every turn, it seems the one common thing everywhere I go when things get *fucked*, is you."

Aemun strolled forward, arms cradling Azhalia while he made little hushing noises. "I am," he said, lowering his voice as he closed the distance. "Very good at getting fucked. Gwen can attest if she makes it out alive. Margaret, if she were still alive. But that doesn't make me a traitor. I've expressed my love for the Ferrucium and King Lodram's rule... and if we don't both walk out of this clearing together, peacefully," his voice became a whisper on the wind, "Dennick will kill all of us."

"No. No. I won't let you talk your way out of this. You led us into several traps. This camp of Enforcers and untethered only the most recent." Lin tried to keep his voice low and level.

"This camp is exactly why Dennick hasn't killed us already." Aemun cradled his child and looked around the clearing. "Evidence of Ferrucium soldiers conspiring with and *controlling* untethered. News to the King's forces, news he'll have to get to someone sooner rather than later."

"I'm sick of your plots and schemes. For all I know, you instructed these men to be here when you sent word to the King's Noose in the first place!"

Aemun stared at Lin for a long moment. "I don't blame you for thinking that. Not one bit. But this time, I'm innocent of these grandiose machinations you place on my shoulders."

This time.

Ethereal light flashed behind the brush and trees where Lin had come from. "And will he spare us when he sees that Tylle is fighting two of his people?"

Aemun's face twisted into a sour expression, and he leaned in conspiratori-ally. "If she takes one or two of them out, better for us. But I feel like Dennick trusts me. The King's Noose *knows* that the Ferrucium has flaws. Shortcomings. Issues with soldiers working with unsavory characters." Aemun shifted the child. "Don't give me that look. I obviously don't mean myself. What we did at the outpost and here to this camp, well, Dennick understands. It's all in the pursuit of correcting King Lodram's forefathers' vision for the Ferrucium at its founding. Go to Tylle. See if she's managed to keep her head. I'll find Gwen."

Lin hesitated. He'd never met a person whose words could become as knotted as this man's. Every word he spoke was with such conviction that it wasn't any wonder he'd been able to convince Margie to become his bound partner, convince Erias to work with him, and convince the King's people he wasn't a rebel. Which face was the true one? The honest one. It made Lin sick just thinking about it. Then another flash brightened the forest ahead, and Lin moved.

A scream, like a feral howl, tore out from where he'd left Tylle.

Lin ran, or at least tried running. The stretch of earth and thicket between Lin and the field Tylle should be at seemed to go on forever. Then he broke through.

Tylle looked rabid, her clothes tattered and matted, her hair flying in loose strands broken free from any semblance of her tight braid. If Lin hadn't seen actual untethered many times over, he would've thought she was one. One of the Noosemen assaulting her rested on their side, a pool of their intestines planted around them like a grotesque flower bed. The other had Tylle avoiding and breaking a flurry of thin, flexible Wefts as best she could. For each she unwove, she took two slices. Some looked deeper than others, blood oozing from the wounds.

The living Nooseman seemed to dance, shifting through well-practiced forms. Fluid, purposeful, and mesmerizing despite the unnatural way the fig-ure moved. Their dark cloak splayed like a viper's hood, and Tylle fell to one knee, her other leg kicked out. A grievous-looking gouge crossed the outside of her thigh near her hip. Neither of the combatants seemed to notice him. The

Nooseman's back was turned, and Tylle's eyes were unfocused, face pale and lit by the glow of magic.

Lin was drained. Both within and without, he raised a hand and winced as he put everything he had into one more Weft. It formed and cleaved through the air, flattening as it went, elongating. The Nooseman turned at the last moment to face Lin, metallic, blood-speckled mask reflecting the light of Lin's Weft.

The attack connected with their side, sparking like it had struck Ferrucium steel. But the Nooseman wasn't wearing armor. Lin's Weft clashed with their *flesh*, just like his magic had against the untethered in Fallo.

Lin pushed his intention. His knees buckled, and his arm went numb, but he slid the razor-edged Weft up the Nooseman's side until it caught in a groove of something under the black cloak.

They launched back, spinning from the force of the blow, and crumpled. Choked wheezing sounded from where they landed.

Lin rushed to Tylle, staggering and fighting against his numb limbs. He'd spent too much time dealing with Aemun. Suspicion flashed through him. What if leaving her here alone had *also* been a part of his plan? If he'd known Noosemen were coming, he could've split them up intentionally.

Pael emerged from behind the wagon, hat missing, face dark. Gwen hung behind him, arms wrapped around herself, hovering like a spirit devoid of body.

"Tylle," Lin whispered, collapsing beside her. "No... no... no. I can't do this without you. Stay with me."

"I'll... I'll watch this one. Might not be finished," Pael called, pointing the crossbow at the wheezing Nooseman.

"Tylle, please. Can you hear me?" Lin took her face in his hands. He wiped blood and grime from her pale cheeks. She was barely breathing. Most of the wounds across her arms and torso looked shallow, but there were so many of them. And several of her deeper injuries pulsed blood.

Her eyes focused, and a groan passed through her lips. "Thank you," she mouthed.

Lin opened his mouth to speak and then shut it. She'd gotten into this state and pushed herself to the brink of death just on the off chance that Aemun would be found a betrayer and finally face the justice he'd been running from, all for him to talk his way out of it.

"Rest," he whispered. "I'll tend to your wounds. I'll fix you."

"And him?" Tylle asked.

Lin licked his lips and met her gaze, squeezing her hand. "We'll talk about it later when you've rested."

The pain he felt in his hand as Tylle squeezed it was oddly comforting. If she still had the strength for that, she likely wouldn't die before he'd had time to triage her. "I'm sorry. What he said made sense. The Noosemen would've come regardless because of the outpost. It was apparently his quick thinking that saved us." *Or this was another part of his plan.* He couldn't say that to Tylle. Not now. Not when she already looked so disappointed and angry.

Tylle shuddered and sobbed softly until her grip on Lin's hand loosened and her eyes shut.

"Did she... Did she die?" Pael asked, shuffling over while keeping his eyes and weapon trained on the Nooseman, still groaning feet from them.

"Sleeping. Get me water and start a fire. We'll need to move Tylle. Gwen, help him, please."

Chapter Eighteen

Bitter Bone

The fire Pael made didn't seem like it would ever warm Lin's bones. His arm and shoulder hadn't ceased aching, and every time he looked at Tylle's face, he felt like he'd failed her. Failed to keep her safe, to find a chance to make Aemun pay when it had been so close to possible. When he'd approached Aemun, there hadn't been any sense of hesitation from the Bludwieve. It hadn't *felt* like his Uethe would hold him back. But it hadn't stopped him from pushing the man from Nebra either. Only once a Weft had been formed had it begun boiling his blood from within.

Pael sat beside the horses, crossbow trained on the Nooseman bound to the nearest tree. Their arms had been tied behind them, and thick Weaves wrapped around the tree trunk, digging into the flesh where their black cloak had ripped.

On a survey, Lin had been right. The majority of Tylle's wounds were shallow, but she did have a deep gouge near her hip, so terrible that Lin had to fashion a tourniquet from cloth to stem the bleeding. Removing the torn scraps that had once been her clothes to treat the injuries felt wrong, least because she was a priestess, but once he did, he stared in awe. Under her clothes, wrapping along her calves and up around her thighs, were countless *intricate* Stitches. The glowing magical lines hummed and pulsed in undulating waves. It made sense. He'd had his suspicions, but he'd been incapacitated the only time he'd been close enough to have felt the magic.

"You really are untethered, aren't you?" Lin whispered. It didn't matter. Not after what they'd been through, but perhaps the term untethered had actually been warped, twisted into something it was never meant to describe. Or the Ferrucium over-used it as a blanket statement. Lin *had* seen monsters. Fought them. The brutal, magic-laced *things* that had once been people. Tylle still held her sanity. And what was Lin, if not untethered by the Ferrucium's rules?

While the tourniquet helped slow the blood loss, no bandage or dressing would be enough to close the wound at Tylle's hip, even if Lin had gut threads and bone handy to stitch it closed. He was too inexperienced with the tools and far from being a physiker. Instead, Lin exhaled and imagined a Needle and Weave, threading the magic through the wound. He made the Fell-Bindings, the act oddly easy for something that should be so blasphemous. Lin swallowed against a lump in his throat, realizing this time he had broken the Binding Tenets entirely of his own accord with no coercion or test of loyalty.

Aemun slunk about near the back of the wagon. Gwen had returned to him at some point, and he'd shown an unusual act of kindness as he draped a thick blanket over her shoulders. She huddled close to him and looked as if she offered to take the child, but he shook his head and kept the baby close to his chest. When Aemun noticed Lin staring, he nodded, face expressionless.

Lin shook his head and focused back on the work at hand. Stitching the one wound wasn't enough. An odor like damp iron wafted up as he toiled away, and Tylle groaned as more of her skin pulled together. If any of her bones had been nicked, there wasn't much he could do, but he had to try. His hands ached as much as his knees, but when the first birdcall of the morning eventually sounded, Lin thought he'd handled all Tylle's life-threatening wounds. Rolling her and bandaging her back proved difficult, but he managed. It gave him a view of the numerous scars he hadn't known she had and the patterned Stitches starting at the base of her neck and splitting into two paths down the back of her arms. Interweaving triangles woven into each other, interlapping. *Beautiful*. Similar to Velkath's symbol if any section were separated from the whole.

"You'll be alright now. I hope," Lin whispered. Rising to his feet brought purple stars swirling through his vision, but after a few deep breaths, they settled into spots that drifted only when he moved his eyes too quickly.

"You're a better physiker than I expected." Tylle sounded as near death as she looked.

"Most physikers don't use magic."

Tylle's pale lips parted, but she didn't speak.

"I... I'm sorry." Lin glanced to where Gwen huddled against Aemun. "If the roles were reversed, maybe you could have found a reason to do it. End him, I mean. But his excuse made sense."

"He is Ferrucium. His family line dates back to the first betrayers. He knows well how to move hearts. Next time there is confusion, it might be best not to let him speak."

Next time. There would be a next time, wouldn't there? Another moment of uncertainty. Confusion hovered around Aemun like fog on a riverbank, obscuring the truth. Odds were, it was precisely what he wanted.

"Ughhh," the Nooseman beside Pael groaned.

Pael twitched and readjusted the crossbow from where it had slipped off his knee.

The way Tylle looked at Lin, he knew she resented him. Some small amount, at least. But she'd never say it, judging by how her thin lips pressed into a line.

Lin tried to hold her gaze but blinked. Tears stung his eyes, and he turned rather than let her see him. There had been periods on the road when Lin had been tired or sore, but the last span had been a different beast entirely. Exhaustion gripped him so tight that he wasn't sure it would ever let go. He tapped the back of Tylle's hand twice, then rose and, aching with every step, stumbled over to the Nooseman.

Aemun swaggered over, shoulders back, looking as rested as someone who hadn't been in a battle the night before. He smiled and knelt on one knee before the Nooseman, leaning in slightly. Azhalia wasn't in his arms.

Behind the Nooseman's flat metal mask, he groaned deeply. The mouth slit was coated in dried blood, and the eye slits were dark.

With a flick, Aemun slipped the mask off and tossed it into the grass near Lin's boots. A gaunt face stared back, eyes unblinking and deeply inset. The man had cracked, pale blue lips. His flesh was ashen, flaking gray, and what hair he had looked like brittle straw.

"Do you speak Danican?" Aemun asked.

"Yes," he replied, his accent thick like merchants and emissaries from Ladrica. But despite the sickly complexion, some of which were signs of a long-lived Binder and the accent, the man looked Danican. His dark eyes shifted to Lin, then to the campfire where Tylle rested.

"Oontethyrd." He played with the word, mouth twisting into disgust.

"You have a name?" Lin asked.

The man snorted and spat out reddish spittle, most of which fell to his own dark robes.

"He is nothing. No one. A nameless knot that forms the noose. Is that correct?" Aemun tilted his head to the side and looked as if he might lean in further.

Despite being bound, the Nooseman shrugged. His split lips puckered, and his nostrils flared as if he smelled something foul.

"Shoot him," Lin said. "Put him out of his misery." It was bad enough that they had a single dead Nooseman. The longer they waited, the sooner Dennick might return and realize Aemun had played him all along. *If he was the one Aemun had been playing for a fool.*

Pael's finger resting on the trigger mechanism twitched.

"Wait," Aemun snapped.

The Nooseman smiled, the bones in his face pulling his flesh tight. "I expect not to live. But you should do the same—all of you, especially you." He narrowed his dark eyes at Aemun.

Pael looked from the man to Lin and back again.

Lin rubbed his temples. "Why?"

"Feroocioom." The man stretched the word out. "No."

His breaths were steadily becoming heavier, each one followed by a rattling hollow sound. "I am blessed. Loved by my King. I am not a nameless knot. I am Borrick."

Lin frowned.

"Fucking Nooseman," Pael muttered, leveling the crossbow.

Aemun raised a hand and looked as if he might slap Pael. "We could take him as a bartering chip. Neither of you thinks far enough to get out of the blowing wind to piss."

Pael licked his teeth and shook his head. "Way too dangerous."

Lin nodded. "No. Kill him. If we take him with us, and he gets free while we sleep, we're as good as dead. If we keep him bound and Dennick returns and frees him, we're dead. If—"

"Yes, I get it. Fear of the King's Noose has you afraid to sleep at night with one nearby already suffering a grievous injury. But if we're expecting him, we could use Borrick as bait. Don't be so simple-minded all the time!" Aemun's face turned a bright red as his voice raised, and he grasped and plucked several grass stalks.

"Dennick. He will kill you all. He is *blessed*. He is *loved*. He doesn't trust you. Not since we first met you. *Aemoon*." Borrick worked his way through the sentence, the same skull-showing smile forming. He nodded, blood-stained teeth flashing through the grunts of pain as he shut his mouth. A chuckle escaped him, the laugh turning into a choke, and then he spat out his tongue. Blood spilled from his mouth like a dam breaking.

Aemun's face went white, and he stared at the meaty pink chunk of tongue that sprouted from the grass near his boot. "You dirty fucking untethered," he whispered. "You filthy, low-born swine!" He rose and moved to kick the body.

Lin got in front of him, nearly taking a boot for his troubles. "We don't have time for you to assault a corpse."

"We didn't have time for you to spend all night breaking the Binding Tenets, but you did!"

"Would the two of you act like you have common sense for once?"

"I don't need a Duke's man far out of his shallow pond telling me to have common sense. All I need from you all is to get me to Erias's little group so I can lead them into the Ferrucium. That's it. I don't need questions. I don't need camaraderie. I need you to follow fucking orders and keep your small, stupid thoughts to yourself!"

"Are you done?" Pael's voice was low, the crossbow slung over his shoulder. "Way I see it, the other one, Dennick, could be back at any point. We need to hurry quick. But with a baby and our best chance against a Nooseman recovering, speed isn't our ally. We take the wagon. You two can ride ahead on horses if need be, but Tylle, me, and the child will be in the wagon."

"She isn't our best chance." Aemun crossed his arms and rolled his eyes back over to the corpse bound to the tree.

"Why do they get to have Fell-Bindings without repercussion?" Lin asked. "Why aren't they considered untethered?"

A laugh slipped from Aemun, and he looked at Lin as if he'd asked the stupidest question one could voice. "They are. But they are taught the Binding Tenets don't apply to them because King Lodram's lineage was given dominion by the Six, and the King's Noose was given authority by him. They are loyal to the King and taught, from a very young age, how awful we all are. You saw the hatred and madness in his eyes. Didn't you?"

Lin wasn't sure he had. Sure, the man *looked* like a monster, but any soldiers who used Bindings excessively could look like he had. Most old Binders lost their hair or found their skin growing ashen, like flakes of chipped iron. "Madness still seeps into them. What keeps them from truly untethering, then?"

Aemun shrugged and picked up the mask, his heel clearly grinding the chunk of tongue into the dirt. "Faith and devotion if the propaganda is to be believed. The Noose itself if you think critically. They kill their own when they start to go rabid. They kill and replace, pulling talented children from the Ferrucium, the same way the Ferrucium pulls children from their homes. Each and every member of the Noose is a Danican native."

"So, all that really sets them apart are the masks and robes?" Lin asked.

"Don't be stupid. You watched them. They're taught things Ferrucium Binders can only dream of."

"You sound envious," Pael said.

Aemun had a reply. It was evident in how the man's mouth twisted in irritation, then slipped into exhaustion. "Ready the wagon. I'll see if I can find one of the horses. If not, I'll ride with my child and wetnurse in the wagon. Hold onto this."

The mask was lighter than it looked, and Lin twisted it in his hands. Specks of dried blood streaked the thin metal. "What I meant... was do the Noosemen keep a writ or something of that nature on them."

"No," Aemun said. "They don't."

Tylle grunted from beside the fire, her eyelids fluttering. Her bandaged chest heaved lightly, and her fingers twitched.

Pael prepared the wagon, hitching one of the horses to it without fuss. Nebra came to him after three whistles, and Lin was glad to see she was uninjured. Each confrontation settled a stone onto his shoulders that never left until he saw her in good health. Of the horses they'd had, it was just the two that came back, so Aemun crawled onto the bench at the front, looking back once or twice to whisper to Gwen.

"What do you think his end plan really is?" Lin asked.

"Nothing good, I'd wager," Pael whispered.

Nothing good was right. "Do you think she'll forgive me?" Lin asked.

"For what? Coming back and saving her life? Or for the fact that this upstarted shit still breathes?"

"I think... her death might've been a trade she was willing to make if it meant killing Aemun. She's been real calm about taking orders since leaving Wellgrove. But, Pael, there's a fury in her that only flickers to the surface sometimes."

"But could you have made the trade?" Pael asked. He was chewing on something like a cow might chew cud, his jaw working furiously.

"Apparently not," Lin whispered.

"You think her sister would've wanted that?"

Lin stared at Pael. For being a shambling man who *seemed* unaware at times, he made solid points more often than not. "I barely knew Margie. But... I don't think so. I don't think she'd have wanted any of this."

"I'd known both of them, little Tylle, better than her younger sister, but neither would've wanted any of this if it could've been prevented. You'd be hard-pressed to find more honest souls." Pael yawned, stretched, and went to the wagon. He walked around it twice, checking the wheels, axle, and undercarriage at various spots.

Lin waited and stared up through the tree branches overhead, like crisscrossing fingers. All he could see when he blinked were after images of Bindings. The flurry of lashes that had struck him over and over again. The Six knew he'd almost died a handful of times. But he hadn't. And neither had Tylle or Pael. *Or Aemun*. Not yet, anyway. And he'd *healed* Tylle. Stitched closed her worst wounds. He never could have saved a life that way if he still followed the Binding Tenets. And if King Lodram could decide that the Tenets weren't necessary for his select group, what made them necessary at all? As light as it was, the mask felt heavy in his hand as he thought about what it all meant.

"Give me a hand," Pael called, waving Lin to Tylle. The two of them lifted her into the back, where she groaned and twitched. They bundled blankets, pillows, and grain sacks around her left side, and Gwen and the baby cuddled up to her right.

Gwen looked as pale as Tylle and just as dirty. The baby cried, and she clutched her close to her chest, shushing her and rocking in the small space between Tylle and the wall.

Lin lifted his left hand and looked at the Bludwieve that twisted crimson around his heart finger. It had hurt him, but only when he'd almost attacked Aemun. Lin closed his hand into a fist and let it fall to his side. It hadn't had a reaction by the creek. So, either it played off his perception of Aemun's behavior, or Aemun had betrayed them at some point between Wellgrove and encountering the King's Noose. He took a heavy pull from his waterskin and wished his headache away. It didn't oblige.

"Riding Nebra or walking alongside her?" Pael asked.

"Riding." It wouldn't feel great, but if speed was as essential as Aemun made it out to be, having him on horseback could make a difference. Even if Lin winced at every bounce and jolt. "I'm going to push Nebra pretty hard, just for a bit, to make sure there are no surprises ahead on the road."

Pael settled beside Aemun on the bench and took the reins. He opened his mouth to speak, but with a sideways glance toward Aemun, he seemed to change his mind. The wagon groaned forward.

Once in the saddle, Lin felt every ache and pain acutely. A fool's dream flashed through his thoughts: returning home. He didn't even really have a home to go back to. Aemun practically promised he wouldn't be welcomed in the new Ferrucium. When he looked over his shoulder, he couldn't see Tylle as bundled in the back of the wagon as she was. His fingers brushed the space of his cheek she had touched early in the night. Dried blood flaked off.

"Hey, don't go too far!" Pael called.

Chapter Nineteen

Bitter Hate

Nebra trotted along the path, barely any direction from Lin necessary. Staying upright in the saddle was a struggle. Moreso than Lin expected, but he'd chewed on the last few scraps of honeycaps tucked into his pack, and they helped keep him alert. Pael's words when Lin had departed haunted Lin more than the balding man could've predicted. He hadn't even told Tylle what Margie had last said to Lin. *Please don't stray far.* Something she'd said, possibly because she knew Aemun might harm her. Or... perhaps she'd planned to tell Tylle she wouldn't leave with her. After all the plotting and planning Aemun seemed to show, it didn't make sense that he'd murder Margie. And that left only one other option. *Tylle.*

Behind, the wagon creaked and groaned along. It was like a constant thundering rumble. Pael pushed its pace, and Lin worried for Tylle's comfort in the rear, especially with the baby screaming as it did. If anyone tracked them, they'd have an easy enough time of it the way the child howled.

Lin glanced behind but didn't see his companions. He'd ridden far ahead, pushing Nebra because she enjoyed it. Pushing himself because he felt he deserved the pain. There hadn't been a long enough moment alone with his thoughts, and every way he tried to imagine what Aemun's *real* end goal was, he failed. Either he was working with the King's Noose to reform the Ferrucium, working with Erias to overthrow the Ferrucium, or playing both of them to his own ends. *Bitter ends at that.*

Nebra slowed, then stopped, and stomped in the middle of the road. Her ears flattened, and she made low, guttural noises. From her back, Lin had a good view of the surrounding area. There weren't enough tree clusters to shelter anyone waiting in ambush. The thicker trees of the forest had given way to thinner, sparser sections, and though the sun was obscured by branch and cloud, the area was lit well enough.

"Come on, girl. If Pael catches up, he'll wonder why I even insisted on speeding ahead."

Nebra's tail swished, and she stomped a hoof again. At times like this, Lin wished there was a Binding that allowed for communication with Nebra. A silly, fanciful thought, to be sure, but one that hadn't gone away since their first escort together. She'd saved his life more than once on the road.

"Nebra," Lin whispered, stroking her neck.

A crack sounded overhead, and Nebra reared up, thudding back down with a skip. Lin braced himself, gritting his teeth and clenching his hands on the reins. Ahead, the branch crashed into the roadway. The end of the wood looked as if it had been sliced straight through despite being as thick as a man's torso.

Another crack sounded overhead. Followed by more and more as if the trees themselves were joints, popping and cracking as the limbs stretched. Lin looked up as Nebra moved forward slowly. She avoided the falling debris, and Lin stared up, mouth agape, as numerous Wefts slashed the heavens apart. He hadn't spotted them at first, hidden in the rays of sunlight leaking through the canopy, but he saw the glimmer in the shadows now that he knew to look for it.

His first thought went to Dennick. But it hadn't even been a day, and if the man chased Aemun, why was he upon Lin and not the wagon? *Untethered.* They hadn't been far from an untethered camp. It could just be a stray monster, Lin the first victim they'd found. Lin swallowed and looked behind him, trusting Nebra to navigate the path.

Turning around now wasn't an option. Not with the road coated in damp, dewy leaves and numerous fallen branches. Lin rifled through his pack and pulled a handful of seeds, swallowing mouthfuls as quickly as possible without biting his tongue. Easier said than done.

The forest grew silent. No more branches hurtled toward the ground. Lin forced Nebra to slow down, watching and listening. Like distant thunder, the wagon rumbled in the distance. And it wasn't slowing. The longer Lin waited, the better his chances were that Pael would catch up. But while Lin waited here, he was a sitting target. Nooseman or untethered, the distinction seeming thinner and thinner. Either way, if Tylle could best either, Lin could. He could handle this. He was a scrapper.

"Show yourself!" Lin called.

"You are the man who killed Borrick and Nordja?" The voice seemed to echo off the trees, accent thick in that lazy, Ladrican way.

"And if I did?" Lin asked.

Twin Wefts cleaved through the air, low and from both the east and west. There wasn't time to move Nebra, but the attacks were aimed at her legs, so Lin focused on unraveling them. The one flying from the west dissolved into sparks, and the leftmost would have caught Nebra if she hadn't moved on her own, throwing Lin off-balance in the process. He tumbled to the forest floor, leaves kicking up and the ground hitting harder than it ever had in the past.

Nebra stood motionless, ears flat, eyes scanning. Lin considered climbing back onto her, but the same issue would exist. She'd be a target. Lin rushed to her, side aching—everything aching—and smacked her rear. "Go!" She took off.

Like a twisted representation of the One, a person robed in all black dropped ten paces ahead of Lin. The King's Noose members had looked terrifying at night, their expressionless masks like a thing of nightmares. But in the early morning light, this one somehow looked worse. Maybe it was because they were alone, or because the sun haloed their head.

"Sight?" the person asked, accent stretching the middle of the word.

Lin didn't reply but sucked in a deep breath, steadying his heart. The surplus of seeds and honeycaps he'd eaten refreshed him, his limbs looser. But loose limbs and being magically healed weren't the same by half.

"You have the Sight?" they asked again, slower and louder as if Lin was stupid or hard of hearing.

Like teeth that couldn't stop rattling, branches clacked and jumped against each other as the ground rumbled underfoot.

"I do," Lin said.

"Hmm." Like unsheathing a sword, the Nooseman placed his hand at waist level and pulled it upward. The motion formed a blade of light. Lin needed to expand his understanding of the magic and fast. The weapon even seemed to have a cross guard similar to a standard-issue Ferrucium sword.

Lin stared, mouth hanging open. The control needed to maintain and move a Binding like that wasn't anything Lin had ever thought possible. A Needle, while a similar concept, was thin and pointed. It broke easily if it didn't pierce flesh, and Six was tiny. This man, this Nooseman, made a full-length fucking sword.

"Borrick and Nordja were good. Strong. *Caring*. You are weak. Scared."

Lin hadn't heard Dennick speak in the forest but imagined this was him. He'd caught up and was staring Lin down behind that cold, emotionless mask. He'd be dead if the person under the mask made it to where he stood.

"Why is the King's Noose entertaining Aemun's plots?"

"Aemun," he said correctly. "Aemun thinks he is a large spider on tiny web. He is a tiny spider on a huge web."

"And you—"

Dennick's shoulders pulled up, and he leveled his blade of light toward Lin. "The time for talking passed. We will rescue the fool, and he will play his part." Of the two Noosemen Lin had heard speak, Dennick seemed better spoken, but that didn't matter if the man refused to exchange words. His dark robes flared out as he lunged for Lin, the edge of his Binding extending into the length of a spear rather than a sword.

Lin focused his intention on the magic weapon. At its core, if it were like any other Binding, it was composed of many complex threads and strands. He focused on those, attempting to unravel the weapon while he side-stepped. It stalled like it had pressed against another blade and sparked, but it stayed intact and pierced the space Lin had been moments before.

"Will versus will," the Nooseman said. "You will never win. You are an errant thread meant to be cut from the Tapestry. I am a thread chosen by the Six."

Could the wagon even outpace this individual? Was Tylle awake and able to assist? There was a heaviness in Lin's heart. Borrick had warned them that their deaths were near, hadn't he?

Lin mimicked the Nooseman's stance and pressed his will into the world. He might not be a thread chosen by the Six, but he'd been selected by Tylle. Taught by her and Denro. And he could adapt. It's what he did. His intention forged into a blade, dull and miscolored compared to the torch of a weapon the Nooseman held. If things went sour, Tylle didn't need him. Her Uethe seemed less strict than Lin's. Pael would survive. He seemed like the type. Aemun. Well, people didn't get to act like he did and get away with it forever. The baby, the precious wailing baby, deserved a better father than that snake of a man. She deserved a mother who was still there, and Gwen, as gentle-souled as she seemed, didn't look fit to care for herself lately, let alone the baby.

Lin didn't need to make it to the journey's end if it meant his allies could. Tylle would kill Aemun and have her vengeance. Wouldn't she? Lin frowned. There was no denying he'd pictured the end of the road beside Tylle.

"Tears won't save you," Dennick said.

"I have no tears for you. These are tears of joy and pride. I've fulfilled my Uethes." Lin lied. He hadn't made Tylle smile. He hadn't removed the Stitches from his flesh. All he'd learned was that the rules need not apply to some people. And he knew failing Margie had been Aemun's fault, not his.

"Blaspheme," the Nooseman hissed. Dennick swept forward, blade aimed at Lin's throat. Lin parried the blow, willing his weapon to remain rigid. Picturing his intention like hard Ferrucium steel.

Both blades sparked and reflected off the Nooseman's metallic mask. Dennick's golden motes of disintegrating Bindings mixed with Lin's sunset-orange ones. Lin shuddered.

Dennick pushed, and Lin strained to keep his blade from being pressed into his shoulder. The Nooseman was as strong as the untethered he'd fought in Fallo—maybe stronger. They pulled apart and swung again and again. Each attack slid Lin back more. And ate away at the edge of his blade, chipping light from it like cheese from a wheel.

With a heavy overhand swing, the Nooseman shattered Lin's blade. He'd imagined Ferrucium steel, but it had been brittle. He thought to his dreams, the blade being dunked in and out of the water, hammered over and over again, breaking, melting, reforming.

Lin flinched and brought his hand up to catch Dennick's attack. His left hand hummed and burned, his Stitches stopping the edge of the weapon from cutting his flesh. It took all of Lin's strength to hold the blade, and, like the untethered had way back in Lyre, he made creeping, mold-like Bindings grow along the Nooseman's weapon. It didn't matter that it wasn't a real sword. Like spreading roots, the magic worked across the blade and formed cracks.

"Clever untethered," the Nooseman said. The blade shattered into fragments of light, but in a flash, Dennick grabbed the largest shards, like pulling threads together, and formed two slender weapons.

But it wasn't the Bindings in the man's hands Lin focused on.

Underneath the leaves and foliage that littered the road, Lin had been working another Binding. It was a Snare connecting to as many roots and stones as possible to make it secure. As the Nooseman stabbed upward, Lin sprung the trap. It was the most intricate magic Lin had ever woven together—excessively so. Knotted sections linked with others, and as it wrapped upward, encompassing Dennick like a net, it resembled a spider web.

Behind them, like a wild boar, the wagon careened down the path, broken branches be damned.

Dennick struggled against the Snare. He was wrapped up completely, and each jolt and squirm only tightened the spreading Bindings. Thinking that most of Lin's ideas and innovations came from untethered was an oddly sick realization.

"Cheap tricks won't save you. I think you are not the one who bested my comrades."

And it was true. Even as the Bindings ensnared the Nooseman more with each restrained movement, other pieces broke, snapped, and shattered into shimmering, loose threads. Lin rushed forward and ripped the mask from Dennick's face. He could practically be Borrick's twin, except the gauntness of Dennick's cheeks was more pronounced on his narrower, more pointed face. Blue-tinged lips cracked and peeled, and spit dribbled from the edge of them.

Lin held the mask flat like a spade and swung the dull edge at Dennick's nose.

Bindings flared to life between them, like a pane of ethereal glass had rested inches from Dennick's face and shattered at the mask's impact. Shards of broken light danced outward from the force, and the metal mask crunched into the Nooseman's nose.

Lin didn't have time to think about that strange interaction. The wagon hadn't stopped coming, and though Pael might not have the Sight, Aemun did. Either way, missing the hum of energy from the sprung trap or the floating Nooseman should be impossible.

Lin waved at Pael to go wide of the path and hoped the man saw him. When Lin turned back, Dennick was gone. The threads of magic that had held him in place floated on the breeze. Lin's hair stood on end, and he shifted, terror seeping into his bones. He'd hoped the blow from the mask would've knocked the One-loved person unconscious. Lin grimaced and looked at the trees. A Weft could fly out from anywhere and injure one of the horses. Even a Weave could catch a hoof and send them tumbling. Or the odd mixed conjuration the Noosemen were capable of.

The wagon crunched along, wheels crashing over smaller branches, horses stomping and charging ahead. Pael controlled the reins and didn't slow more than necessary to avoid the most obtrusive branch in the road. When he locked eyes with Lin, it seemed they understood each other. The man hunkered down on the bench and yipped the reins. Aemun wasn't beside him.

"Yah," Pael screamed.

Lin ran alongside the wagon, barely keeping up. In the shadowed back of it, he thought he could see Tylle's eyes staring at him. Judging him. Lin jumped in, vaulting sideways and pulling a wound at his side. He barely caught hold of a lip around the opening and hung there, ass out in the air as the wagon rattled left, then shifted right.

Lin raised his foot up, then his boot slipped, and he hung in the air momentarily before a hand shot out and grabbed his flailing right hand.

Aemun silently pulled him in, expression as sour as Lin had ever seen.

When Lin collapsed inside, his heavy breaths came out in clouds. He saw Tylle sleeping, the baby's bundle beside her in a makeshift crib. Gwen's back was to the baby and Tylle, her face practically touching the wagon's wall.

"Another one," Pael yelled back. His voice was barely audible over the wind, wagon, and Lin's wheezing breaths.

Lin stumbled over Tylle's nest. He might've stepped on her on his way to look past Pael. His limbs had gone cold.

"Same one," Lin said. Dennick stood in the middle of the road, maskless. And all around the Nooseman, Bindings shone in the early morning air like a gate made of edged light.

"You didn't kill him?" Pael's voice frayed at the end, and his hands trembled.

"No, asking that of him would've gone too far. He's just a simple, stupid Escorter." Aemun had stepped up and pushed Lin to the side, eyes wide as he saw what Dennick had formed. "These men truly are monsters."

Lin looked back at Tylle and wished she were awake. "She made beating them look easier than it actually is. Nowhere to go but through."

"Through what?" Pael asked.

Lin shook his head and stood up fully. His footing shifted with every bump and rut, but he held himself as still as possible. He swayed. He'd been ready to die if it meant they could get away, and that hadn't changed. Breaking all the Bindings wasn't necessary. Lin only needed to shatter enough of them so the wagon could barrel through without damage.

"Faster," Lin said. "Don't slow, no matter what."

"Have you lost your mind? We'll be diced like fish in a barrel!" Aemun tugged at Lin's sleeve. "Steer away, old man!"

Pael replied something, but Lin couldn't make out the words as the wind whipped around his ears.

Lin pressed his left thumb against his index finger and envisioned his intention flooding into the world from the circle. He sent wave after wave of heavy, solid Weaves the width of the wagon ahead of them. Like waves crashing against a stone wall, they shattered against the gate the Nooseman had conjured. Lin pressed and pushed and felt his blood growing colder by the moment. His toes and fingers had gone numb long ago, but this was the first time his heart felt like it might be missing.

To think monsters like this existed. Lin shuddered, and his right knee buckled. *'By being more of a monster than my enemy and more of a savior than the man who thought to save me.'* Tylle had said that, hadn't she?

Lin gritted his teeth and forced himself to stay upright. Even if there was more room on the roadway or an alternate path, the wagon was too close to the Nooseman and his blockade of Bindings. *Wefts.* Lin frowned. After everything he'd seen the man do, he wasn't sure the Ferrucium's simple classification made sense anymore. He dropped his hand to his side and imagined the opening of the wagon as a focus. More Bindings blinked into existence than Lin had ever made at once. Hundreds twisted and rotated around the entirety of the wagon. He imagined the wind pushing them, spinning them around him like a vortex. Lin made a cocoon of magic. Another trick taken from an untethered.

"You'll kill yourself." Aemun wouldn't shut up. So, Lin tuned him out. The man had gotten them into this situation, and rather than help, all he'd done was complain.

Trees and the road alike cracked, and the air warbled at the force. As wild as the outside looked, Lin's insides felt even more discordant. Spots of him were cold, and that sensation ebbed and flowed in pulsing waves throughout. And his heart *hurt* whenever the feeling returned to it. A stinging, biting pain every time it beat.

The wagon slowed, bucked against something. The cocoon pressed inward, back toward the horses, and then, like a spring being released, they barreled through the resistance. Lin kept the sphere of Bindings spinning around them until his vision pulsed from purple to black, with spots obscuring what he saw. He slumped to the side, chest heaving, nearly tripping back over Tylle and the baby.

"You look like shit," Pael said. Which felt odd coming from the man as he had dark bags under his eyes and his hands trembled.

"Feel like it." Lin eased himself onto the bench beside Pael and looked around. The trees had given way to scattered hills, brush, and an expanse of blue, cloudless sky. Based on the sun, it was past midday. *Had he kept it up that long? Is that why he felt so hollow inside?* "More. There will be more. Or the same one."

"Scary stuff. Never seen someone so full of hatred they'd try to stop a rushing wagon barehanded," Pael said.

"Imagine being Sightless. Not knowing how close to death you ever are at a given moment." Aemun patted Lin's shoulder. "You stepped up to the challenge and saved us."

"Bah. A dagger in the throat when you ain't expecting it can kill a man just as quick as a Binding in the ass." Pael forced a chuckle out, and the man's words brought an echo of a smile to Lin's face.

"True," Lin coughed out. Of course, Pael hadn't seen all the Bindings. "You felt the magic, though, right?"

"Hair wouldn't lie flat for a while if that's what you mean. But yeah, we barreled past the pale fuck. He got thrown to the side and chased for a while, but we outpaced him. Hobbled along like his ankle might've been hurt. But I think you're right. Not like to leave something, someone, like that behind for long."

"Aemun," Lin said weakly. Everything hurt, even his insides. He felt like he'd been scraped out, made raw. "Dennick said he wanted to rescue the fool. I'm assuming he meant you. Why would he think you need to be rescued?"

Aemun squeezed Lin's shoulder one last time and pulled his hand away. "I don't know. He either rushed to stop us because he saw through my plan and wanted to question me... or... I really can't imagine why else."

"He said you're a tiny spider on a big web."

"I'm sure he's right. If anything, this little excursion has proved beyond a shadow of a doubt that I am well and truly out of my depth. I never could've done what you did back there. Let's hope that the people Erias has put so much faith in are as capable as he's made them seem."

Pael grumbled under his breath and glanced sideways at Lin. "You need to rest. You look paler than a fresh moon. And thank you, boy."

"Thanks for what?" Lin asked.

"You waited for us. Could've tried to run away ahead, but you waited. Yer horse dead?"

Lin shook his head. "Think she got away. If I'd stayed with her, I think she would've been killed to keep me from fleeing. This isn't over. Noosemen... they're more untethered than not. He'll catch up. Even if his ankle was injured."

"And hopefully, you and her will be rested when he does. Or we make it to Erias's people before he does. Or..." Pael let his sentence fade.

"Or we die," Aemun said coldly.

Chapter Twenty

Bitter Blood

Lin jolted awake with the feeling of fingers tightening around his throat. But they weren't fingers, just the hard edges of a blanket that had seen better days. It smelled like it'd been soaked in sweat and left to the elements, which made sense once Lin felt the way his clothes stuck to him. His bones ached, and there was a hollowness in his gut that bit at him from within as if it might swallow him if he didn't feed it. He shifted on the uncomfortable bench, his arm brushing against Pael's.

"Bad dreams?" Pael looked at him from the corner of his eye. His hat was pulled low against the bright sun.

"Hmm?" Lin winced as his shirt pulled against flesh where blood had dried.

"Squirming and shaking in your sleep as much as a dog that's been kicked one too many times."

Lin narrowed his eyes and wondered how many kicks the man thought a dog might need. "I... I was a sharp blade, but I kept breaking. Over and over and over again. It's the same dream I've been having, and each time I get further along in it, it seems like the steel—I think it's steel—will hold, and each time it fails." Lin looked back and saw Tylle had moved. Her back was now to the front of the wagon, and she was propped up so that her head rested upright against a pillow. Gwen hadn't moved from where she'd lain earlier, and only the faintest rising and falling of her chest indicated she was even alive.

Pael noticed Lin's confused expression and shrugged. "She complained about the little one's noises. Insisted on sitting up and moving a bit." There wasn't a bite to his tone, not a fully toothed one in any case.

Aemun held the child, gaze directed out the back of the wagon.

A slash of light cut through the top and side of the wagon's wood toward the back end. Lin stood uneasily and, careful to avoid stepping on Tylle or Gwen, made his way to the back. Aemun blankly looked at him as Lin stepped by. It felt like the back of the wagon was a home for silence. Even the sounds of the wheels underneath were dim and distant, afraid to break the morose mood. It wasn't that the wood was exceptionally thick, but the fact that a Weft had sliced through it in the first place caused Lin to pause and stare. He was sure it hadn't been damaged before he'd conjured the cocoon of Bindings. So, either he'd done it inadvertently, which he didn't believe, or Dennick managed to rip through the back of Lin's defenses *and* carve into the fleeing vehicle. Lin swallowed and touched the gouges in the wood. Outside, the view helped Lin's stomach settle. Though there was plenty of brush, if someone approached from behind, there'd be no real place for them to hide.

"I'll need to stop soon and water the horse. Shouldn't take long, but it might. So, keep an eye out for water."

What Pael wasn't saying was the worry that whatever time it took them to stop, the King's Noose might find them and tighten around their throats.

"We'll manage," Tylle rasped.

"You're awake?" Lin leveled a grain sack and slowly lowered himself to sit atop it.

"No," she said. A wry smile slipped onto her face. In what light came through to shine on her, she looked paler than usual, like a faded version of herself. "But I had the worst dream."

"Was it of a blade being made and broken?"

Aemun chuckled, and when Lin looked at him, he shrugged.

"No. You betrayed us. Betrayed me," Tylle whispered, wet, dreary eyes locked onto his.

Lin stared back at her, refusing to blink. "How so?"

"I don't recall. But it broke what few pieces of my heart remained."

"I wouldn't. Not now," Lin said. He fought the flush of indignation that crept to his cheeks. After everything they'd been through, how could she think to speak such a thing? To doubt *him*.

"You say that. But when put to the test, can you be so sure? What hard choices have you made? What sacrifices?" Aemun asked, his voice low and bitter-sounding.

"I... I've sacrificed plenty."

"You've fought, certainly. You've struggled, no doubt. But you haven't sacrificed to see this thing through to its end, to fulfill some distant ache in your heart."

"Of all people... you don't get to talk about sacrifice," Tylle growled, shifting to press her shoulders back against the lip of the window.

"I've lost more than most to see the Ferrucium changed." Aemun stared at Tylle, lips pressing tight and jaw clenching. He rocked as the baby stirred in his arms.

"Enough of all that. We can measure losses later. You know, I've found having a bad dream, especially at my age, is a lot like having bad gas," Pael called back through the window.

"It's uncomfortable, then passes?" Lin said.

"It, sometimes, warns of worse shit to come," Pael cackled.

Lin watched Tylle, her pained smile and frustration gone. She stared at him, dark eyes resting on his hands.

"I know it was just a dream. And you've made an Uethe and have a Bludwieve to show for it. And you've... well, done far more than I could've ever thought you would back in Lyre." Tylle shifted her arm and rested her hand on Lin's leg.

Behind the touch and her words, Lin couldn't shake the feeling he'd failed her again, somehow. It seemed like that's all he'd really done since departing Lyre. Protecting Margaret had gone about as poorly as it could, seeing as he'd sworn an Uethe to protect her killer. But Tylle had seemed eager for them to go down this route. They'd give Aemun enough rope, enough loose rein to hang himself. And that certainly seemed to be the case as the King's Noose pursued them. The problem was that Aemun's rope seemed long enough to hang all of them. Lin leaned his head back against the wooden sideboard and stared at the sky through the missing chunk. The fingers of his right hand brushed the joints of his left, and he let himself settle into the silent company of those around him.

They stopped only once Pael spotted a pitiful creek cut beside the western edge of the path. While they were there, Lin watched for Nebra, whistling loudly for her despite Pael's chastising looks. He hoped she was out there, safe. But after allowing the horse water, oats, and a short rest, Pael ushered the lot of them back onto the path, pushing hard to widen the stretch of road they left behind.

Lin rested with Tylle in the back, eyes open for any sign of Nebra or Dennick. Every so often, she'd startle awake with more color to her cheeks than before, and the most recent time, she'd sat fully up as if she hadn't taken multiple, grievous wounds a day ago.

Gwen watched her wake and shivered, shifting to turn her back to them both. Lin had been shocked when she first moved from the wagon during the earlier stop. Something was off about the woman. Clearly, she hadn't expected the sort of trials that had befallen them... but even so, she seemed of a poor disposition for life on the road.

"Have I offended you?" Tylle asked.

"In many ways," Aemun grumbled, pulling his legs closer together so that Tylle's barefoot feet didn't touch his boots.

"Her," Tylle clarified, jutting her chin weakly at Gwen's back.

"She's sick."

"Sick?" Lin asked, studying her.

"Here." Aemun touched his head and shrugged. "But as far south as we are, the next large place with a physiker who might see to her mental anguish... is the Ferrucium."

Lin stared at Aemun, gaze sliding down to the swaddled child at his breast. "And if we need to abandon her?"

"Then we do what we have to. But she has been competent in caring for my child, and I owe her at least that small kindness." Watching Aemun sigh, shift, and sulk made Lin sick. In a blink, the man pulled a flask from under his cloak and took a large pull. The smell of spiced wood and strong liquor wafted through the cabin. "Care for some?"

Tylle shook her head, letting her eyes flutter shut. Her hair was matted and greasy-looking and her skin had a paleness to it that made her look closer to death than her little steps of recovery might indicate. She was better than her current state, better than traveling trapped with a man who killed her sister.

"Would... would you want me to braid your hair?" Lin asked.

Aemun snorted, a look of disdain flashing across his face.

Tylle blinked open her eyes and stared at him. She ran a hand through her tangled hair. She winced as her fingers snagged past her ear and nodded. "Didn't think you knew how the way you talked about Nebra's mane."

"You might have to talk me through it," Lin admitted.

"If you two plan to rut, please warn us so we can ensure our stomachs are empty." Aemun rolled his eyes and kicked his boot out so that he displaced Tylle's foot.

Tylle ignored the man and nodded at Lin, and soon Lin seated himself behind her, weaving strands of her hair into a simple plaited braid. They couldn't wash it, but once Lin brushed her hair, it wasn't as bad as it first looked. Straightening the matted sections proved challenging without a thick comb, but Tylle was patient in her explanations and Lin gentle in his attempts. Aemun made snide comments throughout, and by the time Lin finished, it was clear the man was drunk.

"Want me to do yours?" Tylle whispered.

Lin frowned. "I didn't think it was long enough."

"It wouldn't be like mine, but you've got good hair for it. Strong Danican roots."

"We all have strong Danican roots. Every fucking one of us. Braids mean things, Escorter, and you haven't earned it. She hasn't earned it. None of you fucking untethered have earned any of the... the fruits this coup will bring. Freedom from the King. What does that even mean to any of you?"

"You mean to say freedom means more to you, the one with the golden spoon up his ass?" Lin snapped.

"I am constantly told my place. Told how to act. Told how to present as a grandson of Weaver Azhura. Freedom to me is being able to *finally* live my own life. And you'll get rewarded for having suffered some wounds, insults, and exhaustion. Bah."

Tylle had grown very still, and Lin stared at Aemun's hands. He waved them around as he spoke, accenting points with a finger or fist, but sparks glittered from his quickest motions. Aemun was close to Binding without a focus. Which meant he probably knew how.

"Bah," Pael echoed Aemun's last word. "You'd have better luck braiding my beard than that boy's head."

Tylle turned from him but shifted to look over her shoulder at Lin, the pillow moving between them. "I could do it."

"The One take the lot of you," Aemun cursed under his breath when none of them returned his energy. It seemed the man was trying to pick a fight, but his eyelids had started drooping, and his words were slightly slurred.

"Aemun," Lin whispered as he moved to trade places with Tylle. "Can I hold her?"

Aemun's eyes grew large, and his lips twisted into a snarl before he seemed to realize where he was. "Take her." In moments, Aemun snored gently, flask in one hand, a corner of Gwen's blanket slung over one shoulder.

Taking the child was oddly like reuniting with an old friend. Her eyes still hadn't fully opened, and she made sad, suckling grunts as he pulled her close to his chest and eased back into Tylle's lap. Lin was careful to avoid Tylle's legs, and she pulled him back so that his head rested in a similar manner to how she'd cared for him in Fallo.

"Don't stare at the baby. Watch the road," Tylle whispered.

"Do you think she looks anything like Margie?"

Tylle's fingers were slender and deft, and that hadn't changed despite her current condition. But her motions slowed, and her answer was quick and short. "No."

"Not even a little?" Lin thought the bridge of her nose—

"Not at all. Please, don't ask again."

It was like Lin's back was to a snowbank, cold and unwelcoming, and he held a miniature campfire to his chest, warm and inviting. And Tylle spoke like the two couldn't coexist.

When Tylle finished, she didn't say a word but shifted to lie flat. But with Lin off to the side, Tylle elevated one leg using Lin's. He let her, resting his left hand near her leg.

"Thank you," Lin said, running his hand over the narrow, tight braids.

Tylle nodded and shut her eyes. It was entirely possible that exhaustion had gotten the best of her, but that didn't bode well if Dennick was closer than they'd hoped. Lin had barely survived the fight to run, and he didn't feel like he was in a condition to defend them again. His tricks and tactics wouldn't fool the man twice. He was sure of that.

"Gonna keep pushing through the night," Pael said, voice cracking as he raised it.

"Let me know if you need to rest," Lin replied, shifting his leg from underneath Tylle's once it began falling asleep. His numbness of limbs hadn't faded, but it had lessened substantially when he ate salted meat earlier in the day.

"I was using that," she groused, a smile touching her thin lips.

"No wonder it feels so tired," Lin said.

Tylle turned to face Lin. "Thank you for letting me do your hair. It really suits you better than the loose straw look you were attempting to pull off before."

Lin waved his hand. He'd wanted to learn how to braid Nebra's hair since before Wellgrove, but he hadn't had a chance to talk more about those things. Aemun was right. He hadn't considered some of the deeper meanings behind a lot of things in his life. And the more he learned about what the Ferrucium kept from the Binders en masse, the more at a loss he felt. "No, thank you for showing me. And for letting me do *that* to your hair."

Tylle chuckled. Her complexion continued to look better, brightening. The sleep she took intermittently likely played no small part in that. She ran a hand over her own braid, and her smile grew larger despite the sadness in her eyes. "It's the same as when my sister would practice on me. Eventually, it gets easier."

"Could I use the same braid for Nebra?" Lin asked. "When we find her?"

"For now, but can you guess why not for the long term?"

Lin sighed and narrowed his brow, resting his left hand on his head. Underneath, the wagon continued groaning along with the chirping of insects.

"Why?" Lin asked.

Tylle shrugged at him and raised a brow. When she shrugged, her bandages shifted slightly, showing the top portion of the Stitch along her side.

"Because the braids have meaning. And a practice braid isn't fit for Nebra, or you for that matter," Lin guessed.

Tylle nodded. "But that is alright. Until we retake the history of our past and our *future*, a simple braid is all we need to wear."

"You two are exhausting. Really. Disgustingly so. At least have the decency to do heretical things behind closed doors. A Ferrucium soldier shouldn't braid their hair." Aemun had apparently woken and seemed just as irritable as he had been before he'd fallen asleep.

"You said it yourself: I won't be a Ferrucium soldier once this is all done."

"Must you be so dramatic? Should everything I say be literal all the time? Six, you don't think past what you're told, do you?"

"Perhaps it's hard for him to do that when he's only recently learned things he's been told as facts his entire life are lies."

"Perhaps shut up? In his position, that would make me think even *more* critically. What if I meant to elevate you beyond a simple Ferrucium soldier? Or perhaps I'd assumed you'd have a position in Erias's little circle. Any number of things that didn't literally mean ex-communication."

"You're troubling the child," Lin whispered, easing the bundle left and right as the baby cooed. "And don't speak to her that way."

"Or what? You'll attack me?" Aemun asked, chin and nose both higher in the air than they had any right to be.

"Noone is attacking anyone," Pael yelled, stalling the reply on Lin's lips. "Better to air this out now than to be at each other's throats, though. That's the mentality that helped Erias and Duke Hollander, at any rate."

"Duke Hollander... does he also aid the rebellion?" Lin asked.

"Aid?" Pael chuckled and turned his attention back to the road. "Erias Well-grove and Old Hol, they *are* the rebellion—to an extent, the mind and heart, if you will."

"Can't leave me out of the mix now just because you don't like me," Aemun said.

"Oh, too true," Pael called back. "If we have the heart and mind accounted for... hmm... oh right. You're the pus-dripping cock of the rebellion."

Aemun smiled at first, but it gradually slipped from his face like leaves falling from a dead tree. Lin smiled at that, thinking critically and all.

"Am I misremembering, or did you say that each Fell-Binding on you was placed there because of a lie?" Lin leaned over and asked Tylle. He gingerly touched her side, letting his fingertips trail at the bandage where a dull, golden triangle point shone.

Tylle was quiet for a long time, each bump and rattle of the wagon a different declination of the silence. "You are recalling the tale of Vellyr and his many Inlays. Though, I may have unintentionally misled you concerning my own."

"If they aren't placed for each lie, what then?" Lin asked, pulling his hand away and leaning to better view her face.

"Strength and speed are Inlayed along my arms and legs. Balance is at my back. Wisdom, if you were to lift my hair, though the benefits of more ethereal Inlays are less noticeable. There are other, small changes here and there that are harder to describe."

Lin nodded as she pointed, to the best of her ability, at each one as she spoke. What she'd described solidified a thought that had been playing at the back of Lin's mind for a while now. Different Stitches, Inlays as they were, did different things. It was a simple concept that extended far beyond the initial combat variety he'd been taught by the Ferrucium. Wefts or Weaves. Those had been his world. Then he'd seen the whip-like razors untethered created. The net-like collection of threads. Stitched flesh, patterned flesh, seemed to improve combat prowess. *The Bludwieves.* It led to the question: how many other forms of Bindings were there? How many different colors were visible to someone blessed with the Sight if gold and crimson could be seen?

"And if I worked a Binding into my flesh, I'd be stronger? Like the King's Noose?" Lin asked.

"Sure, the right one. The magic comes from the patterns and the intention placed into them, like the Bludwieve.."

"You'd truly break the Binding Tenets. No going back. No allowing yourself to doubt whether the Six are or aren't real or what you might be doing to the Grand Tapestry by Stitching yourself." Aemun's tone was level, flat, and practiced. As if he'd had this exact conversation before.

But Erias had said he'd tell him how to remove it. Or, even if they couldn't be removed, hadn't he already managed to ruin the Tapestry if the Six truly weren't just sad copies meant to steal the history of Danica's past?

"How did you decide you wanted to mark yourself in so many different ways?" Lin asked.

Tylle sucked a breath in, but instead of letting silence fall, her cheeks flushed. "How does anyone make such a large decision? I prayed. Then I prayed some more. Then I doubted myself and all the good I might do."

Pael's hat bobbed up and down as they hit a rough section of road that could've doubled as a washboard.

"And?" Lin asked, leaning forward, painfully aware of how close he was to Tylle as she bore such a private part of herself to him.

"And I decided I trusted myself enough not to go mad. I trusted the dream I held here," Tylle whispered and touched the space where her heart rested, "And the faith that powered it."

Lin nodded and forced a smile. It wasn't that he didn't understand—he knew exactly what she meant. But in all his life, he'd never had a faith quite so strong.

Eventually, Lin switched with Pael so the man could stretch his legs. The fresh air was a comfort, and even as cool as it was, the wind felt refreshing across his scalp. Lin took the reins into his right hand and raised his left to eye level. The Stitches along his fingers and wrist were basic. Single lines. They'd never looked like anything other than *basic* Bindings to him. Still, now, after speaking with Tylle, he studied them closer. Sure, the linework was simplistic, but the lines were symmetrical, and... he looked closer. Surprisingly complex.

Tiny interlocking circles wrapped themselves through the glowing lines. Were these the signs of strength? He flexed his fingers and shook his head. No, he hadn't *felt* any stronger.

"They are... as you call them, Stitches. Nothing more, nothing less." Tylle's voice was soft and accompanied by the groaning of wood underneath her foot as she crawled through the wagon opening. A blanket dragged behind her like an oversized cape.

"Should you be moving?" Lin asked, realizing what she'd done as she settled beside him on the bench and placed her thick, warm blanket squarely over his shoulders.

"I feel far better than I did even earlier today." Tylle sighed and leaned into him. "You really want to work Inlays on yourself?" She sounded doubtful.

Lin raised his left hand up and studied it longer. "I don't know. Maybe. I think so. If I don't, I can't stand with you. I can't help you find justice. I barely survived. And..." Lin looked over his shoulder into the dark wagon, lowering his voice to a low whisper. "Aemun is too cunning. If he betrays Erias—When he betrays Erias, I might not be able to stop him how I am now. And if it can be undone later, if Erias can rid me of my Stitches, then what's the harm? And that's not even thinking of those Noosemen. It was like in Fallo all over again. Who knows how many more of them they'll send? Or why they were really working with Aemun, to begin with."

Tylle raised her eyebrows and nudged him. "You fought one?"

Lin nodded, realizing they hadn't spoken much about it, and she'd likely been unconscious. "I fled from one."

"The fact you're alive to say you fled is a victory. In some ways, they are untethered and it is similar to Fallo. But also, no. This time, *you* saved *me*. Us." Tylle yawned, and even more of her weight settled against Lin's side. "Aemun will continue to do as he does until his back is against a wall. And if the King's Noose still chases us, we must be ready."

"Cornered animals are often more dangerous," Lin whispered. Though, if he meant Aemun or themselves, Lin wasn't sure.

"Lin, I feel like you think I underestimate this man." Tylle's voice had dropped lower than a whisper. "He killed my sister, a woman just as skilled as myself, even if she didn't want to Bind to preserve her and the child's life. He has escaped several situations through guile, status, or skill. Aemun isn't weak, even if he carries himself softly at times."

"If he is so dangerous... why'd you send me after him back in the woods?" Lin asked. He turned to face her entirely, and she stared up at him.

"Because I believe in you more than I fear him. I told you... I trust you."

They were so close Lin could taste her warm and slightly sour breath. After a pause that lasted far too long, he pulled away. "Can you teach me the patterns for strength and speed? I think I'm ready," Lin whispered. If he failed to keep anyone else he cared about safe, he'd never forgive himself. He was tired of failing.

"Are you sure?" Tylle asked. She rested her head on his shoulder, eyes on the road ahead.

"As sure as I can be." Lin cocked his head to the side and laid it on hers. "I don't think I'm worried about becoming untethered."

"Don't think like that. You still *could*. Madness can seep in when you least expect it. Just because the Ferrucium has weaponized untethered as a blanket term doesn't mean they aren't real."

"I thought you were trying to convince me to do this?" Lin asked.

"Not at all. It's your decision. I'm not here to tell you if it's right or wrong."

Lin licked his lips. "Which one is easier?"

"What? Being right or wrong?" Tylle asked.

"No. Speed or strength," Lin said.

"You can do your right arm with Inlays of strength while we ride. Legs may be harder with the bigger muscles and length of them."

"That's odd," Lin chuckled.

Tylle paused, then nodded gently. "I suppose so. Give me the reins."

Lin did as she asked and stretched out his right arm, sliding it out from under both blankets.

"Intention and pattern both matter. You can try tracing the patterns with your finger as you work the magic in your mind."

"And what happens if I mess it up?" Lin asked.

"It won't take to your flesh if it isn't done right. Even simple Bindings fade and falter when they lack intention or focus, right?"

Lin nodded. It had been a long time since he'd had to think about even a simple Binding failing, but the first several months of Ferrucium training involved repeatedly forming Weaves until one could do it without it sputtering out immediately.

"Focus your mind. Arrest your thoughts other than those of strengthening your bones, muscles, all of it. Put your intention towards that. And draw your first knuckle along your flesh like this."

Tylle took Lin's right hand in her left and pressed so only his index knuckle protruded. She dragged his hand like a quill in interlocking circles. Over and over again, her eyes did not leave the road once.

"That's it?" Lin asked.

Tylle grinned and shifted her eyes, finally staring up at him from the side. "Do it one hundred times and ask again if that was all it involved."

Chapter Twenty-One

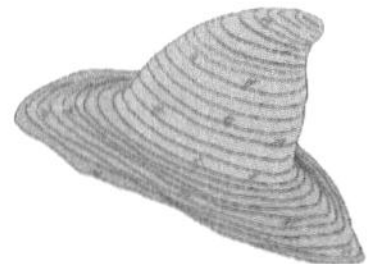

Blessings of Hope

Whether Tylle had been jesting or not, Lin lost count of his attempts to work a Stitch, an Inlay in her own words, into his flesh some point after the fiftieth. Shimmering strands of golden, concentric circles would pulse into existence, some stretches of flesh holding the light more than others before fading entirely. The first attempt seemed the best. Beginner's luck or fool's arrogance, apparently. He'd shuffled out of the blankets early on, and now his shirt stuck to him with sweat despite the biting morning air. There'd been no sign of any Nooseman, untethered, or wayward travelers. The further they got from Wellgrove and the wooded area in which they'd been confronted by Dennick, the less sure Lin was that he would find Nebra. Any number of things could've happened to her, but this still wasn't the longest stretch they'd been separated on a mission, not yet.

Lin dragged his knuckle up the length of his arm, the skin tender. He brushed it in tight, accurate circles.

The glow started softer than his previous attempts like the light was simply staining his skin as leftover rays of a sun that had set long ago. He cursed under his breath but continued. Pulsing like it was attached to his heartbeat, the light thrummed in and out of existence. Was it a timing issue? From the start to the end of the process, he traced over thirty overlapping circles and couldn't help but wonder if he was moving too slowly.

He reached his wrist and wrapped the pattern, closing it off. Both hands trembled, and he stared at the tracings. Three held breaths, and they hadn't faded.

Tylle yawned beside him. "Done?"

"I don't know," Lin said. "First time the lines have stayed longer than it took to place them."

Tylle started to run her hand along his forearm, touching his wrist, but he jerked away. Her brows pinched together, and she shook her head and teasingly asked, "Why'd you do that?"

Lin looked down at his arm, which he'd pulled protectively into himself, shielded by his other arm.

"Think a single wipe of my hand might undo whatever you've done?" Tylle looked like she was fighting to keep back a smile.

"No," Lin whispered. "You just ran your hand right over them. And…"

"And how many times have you done that, caressing the ones I did to heal you when you thought I wasn't looking?"

Lin's cheeks grew hot, and he darted his eyes from her face to the road. "I didn't think about that."

"You wouldn't have any better luck running your hand over your face and removing your eyes. If it's set in the flesh, stitched under the skin, and into the muscle and bone, it is a part of you. As far as I know, it'll take more than a handwave to rid you of them."

Lin glanced at the scar along her chin and thought about how close they'd been the night before. Had she wanted him to kiss her? Did she want him to now? *Do I want to?* Once this was all said and done, he was sure they'd have a chance to talk about feelings and whether she even had any for him.

"What you call Stitches are a deeper sort of magic. Inlays, like Bound Metal, are older than the Ferrucium's imposed Bindings through the Accords. As old as Wievings, if not older. *That* is partly why the Ferrucium fears it so."

Lin forced himself to relax and eased his right arm beside her, nodding when she placed her hand near it. "So, I did it?"

Tylle nodded and ran her fingers across his arm, not entirely tracing the Inlay how someone with the Sight would, but slowing any time she grazed the pulsing lines. "My first one took longer."

"I don't believe you," Lin said.

Tylle shrugged and released his arm, settling back into the bench and gingerly stretching. Every time she moved, it seemed her injuries improved.

"We'll get there before he finishes the next limb at this rate," Pael called from the wagon's interior. "Which still wouldn't be soon enough at the rate we've gone. I should never have let you take the reins, like to be caught and killed by that Nooseman, way you've crawled us along like a bloated worm."

"Pael—" Tylle started but stopped as Lin raised his hand.

"No, he has a point. Do you think you're well enough to ride?"

"I'm well enough to run if I had to," Tylle said, shifting out of the blanket. She pushed her shoulders back, chest pressing forward in defiance. Her jaw was tight, but there was no mistaking the determination in her eyes.

"Give me the day to finish my legs, and we can run ahead."

"And what good would that do the rest of us? If you two go darting off like fireflies? Hmm?" Pael spoke as he made his way to the mouth of the wagon, face squished into a miserable-looking patch of wrinkles and scratchy beard. His eyes were dark, face covered in shadow.

"Did you wake up on the wrong side of the wagon?" Lin asked.

"I awoke thinking I was home, surrounded by the comforts of good living that I'd earned prior to all this... *nonsense*. Only to realize that I wasn't there, on my soft, still bed, but on the slowest *crawling* wagon I've ever had the misfortune to find myself on. We were given a duty by Erias. All this—" Pael waved his hands in short flurries, lips curling into a sneer "—is excess, secondary, *unneeded* to finish that main duty but certainly slowing execution of said duty. And to make matters worse, last I knew, we were running for our lives."

Aemun coughed from the back of the wagon. "Don't forget blasphemous."

"Oh, shut it," Pael snapped.

With a firm hand, Lin pulled on the bridle and slowed the horse. "We should be coming up on a village. Saw smokestacks earlier. Drive us through, and I'll finish my work. I'm sorry."

Pael didn't respond and barely shifted out of the way as Lin pressed into the back of the wagon. The older man might be saying sharp things, but he had a point. It didn't matter what Lin and Tylle could do alone; they weren't an army. They certainly weren't the group Erias thought capable of overthrowing the Ferrucium alongside Aemun.

Lin shook his head and settled amid the baskets and bags of cargo. He pulled his shirt off and stared outside the wagon's back, watching the dirt path snake away as the vehicle picked up speed.

If his right arm had taken him most of the night, he didn't want to think about how long working his left would require. Lin gritted his teeth, cleared his mind, and drew the patterns along his flesh with care and intention. If a year ago someone had told him he'd be protecting a Weaver's family member as they headed to overthrow the Ferrucium's ruling class while Stitching his flesh, he'd have suggested they visit a physiker.

Lin threw himself into the work, putting aside everything from his mind. He just needed to survive long enough to remove the Stitches. *If they had to be removed at all*. It was a thought that had sunk into his mind like a Stitch into flesh. *If* Tylle and Erias were telling the truth, and Aemun's own confessions seemed to support that, then bearing these markings didn't make him untethered. Didn't desecrate his flesh in the eyes of any real Gods. Didn't ruin the Grand Tapestry.

Hours passed in a blink, and only the wagon slowing to a stop pulled Lin from his work.

Surprisingly, the terrain had changed. The rocky, brush-covered hills gave way to more striated earth, with bands of red clay showing where the outcrops of stone grew too high. And the sun had somehow gotten to the left of them, causing the wagon's shadow to cut aggressively right.

Lin struggled to move his legs. They'd gone numb, sitting cross-legged as he had been. He hadn't thought he'd been out of it for that long, but when he looked down, Inlays lined his entire left arm. He'd done it.

Flexing his fingers, he eased onto his palms and forced his legs out from underneath him, slapping the tops of his feet to wake them. He needed to start on his legs, but his stomach growled, and Aemun complaining from the bench up front made him uneasy. Something about armed men.

"Afternoon, strangers. Might we water our horse for a moment?" Pael called to someone off to his left, judging by how the man's hat turned.

Lin leaned out from the back, careful not to step on Tylle. A small collection of men had gathered, blocking the road. Farmers, by the tools at hand. Bandits by the expressions they wore. But behind them was a village, and unless they'd taken over the entire place, they likely weren't robbers.

Tylle slept flat on her back, and Gwen faced the wall as she had for most of the trip. He meant to speak with her, to see if she needed anything, but every time he caught her looking toward him, she frowned and hid her face under her arms.

Whoever Pael had spoken to seemed to say something, but the response was lost to Lin.

"I appreciate the help!" Pael said with a wave of his hand, then in a hushed tone, "None of the folks look too happy. But we won't get anywhere meaningful before nightfall either way. The horse here needs a break, and I need to stretch my legs." Pael looked at Lin from the side of his eye before sniffing hard and turning away.

"Where are we?" Lin asked. From the opening in the rear, tightly packed homesteads could be seen. Closer to each other than Lyre's or Fallo's homes. Men and women clad in sweat-stained, baggy shirts and trousers toiled in fields that looked like they'd already been stripped for harvest. The nights had grown cold, but surely, they hadn't been on the road so long that the fall harvest had begun. Riversbend had been throwing a festival, though.

"Nowhere that matters," Aemun said.

"Every village matters," Pael corrected. "Even the ones like this. Especially the ones like this."

Lin watched silently as the man's hat bobbed while he unbridled the horse and led it down the road to where the water likely rested. "He's... a man of fickle moods."

"We had a pleasant enough time while you ladies rested in the back." Aemun scratched his chin and wrinkled his nose as a breeze blew toward them from the gathered men. "Can we help you?" He asked with a raise of his brows when it became clear the group wasn't disbanding.

"Might. Where you coming from?" a broad-chested man asked. His shirt had seen better days, and his expression was as sour as rotten fruit. His hair was as light as Aemun's, and his skin was tanned and wrinkled from a life spent in the sun.

"Fuck that," a scrawny man replied. "Where you going?"

"Coming from Wellgrove. Heading south," Lin said. He straightened his back and took several unsteady steps toward the group. Each step helped jolt the feeling back into his numb legs, but there was an emptiness at his core that didn't do the same.

"Not much south. We don't mind people passing through, but last time a wagon like that pulled through with men wearing fancy robes like your friend there, my son was taken from me." The scrawny man spat. His facial hair was thick at his chin and above his lip, but that was it. Even his eyebrows looked sparse.

"And if we are Ferrucium?" Aemun asked, rising. His bright red, silken cloak was like a gash of blood against the drab, beige fields.

Whispers came from the back of the group. "Then we've got complaints."

"And we've got ears to hear them," Aemun said. "Give voice to your qualms."

"We have complaints, not *qualms*," the broad-chested man said, frown lines etching his face like stone. "We are tired of watching our young ones being taken!"

The other men cheered. There were eight, counting the two who'd done the most talking. Three rusted sickles and two hoes were all the tools spread between them, but the barrel-chested speaker looked like he could quickly kill a man bare-handed.

"Jev, wait," an elderly woman called. She shuffled to the front. Her clothes were coated in dust but had stitching proving they'd once been finer than typical homespun. She carried herself regally. Her eyes were a bright, midday blue and scanned from Aemun to Lin and then the wagon.

"They aren't the ones who take. Though they're in odd company."

An uncomfortable period passed where the group of eight pressed tighter in a half-circle around the wagon, but the woman stepped between them all, and the tension dispersed.

"How can you be sure," Jev, the thick-chested man, growled.

"You know Momma Lessie ain't ever wrong about them sorts of things," one of the younger men gathered said, his eyes large and wet, as if the thought of violence breaking out were too much for him to bear. Lin had seen plenty of eyes like those in his training at the Ferrucium and plenty more since. Odds were good Lin had even worn that same worried look over the last few days.

Momma Lessie stared. The lines of her face were like the rings of a tree, and she had all the poise of a great, unmoving oak.

The wagon creaked. Tylle exited, limping slightly, one hand holding her hip, the other holding a waterskin to her lips. Although she'd moved more recently, it was still a shock to see her walking on her own.

Momma Lessie narrowed her eyes at spotting Tylle. "Very strange company. I..." She wet her lips and looked like she struggled to find the right words. "I love your braid, though it might be tighter so it doesn't come loose. Would you allow me to fix it?"

From the angle the old woman stood at, her braid, simple and unadorned, showed over her shoulder. Her hair was white-mottled gray and shorter than Tylle's, but she touched it with pride as a gentle, knowing smile formed on her lips.

"While I would love that, I don't know if we have time," Tylle said.

"Lessie," Jev growled.

"Jev." While not nearly as low or menacing, Momma Lessie's voice sent a chill across Lin's shoulders. "Take the boys and bring any provisions we can spare. Please."

Lin watched the man's stern expression shift as his eyes narrowed, widened, and rolled. His shoulders were tight back, and his jaw and fists clenched so hard it was a wonder his bones didn't grind to dust.

"We've had a hard time lately," the wet-eyed young man said as if he needed to explain. "Won't be much to spare."

Tylle nodded. "Suffering, large or small, affects us all. I may not look like it, but I'm a priestess. If you have a holy house, I'd love to sit and pray for you and your people."

"I'll take you there. The Six and One watch over much of Danica these days, but we remember the old ways, and Velkath would be happy to hear you from this humble home."

Aemun's lip twitched, and he shook his head. "Heretics."

"How can you say you know we are shackled as a people by King Lodram and not think there is a chance that what we've been taught in the Ferrucium is a lie?" Lin asked, shifting to meet Aemun's eyes.

"I don't plan to argue the studies of Gods with an Escorter whose education doesn't go past basic principles. I studied with the Fentian scholars. I've sat at tables with wise men and kings. I've seen the Six in dreams, and knowing Danica as a whole has been yoked and shackled through the Accords by its own power doesn't make me believe in the Six any less. My faith is made of sterner stuff than to be swayed by a thin-boned, hard-edged priestess."

Lin held his tongue, too tired to argue. Then said, "I've always wanted to meet the scholars of Fentis. I've heard the academy overlooks the southwest ocean and towers over everything in the area."

"The Pellic Sea," Aemun said, softer. "It was a pleasant time. It's probably my favorite memory from my youth. Once this is all done, I look forward to returning. I think the committee that leads the scholars will be more than eager to help in the reformation of Danica."

The Fentian scholars were men and women who'd given themselves to study. A number of them were once Binders, sworn to the service of the Ferrucium. But in becoming a scholar, they were sworn to a loveless, partnerless life. Some saw being sent to Fentis as a punishment. But Lin had always marveled at the stories Denro told him about the towers, sea, and people.

Jev approached, a limp sack carried in his large hands. The rest of his crew followed behind, but the only other person holding anything was the young, wet-eyed speaker from earlier. A small fruit basket was clutched tight to his chest, brushing against the dirty tunic.

"Not as fresh as most would like... and if you don't eat them in the next few days, probably give 'em to the horse."

"Rusty," Jev said.

"What?" the young man replied with a grin. "Figured I'd let him know."

"Speaking of horses," Lin started. "You haven't seen a lone mare, chestnut-colored, dark saddle, come through. Have you? She'd be a bit older, white splashed across her face."

"Plenty of horses look—"

"Oh, she's yours?" the young man, Rusty, said excitedly.

"Gods damn you, boy," Jev cursed. He dropped the sack to the dirt, a cloud of dust kicking up, and moved like he might strike Rusty. Despite his exhaustion, Lin was quicker. He moved between the two and stood there, matching Jev's glare.

"I... I'll go fetch her," Rusty said. He sat the small bushel down and rushed away.

"Lessie ain't the end all be all," Jev said.

Lin nodded. "I'm sure she's not."

"I could kill you where you stand."

Lin nodded again. "I'm sure you could." He kept his voice level and his body language flat. But without *intention*, a Weft hummed into existence near Jev's throat.

Aemun whistled from behind him, but Lin didn't pull his eyes from Jev.

If the man felt the magic, he didn't react. His dark eyes were wild and stabbed into Lin, his lip twitching.

Slowly, Lin bent down and picked up the sack the man had dropped. He felt a few loaves of hard bread within. He braced for an attack, but the others behind Jev spoke softly, pulling him back and away. Pael came back, the horse in tow, and shortly after, Rusty returned, Nebra behind him. She looked healthy and approached him quickly like he hadn't struck her rear to make her flee. He checked her over. No wounds, nothing. She was alright. Six, she was alive.

Lin blinked, not wanting to cry before Jev or his gaggle of men. "Nebra," he whispered.

Nebra sniffed at Lin's hands, the Stitches along his arm tingling at the contact. When this was all done, she deserved a good ride—a good rest—unburdened, like when they'd be between escorts, and the threat of enemies hadn't seemed so real. But, of course, there had been enemies all along, festering in the spaces Lin couldn't see.

"Thank you," Lin said. "For being a good, honest man and bringing her to me."

Rusty shrugged. "Momma Lessie would skin me alive if she knew. I could tell by her expression that she liked the cloth you all were cut from."

"Well, I'm sorry for any extra burden we may have placed on you for this," Lin said loud enough that he hoped everyone would understand precisely what he meant.

Chapter Twenty-Two

Blessings of Bone

"You act like the prayer took long," Tylle said. She shifted in her seat, straightening her back and turning just enough to stare into the wagon where Pael rested.

It hadn't. Not really, but each passing delay seemed to drive a nail of sour spirit and poor attitude deeper into Pael. That, on top of Aemun's occasional rude comment, whenever an actual conversation started, had seemed to put Pael on an edge the man might walk right off of.

And Pael's mood stung underneath Lin's skin like a splinter. Even if the man had reason to fear what may be following their trail.

"I didn't say it took too long. I said we didn't have time for it. Barely had time to stop for water or... You know it doesn't matter. I'll take over again soon and compensate for the lost time."

"We needed to stop. You know that as much as we do. And if Tylle praying for them brings them some small comfort, isn't that better than nothing?" Lin asked.

"Better than nothing. The words of a man who can't look past his station," Aemun said.

"Do you ever stop and listen to yourself, you condescending shit? Hmm. So, you've got Erias's ear. You've got his help and, in doing so, will be drawing out his best fighters. It's all too convenient. All of it."

Lin tensed. Pael had kept his thoughts reasonably close to his chest, but this was the first time the man had voiced what Lin had been thinking. Lin needed Aemun alive so that Erias would remove his Stitches or tell him how. But if Aemun *did* betray them, would Erias still reveal the process? Or keep him shackled?

"Pael," Tylle whispered.

"Little Tylle, I don't know how you've done it. Swallowed all the rage and fury to sit beside this man. He killed Margie. And that's all fine and good. People die. I've lost more loved ones than most of you've had. But to do that and *sit* there acting like he's better than us 'cause I don't always wear leather boots? Or 'cause I'm not from some bloodline of betrayers."

"My family has sacrificed more than most to keep Danica free. I wouldn't expect you to understand."

Pael moved in the back, and the wagon creaked its complaint at him doing so, but Lin couldn't see him and didn't dare take his eyes off the road as the wind continued to gust hard against them. The horse pulled the wagon along steadily, and the dark clouds overhead promised a long night, even if the heavens didn't drown them. What few pitiful trees had been scattered closer to the town earlier in the day had given way to entire, bleak stretches of shrubs and craggy outcroppings.

"You know," Lin started. He ignored Tylle's hand as she touched his shoulder. "For a man who seemed so carefree when we met, you've been on edge lately."

"Oh, have I been?" Pael's raised voice carried from the back.

"I mean the both of you back there, actually," Lin said.

"Both of you, stop it." Tylle's hand squeezed. A light pressure but one meant to draw Lin's eyes to hers. She shook her head when he finally glanced her way and mouthed the word, *"Please."*

"Was I carefree when I led you and Tylle, stealthily, to the Duke's manor after having your nose at the end of my dagger? Or perhaps it was as I, despite my better judgment, aided you in fights against people I've got no business fighting? It's not like any of us got out barely alive, right?"

Aemun didn't respond, but Azhalia did, crying in rhythm with the rocking of the wagon. His voice carried as he made shushing sounds.

"And if you could silence—" Pael started.

"Apologies. My daughter is starving!" Aemun snapped. "If you've got a teat she might suckle upon, please produce it. Otherwise, keep your barbs directed at me, even if you know she might be an easier target."

Lin hadn't considered what Pael might be going through. There was the shared journey, but he didn't have the prowess or powers that Tylle had or that Lin was developing. Was he skilled? Yes. But it seemed to be in subterfuge and close-quarters combat against non-Binders. And besides, Lin certainly hadn't thought Gwen had stopped feeding the baby. Though she'd barely cared for herself, as Lin considered it. He looked at Tylle, catching her eyes.

"I can't," Tylle whispered curtly, with no further explanation.

Lin nodded. He wasn't entirely sure how it worked, but he didn't think Tylle would let her sister's child go hungry if she had a choice.

"Pael, what does being a Duke's man mean?" Lin asked. "You've called your-self that several times, but I'm not sure I ever stopped to ask."

A sigh carried from the back of the wagon. "A Duke's man is many things. I've brokered peace more times than I could count on one hand… and ended twice as many lives as that. I've seen the tallest peaks you could imagine, negotiating trades, and I've been in the darkest cellars, punished on the whim of rivals." Pael's voice grew closer. He rested his chin on folded arms, level with Lin's and Tylle's shoulders. "It means that I've taken an oath, and despite my outward appearance or what you think of me, I have a duty. But I'm hungry, and my joints ache. I've grown old in my service, but all that means is that Venya, bless her, still loves my dice. So, if I seem on edge, it's because I am. I'm sore and afraid and *tired*."

Lin had heard a speech like that once before from Denro. Every time he'd seen his older friend, increasingly grayer hair sprinkled his head, and wrinkles had snuck onto his face. Growing old hurts. Even at twenty-seven passes, he knew that much, but Lin couldn't imagine the strain Pael was putting himself through to keep the pace they had. Even in a wagon, the bumps and jolts of travel had a way of sinking into your bones.

"You told me you were loved once but not liked. Do you still feel that way?" Lin asked.

Pael chuckled. "Getting stuck doing this mission? Doubly so. I'm sure all the Gods are laughing at me from where they sit. But I'm alive. And I have the chance to keep fellow Danicans the same."

"Velkath and his brothers and sisters have better things to do than stare at a dirty old man," Tylle said. She raised a brow and let her smile travel from her eyes to her lips.

"That is exactly why they love me but don't *like* me. I'm sure they do watch from wherever they take their shits. They've seen things that might make a midwife blush, a physiker weep, a Binder Stitch their eyes closed forever watching me. For you have the right of it. I am a *dirty* old man. But that's the trick. Venya knows better, but most?" Pael tapped his nose before grabbing both of them by the shoulder. "Most don't expect the vagrant to be a spy. Especially not an endowed one who can talk his way into no less than three *separate* Duchesses' chambers."

The baby's cries softened marginally, and Lin heard Aemun whispering but couldn't make out the words. Perhaps Aemun focusing on the child was a boon rather than setting Pael off even more.

"You sound like you believe in Venya at least, if not Velkath and the others," Lin said.

Thunder boomed, and Lin flinched at the sound. But whatever storm brewed overhead seemed to pass quickly enough that the torrent of rain swelling in those gray clouds would fall well behind them.

"It's impossible to believe in one without believing in the others," Tylle said.

"Or foolish. But I neither make a habit of attempting the impossible or claiming the title foolish. Truthfully, I care little about either faith. And If I did, I'd rather think I would make a decent preacher," Pael said, releasing Lin's shoulder and patting Tylle's.

"You help the people in other ways... and that's more than enough," Tylle replied.

Pael shrugged. "Let me take over. I've rested long enough."

They barely stopped long enough to swap seats and pass the waterskin around before they moved again. The wind whistled through the crags in uneven tones, and sprinkle drops fell, pushed at them by the gusting wind. Aemun didn't move from the back, but he forced Gwen to sit up and drink water. Pael took the lead, and Lin rode on Nebra for a bit, taking comfort in her warmth despite the chill, nipping wind.

"You said earlier—" Pael called to Tylle, who had moved into the back of the wagon to lie down "—that I helped people, and that was more than enough."

"Yes?" Tylle asked. She sounded as if she'd been pulled from the grip of sleep. Lin sidled Nebra to the left of Pael.

"I was thinking. I do help people, but I do it for myself. Not because I care about some stolen history or because I think it's what Gods or men might want me to do. I just want to do right by those who've done right by me."

"I think I know what you mean," Lin said. He needed to start work on his legs, but the numbness near his core hadn't really gone away. It was like he had a hole resting just above his navel.

"Do you?" Pael asked.

"Since I can recall, I was told it was my job to help people. Protect them. Be a Binder of the Ferrucium—a soldier. But then I was an Escorter. Traveling from city to city, protecting other Binders who, for whatever reason, couldn't protect themselves. And this was *before* the untethered seemed as large of a threat. I never stopped to ask why we weren't tasked with protecting the villages. One Binder per village doesn't seem so much to ask. But I only helped where and when I was told to. And so help me if an untethered did cross my path. My justice on them was swift... and merciless." Lin blinked at the sting in his eyes and pulled the blanket cloaked around his shoulders tighter so the new Inlays on his arm were visible. They shone golden and bright.

"You aren't untethered," Pael said. "I don't know that one of them murderous fucks would opine about failing to protect innocents. They seem too busy attaching limbs to walls and wiping out whole villages."

"I wish I understood them. Understood why they attack the way they do," Lin whispered.

"Instinct?" Pael asked, rubbing his eyes with his free hand and pinching the bridge of his nose.

"Tylle said they are focused only on violence and inflicting pain."

"In my long years, I've noticed something... and I don't know if it applies, but lumping together all *untethered*, or all Reds, or all noblemen, or all the working class, well, it doesn't do anyone any good. Sure, you can say all working-class wake before the sun, but that doesn't consider the midwife who alternates to watch the babies at night. And just 'cause something *can* apply as a broader statement, well, it would be a bit ridiculous to think they all wake up at the *same* time for the *same* reasons."

Lin nodded. "So even if untethered are all full of hate and fury, it might not be for the same reasons?"

Pael shrugged. "I just know you aren't like most Reds I've met or untethered I've seen."

"How so?"

"You're still alive." Pael cackled and dug a nail into his ear, twisting it back and forth before removing it and examining the wax buildup on its end.

"We'll see how long that lasts," Lin muttered.

"Same." With a slight nod of his chin, Pael looked away, his shoulders slumped forward. He scratched the hairs on his chin with his free hand and drew his wide hat lower onto his brow.

Stitching—Inlaying his arms had been about strengthening them, bones and muscles and all. And, even hours after finishing, they felt the same as they had before he began. Lin didn't *feel* stronger. But the magic was drawn across his flesh like shining tattoos, and there was no denying the thrum of energy coming from them.

Eventually, Lin let Nebra walk alongside the wagon alone and crawled onto the bench beside Pael. Light rain droplets fell for most of the night, each a miniature test of Lin's concentration as he traced the patterns along his legs. Over and over and over until his feet had numbed and his back ached. The entire process involved more movement than his arms had. The motion felt like rowing a landlocked boat. Even Pael, sitting not more than a foot from him, eventually faded from Lin's notice. Like a string drawn taut, the Inlay stiffened and shimmered into existence. Lin's breaths came and went quickly as if he'd been running the entire time, and there wasn't an inch of flesh not coated in sweat. Counting the Bludwieve, this was the fifth time he'd worked a Binding onto flesh, *into* his flesh. The muscles on his right leg tensed and pulsed. The cramp rolled through him and pushed back down to his foot. Then he repeated it all onto his left, without break.

The work passed in a hazy blur. He only came awake at a shake from Pael beside him. Gods, he was sore. Bones, jaw, limbs, chest. Everything ached.

"Probably best to clothe yourself," Pael said. His voice snapped Lin's focus outward to his surroundings. He'd worked in a daze, and his legs glowed with patterns of magic—straight down the center, like a map of his bones.

Sheets of rain bombarded them, and lightning danced like Bindings through the clouds. The wagon was stopped under a canopy as thin as Pael's hair that did nothing to stem the downpour. They hadn't outpaced the storm after all.

"Water," Lin whispered.

"Put on pants. Somethings wrong," Tylle said. She wore a thick, unadorned, black leather coat, two sizes too big for her, and with a hood that covered most of her face. Her boots were mud-caked, and she stood beside Pael. When she'd dressed and where she'd found the cloak was lost on Lin. He'd been too focused, and the looks on their faces at present worried him.

"Why'd we stop?" Lin asked.

"Shhh," Pael said. "You're talking too loud."

Was he? Lin worked his jaw and swallowed, throat sore. "Sorry," he said softer.

"Eat this. Drink this. And wait here." Tylle handed Lin two apples and a sour-smelling waterskin.

The world exploded with light. Whip-like Wefts tore into the wagon like a bolt of lightning crashing from the heavens. Lashing after lashing seemed to strike from above.

Pael's face lit with ethereal light, and Lin knocked the man over, tripping more than tackling. They rolled in the mud as more Wefts cut the air where the man had stood. The baby wailed, and Gwen shrieked within the wagon. Aemun launched out of the rear, sword drawn, swiveling. Each flash of light painted the rage and fury of his features.

Lin wiped a wet glob from his face, body heavier now that he was coated with mud. His tunic clung to him, and his small clothes plastered to him like he'd soiled himself. Everything hurt. And the assault didn't stop.

Lightning crashed in time with the closest flurry, and the horses, Ferrucium trained or not, spooked. They neighed and stamped, and the wagon groaned.

Lin pulled himself up, and Pael... Pael was gone. The old man had disappeared, and amid the downpour and darkness, he'd either blended in with the dark or dirt. Staggering to his full height, Lin watched numbly as Tylle matched the assailant blow for blow on top of the wagon. She moved slower than when she last fought, favoring her left side over her right.

"Tylle!" he screamed and limped to get a better angle.

She ignored him. Wefts and Weaves clashed and dissolved too quickly to track where one began and the other ended.

Lin focused and, arm growing icy cold, formed a Weft. It was faded and colored like dirty water and smelled like rusted iron. He aimed, loosing the sad Weft at the attacker's side. It found purchase, sparking against them before crumbling into brown flecks that faded in the rain.

Tylle stabbed forward, dagger in one hand, Wefts created and thrown with the other. But where she seemed slower, more cautious than Lin knew her to be at her best, the assailant was quick. The bursts of light from above made Dennick's pale face all the paler. Robed in heavy black clothes, he looked nothing short of the One Shadow. And he'd found them.

Lin circled around the back, blinking as the bright Bindings and rain stung his eyes. Aemun had disappeared into the wagon, likely to protect his child. Lin slung another Weft, as ruined looking as the first, at Dennick. The Nooseman didn't even react as it shattered against his shoulder.

Stilling his trembling hands seemed impossible, and the world pulsed purple around him. Tylle was forced back one step, then another, and finally, they were too far on the other side of the wagon top that Lin had to move again to see them.

"Stop!" he screamed. "Fight me. I'm the one you want!" He tried to make another Weft, but it flickered out as it formed, motes of ethereal light drifting away.

"Please!" Lin fell to his knees, and his leg cramped. He shouldn't have pushed himself like this. He should've known better. He crawled around the wagon, muck sliding between his fingers as he dragged himself. He'd failed Margaret. What would he do if he lost Tylle?

Even pulling the apples from the greedy grasp of mud proved hard, so Lin began biting into them where they rested. Grit crunched as he chewed, and the apples themselves were sour. As bitter as his failure.

Lin rolled onto his back and raised a hand.

Tylle and Dennick were gone. Bindings flashed from behind the wagon and tree it rested under. Their feet were visible, and Tylle had grown even slower. Every push from Dennick saw her give up more ground.

Lin willed his Weft to cut underneath the wagon, but as it sliced toward them, it faltered and dissipated into a trail of slow-dying sparks.

"Tylle!" Lin screamed again. "Aemun! Pael! Help her!" But he hadn't seen Pael since they were first attacked. He was alone, and Tylle would die because of his weakness.

Chapter Twenty-Three

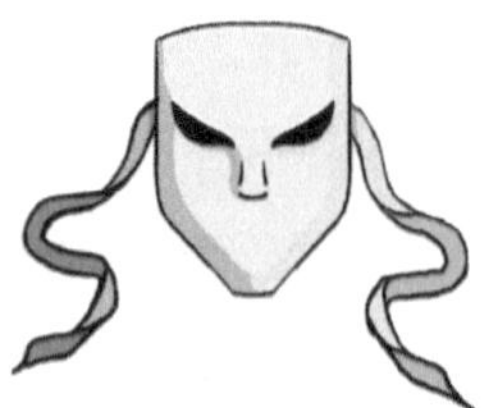

Blessings of Hate

Lin hated himself for being weak. He couldn't lift his exhausted limbs. His arms were coated in a layer of mud that obscured the Inlays along his flesh, but smears of light broke through bright in the darkness. Each time he tried to form a Weft, it looked more fragile than the one before. His chest was cold. How had he ever thought he'd be capable of saving the lives of those he cared for? Lin gritted his teeth and forced out a scream. Tylle was fighting injured because he hadn't been strong enough to stop Dennick at their last encounter.

All of this was because Lin hadn't stayed close when Margaret begged him to. What good were these One-loved Stitches if they didn't make him stronger?

Lin rolled onto his stomach, pulling himself along towards the wagon. His Bludwieve, a red stain against the muck, mocked him. Protect Aemun. Ensure he makes it to the Ferrucium. Who was he to protect anyone if these monsters were what constantly stood in his path?

Screams carried on the wind. Tylle howling. Lin's nails ached from the wet earth pressing underneath them. He could see her on one knee, weapon angled up. Dennick had formed a Binding Blade and swung it at her throat.

Lin screamed, willing his eyes to remain open. She didn't even look his way. Then, a flash of light and a crash of thunder. Lin had never seen so many untethered in one place other than Fallo. They glided like a raft on water, each marked differently. Six of them moved toward Tylle and the Nooseman.

"No!" Lin's scream tore from his throat with jagged nails, and he gagged as if the taste of mud and failure had been scraped from within him, thick on his tongue.

The fluid lethality that dripped from Dennick like poison on a blade was gone, replaced by furtive, quick motions. *Scared* motions. But Lin could understand why. Untethered were rushing Tylle and he en masse. Lin tried to drag himself up but slipped face down, and now his arms, which should have been iron-strong, felt like lead, useless to pull him any further through the mud.

"Tylle," he choked.

"She'll be alright," Pael's voice trembled from beside him. The old man shook as he gasped in raspy, uneven breaths. He was dark as night, coated in mud and soaked from the rain. Clumps hung to his scraggly beard, and his wide-brimmed hat looked like it might fold at the edges from the water pooling at its sides. "You'll be alright now. Drink and watch. This is why Erias wanted us to get Aemun to *them*."

Lin wiped his face and struggled against Pael's gentle touch. He pushed away the sour-smelling waterskin and raked the mud with his nails. "Help her!"

"I did all I could," Pael said. The old man pulled Lin, gentle grip freezing solid like winter had set, and embraced him. "Now watch."

Pael lifted Lin's chin and forced the mouth of a waterskin to his lips. The liquid burned. Warmth flared through his mouth, throat, and insides as it settled into him. He gagged, but after ten beats of his heart, the heat crept into the numbest parts of him. It hurt. A sharp, stinging pain. But he could feel them, and that's what mattered. With this, he could fight. But his limbs wouldn't listen to him.

"Pael," Lin choked out. Help her." From where he sat, cradled in Pael's arms, he watched as the untethered trapped the Nooseman. They moved in tandem, pressing Tylle away and taking her spot, surrounding the Nooseman like a pack of baying hounds might a fox.

And it was over. A blink and Dennick's figure flashed away in a flurry of Bindings. Wefts, Weaves, and those strange in-between ones Lin hadn't quite figured out how to form.

"What?" Lin forced out.

"Binders, like Tylle. Like the King's Noose, I reckon. Call them the Duke's Web if you want. But they have no formal name," Pael said, clutching Lin and rocking in the mud.

Tylle rose and eventually limped to where Lin sat.

"Tylle," Lin started.

"You're pale and trembling. You overused your *spul*," she said, speaking like she was chastising a child. She held her side and grimaced as she stared down at him.

"I was trying to save you."

"You were trying to go mad, and I didn't need saving. Your mission isn't to protect me. It was to get Aemun to them." Tylle jerked her chin at the group that approached and Aemun, who stood at the window to the back of the wagon, his child cradled tight to his chest.

"I'd never choose him over you," Lin said weakly.

Tylle grabbed his left hand, but instead of a gentle grasp, she squeezed and forced his ring finger out from the rest. "This says otherwise. You *must* take this seriously. If it comes to me or him, as long as you bear this, you have no choice."

Lin couldn't take his eyes off her. She was pale as a corpse.

"I... I'm sorry. I thought I lost you."

Tylle's jaw set, and she didn't reply, dropping his hand to the mud. Small wonder Lin wasn't sure if she felt any attraction to him, the way she acted. But how could she ask him to choose Aemun over her?

"Can he walk?" Of the untethered who had arrived, most seemed to fall back. But one, a woman barely shorter than Tylle and more muscular, stood beside the wagon. Her hair was shaved on the left side, with a lone, tight braid trailing down the right. She wore dark leather, and of the gathered untethered, she had the fewest visible Stitches.

Aemun appeared from the wagon, looked around, and cleared his throat. "He isn't needed moving forward. He's proven, more than once, that I can't trust my or my child's life to him. I'd feel far safer with the lot of you and those two."

Lin stared up at Aemun. The snake didn't even look down at him. "I was sent by Er—Grovetender to escort him to you and then to the Ferrucium. Not to fight, but to protect him."

Pael patted his shoulder and helped sit him up against the tree.

"And I don't want *your* protection. You Stitched your flesh seemingly without care for what the repercussions could be if we were attacked. Which we were. Knowing the King's Noose hunted us. You've shown a lack of foresight time after time, and I refuse to let everything I've risked my life for be thrown away by a careless fool!"

"Are you positive?" the woman asked, tone neutral.

"I am. Am I wrong in my claims?" Aemun jerked his chin at Tylle.

Tylle licked her lips and pressed a palm to a cut along her forearm. She stared at Lin silently. Then, she shook her head.

"If you... if you don't let me go, then what was the point? What was the point of any of this?" Lin knew his voice peaked. He tore at the ground until his fingers were raw. Roots and stones catching and cracking his nails. "What was the point?" he said softer, weaker.

"We need to go. Should we kill him to keep his tongue silent?"

Lin blinked. The words couldn't have been meant for him, but then why had Pael and Tylle moved ever so slightly away? Why had a separate woman, an untethered with wild Stitches across her face in uneven patterns, moved closer with an expression of pity and disgust?

"Perhaps," Aemun said.

"No. Lin doesn't deserve that. We will get word to Erias that he needs to be reclaimed. Lin, are you listening?" Tylle had moved between him and the woman. She snapped her fingers. "Rest. Recover your strength. Erias will uphold his end."

"Pael, take the wagon. Let me speak with him privately for a moment. Don't stray far, but give us space." Aemun knelt in front of Lin, and in moments, the wagon groaned away, the horse seemingly eager to get out from under the tree as the rain slowed. The untethered, the Duke's Web, moved with the wagon, though the wild-eyed woman didn't stray nearly as far.

"I told you, didn't I?" Aemun said in a hushed tone.

Lin tried to steady his breathing, but it felt like every time he sucked in a breath, it was leaden, airless. "Told me what?" Six, he sounded pathetic. He didn't even have enough energy to feel rage.

Aemun leaned in. "That there wouldn't be a place in the Ferrucium for you." Aemun's fingers brushed Lin's cheek, warm. Then he gripped, squeezing Lin's face like he were a dog. "I could never have respected you, even if you'd killed Tylle in Lyre. A man who quits his convictions over petty things like truth and honor has no place in the coming war."

"You can't!" Lin hissed between forced-shut lips.

"Stop me then," Aemun urged. "Hit me. Throw a Binding my way. Kill me." He released Lin's face, tossing his head back against the tree trunk.

Lin tried. No Weft formed, and he couldn't move enough to even lunge at the man.

"Good luck," Aemun said, smirking.

It didn't take long for the group to disappear entirely from Lin's view. He slumped against the tree, arms in his lap, fingertips throbbing. Nebra, bless her, had come to him at some point, waking him from the trance he'd fallen in. Her tail swished near his face, and he looked up at her, surprised to see her.

"You. You can go too," Lin whispered. Then, a sob racked him, and he pulled his knees up to his chest. He hadn't thought either Tylle or Pael would agree to leave him after everything they'd been through. But they had and hadn't looked back. All because he blasphemed. They wouldn't have abandoned him if he hadn't Stitched his flesh. But Tylle had been the one to teach him. It wasn't fair. He'd be reclaimed, whatever that meant. And Erias would... Erias *might* teach him how to remove the Stitches. Lin doubled over, leaning to the side, and vomited, then he curled into a ball near the base of the tree and convulsed until he passed out.

Songbirds woke him with the rising sun. Though the world was a mottled gray, the sky was a pale winter blue with a promise of warmth. Nebra grazed nearby, and ruts cut through the muddy path, revealing the route his allies had taken the night prior.

Using the tree, Lin got to his feet. He stretched and regretted it as his mud-laden underclothes chafed against his thighs. His wounds, caked in mud, felt better but still pulled painfully. His cheek throbbed where Erias had struck him, and his shoulder, where he'd been bitten in Lyre, felt stiff. He'd been in bad patches on escort missions before, but never like this. Never abandoned by allies. Lin cocked his head to the side as he considered Fallo. Aemun had left him then. But did he even consider Aemun an ally now? No. Not one single bit.

A survey of the area revealed mud-coated apples, one of which had been crushed underfoot, and Dennick. His dark robes were in tatters, his face a latticework of slashes. His nose was swollen and crooked, but despite all the injuries, his chest rose and fell slowly.

Lin looked around for a blade, but there was none. His had been in the back of the wagon, belt and sheath undone so he'd be more comfortable. He shambled over to him and knelt beside the man.

"You were used," Lin whispered.

"K… kill me."

"I will. But can you tell me something first?"

Dennick sucked in a wheezing breath. A bloody bubble formed on the exhale.

"Aemun. He sent for you, no?"

More heavy breaths. More pained grunts and wheezes but a stark lack of reply. Lin sat in silence, letting it seep into him until he eventually looked over at Dennick. He'd stopped breathing. Stopped fighting. It felt odd to look at what was left of the man's face and see traces of humanity there. Lin didn't know much about the King's Noose but doubted members had a family. Lin stripped the man. He'd wash the tattered robes when he could but slipped into them all the same. As caked in mud as he was, it didn't seem to matter that the strips of robes were heavy with blood and muck.

Moving Dennick wasn't an option, and he didn't have a way to make a pyre. So, he closed the Nooseman's eyes and prayed for him to the Six. Lin didn't know what to believe regarding the two religions, but he knew the Six had always been there for him when he needed them. He didn't plan to begin praying to

Velkath or his brothers soon, that was for sure. Since learning about that secret faith, his life had been pretty shit anyway.

Lin rummaged through his saddle pack, looking for anything he could eat that didn't need to be prepared. He was out of honeycaps, nuts, and dried meat. His waterskin was empty. But tucked at the bottom, resting just on top of a thin metal mask Lin was sure he hadn't had in the pack before, was a corpse-seed. The sweet juices exploded in his mouth, the smell not nearly as pungent as it had been the first time Lin had eaten one.

Tylle. She'd left the mask. The seed. She'd known Dennick was still there. But why? The answer was obvious. She had to have assumed this was somehow part of Aemun's eventual betrayal, part of a grand plan. *Or?* Or she just hadn't wanted to leave Lin to fend for himself in the state he was in but couldn't stay. Perhaps she had *wanted* to stay with him. Lin licked the sticky fluids from the corpse-seed off his hands and steadied himself against Nebra. Whatever it was, Lin couldn't turn back now. Wouldn't. Tylle needed him. *He* needed her. Aemun needed to die, even if he couldn't be the one to kill him.

Using Nebra as a big, slow-moving crutch, he followed the trail the wagon had left.

Chapter Twenty-Four

Blessings of Blood

Lin could tell he was only a hard day and a half's ride from the Ferrucium. But it would take him three long days at the pace he'd managed since leaving Dennick's corpse. Especially since Lin struggled to convince himself to leave the slow-moving creek Nebra had led him to. The water gently kissed his skin, soothing his sores in a way he hadn't felt since before Lyre.

"Think you'll be done soon?" a high-pitched woman's voice asked. It came from a thin tree branch that swayed feet above the water's surface. She was lithe-looking, and the branch looked far too slender to support even an acorn's weight, yet she lounged along it with barely a bend.

The creek, more a run-off from some water source better deserving the title, was surrounded by brush and stony outcrops, with only scarce, weak trees shading the leftmost side.

Lin froze, floating face up in the water, and stared at her. He'd seen her before.

She was covered head to toe in Stitches, the skin of her face crossed by uneven horizontal lines of bright magic. She was the one who had asked if he needed to be killed.

"I don't know," Lin said. He hadn't tried Binding since resting, but he felt like his spul had recovered enough to at least form a Weft if it came to that.

"You don't look like a Nooseman," she said whimsically. "Even if you took his mask and robes."

Lin dipped his chin underwater, then glanced to where Nebra grazed.

"I left it all in your pack. I'm no thief, after all. You don't smell like a Nooseman, either. Mint, cold, and rust. You smell like dust, travel, and dreams—nightmares even."

She dropped forward, catching the back of her knees on the branch and hanging upside down to stare at him. Her tunic and cloak shifted down, showing a stomach lined with more crooked Inlays. "Name is Denny. You?"

Luckily, the water wasn't crystalline, and Lin only needed to shift moderately to ensure he was modest. "Lindel."

"Lednil," she giggled, letting her fingertips skim the water. "Why are you following us?"

"I didn't think I was." He lied. Of course, he was following them, albeit far slower than he would've liked.

"You are. Carine, our boss, left you there at the tree. So... why are you following us?" Her tone had dropped, any hint of mirth gone as she repeated herself.

Her expression didn't match her tone, though, as a wide smile formed on her narrow face. The smile reflected on the water's surface, sending unease rippling through Lin like the rings formed every time Denny tapped the water.

"I don't trust Aemun to honor whatever agreement he's made with Grovetender."

"That is Grovetender's problem."

She wasn't wrong. But it didn't matter. "I didn't want to leave my two allies alone with him."

"A better reason. But you might give our movements away, limping along like a lame dog behind us."

Lin rose, feet digging into the silty bottom of the creek bed. "Aemun might've dismissed me, but I escorted him through my agreement with Grovetender. They may be partners, but one doesn't speak for the other."

"Best reason. I haven't told anyone else you were following, but I have to tell Carine. If she wants you put down, I'll be back." Denny righted herself on the branch and shook her head.

Lin hadn't noticed before, but he squinted and confirmed his suspicion. "You've Stitches in your eyes."

Denny nodded. "*Inlays*. And you have them in all the same old boring places. I'd hoped you might have some on your nethers, but oh well." She giggled and jumped from slim branch to branch as if they were stones, and she was crossing a stream.

Lin looked into the water, blushing despite the small clothes he'd kept on. *The Duke's Web.* Lin sank back into the water, the breeze raising prickles along his arms. He looked down at the man on the surface, who stared back. His cheek, swollen and split, was an irritated red. Physiker stitches would have kept it from scarring half as badly as it looked like it would. Lin never had a beard, unlike Denro's, but scraggly hair, as rough as the brush around the creek, covered the lower portion of his face and even some of his neck. He didn't look like himself. Didn't *feel* like himself. When it was all said and done, when he removed the Stitches from his flesh, would he even want to go back to his life? No. Not if Aemun was the one pulling strings in the Ferrucium. He wanted—needed to talk to Tylle. If her fight were over, her vengeance unobtainable, would she also want to run from it all? *With him?*

Drying off proved a bitter experience, the chill air reminding Lin that the north's cold crept behind him across Danica.

***

Lin rode easy at first, Nebra patient despite her desire to run harder. She tested him once or twice, and when it felt like he wouldn't rattle a lung loose or open a wound at the pace, he let her take complete control. He'd wrapped himself up in the tattered, washed Nooseman's robes and could only imagine how frightful he might look to any who saw him. When his body couldn't take more, he reigned her in and slumped forward in the saddle. They passed farmlands, split paths interrupting the way with signs pointing to small towns and smaller homesteads. But Lin stayed on the main road, pushing toward the Ferrucium. It wasn't visible yet, but its towers would be by the next day if he managed his pain and exhaustion to match Nebra's energy. He played with her mane, imagining the hanging net Tylle had formed in her horse's braid on the road to Wellgrove. It helped pass the time, looping and twisting her mane. It looked similar to what he had envisioned when he was done, even if it didn't hang entirely flat.

Lin found a wide, level stone that jutted at an angle to keep the wind at bay. It housed remnants of a fire pit but not enough markings to know if it had been Aemun's large group. He tended to Nebra and lay his back to the stone. The sky was cloudless, the moon a sliver, the stars swimming above like fireflies caught in rare volcanic glass.

"Camping here?"

Lin jolted up.

Denny stared down at him, crouched atop the jagged tip of the overhang Lin was sure was flat.

"If that's alright."

"It is. Carine told me that if you weren't at least a half day behind us, I should break your and your horse's legs."

Lin tensed and imagined how this fight might go. She had the high ground, but if she planned to assault him, she likely would've already.

"And if I'm closer than that?" Lin asked, shifting so he could roll away from the spot if he had to. He could try to crush the stone and use the resulting dust cloud to escape.

"Feed you." Denny dropped beside him in a blink, her Stitches bright in the half-enclosed space. She had a rucksack over one shoulder and shifted it to her front. The scent of spiced meat, not fresh but seasoned well enough that it didn't matter, drifted from the bag. "Hare. Some honeycaps. Mushroom stew, the stuff the old duddy gave you by the tree."

Old duddy? Surely, she meant Pael. Not killing him was expected. Feeding him? Lin shook his head, bewildered. He took the offered food and wasted no time tearing into the strips of meat. "Why?" he asked, between chews.

Denny shrugged, her big eyes wet and bright from the Stitches in them. The only other person he'd seen with Inlayed eyes was Dennick. Lin shuddered at the memory.

"How... how does that work? Isn't everything overly bright?"

"Nah," she said, not elaborating. "Once you eat, I'm supposed to see how useful you are in a fight."

"As in, test me?" Lin asked. He drank the stew down, barely having to chew at the gritty bits of mushroom. He cupped his hand under his chin, catching the stray brackish green droplets that slid from his mouth.

"Basically. Cause if you can't handle yourself in a fight." Denny imitated the sound of a breaking bone and mimed it as if her hands were doing the snapping.

"I could Stitch it."

"Stitch broken bone? You'd have better luck Stitching the moon to the heavens."

"I'd... find a way," Lin whispered. His limbs tingled warmly, similar to how it had felt when Pael force-fed him. "If you can Stitch your eyes..."

Her hand shot out so fast that it left a trail of light in the air from her Inlays. She held a finger to Lin's nose, pressing a dirt-lined nail into the tip. "Stop mentioning my eyes. Stop it. Carine told me to test you. She said, Denny, don't go overboard. Denny, don't hurt him if he's close. Denny, are you listening? Denny, do this, and you'll get first kill when we infiltrate the Ferrucium. But if you mention my eyes again, I will take yours and wear them as earrings. And deal with her disapproval later. Understand?"

Lin stared into her eyes, the pattern of Stitches like a forest of golden trees blooming from a center of milk-white. "I understand."

"Stand up," she said, a smile flicking onto her face. Lin realized when she smiled that the horizontal Stitches across her face became even less level. And when she'd looked deadly serious just now, frowning and angry, they'd been perfectly straight from cheekbone to cheekbone.

They stood across from each other, Lin wishing he had a bladed weapon but feeling like the food had already restored his spul as much as it could. Denny didn't have a weapon either; her hands were empty and held up in some fighting form Lin hadn't seen before. Her palms facing outward, her hips set back and low. Her cloak hid most of her body, but she wore similar leathers to Carine's underneath the fabric.

Denny's weight audibly shifted, gravel crunching underneath, oversized cloak rustling against its folds.

Lin smiled. She was capable of making sound, after all. Then, in a blur, her foot crunched into his shin, just below his knee, and pain blurred his vision. The impact slid his heels back, and dust scattered from his borrowed trousers.

"You'll want to block the next one better," Denny chided.

She was at his chest in a blink. Two strikes barely blocked by his forearms. Then she twirled away, cloak fluttering. Her smile was vicious and exaggerated her Stitches into sharp angles.

Lin charged forward and sent out two Weaves. One flew high towards her throat, the other lower towards her knees. Both were thick and band-like in an attempt to hinder her movement. But she clearly possessed the Sight and tracked the attacks. Then, he broke the Weaves, unraveling them with a thought. The shattered ethereal light scattered like golden dust.

Denny cackled and ducked away from the Weft Lin had formed amid the distraction.

"First Reds I ever fought didn't realize I had the Sight until they were dying," Denny whispered. "And really I didn't have the Sight until I started living." Like a snake's skin, Denny shed her cloak. Her Inlays crisscrossed along her arms, blurring and forming patterns in the air as she moved her hands.

"You think I rely on my Sight too much?" Lin asked. He cleared the space between them and caught one of her arms, yanking her toward him. Where his Stitched palm met her Inlayed flesh, their skin buzzed, the magic reacting as if he held a hornet's nest.

Denny shrugged and twisted.

Moving his feet in time with hers, Lin followed and pinned her arm against her back. Sweat stung his eyes, and he tried to wrap his other arm around her throat, but the back of her skull crunched into his nose. He wanted to pull her into him, but she threw her head back for a second blow. Lin released her with a shove and ducked. Her heel curved through the air in a kick that seemed impossible from the angle she stood at.

It was like catching a snake by its tail instead of the neck. Lin was likely to keep getting bit.

Lin exhaled and spat out the blood he tasted. "I didn't think we were trying to hurt each other," he called.

Denny touched the back of her head and frowned. "Your face isn't as soft as it looks."

Lin circled her, arms up. A seed of doubt grew inside him. What if he'd done his own Inlays poorly? And that was why he was so outmatched? He didn't feel any different, any stronger.

Twin Wefts slashed through the air, cruelly sharp. More and more flew at him, each set growing slightly darker than the last. Lin ducked, broke apart the closest set, and tripped, causing the third pair to skim his shoulder.

Not moving felt like the best option, and the stars spun overhead. The back of Lin's head throbbed. He must've struck it on the ground when he tripped. He knew he wasn't as skilled a fighter as Tylle. But she moved gracefully, and her Inlays seemed to compensate wherever her martial prowess failed. Denny was even more capable. More explosively violent. Lin gritted his teeth and pushed himself up.

"You aren't in tune with the changes you've made to your body," Denny said. Her chest heaved, and she shifted around him like a predator would wounded prey. "But you've got some skill."

And? And Denny was an excellent fighter. But her Binding skills didn't seem creative or well-made. Sure, she crafted several Wefts in a flash, sharp as any he'd seen, sharper even, but that was it. She'd laughed at his unusual use of Bindings, thinking he had done it when he realized she had the Sight.

Lin stood and studied Denny.

She'd approached silently and moved her hands through that same pattern with such speed that the Inlays on her flesh created a ring of concentric circular trails in the air.

Lin wiped his mouth with his hand and nodded at her. He rushed forward, sending a bright gold latticed Binding that stretched wide. It was like a blanket of crisscrossed Weaves.

Denny's eyes widened, and she rushed toward the net-shaped Binding.

Lin prepared a Weft, thinking she meant to leap over the net, but Denny charged headfirst. She pressed her hands into the openings and pulled at the disparate threads. It felt like someone was pulling Lin's arms, not painfully, but to get his attention.

That's new. Lin frowned and steeled himself, pulling his arms back and resisting the phantom force.

Denny struggled, pushing deeper as the magic wrapped around her. The Weaves were flexible, not shattering or unraveling. Then, her face was pressed into the net, and she fell to the ground, straining the entire way down.

Lin stumbled over to her and stared down at the wild-eyed woman. "You're better than me," Lin admitted. "I need to learn from this. I *will* learn from this."

"Why... why won't it break?" she hissed. Watching her struggle sent a pang of guilt coursing through Lin's chest. As skilled as she was, powerful as she seemed, she couldn't free herself of the clinging magic.

"Does this mean you won't be breaking my legs?" Lin asked.

Denny giggled, the mirth turning into a cackle after a moment. "No. I won't be. But death is never far from those close to me."

"Right." Lin hesitated to drop the magic. "But you won't be killing me... today, right?"

Her smile fell away with her laughter, but her eyes twinkled with the promise of mischief, and she nodded. "The Red might want you sent away, but I think Carine would be happy to have you join us."

"Join? As in permanently?"

Denny shrugged as the net dissolved. "As permanent as any of the rest of us are."

Chapter Twenty-Five

Burning Hope

When Lin woke, he looked for any sign of Denny. She'd left before Lin fell asleep with the promise that she'd return with any final requirements or suggestions from Carine. Before her departure, they'd spoken of small things like where she was from and her favorite memories. Most of which involved killing Reds. A point Lin didn't love. But Denny insisted it was water under the bridge and that she had absolutely no intention of murdering anyone else once the coup had finished. Lin had slept worse than usual, and he was confident it was her fault. That or the mushroom stew he'd consumed, which had certainly warmed his innards but made his guts queasy.

With no sign of her, he packed up and took to the road with Nebra. It wouldn't be long before he'd see the red stone Ferrucium towers tickling the sky. He'd put a salve on his shoulder where Denny's Weft had nicked him, but riding made the fabric of his cloak pull uncomfortably. If it weren't so cold, he'd have gone topless to let the wound heal unperturbed.

He kept thinking back to what Denny had said. Joining the Duke's Web hadn't even crossed his mind. But odds were, it had been Tylle's. Or better odds were that she was already a member. What did that mean for her plans after the coup? And all of that was based on the idea that Aemun would hold his end of the bargain, whatever that was, and not betray Erias somehow. Would Lin, once it was all said and done, belong anywhere?

Confusion and then regret flashed through him like Wefts slicing flesh. Denro had always made him feel like he belonged. And what would his mentor think if he saw him now? Lin hadn't recognized himself looking into his murky reflection on the creek. Denro, a Ferrucium soldier to his core with the Sight, would attack him immediately. If Denro were at the Ferrucium hold, he'd stand against the intruders and likely die for his efforts. The soldiers, even the Enforcers, weren't trained in a way capable of matching the untamed ferocity of Carine's group. And that made Lin consider Tylle's version of history all the more plausible. Why wouldn't the Ferrucium want its soldiers to be as capable as possible? As skilled as the King's guard or the brutal monsters that were actually untethered. To keep them under control. To be able to put their polished boots on the unwashed necks of the common person any chance they got.

Lin swallowed the lump in his throat. He was culpable. He'd killed untethered in the name of the Ferrucium. But if the unrestrained Bindings— Wievings— caused untethering, wouldn't the control be justified? Fallo had been a massacre.

Off to the side of the road, whimpers caught Lin's attention, barely audible over the sound of Nebra's hooves and the wind.

He slowed. Bandits weren't likely this close to the Ferrucium hold, but a random person whining in the brush was even less likely. But there she was. *Gwen*. Huddled to herself like she was surrounded by wolves that might snap at her every move.

"Gwen?" Lin dismounted and rushed to her. Her pale skin was free of wounds, her eyes wet and red and overflowing with tears. If she heard him, she ignored him. Rocking, she clutched scraped knees to her chest. "Gwen?"

Gwen blinked, looked up at him, and collapsed into his arms. He'd expected her to pull away or flee at the sight of him, robed like a Nooseman as he was. That and the fact they'd barely spoken, much of the time spent together. A polite word here or there. A glance.

Lin squeezed her shoulders. "What happened? Where is the baby? Where is Aemun?"

She squirmed in his arms as if her flesh were covered in ants, and her whimpers turned into deep, shaking sobs. Aemun had said he wanted to see her treated, see her mind eased. Once again proving he ran from problems more than he solved them.

"I'm sorry. H-h-he said I couldn't be trusted. Said I c-c-couldn't help Azhalia. She wouldn't make it without me."

Lin stared at her, at the pain in her eyes. Now that he heard her speak more, she couldn't have been older than eighteen passings. And she'd been scooped from whatever town, likely Riversbend, to aid Aemun, only to be left on the side of the road like a lamed horse.

"Okay. It'll be okay. I saw some smokestacks climbing up earlier. We can get you some food and water."

"I..." She clutched at him tighter. "I told him I could be. Told him I was worth taking."

"You don't have to explain." Lin tried to ease her grip, but the more he pulled away, the tighter she squeezed. Sobs like gasped breaths tickled his ear. If she had been like this constantly since they'd separated, it was no wonder Aemun left her at the side of the road, as cruel as he had proven himself capable of being.

"I'm sorry. I'm so, so sorry." She pulled one arm into herself and fiddled with Lin's robes, cold fingertips tracing his ribs. Her lips brushed his neck.

The hair on the back of Lin's neck rose, and he pushed her back as hard as he could. The nails of one of her hands raked a gouge along his neck, and her sobs turned into furious screams. Lin pressed a hand to his stomach, rising and stepping back. He pulled it away and looked at the stain of blood on his fingertips.

The dagger hadn't gone deep, a flesh wound if not slightly worse, but she'd stabbed him. "You stabbed me," he said, still looking at his blood in awe.

"Lord Aemun said—"

"Oh, he's a *Lord* now, is he?" Lin snapped.

She cowered back, dragging herself away and brandishing the little dagger, tip smeared red as if it might stop Lin if he felt like ending her pathetic life. "He said if I killed you, I'd be worthy. He said to watch for you and slow you and..."

Lin felt a rage begin churning in his chest, bubbling out of him like over-boiled water. "You idiot. After everything you've heard and seen and *felt*, do you think anything that man wants is worth doing? He killed Azhalia's mother. He left me for dead. He…" Lin sucked in a deep breath, realizing how loud he was being. Realizing he was admonishing himself as much as her.

"He had to do all of that. He swore. He's a good man. He cared for me until I stopped caring for the child. I c-couldn't. Nightmares haunted me. They still do. Of people dying so violently. I'm sorry." The last word dragged out of her the way a hungry dog might plead for food. He had intended to let her ride Nebra to the nearest village or town but that urge to aid her was gone now.

"If you believe all that to be true, rare Ferrucium children can sell the golden silk they spin for fortunes. Imagine how wealthy you might've been if you simply stole the child."

Lin left her, sobbing feet from where she'd originally sat. His side ached, but his neck stung worse, and mentally, he added the wounds to his running list of reasons why Aemun had to die. He'd convinced himself. Tylle didn't trust him. Carine seemed to have her doubts based on the tidbits Denny had shared. All he had to do was find a way to circumvent his Uethe, or more likely, be there when Aemun proved without a doubt his betrayal. Lin swallowed. Wasn't that a clear sign that Aemun did plan to betray them, trying to remove Lin permanently from the picture? It also could have been a simple ploy to rid himself of Gwen. Covering two options with one choice seemed something the man might smile at himself for.

***

The sun was setting on the horizon. Striated clouds hung low as if a giant had scratched through the heavens, disturbing the serene sky. The wounded, irritated red sky blended with the dark lavender fields of wildflowers to the west, stretching to the far hills. Soon enough, farmland would occupy the last leg of the journey to the Ferrucium hold. By now, Lin had expected to see the tower tips, but his pace had been too slow. If he rode through the night, which he planned to do, he'd see the sun impaled on the distant towers come morning.

Lin approached a crossroad and spotted Denny as if she had appeared from thin air. Sweat beaded her brow, and the manic countenance he'd grown accustomed to seeing was flat, even dour, making her stitches a straight line across her face.

"You kill her?" Denny asked.

Lin slowed Nebra, eyeing Denny's rucksack and wondering if she'd brought anything for him tonight. So, she'd known Gwen had been left behind as a trap for him. "Considered it. She's just a silly girl, fooled by a cruel man."

"Moon-touched if you ask me," Denny said, which seemed odd coming from someone who acted so erratic most of the time. But you didn't ask me." She shrugged. Denny looked tinier than usual while Lin sat atop Nebra. "Had to let it happen. Carine says Aemun won't accept you back under any circumstance. He says he knows something of "the old ways" and that bonds that shouldn't be broken might be if you rejoin as you were."

"Then I'll be a shadow, following until needed."

Denny looked up at him and shook her head. "Not a light in existence that might make a shadow as deep and dark as you."

Lin frowned at that. Occasionally, she said odd things that made his skin crawl and his teeth ache.

"But," she said slowly, "coming back as something different is good. Necessary even." She slipped to his side and pulled Dennick's mask from his bag, lifting it into the air, letting the sagging sun reflect on the hard edge of the metal.

"I can't pass as a Nooseman."

"You wouldn't even try?" Denny tilted the mask to the side and placed it over her face. "Do I not look like a Nooseman?"

She did. Six she *did*.

"Aemun will recognize me. Or, at the very least, he will think it odd that a Nooseman shadows him into the Ferrucium."

"Would it be odd? Carine says he called down the last few. Makes me wonder how he had that sort of pull. What sweet whispers left his lips to bring them from Ladrica? His lips do look like they'd make sweet things— promises, kisses, poison."

"Poison is right. But there is a chance, slim as it is, that he won't betray Erias."

Denny stopped walking and handed the thin mask to him. She stared up at him with those big, bright eyes of hers. "You look like your lips might make sweet things, too, if given the chance."

Lin's cheeks grew warm, and he pulled the mask to his face to conceal the flush he was sure he had. Denny was wild, smelling like evergreen trees, silt, and ash all at once. He hadn't thought of her as anything but a soldier.

"You aren't far. We made camp underneath the thinnest, tallest tree in the area. If you rode your horse hard for the next stretch, you'd catch up before we left. But we haven't been resting long."

Lin thought he knew precisely which tree she meant. If it were, he'd dreamt of climbing it ever since spotting it in his youth.

"Is the baby alright?"

"As alright as a motherless child might be. Prish, one of ours, offered her breast to it if only to have its wailing quieted. I didn't even know Prish had a wee one, but apparently, she does. She's always out and about for stints at a time, though not surprising. It could be Jun's the way those two eye-fuck each other all the time. I'm rambling, sorry, just not ready to run back."

Lin frowned at that and glanced back along the path they'd come. If that were the case, did that mean Gwen had a baby of her own as well?

"Did you say run back?"

"Don't see a horse, do you?" Denny squinted at him. The Stitches across her face skewed and stretched as she smiled.

"This might be a weird question, but can you feel your Stitches? The Inlays, I mean. Like the patterned ones along your arms and legs." He kept the mask close to his face, looking into her eyes and looking away just as quickly in case she assumed he'd meant the Stitches in them. Not that he wasn't curious about them, too.

"We've all talked about it in one way or another. Hugo says his Stitches feel like a thin, soft, and gentle layer of cloth. Prish doesn't speak. Can't actually.

And when she signs, it's never about her feelings. Jun mentioned his Inlays felt like a too-close shave. Mine? They feel like frozen needles. I can't feel the area, but I know the magic's sticking into me. And I can tell there is an absence of warmth. You asking 'cause yours hurt or something?"

Lin felt them hum like strings pulled tightly when he touched them, but he didn't feel *them*. "No. Not painful. When I touch them, I feel the hum of Bindings like I would when forming them. But I don't feel any stronger, faster, nothing like that. If I didn't have the Sight, it would be possible to forget I had them at all."

Denny cackled, high, and hitched. "You think you'd keep up with me if you didn't have those. You think you'd be able to take a single punch?"

He'd taken plenty of blows from larger people long before he'd marked his flesh. Then he thought back to the overwhelming force of the untethered's kicks in Fallo. Bone-rattling. "Maybe," he said softly.

"Let me see your arm," Denny said.

Lin obliged, sliding the robe's sleeves up and revealing the stretch of glowing patterns along his bicep down to his wrist.

Denny slid her fingertips along the length of the markings, her calloused hands rough. "The patterns tell a lot. The scars even more." Lin was doubly glad for the mask and cleared his throat. "They seem normal to me. I'd wager you need to get accustomed to them. Loosen your muscles, and train with the changes. It's like picking up a weapon you've no experience in. Holding it is easy for most. Using it harder. Using it well, impossible for some."

He doubted he'd have the Inlays long enough to master the differences in his body that came with them. But he'd accepted that the magic was necessary if he were to see his path to the end. And if Erias was already helping him rid himself of the ones Tylle made to mend his flesh, removing the others should be easy enough.

"Makes sense," Lin said.

Denny held his arm, fingertips brushing the pattern. "I... I really don't trust him. Aemun, I mean."

"Me either." Lin pulled his arm back and let the mask fall from his face. "But Grovetender has a plan, right?"

"Even if he didn't. Carine would. Gods only know where we'd be without her." Denny stretched, her sleeves brushing the dirt as she doubled over.

"Gods. Velkath and his kin?"

Denny looked up and bared her teeth. "No. I prefer my gods faceless. That way, when I disappoint them, I know they can't look upset."

Before Lin could reply, she was off. Denny didn't run quite as fast as Nebra at full sprint, but she was silent, her steps only on the driest bits of the road, making a soft sound and a puff of dirt. Once she was gone from view, Lin slid the cold metal mask fully onto his face. The slits, thin as they were, still gave him an unhindered view of the stretch ahead of him. Everything below his torso was visible, but the heavens were blocked from his vision entirely. It was as if the one who'd made the mask hadn't wanted the King's Noose to see the stars. To see the sun. Or have a single view capable of making them dream.

Chapter Twenty-Six

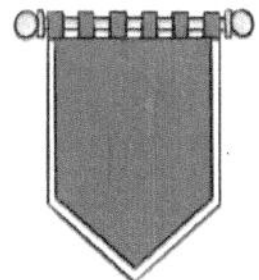

Burning Bone

Lin rested on a thick branch high above the camp. Denny had been right. He'd run Nebra hard until he saw the smoke, then let her loose. He spent more time telling her goodbye than he'd admit to anyone other than perhaps Denro. But they weren't far from the Ferrucium hold, and Nebra would be unmistakable. Even if the mask Lin wore fooled anyone else.

What he hadn't expected was his traitorous horse trotting into the camp not long after he'd released her. At least he'd removed her saddle and bags, but now she grazed down there with the rest of them.

Hopefully, they'd all think Lin was dead. Save, of course, Denny and Carine. Lin tried to spot the two of them, but the branches and other, shorter trees obstructed much of his view.

Climbing the tree had been easy, shambling from the lower branches of shorter trees further away from them. Lin imagined he moved as swift and silent as Denny the day she'd left the creek, but he knew he made more noise than she likely ever would. The hilly fields and brush of the last few days were separated from the farmlands by this pocket of trees, larger and sturdier than any others Lin had seen on his travels.

From his vantage point, Lin stared at the tips of the Ferrucium's towers. Aemun and the group would be at the gates come this hour tomorrow. And then, one way or another, this journey would be at its end. Either Aemun would reveal his betrayal, whatever plans he's had in place, or the coup would happen without fail.

A strong breeze swayed the treetops, setting the broad leaves rustling like sheets cast off by a passionate lover. Lin pulled the tattered robe tighter around himself and wondered about the man it had belonged to. Dennick had seemed like a murderous bastard, to be sure, but hadn't Lin proved himself to be the same? It was easy to imagine himself in a similar place. In fact, if Lin squinted, being a member of the King's Noose didn't seem so different from being a Ferrucium soldier. Aside from the Noosemen being allowed, encouraged even, to work Fell-Bindings into their flesh. Dennick had likely been taken by an Evaluator, made to feel at home in the Ferrucium hold, then taken again and made to break himself to fit into another mold. But wasn't that what Lin was doing? Breaking himself, piece by piece, belief by belief, to fit into the thing he needed to be to survive this? Or perhaps he wasn't breaking so much as shaping. Tylle had called him flexible of mind, after all.

Lin absently stroked his left hand, listening as the voices carried up from the camp below. A fire, not large enough for all of them, sent shadows dancing through the limbs. Then, the baby cried. It started low, rising to a wail that crested and crashed against the surrounding copse. As awful as it was to hear, he'd missed it. Not the way he missed Denro, not the way he longed for Tylle's company, but Azhalia had become a comfort to him. And his chest was cooler, numb, for not having her pressed against it.

The sun hadn't broken the horizon when the camp broke underneath him. If anyone was set to scout, they didn't notice him or make it known they had. But he stayed to the darker parts of the trees and kept the black robes as tight around him as possible.

Lin stopped at the edge of the forest, where the trees thinned as much as Pael's hairline. Beyond that point, he'd be exposed to the early morning light. Exposed to the group. He shuddered, thinking about what happened to an actual Nooseman when they set upon him. His heart caught as he spotted Tylle. He leaned forward. She rode Nebra. His smile recoiled as the cold metal of the mask against his mouth surprised him.

The group moved at a sluggish pace, except for one person who might've been Denny, who went running ahead. A second person split from the group and headed more easterly. Based on the Stitches visible, it wasn't Aemun or Carine, and Pael was likely still driving the wagon forward.

Lin pulled the mask from his face and held it, staring at the flat metal. The slit for the mouth had built moisture around the edges. Had the masks been made to be reflections of the Six Faceless Weavers? If so, had Carine's group killed a God? Not likely. Dennick, for all his prowess, seemed to be a man. A monstrous man, but a man all the same.

And now Lin wore his shed face. Their positions could have been swapped easily enough. If Lin had been taken as a child a second time.

Once the group had become little more than specks, Lin dropped from the tree. This obviously wasn't how he'd planned to return to the Ferrucium, but a piece of him was glad to be headed back. It'd been too long. But even as he thought about returning, fear nestled into him like one of the thinner tree's many needled leaves. He wouldn't belong. He'd never belong again, not until he removed the Inlays.

Lin touched the oldest Stitches, the ones Tylle had done to fix his broken fingers. Standing in the shade of the copse, he felt like a tree himself. A stunted one with gnarled roots anchoring him firmly in place, fighting to feel the light but unable to break out. He placed the mask back on, metal cold against his cheeks. Straps of leather cord dug uncomfortably into his flesh where ear met scalp.

Then Lin ran. Even riding Nebra, he'd never felt so free, wind sneaking in through the slits of the mask and stinging his eyes. The farmlands opened up to him, and rather than run along the road and risk being spotted, he darted into the fields.

Harvest had already happened, leaving the stretches of soil barren save for the occasional worker plowing. When they spotted Lin, they more often than not turned away, marking the sign of the Six, as if he were the One themself, come to whisper their names.

Lin had doubted that the Inlays did anything. But after vaulting up the trees in the night and now running without stopping for the better part of the morning, he believed in them. And it seemed Denny had been right. The more he ran, the more he stretched his body and mind, the more comfortable he felt moving in general. He should have been sore, exhausted from all the travels up until this point, but somehow, he wasn't. If anything, when he'd rested high in the boughs of the tree, he'd felt refreshed.

It was like his Stitches had been threads of light, far heavier than they had any right to be, but now his body had started adapting.

Lin ran through the day, only stopping twice. Once to drink from his waterskin and eat from the rations Denny had last given him and again to let the wagon get far enough ahead of him that he wouldn't be spotted. The last stretch would be the hardest to avoid being seen, but thankfully, they reached the open fields that surrounded the red Ferrucium walls at nightfall.

Lin stared up at the sky, a soft curse escaping him. He licked his lips; they were dry, and he felt a shallow split had formed on his bottom lip. Cloudless. Moonless. The sky was a vast ocean, lit by enough stars to make a man think he'd seen them all. The scent of salt hung heavy on the air, the breeze rolling off the southeast expanse of water that Lin could never remember the name of.

Binders didn't do well with open water. Superstitions were passed down from senior soldiers mostly, but Lin had never pressed his luck. That and the fact that only the Weavers were even allowed to own a ship. Not even small fishing vessels were allowed which meant any fishing was done off the coast. But now, knowing about the dukes, Lin was sure they'd have a ship or two secreted away somewhere. Odds were, it was all just another way of keeping Danicans shackled. Lin frowned. After all, if the sea was so terrible, why'd the Ferrucium hold been erected near a cliffside overlooking a cove?

Bush fronds tickled his arms, and the cold scent of summer's rotting corpse hung in the air. Ahead, the group pushed forward.

If there were to be a betrayal, it would likely happen just inside the imposing walls. Walls that, while not as tall as the towers, made nearly every other building out across Danica appear tiny by comparison. Red slabs of stone that hinted at the bloodshed that might occur within. Just through the gate, the path would open into a square overlooked by high walls perfect for archers to rain death down from.

Lin judged the distance, a thought dawning on him. He'd been going about this all wrong, and the sudden realization felt like a stone crushing down on his shoulders. He'd thought following them was the right choice, seeing as he'd needed to catch up. But slipping in first, ensuring there wasn't a trap laid, would be best. Their pace, while not leisurely, was stealthy. If sentries watched the road, the group shouldn't appear suspicious.

To Lin, the world was a blur as he sprinted, eating at the space between him and the towering walls of the outer hold. He hadn't considered what he'd do once he got there, but as the wall came closer, looming, it clicked. A macabre image of Fallo and the limbs and bodies stitched to the buildings flashed through his mind. Lin would use Wefts to climb. He just needed the magic to hold when it stabbed into the stone.

Lin slowed only enough not to break his bones if his plan didn't work. He'd gone wide, around to the southeastern side of the walls so that he didn't risk crossing in front of the group or where any watchers might be looking. And he leaped. Stone met foot, neither giving way, and then he sprang upward. Muscles ached, bones throbbed, but he flew. He formed a small, thick Weft in his hand, imagining a climbing piton. It bit into the crevice between stones and held. He hung there, breaths coming heavy. Then proceeded up. Binding after Binding bit into the outer face of the wall, silent despite the force necessary to press the magic into the wall. It was similar in execution to the Blade he'd been able to form.

He swung, stabbed, swung, and stabbed until he hung so high that falling meant more than breaking bones.

At its core, Lin felt like he understood what was happening. Magic was woven into reality. Reality was bound to his intention. Soldiers were taught Wefts and Weaves. And warned of Needles and Fell-Bindings. But the world was so, so much wider. Blades and Nets and Snares and now tools to climb—the Binding he stabbed shattered against the rock, exploding into bright motes that stung his eyes from the proximity.

Lin hung by one arm. He wasn't far from the top. Another Binding or two at most. He didn't look over his shoulder or down. The inside of the mask had grown damp from his breath. His nose rubbed against the flat of it. A wry chuckle slipped from him. By the time he took the One-loved thing off, he might look like Lyre's Alderman. He steeled himself. Now wasn't the time. He swung up, forming the Binding and stabbing in one motion. The magic sank in slowly, struggling to anchor. Lin wasn't sure why, but the sensation reminded him of Erias's ring, of those strange doors.

Bound metal. Could the heights of the walls be enforced with the same properties? Possibly. But the stonework didn't look different. And Lin had never known stone that a Weft or other Binding wouldn't bite into.

Lin braced his legs against the wall and lunged up. If the stabbing hadn't caught anyone's attention, his crashing over the lip of the wall in a tumble certainly should've. He came to his feet as swiftly as he could, and the sound of boots on stone and whispers confirmed he wasn't alone. A pair of guards, one holding a lantern and the other a crossbow, stared at him from mere steps away.

"Wasn't sure when you'd get here."

Lin cursed. He'd hoped to avoid hurting any of his brothers. But they'd *expected* him? Had probably watched him climbing the walls and waited with weapons and—

"Preparations are ready for Lord Aemun's arrival. The path is clear for you to get to the Chamber of Judgement unbothered. And, of course, if you have to kill any besides the Weavers, Lord Aemun understands."

Lin stared at them flatly, and when he didn't say anything, the younger-looking of the two added, "Not that we presume to tell a Nooseman how to go about a job."

"Right," the other said with a nod. When Lin still didn't speak, he furrowed his brow. "Maybe he doesn't understand us?" he said softer.

Lin swallowed and raced to catch up with what was happening. Of course, they thought he was a Nooseman, dressed the way he was. But these soldiers knew Aemun's plan. *One* of Aemun's plans. Did that mean there was an actual member of the King's Noose coming? *Or already here?*

"Oonderstand." Lin stretched the words the way he'd heard the Noosemen speak. Hopefully, these two had the same lack of experience concerning the King's Noose that Lin had once had.

"Gives me the creeps," the man holding the crossbow whispered. He smiled, as genuine as Lin's forced accent.

"Creeps?" Lin asked, cocking his head to the side.

There'd likely never been a man gone paler in such a short breath. Even the warm flush of the oil lamp couldn't add color to his cheeks.

Lin turned, smiling invisibly under the mask. His path forward seemed clear enough. Get to the Chamber of Judgement, the very place he'd planned to take Tylle back in Lyre when he thought her the murderer. An idea, like a nagging splinter under a nail, stuck into him. What if... what if the Weavers knew of a way to remove his Stitches? What if saving them allowed him to save himself? Tylle would never speak to him again. His Bludwieve and Uethe might not even allow it if it meant ruining Erias and Aemun's plan. But somehow, Aemun had already gotten to some of the soldiers. *Lord Aemun.* A Ladrican title. Danica had no lords.

"Oh, and avoid the main route if possible."

Avoiding the main route meant staying on the outer stretch, circumventing the expanse that stretched between the walls of the outer hold and those of the inner hold. Lin slowed, straining his vision to scan the breadth of the wall. Soldiers, many of them, with crossbows and hooded lanterns. It *was* a trap. Lin slowed and then turned, returning to the men.

"Yes?"

"Your preparations?" Speaking stilted and stretching out his words proved more challenging than Lin expected, but he pushed through it.

"Our preparations?" the pale guard asked. His thin lips pressed into a nervous line.

"He means are we ready. Course we are. Lord Aemun will be pressing through. We make sure no unwelcomed continue with him. Then our lot press in behind and aid in the Chamber of Judgement. Some may have lost their way, sir, but Lord Aemun has his faithful who will see King Lodram's vision returned two-fold to the Ferrucium."

Lin slowed his breaths. *Unwelcomed. Vision.* There was a chance Aemun lied to these men like he claimed to have lied to the Noosemen, but Lin had no room left in his heart for uncertainty. At every turn, vengeance and justice slipped through his fingers like spilled blood, and he was sick of letting platitudes and lies stem the bleeding. Aemun may not be lying to Erias and Carine and Tylle and Lin, but he was a liar. *And he couldn't be trusted.* Did this not count as betrayal?

When Lin didn't reply, both men shifted. "Not that we think you need the aid. Climbed a whole damned wall alone. Can take care of some threadbare remnants."

Lin heard what the man *wasn't* saying. He thought Lin was a monster.

And Lin had to agree as he slit both guards' throats in one swift, effortless motion with conjured Wefts. Whatever Aemun's plans entailed, it wouldn't— couldn't— involve any of the soldiers lining the walls.

Chapter Twenty-Seven

Burning Hate

Thirty. That's how many lives were snuffed out because of Aemun's treachery. Moreso, if Lin considered the lives taken on the road to reach this point. If he let his mind drift to Margie. Gwen, if she hadn't survived. Lin had left the outer gates open, swooping from shadow to shadow like a hawk diving the cliffs to catch fish. The soldiers, those who saw him, didn't react until it was too late—until golden Wefts splashed crimson.

By the time Lin had cleared the parapets lining this outer wall, a storm cloud had amassed off the sea. The breeze rushed from the swelling clouds as if chased and uncaring of the cliff that should have prevented its ascent. Perhaps Lin could be like the breeze—invisible, constant, and cold.

Lin blinked away tears. These men and women, perhaps, didn't deserve their fate. But... maybe Lin hadn't deserved the fate foisted onto him either. Maybe fate was a fickle thing no better than the breeze.

The sound of a wagon wheel on a cobbled stone pulled Lin from himself, from the roiling twist of storm clouds within his mind.

Lin stared over the edge. He'd left several of the hooded lanterns alight around the wall, but he pressed into shadows now. Watching for Aemun's reaction.

Pael drove the horse forward, wide hat hiding his face from view. A woman, side of her head shaved, sat beside him. Carine. Tylle rode atop Nebra, strides abreast, clothed fully so that not a single Stitch glowed in the darkness. Denny was nowhere to be seen, but the wagon was flanked by several others. A man larger than most Lin had seen, neck as broad as his huge biceps. And lined in horizontal Stitches that flexed at every movement. A shirtless man flanked opposite of him, all corded muscle and sparse Inlays lining his flesh. He was darker skinned, bald, and moved like Denny. Which left Denny and the silent one missing. Prish. They could be in the wagon.

Lin wanted so badly to rush down there and speak with them. But rushing there wouldn't do anything for him. He needed Aemun to reveal his entire hand. And that seemed like it would take place inside. So, he dropped from the outer hold's walls and moved between the vendor stalls that lined the marketplace housed within. During the day, trade would take place inside these walls, markets, and occasional festivals for the people who tilled the farmlands. Festivals Ferrucium soldiers were only meant to observe, not attend.

Shops and stalls gave way to homes, some lit by lamplight from within despite the late hour, some with the unsettling glow of Wanderer's Ore. And then he was to the inner hold. These walls were scalable, but doing so wouldn't get him near the Chambers of Judgement. And he hadn't spotted any guards stationed on the parapets that wrapped the towers. Only untethered would be mindlessly foolish or violent enough to attack the Ferrucium head-on, and even then, they'd never moved in numbers enough to do so without being slaughtered.

Lin slinked into the torch-lit halls of the inner hold. Aemun might grow suspicious if he didn't see his planted soldiers, but surely, he wouldn't show his hand prematurely to Carine and her group.

He passed the kitchens. The halls of the inner hold were more familiar than anywhere else to him. Memories of running through them with other recruits. Getting chastised. Doing it again, then being beaten. Every doorway he passed brought back long days and hot nights. Poor food and poorer companions. The training yard was out the hall to his right. And the scent of Denro flooded him. Of his mentor's alcohol-tinged breath, the faint smell of burning leaves, the oil he slicked his hair with. Six, he hoped Denro wasn't here.

Then, he was at the Chamber of Judgement, a room where crimes were weighed, lives were taken, and decisions were made by the three Weavers, the council that ran the Ferrucium according to King Lodram's wishes.

The doors loomed large—larger than they even had when Lin was a child. On the surface, it didn't look nearly as ominous as Erias's door and certainly didn't give off the same skin-rippling sensation, but dread built in Lin all the same. No matter what Aemun's plan ultimately was, Lin was positive that death and pain waited behind those ancient, dark doors.

With a deep breath, Lin pushed.

Three people, two men and a woman, sat on a platform feet off the ground and set into the back wall. Weavers Danur, Azhura, and Grott. The two men sat on either side, with Azhura in the center. Two guards flanked either side of the platform, facing straight ahead toward Lin. Spears held in hands as they stood at attention. Lin glanced to either side and noted two more guards. Four in total. All were marked as Enforcers based on the insignia shaped like talons stitched onto the upper arm of their sleeves.

There had been a time, not so long ago, when Lin would've feared that marking. Would have bowed at entering the presence of the Weavers, even as they sentenced a brother or sister or stranger to death. But now, the Weavers bowed to him.

All three touched their wrinkled foreheads to the silky, smooth pillows they sat upon. All four guards tapped the butts of their spears to the marble floors in a pattern of one, two, and one strikes. The Weavers looked up in unison.

Lin approached them like he belonged. Back straight, eyes flicking from the seated Weavers to the standing guards, to the veins of ore in the marble that glowed faintly like sunflowers at sunset. It was the glow of magic as if the stone floor itself were made of Bindings. Much the way honeycaps seemed lit like honey caught in a ray of sun.

"Welcome, honored one," Weaver Azhura said. She smiled, her ashen gray skin stretching tight. Her robes were sheer, colored like thinly sliced flesh, revealing every sag, wrinkle, and beauty mark she might have. Grott and Danur wore much the same on either side of her. A testament that they were true upholders of the Binding Tenets and flesh clean from the impurities of Fell-Bindings that might mar the Grand Tapestry. And yet they'd prostrated before someone clearly marked with those same impurities. Rage bubbled up within him, but he held himself back.

Lin didn't know how members of the King's Noose treated the Weavers and thought back to the way the Ladrican emissary spoke to Duke Wellgrove. He gave a brisk nod and waited ten steps from where the Weavers sat. Underneath him, the tiles slanted to a drain, and the porous stone had long ago stained red from the countless executions.

Behind the Weavers was a tapestry, the length and width of the wall. It depicted the alleged first Binder, the founder of the Ferrucium. A dark man draped in clothes dyed a deep red, far darker than the soldiers' cloaks were. Intricate golden patterns were shown at the center of his palms, and a swell of darkness rose at his back. In Ferrucium teachings, the first Binder was blessed by the Six. Tylle had named Vellia, a *woman*, as the first Wiever. But a member of what would later be bastardized as the Six. Lin shook his head.

Azhura tsked at his motion and straightened. She had always been the mouth for the trio, quick to reprimand Ferrucium soldiers. "We hope we have not offended you somehow."

"No," he forced the word out, stretching it in his pretend way. "Amoon has requested, entreated, that I visit you three."

"As he told us when he sent the letter," Azhura said after a moment. Her eyes were bright and angled sharply, but she nodded as if she believed Lin wholeheartedly.

"Did he tell you why?" Lin did his best to sound menacing. *Threatening.* If he could perhaps get some sort of truth from the Weavers, then he'd know what to do when the group rushed in behind him.

"He couldn't tell us the actions of the Noose any more than we might guess the pattern of the wind." Azhura chuckled. When Lin didn't react, she added, "So, no, honored one."

Lin nodded. He didn't know how to proceed. He'd gotten this far. Killed so many of his sworn brothers and sisters, but now that he was here, what was he meant to do? If he killed the Weavers, perhaps even if Aemun planned to betray Erias's people, he'd pivot. Work with Carine and create a real structure for protecting the Danican people without the forced enlistment and taking of children. Without the potential rules meant to keep them from growing to their full potential as Binders.

"I've come to kill you," Lin said.

Azhura's smile died slowly. "I've not met a Nooseman prone to jesting."

Grott and Danur whispered, hands held to their faces, just behind Azhura. They leaned over, bellies exposed, throats tucked but as vulnerable as any of the soldiers he'd killed on the walls to make sure Carine's group wasn't attacked or trapped.

"On King Lodram's authority?" Grott asked. His voice was higher pitched than expected, and Azhura shot him a look that could have flown from a crossbow.

And the doors behind Lin exploded inward. Lin shifted, expecting Tylle or Carine, but flinched back as a Weft, cruel and thin, ate the air in front of him.

A Nooseman, lithe and robed in shadow and starlight, darted in. They wielded a Binding Blade, like Dennick had made, and rushed past Lin as he stumbled back. So, Aemun did have multiple plans working. He had the rebels and the King's forces both pressing the Ferrucium at once.

The Weavers hadn't moved, but the guards had.

Enforcers rushed to stop the Bindings cutting the air to the Weavers, Ferrucium-steel spears clashing then breaking the Wefts. Then, one Enforcer took the Blade to his knee and a spinning backhand that sent the soldier crashing into one of the six marbled columns lining the room.

Lin regained his footing and charged into the melee. He had wanted to see the Weavers' reactions to know if any had been working with Aemun, and all seemed concerned by Lin's statement and terrified by the attack, even as they sat there watching their guards fall. Another soldier was dead or dying but unmoving all the same. Lin took the man's spear, which had rattled to the tiled floor near him, and threw it with everything he had at the Nooseman.

The Nooseman moved preternaturally fast, and the spear stabbed into the tapestry through the man's face. They stared toward Lin for no more than a breath, then continued the assault, disposing of the last two Enforcer guards with Wefts that split like threads untwining, catching both guards in the throat.

"Wait!" Lin shouted as the Nooseman placed a single foot on the platform the Weavers sat on.

They waited, turning to face Lin. And even with their back partially turned, the Weavers were motionless.

"You're not Dennick, though you wear his face."

Lin froze. He'd seen the masks. They were all the same, flat metal. No markings. Nothing. *That he could see.* "I killed him," Lin lied.

The Nooseman nodded. A Weft, fast as a guillotine dropping, took the head from Weaver Danur's shoulders. "Good for you."

Azhura didn't flinch as blood sprayed her face, and the body collapsed beside her. Grott didn't keep his composure half as well and rose, getting a whole four steps before Azhura pulled a sharp, thin sword from seemingly out of nowhere and cut the back of his calves, collapsing him into screams. She placed the blade on the empty cushion to her side and placed her brow against the bloody satin pillow, hands out, fingers splayed.

"Please. I believe the King's Noose is being used. We are all being pitted against each other... to start a conflict. To serve the goals of one man." Lin raised his hands and showed his palms. "Please, just speak with me for a moment."

"You speak of Aemun?" Whoever this Nooseman was, their accent wasn't nearly as thick as the others Lin had met.

"Yes."

The Nooseman stared at Lin long. Too long. It was only a matter of time before Carine's group came crashing in. Lin needed confirmation. Hard evidence of Aemun's treachery. Without a word, a Weft, whiplike this time and blurred from the speed, shot toward Azhura's neck.

Lin tried to break it, snapping his fingers and picturing the unnaturally fast attack breaking into dust, but it wouldn't unravel. Azhura didn't move until the last second, and once she did, the attack lashed across the edge of her blade, breaking into motes of golden dust. A gash welled with blood along her back, her robe sliced cleanly where the magic bent around the blade's edge before shattering.

"I gave up my life. My family. Our people's freedom for our people's peace. I will not die quietly like a sleeping dog or fleeing like a coward." Azhura rose, flaps of her robe opening to expose the stomach of one who hadn't wanted for food in decades and the torso of a fighter who might've been striking in her youth.

Lin took the chance to attack. He sent three Wefts, two horizontal and one vertical, slashing toward the Nooseman's side. One sweep of their Binding Blade broke all the attacks, but Lin had expected that. He rushed forward and created his own Blade, his attack parried but not shattered. He used the length of the magical weapon to keep his distance, and Azhura pressed the Nooseman from the other side.

This journey had many firsts, but never in Lin's whole life had he thought he might fight alongside a Weaver. And he was underwhelmed. Compared to Carine's fighters, compared to the monstrous untethered he'd encountered, and now every Nooseman, he knew what the peaks of Binding seemed to be. Weaver Azhura was an amateur. But her age belied her speed, and her slashes were well-placed. Most importantly, she seemed to be gaining speed. Her assault quickened, pushing the assassin onto their back foot so that Lin could press them from the other side. He stabbed forward, catching the Nooseman in the ankle and raking the Binding Blade upward.

Like a swelling cocoon, the Nooseman summoned a swirl of Wefts to cut the air around them. And just as quickly, the Wefts petered out, shattering and failing—all of them, Lin's own blade included.

The three of them stood there. Azhura looked confused but swung her Ferrucium-steel blade downward, ready to take the Nooseman's head.

"Enough!"

But none of them had spoken, and Azhura stopped her swing an inch from the Nooseman's exposed neck.

Aemun, robed in a similar sheer cloth that looked every bit of blood-soaked spider silk, sauntered in. "Grandmother, lower your blade and see your life spared. Noosemen, there seems to be some confusion over the nature of your roles. Step aside."

His last words were said with such authority that Lin almost did what he asked. But the other Nooseman, the real Nooseman, hadn't moved, so Lin stopped himself.

"Step aside," Aemun repeated himself. Behind him, movement drew Lin's eyes. Denny, wild-eyed and frowning, had rushed into the room, tailed by the boulder-sized man and the lithe, Inlay-striped man he'd seen earlier. That left Carine, Tylle, and the silent one, Prish, unaccounted for.

The Nooseman did. Bloody footprints from their boot stained the marble tile as they slinked back from the platform. Lin mirrored them. He wasn't sure why the Bindings had all failed at once, but he was sure it had something to do with Aemun and perhaps Bound Metal. Though, he didn't feel his blood roiling or skin crawling.

"Aemun. Son of Frellus. *Grandson*. You step into this hallowed chamber and give commands. You wear the silks of Weavers. You bring fighters covered in Fell-Bindings, ruining the fabric of their places on the Grand Tapestry. And above all that, you bring in Bound Metal, that foul, dark magic."

Aemun nodded at Azhura's accusations, an easy smile forming on his lips. He looked every bit like he belonged up on the platform.

"I wear the silks of a *Lord*. I give commands because it was my lot in life to do so. Grandmother, step down from that platform, and you will know comfort and luxury for the remaining time of your life." Aemun waved his arms wide as if to encompass the entire room. His soft-looking sleeves slid up his forearms, revealing dark gray lines raised on the flesh of his right arm. Black, faintly fuzzing lines that seemed to absorb nearby light.

Lin's stomach twisted as he looked at the dark bands—Bound Metal—placed into his flesh. They'd only been separated for a few days. And Carine had *let* him do that?

"Monster," Azhura whispered.

"Me?" Aemun's voice lilted. "No. If you ask the Ladrican King and his forefathers, *we* are the monsters. All of us. This—" he looked at his right arm "—is *evolution*. I won't ask you to abdicate the platform again."

"Tell me," Azhura said, rising to her full height. "Was this King Lodram's doing? A traitorous Duke? Or my own failing?" With each question, she stepped forward until she was fully off the platform and no longer between Lin and the actual Nooseman.

"We all have our places in the Grand Tapestry. You haven't failed me. You've failed yourself, and I forgive you."

Lin's limbs had never felt heavier. It was as if metal bands had wrapped them, crushing his joints. By the looks of discomfort plain on Denny and the other two, they felt it as well. Whatever Aemun had done with the Bound Metal, it was affecting all of them. Weakening them, or at least the benefits their Inlays granted.

"Aemun. Grandson. What you do is treason."

"You taught me better than that, Nani. What I'm doing, what I've done, is tended the loom. Replacing the strings too old to be useful. Scraped away the rusted bits. Added a splash of varnish and reworked the wooden supports."

Lin looked down at his Bludwieve. If the other magic worked into his flesh had lost strength, it stood to reason that the Uethe preventing him from harming Aemun had as well. And even if it hadn't, wasn't this a confession? He wasn't replacing the loom. But repairing it to his own liking.

Steps so silent they were only marked by shadow came from the shattered door. A woman, Inlays glowing faintly, stepped through, a baby— Azhalia at her breast. Once she entered the room fully, her movements slowed, and her Inlays lost some of their glow, but she pressed on until she stood beside Aemun. Her hair was simple, cut close to the scalp, and colored a deep brown with streaks of gray. Her lips—Six, Lin had to look away. Her lips were Stitched closed.

With his left hand, Aemun took the child. He walked past Weaver Azhura to the tapestry and leaned against the wall underneath it. "Let the threads be snapped." He snapped the fingers of his right hand, and the Chamber of Judgment exploded into light.

Chapter Twenty-Eight

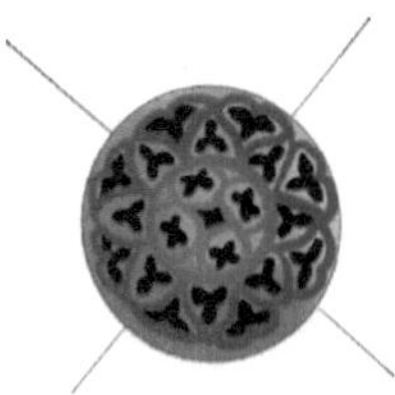

Burning Blood

Lin's mask shielded his eyes from some of the light. Not enough to keep him from going blind for a moment, but enough that when he opened his eyes, he saw the Nooseman rushing toward Denny as lavender dots danced around them. The Nooseman had a Binding Blade drawn to their side and moved as if wholly unbothered by whatever Bound Metal trick Aemun had pulled.

"Hugo, Denny, Jun, Prish. Bite!" a commanding voice yelled through the doorway. Tylle and the shorter, more muscular leader, Carine, rushed into the room. Both were covered in blood, and Tylle's Inlays glowed faintly underneath the gore and ripped fabric of her clothes.

Carine's group moved in unison—all except for the Stitched-mouth woman, who hesitated. Prish, the one who'd cared for Aemun's child, the one who'd apparently run off to hunt, the one who now sent several Wefts aimed at Carine—another betrayal.

Lin sent three Wefts slicing across the marble tiles toward the Nooseman. They weaved behind a column, and the Weft sank in, biting until it seemed to strike a vein of ore and shattered. The Nooseman howled and pivoted, launching themselves at Lin. Lin avoided the first two strikes, ducking and shifting his weight to the left, but the Nooseman split their Blade in two and pressed the assault harder. Lin caught their left arm and twisted it, ready to snap the elbow, but he'd been too slow, and the sharp Blade in their right hand caught him across his mask. It sparked and hissed and then exploded in both their faces.

The crack that sounded could have come from his skull, the way his brow throbbed, but the mask fell to the ground in two pieces, clattering on the tile and cracking the stonework. A scream erupted from where Carine's group had formed, and Lin struggled to spin the Nooseman around to see. They kicked and punched, and Wefts were sent wide by the slimmest margin, but it seemed like Lin actually had the upper hand. He was stronger, though barely.

"Aemun has..." Lin grunted, straining to throw the Nooseman onto their back. "Betrayed the King. Betrayed *us*."

Someone or something struck Lin across his back, sending him tumbling and sliding across the tile until he thudded into the raised platform. He'd lost his grip on the Nooseman and prepared to unravel any stray Bindings that might be flying at him. But the air was empty of magic, at least near him.

Tracking everything, everyone moving, with the Sight proved a challenge in the half-lit room. The Chamber of Judgement had turned into a battlefield of bright lights, blurred bodies, and blood splatters. Prish was a storm made manifest, blocking blows and Bindings from both Jun and Denny. She moved like she could see the future, always two motions ahead of the other two.

Doors at the sides of the chamber opened, ones Lin had only ever watched those sentenced to judgment come in from, and red-swathed Ferrucium soldiers spilled in like a sea of blood.

Lin climbed to his feet, a hand helping him up. Tylle was there, all concern and rage on her gaunt face. Six, she looked paler somehow. Leaner. *Hungry*.

"He's betrayed us."

"It was never a matter of if but when and how. I think he always planned to have the King's Noose give chase and take out the Weavers," Lin said as he watched the Nooseman scramble to their feet. Each hand conjured a Binding Blade, more ochre in color than the pure gold it had been before.

"Didn't get all the Weavers yet. Erias might want to strike a deal with her. We need to keep her alive," Tylle whispered. "Go. Get Aemun."

Lin's heart fluttered as her hand squeezed his arm. "We should go together."

As the soldiers pressed in, Carine broke them like a cliff-face breaking waves. She kept her back to one of the marble columns lining the chamber and sent low sweeping Weaves and fast speeding Wefts, breaking ankles and slicing throats or breaking against Ferrucium Steel. Jun and Denny both looked fatigued, Prish pushing them more and more away from Carine and the large man's corpse. Six. That must've been the scream. Prish had managed to kill one of Carine's people.

"Go!" Tylle said, releasing his arm.

Aemun leaned against the wall, baby in one hand, a small dagger in his other. He stared at Lin, his lip curling, and shrugged.

Then the Nooseman was on Lin again, Blades a flurry of slashes and strikes. The Nooseman was adjusting the length with each strike, cutting air the first time, widening the blade, and catching cloth the next swing; then Blade bit flesh along Lin's side. Not terribly deep, he wasn't gutted, but Six, it stung as if the strike hadn't been a flat, clean cut. As if the Blade had teeth that ripped flesh.

"If you flee, you can warn King Lodram of Aemun's treachery," Lin said. He'd made his own Blade, still a poor imitation of the skillful mastery of control that the Noosemen employed, but it parried well enough and kept their Blade from tasting Lin's blood again. Lin gasped in a breath and countered, swinging his own strike low and flat toward the Nooseman's right ankle.

The Nooseman limped out of the distance of the strike, favoring their left side, and the odor of old blood wafted up. "Betrayal takes trust. Betrayal takes expectations. My King let this man's words sweeten his tea for a time, but King Lodram is immune to the venom this one spews. I am here to see that the pieces falling do so where the King wishes." The Nooseman spoke flatly, with no emotion behind their words. Then they spun around Lin, far faster than Lin thought them able with their limp, and stabbed downward. Lin's robes pulled and ripped as the Blade pinned him to the floor.

In all the chaos, Weaver Azhura had moved to the side, but she hadn't lowered her blade, and her eyes were aflame with indignation and fury. And she smiled as the Nooseman rushed her again. Lin had seen that smile before—at judgments—on Aemun's face. It was an inherited, joyless thing.

Tylle rushed to Carine's side. The swarming soldiers had thinned, but Prish moved through them like a shark through water, avoiding their attacks and striking at Carine every chance she found. Lin ripped the robe off and thought to crash into the mob. But Tylle had suggested keeping the Weaver alive, and though her swordplay rivaled most Lin had seen, she was old. And she didn't have the benefit of Inlays patterning her flesh and bolstering her prowess.

"I knew one of you would tighten around my throat one day," Azhura growled. "Always tightening. Limiting our borders. Limiting trade. Choking us from the rest of the world one decree after the next. Never did I imagine the final knot would be tightened from my own blood." Her chest had begun heaving, and her sheer robes were tattered and stained heavy in places along her arms and sides.

"Monologues are for despots, Nani. If you'd have simply sat down and laid the blade down, the last bit of your life would have been comfortable." Aemun narrowed his dark eyes, tracking Lin as he rushed to the Weaver's side. And you. Subterfuge doesn't suit you, Escorter. Knowing you wore a dead man's mask leaves a bad taste in my mouth."

Lin bit back his reply. Azhura was being pushed back. Her blade purely focused on defensive motions.

"I knew you were untethering. Breaking the Binding Tenets every chance you got, but to blaspheme against the Six by wearing one of the Noosemen's masks?"

Lin aimed a Weft for the back of the Nooseman's knee. The Nooseman dropped as the magic cut tendon and joint. Azhura's blade found their neck. The slice was clean and deep, and the Nooseman didn't put a hand to the wound. Instead, they worked a Needle, brown and brittle, forming it in an instant and stabbing it up to the folds of flesh hanging at Azhura's throat. It made contact but, like a dead, dried reed, broke. It crumbled into dust toward the floor, ugly compared to the sparks of fresh Bindings exploding.

Azhura leveled her blade at Lin's chest as the Nooseman collapsed. She turned to Lin and hissed. "You aided me after claiming you came to kill me. Why?"

Lin licked his lips and tasted blood. "I'm no Nooseman. I... I made an Uethe to protect Aemun." An idea sparked within Lin, like the striking of a hammer on steel. "I was an Escorter. Woven into this conflict."

A look of realization flashed across her face, and she lowered her blade a half inch. "You're the Escorter who was assigned to bring him and his partner home. You've untethered."

"I will remove them!" Lin screamed at the Weaver. Something he'd never thought he'd live to do, let alone take a breath afterward. "Surely you understand what a means to an end means. To free my flesh, Aemun must be protected. I hope you understand." Why was Aemun the only one allowed to play games and have plots? Lin was sure Erias did, too, but why was Lin meant only to be a pawn in some other man's game?

Lin attacked. His first strike disarmed her; his second sent her crashing into the rail behind her that separated the chamber floor from the viewing area off to the side. Then he shifted and stood in front of Aemun. He had to put everything into the strike to make it seem believable. The Binding Blade erupted into light and petered out as it grew closer to Aemun and his Bound Metal lined arm. Lin let it disperse and threw a punch at Aemun's face. The man didn't move. Lin's punch went wide at the last moment. He threw another and another, but each attack slipped wide by the barest margin.

"Damn you! One take you!" Lin hissed. He fell to his knees and curled, head touching the cold stone floor near Aemun's boots. The Bound Metal arm would be an issue. The Uethe being faked was not. It didn't compel him not to harm Aemun anymore. However the Uethe or magic, or both, worked, Aemun had apparently broken it through his actions.

Aemun's boot touched the bottom of Lin's chin and lifted his head. "You still think to remove those foul markings?"

Lin nodded and squeezed his eyes, forcing out tears.

"With the actual Nooseman dead, this will get out of hand long before—" he lifted Lin's chin higher "—reinforcements arrive. Come with me. Protect me until we reach my boat, and I will tell you the truth about removing the Stitches."

"Yes," Lin whispered.

"Yes, *Lord Aemun*," Aemun spat. He moved his foot from Lin's chin and let it drop to the floor. He looked as if he planned to say more, then narrowed his eyes and spun. It seemed he'd believed Lin's act. This meant Lin could get him alone and end his life without the threat of Prish or one of the others trying to stop him. Weaver Azhura didn't move, but Lin was sure he hadn't dealt a fatal blow.

The flood of soldiers slowed, but alarm bells had begun to ring, and the scent of smoke filled the air. With the tide of Ferrucium resistance slowing, Carine seemed able to match Prish blow for blow. Denny was on her side, a puddle of scarlet reflecting her pained expression. But pain meant she was alive, and besides Tylle, she was the only one Lin had managed to meet, let alone care for.

"Tylle," Lin shouted. He caught her eyes and pointed at the door Aemun had walked through, hoping she understood what he meant.

The path was dark, lined with glowing veins of iron in the walls. Weaver Danur's head looked like a damp, moss-covered stone until Lin got close enough to see it. He looked back, disgusted by how far it had flown. Then Lin considered the man he was following and reasoned that Aemun might've treated it like a ball, kicking it along the way. The corridor was cramped and narrow and smelled of sea salt mixed with fresh air.

Lin's steps echoed. Each was an accusation that what he was doing was wrong or poorly considered. He needed to catch up to Aemun, but his legs were tired, his lungs screaming to stop and breathe. But every time he considered it, he thought of the number of times Aemun had bested them, and Lin hated that he'd ever let him get away in the first place. Odds were good that the man was planning another betrayal of some sort. Lin hadn't bested him once in the few chances he'd had. What had changed now? *Nothing.*

When he finally exited the tunnel, oil lanterns illuminated a path that wound down to a private harbor Lin had only ever heard rumors of, like a cove set aside just for the Weavers and their closest confidants. Aemun strolled down, his child bundled across his back, and glanced up at Lin.

There, moored at the dock, was a ship large enough to house a small army. Lin shielded his face against the cold wind that whipped against the cliffside, steeled himself, and then jumped with all the force his Inlayed legs could generate. He hoped and prayed to the Six that Tylle and Denny would survive. Carine seemed capable, even if the Stitch-mouthed Prish was a force of fury all on her own. *Shit.* What if this was a trap meant to pull him from them? Tylle had understood what he meant when he gestured to the door, hadn't she?

"I truly do wonder," Aemun called up as Lin crashed to the shoal of the shore. "If you've always been this useless. What if I'd been attacked down the path?"

Lin landed, sending up stones and dust. "You weren't. Tell me how to remove the Stitches."

Aemun smiled. "There have been countless studies done. Not here in Danica, of course. But at King Lodram's court, on Noosemen who didn't survive the training. Or who *barely* survived, only to die in the name of understanding the limits of Danican magic. And, of course, the Fentian scholars, with more humane methods. If anyone truly knows, it would be them. You know, Bound Metal is a strange thing. Erias thinks it is old magic. My Nani thinks it is foul, *dark* magic. Do you know what it really is?"

Lin tensed, noticing the workers preparing the ship. "No."

"It is nature. It is the soil below and the sky above collaborating to stop Wievers from changing the natural order. It is the natural evolution of magic."

Lin frowned. "What does that have to do with removing my Stitches?"

Aemun snapped his fingers. "Simple, it doesn't. Kill yourself. You want your markings gone? Skin yourself alive and break the bonds that formed with flesh and bone when you worked the magic."

"But Erias said he would tell me."

"Think hard. Did he? Did he swear an Uethe that he would tell you how to remove them?"

Lin clenched his fist, wounds across his chest stinging from the salt spray. He hadn't, had he? Erias had said something along the lines that he'd tell Lin all he knew. Which might mean if he knew nothing, he'd tell Lin nothing. All of this, every bit of it, had been a waste. Erias, *Grovetender*, wasn't some all-knowing man. He was a duke's brother playing at something far larger than he was. "You never planned to work with Erias, did you?"

"No more than you planned to work with me." Aemun shrugged. "I've had a lot of time to think about what you asked. Why did Margaret have to die?" His tone had slipped to something more befitting a eulogy, and his face darkened.

"There is no answer, is there?" Lin whispered.

Aemun looked down at Lin's boots, then up at his face. "No. She wanted me to stop. To leave everything I'd been working toward at the door and run away with her and Azhalia. When I told her to come with me, she refused. We were at an impasse. And I'd worked too hard to end it all there."

"You wept for her."

"I wept for what was lost to me. And sometimes... sacrifices must be made. I knew from the moment I laid eyes on her that she'd take a part of me and never let it go."

"Was it all worth it? I mean, look at you running now," Lin said.

"Repositioning. Soon, King Lodram will send forces. Not a scattered collection of King's Noose, but armored soldiers whom I've witnessed firsthand. They will press the border, bending the Accords. Any semblance of peace we've had will fall. The dukes will make their moves, and the Ferrucium will be lost. And I will be sailing towards the future, waiting for the right time to come in and fix it all. I do all this so that Azhalia might have a better life." Aemun ran a hand across his cheek, and when he looked up, his eyes were hard and emotionless.

"Horseshit," Lin said. Everything up until now pointed at Aemun pulling strings for his own pleasure. What about setting Ladrica to war with Danica made for a better future?

A bell clanged from the ship, and Aemun turned, glancing over his shoulder. "Goodbye, Escorter. Have some dignity and strip the Stitches yourself."

Chapter Twenty-Nine

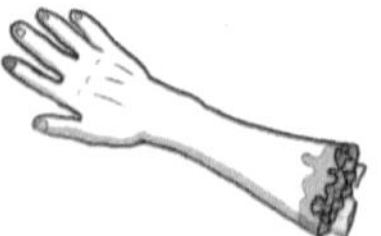

Broken Hope

Lin couldn't move. He'd come here to kill this man. But what was the point? If his Stitches, Inlays, whatever the fuck their true name was, couldn't be removed, what was the point in living? To anyone with the Sight, he'd be a monster. The one thing that had kept him going through all of this, all the betrayals, battles, and blood, was the hope that he might return to a normal life. No. He wasn't being honest with himself. Tylle had been a large part of it before they'd separated, the desire he'd felt for her and the chance to settle down with her and be taught more about Danica's history.

Six, he hoped she fared better than him right now. When Inlays were equal, physical prowess and weapon skill became a factor again, and Prish moved like she'd trained her entire life to take on a group like Carine's.

Azhalia cried. A soft whimper crescendoing to heights that might challenge the stars.

The shoal stones, mixed with chunks of red clay and sandstone, sounded like shattering glass as it shifted underfoot. Sharp bits poked and stabbed through Lin's boot's leather, and he winced as he took a single step forward. Then another. And another. Lin sprinted at Aemun, and the man spun on the dock, right arm extended and palm out to Lin. His arm seemed to have grown ashen and stiff, cracks forming at his joints.

"Not another step," Aemun growled.

Lin took another step. Aemun's arm wavered. Like the waves lapping underneath, nausea rolled over Lin. His flesh, blood and Bindings felt pushed and pulled all at once.

"This is Bound Metal. Studies have been done on this as well. Binder's blood pulls towards it, attracted. Makes them nauseous. Unsteady. But..." Aemun narrowed his eyes and tensed his arm. "It also can push away all that it pulls with the right intention placed upon it."

Lin slid back, stones digging into his heels. His muscles throbbed. Azhura was right. This was dark magic. He gritted his teeth and staggered forward, fighting the sensation that compelled him back. The closer he got, the harder it was to progress.

Aemun clenched his fingers as if strangling a ghost, and the nausea washed over Lin again.

Lin groaned and fought to keep from falling to his knees. "So, you've given up Binding to have control over Binders. Suits you."

A low thrumming whistle sounded from the shore beside them, and Aemun's arm sprouted a plumed shaft. He screamed, pulling his arm toward his chest, the strange effect ending and causing Lin to stumble toward him.

Pael. Lin hadn't thought about the man since entering the Chamber of Judgement, but he'd apparently taken this cove into consideration. Lin wanted to look for him but refused to take his eyes off Aemun. The man's blood, true to his own words, seemed to congeal around the bands of metal on his arms.

"Lin!" Not Pael's gruff voice. Tylle's. He glanced over his shoulder and watched her rush down the hill with leaping strides that took her down far faster than would be possible if she weren't Inlayed. "End this. Now!"

Lin frowned. He turned back to Aemun and took a dagger slice to his chest. Six, he shouldn't have turned to look at Tylle, but just hearing her voice had taken his mind to places he'd rather have been. Without a focus, as he'd learned to do so well, he formed a Weave like a bandage that flattened across his chest. It pulled lightly toward Aemun's wounded arm, but it didn't come away from his flesh. He'd owe Pael a drink once it was all said and done.

"Won't you just die?" Aemun screamed. His voice carried and rebounded off the cliff-side hills that hugged this southern cove side of the Ferrucium.

Lin pulled away and sent two Wefts at Aemun's throat.

They unraveled with a snap of Aemun's fingers, and the man drew his Ferrucium Steel, slashing up at Lin as he cradled his wounded arm. From his back, Azhalia's wailing grew more pitched.

Tylle was beside them in a blink, a Needle in her hand, a ruddy brown color like no Binding ever should be. She was doing the very thing she'd warned him against. Or she was too busy to notice how much of her *spul* she'd expended to end Aemun's life.

Lin rushed forward, forcing the pain in the bottom of his feet to the back of his mind.

Tylle's clothes were ripped, her Inlays fully visible along her arms and side, swirling up to her chest. Her bandages seemed only to cling to her because of the fresh blood that soaked them, and her single long braid had started coming undone.

The sheer robe Aemun had worn still shimmered lightly, draping off his shoulders. His grin devolved into a grimace as his eyes darted between Lin and Tylle. He broke Tylle's Needle with a swipe of his blade, then raised his left hand placatingly and stabbed his sword into the dock. "I've got the babe bundled to my back. We can talk this out."

Whether the men on board were soldiers or simply hired sailors, they hadn't made sight or sound since ringing the bell, and the ship rocked in the water behind Aemun.

"There is no need for more words. Carine has ended the betrayer, Prish. Weaver Azhura is being cared for. Birds have already been sent to Grovetender." Tylle's words were a blood-stippled wheeze.

"So, you'd have my child die here with me?" Aemun asked flatly.

"No," Lin said.

"Yes," Tylle said at the same time.

Lin looked at her. Six, the woman looked tired. So close to the edge of death or unconsciousness that her eyes had lost the light of life that he'd seen so often in them. "You can't mean that. Your sister's child?"

"His child. If it means not letting him flee again." Tylle snapped a hand up and sent two Wefts slicing towards the man. A sickly burned orange color to them.

"You'll overuse your spul," Lin said.

"Ha!" Aemun exhaled and slipped to the side. He darted away from Tylle's barrage as quickly as if he were dancing with a familiar partner and knew exactly where her weight would go and which way she'd lean.

Each Weft she sent out was darker and slower than the last. Like the sun of her soul was petering out.

"If she keeps Binding like that, she'll die."

Tylle lunged toward him and slipped, her left leg giving out from underneath her.

Lin rushed to her side, eyes drawn to Aemun's arm, unable to look away from its dull, dark gray metal. *Bound Metal*. He was sick of it.

Aemun narrowed his eyes and held his blood-coated arm up, running his fingers over the shaft of the bolt and then the metal along his arm itself.

"I can stand on my own," Tylle whispered, working her way to her feet.

"The Weavers were all brittle—hard and strong but inflexible, easily broken when the tiniest amount of force was applied." Aemun hawked a glob of spit. "It would be best to end my Nani before she takes your heads."

His voice was free from pain, from the shaking, trembling rage that Lin had heard Tylle speak with regarding her sister. It was a flaccid statement, devoid of care.

Tylle shook her head. "If she doesn't cooperate. Her fate will be worse than anything you might imagine. Grovetender will want more than your own blood for your betrayal. Cousins. Uncles. Weaver Azhura had two sons and a daughter, did she not?"

Aemun smiled and nodded. "That was her way. You two have followed me like slathering hounds. No matter how badly beaten, you've recovered and pushed your way to me. And now that you're here, what do you hope for? You've killed the leaders, subverted my ploys at weakening your forces, and have me with my back to a boat."

Azhalia continued to wail. It was like a hand gripped Lin's heart and squeezed. Days on the road, that child pressed to his breast, he'd learned that cry. *Felt* that cry.

"Vengeance," Tylle hissed.

Aemun tsked, and anger flashed across his face. "And when I die, no one will be left to speak with or calm King Lodram or his emissaries. Erias is not loved like I am. He doesn't have the King's ear. Neither does my Nani. I'm the only one who can keep these tangled threads from knotting and strangling the lot of you. And you haven't freed anything with this assault. Nothing has changed with this moment. You've chewed and chased at imaginary hands while not realizing the chains staking you to the yard. You don't even know the first thing about navigating the Accords that will be broken—"

"I wanted the truth... and justice," Lin said. He stepped forward, watching Aemun. "And to save Margie's child."

"You wanted the truth?" Aemun leveled his left hand at Lin's chest. The bands of Bound Metal were slick with his blood. "You can still get it. All of it. Kill her, and I'll tell you anything you want to know. You want justice? Nebulous. You want to save *Margie's* child? You would save a baby from their own father?"

Lin looked to Tylle. Her eyelids seemed heavy. But Aemun was stalling. He'd already proven there was nothing he could tell Lin. He'd wanted Lin to have dignity. "Have some dignity, Aemun. You've been caught."

"This... this takes me back," Aemun said, a smile slipping to his face like a wave lapping up against the dock. "Think about how different things would've been if you'd just done what I asked back in Lyre. No Fell-Bindings. No uncertain allegiances. A chance that you'd be on the right side of history." He took a shuffled step back and made shushing sounds under his breath to Azhalia. He was pressed so close to the boat and water that a strong enough breeze might blow him into it.

Another, louder wail from the baby made Lin shift, jaw clenching.

Tylle hadn't moved, but her breaths were low and quick.

Lin shook his head and tried to ignore the distant sounds from the Ferrucium proper and the closer, much more distracting, sound of Margie's child.

"The truth is not worth so much. I'd rather see you dead and stay in the dark than kill someone who means so much to me."

Aemun nodded, his mouth twisting. When his face stopped shifting, his top lip quivered. "Come *unbound*. Escorter. Come to your darkness. All your Stitches and hopes won't stop what's to come. And when Danica is crumbling around you and the people are truly yoked, you will see that the pastures they've had were far better than the cages heading for them."

Aemun lunged forward, his left arm grasping for Lin.

Its tug was undeniable, an invisible pulling at his blood and bones that spiked his nausea. Like pressing a mountain through the eye of a needle, Lin exerted his will. He channeled it into the thinnest Weft he'd ever made, if it could even be called that. No. Lin made a Thread as delicate as a strand of hair.

Watching Aemun move was like watching a dancer perform, even with a child on his back and a bloodied arm. He shifted his weight, took his sword, leaned forward, and stabbed before effortlessly pulling back and regaining his balance. Each stab was accented by the pulsing pressure of his left arm.

Lin's Thread drifted in the air, against his control, whenever Aemun got close with his arm. But no matter how Aemun moved, it continued towards him. Sharp and flexible. It was an extension of what Lin had watched the Noosemen make, but lighter. Lin sent actual Wefts slashing at Aemun, which broke on his blade until the man's brow was beaded in sweat. Aemun was a skilled swordsman, but Lin kept his distance as best as he could. Aemun stabbed and slashed, pushing Lin further and further back. One horizontal slice caught Lin across the arm, the blade clashing and sparking with the Inlays there but not breaking the skin. It hurt as if the bone itself might shatter.

The thread drifted down, drawn to the Bound Metal, and twisted around Aemun's bicep like a thin golden vine. Aemun kicked and struggled as it tightened, then tried to take his sword to the thread. It glowed brighter the more it bit into Aemun's flesh.

Aemun stumbled, gave up attempting to cut or unravel the Thread, and held his sword like he might form a Binding using its hilt as a focus. He hadn't acted like he could still Bind this whole time.

Shit.

Lin tensed his legs and launched toward Aemun, pushing himself across the span between them in a breath. The Ferrucium Steel reverberated between Lin's palms as he slapped the flat of it at two different points. He gritted his teeth and struggled to keep hold as Aemun attempted to free the weapon.

The fingers on Lin's left hand throbbed, the Stitches thrumming at the contact with the steel. As close as he was to Aemun and his Bound Metal arm, he felt like the very bones might be pulled from his hands, and his digits grew cold.

Lin roared, muscles straining. The blade cracked, the sound like breaking ice pinging sharply several times.

Aemun released his hold as the blade snapped.

Shrapnel grazed Lin's hands, but he held onto a sizable piece with his right hand, away from his numb, Stitched left.

Tylle limped towards them, daggers in hand. Her face had become as pale as the new moon, but a new fire had been kindled in her eyes.

Aemun growled and struggled to dig nails under the Thread that had drawn blood.

As graceful as Aemun seemed, the numbness that swallowed all Binders when they over-worked themselves took him like any other. He appeared to trip over his right foot, falling hard onto the dock. He pushed and fell to his knees, hunched over. Azhalia screamed and screamed. And when Aemun looked up, tears had formed, streaking the dust on his face.

Aemun raised his hands to shield his face as Lin crowded over him. A Binding, nearly black in color and odd feeling, blinked into existence near Aemun's right palm.

Lin snapped his hand forward and fell to one knee. He grabbed Aemun's right hand with his left. The magic thrummed as they touched, Aemun's Binding swirling and twisting as the two fought for control. Lin pushed back the idea that he was mimicking yet another untethered as flashes of Fallo filled his mind.

"Stop!" Aemun yelped. "Think of my child. Please."

"It isn't that the untethered are better Binders. It is that their will has hardened along with their hearts," Lin growled. The Binding, black as the sea beside them, started at Aemun's fingers. It twisted and tightened quicker than Lin expected, Aemun's joints popping as each line bit into his flesh. The Binding connected to his wrist and then snapped that back on itself.

Aemun punched across his body with his left fist and kicked and scraped at the dock with his heels. He moved like a child throwing a tantrum, spitting and hissing. Several strikes smacked the side of Lin's face, but each blow was weaker than the last.

"It won't kill you," Lin said. He blinked and wiped the blood from his lip with his right hand. "But it will break you."

Lin released Aemun's hand with a shrug and stepped back, watching as the man struggled to wrench away the intangible magic that wrung up his arm. The Bindings moved as if they were hungry, greedily devouring the surface of his hands and arm. Aemun's entire arm had grown a sickly, necrotic black.

Tylle had, at some point, come to stand beside Lin and rested a hand on his shoulder.

Aemun howled and kicked, face contorting. With a sick pop, his arm finally hung limp at his side.

"Untethered," Aemun whimpered. Spittle flew from his lips, and the word was as limp as his right arm. His left had swelled, and the Thread still grew tighter, blood dripping in rivulets down the wound. It was what he'd imagined when crafting the Thread, but Lin hadn't realized how effective it might be against Aemun's Bound Metal.

"Judge him," Lin said.

"Not even Verbanth, cloaked in his wrath, would judge this man. Wicked Tel'Myr would not cast him a second glance. He isn't worth judgment." Tylle crouched, then stumbled, and came to rest on her knees. She held a dagger tightly, her knuckles white and trembling.

Watching her, a great sorrow filled Lin. It didn't matter what they'd achieved. It wouldn't bring Margaret—Margie—back. Nothing could fill the ache Tylle must feel. Even if he tried with all his might.

Lin inched his way around to Aemun's back, ready to take the screaming baby.

"King Lodram... you need someone to speak to him and his. I... I have his ear. I've had it for years now. I can... I can speak on behalf of our people. But really, this time. Reduce the ire that will flow from him for these actions against the Ferrucium," Aemun said. "You need me," he whined. Aemun fidgeted, rising to his knees and extending his left hand.

Whatever he'd intended stopped as Lin willed his Thread tighter. It had been sinking into his flesh on its own, propelled by the initial command and Aemun's own Bound Metal arm. But not even Lin's best Weft on his best day could make a cut as clean as the one that saw Aemun's arm removed from his body. It thudded to the dock unceremoniously, fingers twitching with whatever last action they'd been about to perform.

The scream that tore from Aemun's throat must have come from somewhere deep within him, for it was a dark, agonizing howl. His right shoulder twitched, clearly his mind telling him to grab at the bloody stump, but his right arm and hand were a twisted ruin and couldn't heed him. He sobbed and screamed, rivaling Azhalia. Snot and blood and spit and, by the smell of it, piss were all fleeing the man at alarming rates.

Lin stepped back at the sight, and Tylle stayed seated, not taking her eyes from the man for even a moment.

"I'm... I am needed if you two wish to survive what will come from this. I am!"

"I don't doubt that Margie loved you," Tylle whispered. "I don't doubt that she asked you to join our cause or that, in her innocence, she betrayed some of our plans. But I don't believe *you* loved *her*. Because if you loved her and could do that, I have little hope for the rest of the world if you could grind it under your heel."

"S-she didn't suffer," Aemun said.

"You let her bear a child, then killed her before she even had the chance to meet it! What greater suffering could a mother have?" Tylle's words came from a hoarse throat.

"It broke me to do that. Tore me apart within!"

Tylle shook her head and stabbed the dagger into the wooden planks of the dock.

Lin watched and waited, breaths coming short, torn between rushing to the wailing child and staying with Tylle. But Tylle sat motionless, staring half-closed eyes at Aemun as if she couldn't hear the babe. Or care at its howls.

Aemun's sobs had lessened, and his blood-stained chest slowed its up-and-down movements. The man was bleeding out, and his skin had become sickly pallor.

"Stitch it," Tylle whispered.

"Me?" Lin asked.

"No. Him."

"B-break the B-binding Tenets? Me?" Aemun asked. His lips were turning a pale pink, and his teeth had begun to chatter.

"Have some dignity. Do it," Lin snarled.

"Bind it," Tylle repeated. "You've done worse under the eyes of Gods and men." She sounded cold as buried iron.

Aemun blinked, fresh tears falling from his face. He shook his head, and a sob shook him. "I don't want to die." He'd turned his eyes toward Lin as if Aemun might find mercy on his face.

Lin met his glossy stare and took a single step forward, but Tylle held her hand up, and he stopped.

"You've been judged, not by the Wievers before you. But by yourself. You're guilty. You know you are."

Aemun groaned, clenched his jaw, and, as if using the open wound of his arm as a focus, began Stitching the grievous injury shut. The edges of his flesh pulled together, tight like an overdrawn string. The magic was as red and irritated as his flesh, and Aemun's skin looked like it might rip away as ungentle as he was. Blood still trickled from the wound, and the injury didn't seem the sort that was perfect for healing through Stitches. He'd been better cauterizing it, but it didn't look quite life-threatening anymore.

Lin watched and folded his arms. He had enough grievances to wish this man dead, but if Tylle didn't want to take her vengeance, Lin could respect her choice. As foolish as it seemed. He'd done all this for her, after all.

It was no sooner than the thought had passed his mind that Tylle had ripped the dagger free from the dock and stabbed it into Aemun's throat from the side. She stabbed more times than Lin could count, ending up on top of him in a bloody, angry mess.

Lin rushed to her and pulled her up and off of him. And she turned on him, dropping the dagger, and hugged Lin. A tight, terrible embrace as she sobbed. Tylle, who was so strong it terrified Lin at times, clutched ahold of him with trembling, bloody hands. He couldn't say anything. He didn't dare. But he held and supported her as she collapsed into him, her knees buckling.

"Why have him Bind his wounds just to kill him?" Lin whispered after enough time had passed.

Tylle grunted, but no actual words escaped her lips.

Lin held her until soft, weak snores replaced shuddering sobs. He shifted so that he could lay her down on the dock. Then he moved to Aemun. The baby, the sweet, tiny baby, had grown silent, but Aemun had fallen onto his side, and his weight hadn't been on her. Azhalia was red-faced, and her swaddle was soaked in her father's blood. The ship's crew might have a wetnurse, but as it were, none were above deck. Lin brought her to his chest, shushing and rocking Azhalia until she seemed to fall asleep.

Searching the boat revealed waterskins, fresh fruit, and a pillow. As well as sailors hiding and a captain who insisted they'd already been paid and could either leave or stay. Lin drank the water so quickly it threatened to turn his stomach, and he gingerly placed the pillow under Tylle's head. Then he crept towards Aemun.

Aemun's pockets were empty, his thin silk robe as torn and ruined as his throat.

Leaving Tylle alone with Aemun, even if the man was a corpse, didn't sit right. Lin looked up the cliffside to the tunnel opening and the high, once seemingly unscalable walls of the Ferrucium.

Lin looked down at the dried blood crusted in his palm lines, then checked the baby's face. Ruined as her wrappings were, her cheeks were rosy and not from blood.

Two horn blasts echoed through the night air and resounded from the cliffside.

Lin considered grabbing one of Tylle's daggers but shook his head. They'd fought enough. He'd fought enough. He stood still for a moment, settled beside Tylle, and lay on his back beside her. The baby was against his chest, and he stared up at the night sky, wishing there was even a sliver of the moon to ease his tension. Once she awoke, he'd ask her the question that was burning into his heart the way Azhalia burned against his chest.

Chapter Thirty

Broken Bone

Tylle groaned and Lin stared at her. He'd been watching her for a while, her soft breaths balanced against the hard slap of wave on wood. Blood stained her cheeks, and the braid the villager had done for her was a tangled mess. But she was alive. And so was Lin. And so was Margie's child.

Pael had come at some point, offering water and more of that mushroom stew concoction. He muttered and mumbled and seemed none too pleased to see Aemun's corpse. He spat near it and looked like he planned to retrieve his bolt from the man's dismembered arm but stopped when he saw the metal bands encircling it. "Plan to keep the metal?"

Lin shrugged, and Pael left it alone, lingering for a bit before leaving up the path to the Weavers' tunnels.

Eventually, the sun broke across the water, blinding at the angle it cut over the rocky cove.

Tylle groaned and twitched and seemed as if she wanted to sit up. Lin placed a hand on her shoulder and whispered. "Don't overdo it." His throat was scratchy, and the words came out as if he'd swallowed gravel.

Lin pressed his chin to his chest and stared down at the light-haired baby he held. He hadn't noticed before, but she looked so strikingly much more like Aemun than Margaret. She'd stopped crying before the sun rose, and now soft, whimpering sounds of sleep came from her. He needed to clean her and find her food.

Despite Lin's attempts to keep her resting, Tylle half-rose into a sitting position and blinked several times before her eyes finally rested on Aemun's corpse. Her eyes had no joy, and her lips became a tight line. "I planned to let him live. I really did," she said. "We'd get information from him and wring the truth from his bones. Erias will not be pleased."

Lin nodded. "It was your choice to make. And I had permission to kill him if he betrayed the cause. He deserved death."

Tylle shook her head. "No. We—I should have pressed him for information. Pressed him into Erias's service. But... but when I saw him breaking the very Tenets that he... that he killed Margie for just to save his own life. I lost myself."

Lin shrugged. "Or you found yourself," he whispered. Lin didn't have the heart to tell her why Aemun claimed he slew his partner. Because she wanted to end his ambitions and settle down with him.

Tylle hung her head and noticed the waterskin resting on the dock between them. She lifted it and gulped down the remnants within.

Lin licked his lips and watched the stream of water that trickled from the corner of her mouth.

"And the Ferrucium?" she asked.

"I don't know. I've had my hands full," Lin said, nodding down at the child.

Tylle let her eyes rest on her niece for the briefest moment before turning away. Her hands folded in her lap, and she craned her neck to look at the tall cliffside and the keep that rested above them. "If we lost, the Reds would've come down here looking for Aemun, no?"

"Maybe. I don't know if Azhura would've let him get away. Blood relative or not. And Pael seemed to be coming and going of his own accord. Not that a pack of Reds would stop him going somewhere he had a mind to."

Tylle snorted in apparent agreement.

"Can't believe he had a ship ready to sail if things went poorly for him." Tylle held the water skin upside down, face twisting in pain.

"He seemed to think himself clever."

Tylle shrugged and sighed before letting her head fall back and staring at the early morning sky. "We should go and see the state of things."

"I... Tylle. I had a lot of time last night to think about things." Lin hoped his hard-beating heart wouldn't wake the infant.

"About what?" she asked. Her weight shifted, and she climbed slowly to her feet, wincing as her bandages pulled.

"Well, many things," he admitted. Some I can find no answer to, but some for which an answer would come swift if I simply voiced the question."

Tylle stilled and looked at him. Her eyes rested on his in such a way that Lin thought he might die for lack of breathing. And then her eyes drifted down to his chest, to her sister's baby that she hadn't once reached for.

"Tylle, we have a ship. With paid transportation to the Pellic Sea, to the Fentian port. We could go, the three of us."

It looked as if she didn't breathe. "I've never sailed, have you?" Her question came after a stretch of silence so severe that Lin would've thought he lost his hearing if the water behind hadn't continued slapping the dock.

"No."

"Lin... there is so much still left to do," Tylle whispered as she stretched to full height. "Aemun's threats of the King's retaliation. The re-education of our people. Teaching about Velkath and his kin. Making sure the mistakes of the false Weavers don't happen again. Rebuilding the villages ruined by the untethered. *Stopping* the untethered."

Lin blinked and stared down at her boots. "I know. All of that is important. But we have a chance here. A chance to get away from it all. We could be a family." He raised the baby slightly, enough to bring the focus to her wispy blonde hair and blood-stained wraps.

Tylle's hands were rough against his as she grabbed them. Calloused and sticky to the touch with dried blood she hadn't washed away. "I'm not ready. And I don't think you are either. There is too much to rebuild, both without and within. But I will make a promise to you."

Lin lifted his eyes to hers. "A promise?"

"We will breathe *together* when we have a moment to do it. And eat and talk and enjoy each other's company in a way we've been unable to until then."

Tylle pulled Lin into a gentle hug, her face angling down to the bundle in Lin's arms.

He breathed her in and squeezed back as lightly as he could. She smelled of sweat, blood, and the lightest fragrance of wildflowers.

"You saved me," she whispered. "In a way, I could never repay."

Lin shook his head, but the words he wanted to speak wouldn't come. He wanted to scream that she'd saved him and helped make him more whole for her being in his life. He finally felt like he'd found someone to whom he could be *bound*. "There is no debt," was all he could say.

"Take her," Lin whispered. Tears threatened his eyes, and the words didn't come easy from his throat. He knew it wasn't fair to think Tylle was taking his chance at a family from him, but it *felt* like that, didn't it? This was the perfect opportunity. And she didn't want to take it. Not with him, at least. Not now.

Tylle pulled away and stared at her boots. An emotion Lin couldn't place flashed across her face. "I can't."

"Now that we found her, got her back, what's the plan?" Lin asked. Azhalia squirmed, shifting slightly in the wrappings.

Tylle seemed to look everywhere but at the child. "We need to... we need to get back up there and ensure the battle was actually won. Aemun might've played Erias against the Ferrucium and King's Noose, but Azhura could still be a threat. Everything else is secondary." She shook her head. "You really shouldn't have let me rest this long."

Lin watched wordlessly as she began walking back up the cliffside trail. He looked back at the ship, but Tylle didn't glance back at him, and after several moments, he followed.

As sore and wounded as they were, it took far longer to climb up the path than either of them expected, but once they hit the tunnel's cool, dank air, their steps came easier.

The Chamber of Judgement felt colder than before. Any color the tapestry at the back once had seemed faded compared to the bright sky Lin had left. The spear he'd thrown still stabbed into the wall, and a ladder had been brought out, soldiers trying in vain to pull the weapon from the ruined tapestry. The sheets cut from it folded and limp in stacks on the floor. Crevices between the marbled tiles looked like dark Bludwieves. Weaver Azhura stood off to the side, hands bound with Weaves, a thicker robe placed over her to cover her bare breasts. Carine sat beside her, looking half as rough as Tylle but doubly as tired. Dark circles under her eyes like grave plots against her complexion.

"You killed him?" Azhura asked.

"I...," Tylle whispered. But Lin nodded and interrupted, remembering Tylle's words of guilt.

"She tried to stop me. But it's ultimately Aemun's fault—all of it. I gave him the same chance he gave me. His last act to save his pathetic skin was breaking the Binding Tenets. And that snapped something in me—like a cord pulled too taut."

Despite everything, Azhura shuddered, then wept openly. Lin wondered what it might feel like to lose a family member. Especially one he likely helped raise. But pity was one thing his heart didn't seem to hold.

"Is... is that my great-grandchild?" she whispered.

"If you see tomorrow and the days after, you still won't have any hand raising my sister's child. Not a single finger will touch her. Not a single sigh of exhaled breath," Tylle snapped at Azhura, and Carine shifted, prepared to get between them if necessary.

Countless corpses had been dragged out, but twenty or so remained. Prish was among them, her Stitched lips grotesque and unnerving. Her throat had a ragged gash across it. Denny and Jun were nowhere to be seen, and the stench of the death-soaked room became increasingly overbearing. "Should we go to the courtyard? Get some air?" Lin asked as he stared at the figure on the tapestry. Heroic smile at odds with the frustrated soldiers yanking at the spear that stabbed through the man's face.

Tylle looked around and took a half-limped step to the door.

"We have a tent with physikers set up just outside the walls of the inner hold. See to your wounds. Pael is coordinating efforts out there. There were some... uncooperative soldiers in the early hours, but they were dealt with. Others surrendered entirely. And still others sided with us, though half-heartedly. Thank you, Lindel, for your efforts."

Lin nodded, realizing Tylle had shambled ahead and ambled alongside her, walking through the halls.

"What do you plan to do now? Become a priestess again?"

"I never stopped."

"Is... is there a name you'd want to call her?" Lin whispered. "Azhalia sounds foreign. Like Azhura, and if you didn't wish her knowing her heritage—"

"I don't know. That bastard named her, did he not?" Tylle slowed before the exit and leaned against the stone wall. A group of three young boys pressed through the hall, soapy buckets in hand. By the cut of their hair and hollow cheeks, they looked like Ferrucium trainees. Tylle watched their backs as they walked over the ruined door and into the Chamber of Judgment.

"Lin... am I a bad person? Do you think me wicked?"

"For Aemun?" Lin whispered. He looked up at her, at the tenseness in her shoulders. "How could I?"

"Whenever I look at that child, I don't see my sister. I see the cost my sister *paid*. I see *him*. I'm thankful you're here to hold her. Because I can't. I won't." Perhaps Lin had ignored it. Tylle had been fantastic with those children on the road, but had she ever even reached for Azhalia when she cried?

Lin's heart sank like a stone in the sea. Her words a snare, rooting him into place. He could understand if Tylle didn't want a life with him, but the baby? "No," he lied. Perhaps she didn't know what she was saying. The stress, the loss, the dumping of all that emotion onto Aemun's corpse, maybe she'd left a bit of herself back there with it. A piece that might take time to return. But if she didn't want to raise the baby and didn't wish to let Azhura have anything to do with her, then what was left?

The walk to the marketplace seemed to stretch forever. Tylle limped along, strides ahead, never looking back, never relaxing. When they exited the court-yard, Lin's mouth fell open, and he shut his eyes. There were far more bodies than he'd expected. He'd done his damage, killing those soldiers who'd seemed to side with Aemun before his arrival, but when Carine said there had been opposition, Lin hadn't expected to see so many of his sworn brothers and sisters piled like logs for winter.

"W-what?" he asked weakly. "So many dead." Lin fought to keep his stomach down. He scanned the faces, searching, praying he didn't see Denro's gray hair and dark skin. He didn't, but the pile, the mound, was stacked tall.

Tylle frowned and shook her head. "Maybe they wouldn't stand down."

A sick knot twisted in Lin's stomach. He nodded toward a black tent that seemed to be a base of operations as soldiers moved in and out. His breaths were coming so fast he was sure he'd wake the baby. "D-doesn't matter now, I guess."

The tent was more of a tarp thrown over one of the last remaining vendor stalls that a fire hadn't consumed. At some point, the flames had been doused, but some sections still birthed dwindling smoke tails into the sky.

Laid out on a table made of stacked crates was a map of Danica, its borders, and the southern sea below it. Pieces were strewn about, most of them green-painted stones. Pockets of red-painted rocks were placed at various intervals, likely outposts, and near the border to the north. As Lin approached, a single soldier in the mottled blue-black livery of Hol's Land stepped forward, blocking his view.

"Tent is for—"

"Grimes, let them through," Pael's voice snapped.

Lin blinked and peered around the soldier to see Pael seated behind the crates. His face was drawn, and his wide-brimmed hat was pulled low over his eyes.

"You look awful," Pael mumbled.

"Thank you."

"Wasn't a compliment," Pael looked up and chuckled.

"For shooting him."

Pael nodded, looked up, and seemed to take in Tylle's and Lin's condition. "Triage is up the way, southern side of the outer hold. Grimes, send the birds out." Pael handed the soldier several rolled parchments.

"If any of those birds are meant for Grovetender, tell him that Aemun claimed King Lodram is already moving. It could have been a threat meant to stay our vengeance, but you never know."

"We are intimately informed on the motions of King Lodram's forces," Pael said. He swung his arm over the north-eastern end of the map at the scattered red stones. "But whether he moves in days, weeks, or decides to wait out the winter matters little. Carine says Azhura plans to cooperate, which is why we have any Reds alive and moving at all. We have Danica back in earnest with this occupation. And we don't plan to give it up so lightly now that we've gotten it." Pael sighed and nodded to a Ferrucium soldier with the embroidery of a captain. "Watch the tent, please." Pael lifted his eyes and scanned the churning crowd ahead of them. It looked like the citizens of the hold, those who worked the fields and managed the actual port, had gathered near the northern gate. His mouth twitched into a frown as he studied Tylle. "Physikers, come on. More of your people are there now anyways."

"Our people?" Lin asked.

"Carine's people."

Pael took the lead. He nodded at any passerby who did the same to him first and kept his eyes down other than that. A crowd of people, likely the citizens and merchants who had made up the population of the outer Ferrucium, shuffled around a cordoned area. The scent of spiced stew and bread carried through the air, vying against the smoke and death that refused to be bullied away by the breeze.

"I never thought the Ferrucium could be wounded," Lin whispered.

"All gods seem untouchable until they first bleed," Pael said.

Tylle snorted from beside Lin. "If they bleed, then they aren't Gods."

Pael shrugged and shook his head, cutting them through an area at the far right side of the courtyard where more tarps had been erected.

"In there. Let the physikers know I sent you." Pael paused, staring into the shadows of the nearest tent. "For what it's worth, I'm glad you two made it to the other side and haven't cracked." He tapped the side of his head and nodded at them. "Little Tylle, If I don't see you again for a while, take care of yourself."

"You too," Tylle said.

Lin remained silent and stared at the back of the man's head as he disappeared through the crowd they'd pressed through to get here. "He seems different," Lin said.

Tylle sighed, but whatever she thought about it, she kept to herself as she shuffled into the nearest tent. Lin followed behind, bringing his arm up to cover his nose as the stench of infection attacked him. There were six cots, side by side, with barely enough space to step between them. Faces with glassy, unfocused eyes stared back at Lin. Not one of them was familiar.

"Lindel." The voice made Lin pause. His heart jumped and rose and then choked him in his throat. It was Denro's voice. Denro was here. He had the Sight. He'd know Lin for a monster. For an untethered. Before Lin could reply, strong arms wrapped around him. Denro squeezed tight, and he smelled like clay and mud and travel and spring despite the chill in the air. Not a bit of his usual fragrances were about him.

What have you done? You were a part of this? You're a monster. All things he was sure he'd hear Denro say. "Six. I wasn't sure I'd ever see you again."

Lin adjusted his arms so Azhalia wasn't pressed so hard between them. "I'm alive. You're alive. I... I need to tell you so much."

Denro pulled back and stared at him, eyes going to all the places his Inlays rested. Denro's smile faltered at the sides, and tears glistened in his brown eyes, but he pressed his brow to Lin's and held his shoulders in his hands. "I'm sure you didn't wander in here by mistake. Go, see to your wounds. We will catch up before I leave."

"Before you leave?" But he'd just seen him again. Denro *couldn't* leave. Not now. Not with Tylle practically saying she didn't have time for him, not with the burgeoning war and the fact that they'd just reunited.

"Weaver Azhura has requested that I visit the Fentian scholars. If Danica is to survive this turmoil, their aid will be paramount. And I've... well, it's not easy to say, but I've given up my role within the Ferrucium. Not exactly by choice, but sometimes even choices not made for us are done in our best interest. I'll be a scholar."

Lin stared at the lines on the man's face, each marking a year or more on the road that could never be replaced. Lin's childhood dream may have been to meet the Fentian scholars and study what they had to teach, but Denro had never indicated it was something he might want to do. "You've been forced out."

A woman on the cot beside them groaned and heaved, growing still after a moment. And the air inside the tent grew more rancid.

"We will talk at length before I depart. But for now, get aid. And I'll handle this." Denro patted a satchel he wore strapped over his shoulder, and Lin realized his mentor wasn't wearing a Ferrucium cloak. Six, without it, he looked somehow thinner and frailer than Lin had expected. His short-cropped beard had lost most of the rich, dark colors it once had and was now a peppered white. Whatever he carried in the satchel, he didn't clarify, and he stepped from the tent briskly without another word.

Aside from the bed's occupants, no one else remained in the small, foul-smelling tent. No physiker.

"He seemed pleasant," Tylle said. "He was your mentor?"

Lin wiped his eyes with the back of his hand and nodded. "Come on," he urged. He took Tylle by her hand and led her out slowly. The more they'd walked, the more pronounced her limp had become. Together, they checked three other tents before Tylle grunted and leaned fully against Lin. Her pressure against him weighed more than all her words earlier. Between her at his side and the child on his chest, he was glad to be alive at that moment.

"Tylle." Jun came into view just as Lin heard him. His face was gaunt, and patches of flesh along his jaw flaked like shaved iron. The gray overcast did little to help his ashen complexion. His arm was in a sling, and the left side of his bald head bore stitches the length of Lin's hand. But he moved without aid and smiled politely when he saw them. He looked at the other wounded people gathered and waiting for assistance and shook his head. "Follow me," he mouthed.

The Ferrucium was rebuilding, not that there was much to rebuild. Aside from the soldiers who'd lost their lives and the fire that had taken out a modest section of vendor stalls, the coup had seen scarce downright destruction. But soldiers and civilians alike worked to ease the pain of a broken peace, even mere hours after the conflict. And all Lin had been able to do was walk, walk more, and finally find himself in someone's home. Based on the layer of dust on the furniture, it had been empty far longer than anything the assault might've caused.

The only things in the room were two chairs, a narrow, low table, and a hearth. There had been three or perhaps four chairs once, but the hearth was lit, and the fire within was eating away at broken pieces of kindling.

Denny lay on the floor, eyes closed, flesh pale, and beaded with sweat. Her right arm was missing below the elbow and bandaged against her chest.

Jun held up a finger to his lips as he led them in. He gestured toward the chairs, and Lin helped Tylle ease into the wooden seat.

Lin stared at Denny. "Will she be alright?"

Jun nodded and ran a hand across his shaven pate. "Should be. Hasn't woken up yet, knocked her head pretty hard."

"Hugo?" Tylle whispered.

Jun looked down, head shaking.

"And Prish?"

Jun grew quiet and then took an unsteady breath. "I haven't solved what Aemun held over her to get her to betray us like that. She hated the Ferrucium, hated the untethered, hated just about everything." He looked down at his hands.

Lin could hear what the man wasn't saying, remembering what Denny had said. The two had been close. Likely lovers. And he was doing his best to hold all the pain back. Prish hated everything except for Jun. Yet she had still betrayed him.

"Denny mentioned you two were close. Did Prish have any family?"

Jun shook his head. "None that I knew about. She couldn't speak, you know. The tongue was removed by Reds for her speaking out when she was younger. She Stitched her lips after that. Barely ate. Lost who she was and became who I knew. She signed, but that didn't do us any good trying to speak to her when she attacked." Jun's hands clenched into fists, and for a moment, Lin thought the man might start crying, but he exhaled and looked up at Tylle. "Let me see to your wounds. I trained to be a physiker long before deciding I was better at hurting people. Or rather before it was decided for me."

"Alright," Tylle whispered and turned to face the hearth. She shifted her tattered blouse off and leaned forward, elbows resting on her knees.

Lin paced, eyes darting back to Tylle's bare shoulders as Jun worked.

"I think I'll go to the library," Lin said softly.

Jun looked over his shoulder at Lin and barely nodded, gut clenched in his teeth as he worked stitches with his hands.

For some reason, seeing this man with his torso covered in Inlays using actual needles and threads made Lin smile. Not everything had to be Bindings and blades.

Lin moved like a ghost, haunting all the old places he'd visited as a child. There were more differences than just corpses and property damage. The more he stared at the familiar setting, the more twisted it became. He walked through the barracks where footlockers and trunks rested in front of cots, past the room he'd spent much of his youth in, through the food hall serving soup and bread.

Two well-dressed individuals manned the library, fitted blouses embossed with crimson stitches. They gave him a look but continued whispering among themselves as Lin stepped past.

Lin walked along the shelves, reading the spines of the tomes, looking for anything that might point toward Danica's true history. He walked past the alcove he'd spent many long nights reading in, searching for something he couldn't even describe. Anything that might prove Tylle correct in her claims. But despite the rows of tomes and the numerous shelves lining the expansive room, that familiar numbness settled over his heart. Azhalia woke, soft whimpers turning into angry cries. Lin held the child, rocking as he walked along the aisles and doing his best to avoid the stares of any who might chastise him.

"Can I help you?" One of the organizers approached, looking Lin up and down. She smelled like fresh-picked berries, but her expression made it clear she thought everyone else *didn't*.

Lin sighed and shook his head, turning away from the imperious woman.

"If *I* can't help you, then there is nothing here for you," she called.

Lin froze and turned his attention to the numerous books organized along the tabletop. Countless volumes of knowledge, each one curated by the Ferrucium. "I think you're right. More right than you might know."

Without another word, he walked from the library. Just by standing in the room, he could tell that there wasn't a single tome in there that might shed light on the truth. He felt it in his gut, as sure as he was that there might not be a chance at rest like this for a long while. Lin also didn't like how, despite all the individuals gathered, not one person asked about the crying child.

"Lin," Carine called from the hall door. She smiled pleasantly, one side of her mouth quirking up. Her eyes sparkled, and speckles of dried blood dotted her face. "Still haven't given that one a proper bath?"

"Oh." He hadn't, of course. Six, what was he meant to do with her? "I will. Or… I'll see that someone does."

Remorse flashed across her face. "Follow me." She led him through the guts of the Ferrucium, and Lin felt wholly digested. Lin wouldn't hazard to guess how she had known where the baths were, but she pulled towels and soaps from a cabinet on the wall and laid them out, gesturing to the water.

He'd never cleaned a child, let alone a baby, and Azhalia fussed and squirmed. Eventually, her father's blood was scrubbed tenderly from her chest and brow, and her soiled underclothes were changed and replaced with Carine's aid.

When they were finished, Carine sat to the side, bare feet dangling in the now murky water.

"Thank you," Lin said, clutching Azhalia tightly. She was crying, and she was likely hungry since she'd just been cleaned. He'd find a wet nurse.

"Of course. I wanted to offer you a spot in our little coterie. We've lost members we could never replace. I've known of Tylle for a time, and our talks on the road have led me to believe she'd be willing. But I barely know anything about you."

"And yet you'd offer me a place among your group?"

She twitched her left foot and pulled it from the water to rest with one arm dangling across her knee.

"Where else would you go? Azhura will be a figurehead if things go as planned, will work with the dukes and Erias, and things will change, but it will take time. It will take more than a coup to make Danica safe for people like us."

"I…" Lin struggled to find the words. "I wanted to remove all my markings, and Erias implied there was a way, but Aemun shed light on the truth of it."

"Do you know what's worse than trusting the tongue of a liar?"

Lin looked up at her sharply.

"Trusting the tongue of a liar who has proven time and time again to be just that. What did he tell you?"

"To flay myself alive," Lin whispered.

Carine nodded. "That might be a way, to be sure, but I've heard rumors that the Fentian scholars stopped doing that decades ago. They'd found another way. All they do is study magic and nature and the laws that govern both."

Lin frowned and cocked his head to the side. "I didn't know they studied the Binding Tenets."

"No. The real laws. The ones put in place long before faith ruled the Wieving of our people… this might be presumptuous… but I think I'd have an assignment for you if you're interested. It would allow you to be far from Grovetender's branches as he calms himself from losing the chance to interrogate Aemun."

"So, a forced exile?"

"No," Carine stretched out the word and tapped her knee. "A journey to meet the scholars of Fentis. We'll send a bird with the news, but putting a face to the crisis, someone so earnest in what being a Ferrucium soldier was meant to stand for would surely work better than words on parchment."

Denro was going there. He'd said as much. A lump formed in Lin's throat. It was something he'd always wanted to do. And Carine seemed to be doing him a kindness.

"Work better toward what end?" he managed to ask around the tightness rising out of him.

"Toward aid against Ladrica. The more I consider it, the more I'm sure there isn't a single person more suited to this task. I'll be busy working with Weaver Azhura to ensure the occupation continues running smoothly." She leaned in closer and whispered, "Though I don't trust her nearly so much as she expects I do. Jun and Denny will be training anyone who wishes to Inlay themselves. And Tylle will teach the old ways and take any newly recruited children back to their homes if they want."

Lin nodded and pulled Azhalia up to his shoulder. "I'll do it. I'll go, but after I deliver the message, I'm done. Deal?"

Carine dipped her foot back into the water and kicked it at Lin. "There will be a war. Aemun ensured that. We can't afford not to have you. Will you at least consider fighting? I saw what you were capable of. A little more practice, and you'd be as good as any of us."

"Answer me this. Are you a Wiever or a Binder?" Lin shielded Azhalia from the water drops, the coarse towel used to dry her now bundling her.

"I don't care what they want to label us. Tylle is rooted in the old ways, old teachings. Me? I'm a survivor. You?"

"Sometimes I feel like a loose thread, waiting to be snipped or tugged past my tearing point. Other times, I feel like an anchor line, holding the whole thing together. But... the more I think about it, the more I like the title Wiever." Lin stared down at his hand that had started it all. The Bludwieve, representing his Uethe, hadn't gone away. Maybe the Fentian scholars had an answer for that, too. Or perhaps he'd find more questions in their ivory tower by the sea. But even if it meant leaving Tylle, leaving the Ferrucium, he had so much to tell Denro that it made the idea of departing a tiny bit tolerable.

Carine rose and offered that same polite smile. "I'll draft a letter, and we can discuss talking points before your departure. And feed her. I'm sure she hungers for far more than the rocking of a Wiever."

"And what am I going to do with you?" Lin whispered into Azhalia's ear.

Epilogue

A Beautiful Tapestry

Lin slowed Nebra, easing her over the hill and bringing the entire city of Fentis into view. Tips of ivory-tipped towers had been visible since midday. Still, as magnificent as they appeared, they didn't do justice to the sprawling cityscape surrounding them. Turrets, walkways, and bridges dominated the view, and the closer they got, the harder it was for Lin to breathe. He leaned into Nebra, stroking her neck. The past weeks had been all Lin might've ever hoped for. No escorts. No untethered. No worrying that he was hunted. Just him, Nebra, and Denro on the road.

"It's beautiful," Lin said. He wished Tylle was there to see it with him. But Mellyr, the name he'd decided for Margie's daughter, which suited her far better than the foreign-sounding Azhalia, kept him plenty company. She pulled on his ear and made a garbled cooing noise from the bundle on his back.

Denro had taken to the child immediately and had even proved himself to still be a proficient educator by teaching Lin proper ways to hold her so that her head was supported. Clean her so that a rash wouldn't develop. Sing to her so that she might sleep. Though Denro's deep baritone proved far more capable no matter how hard Lin tried.

But as they'd gotten closer throughout the day, Denro's demeanor had shifted. He hadn't voiced awe at the towers or sights around it and shifted nervously in his saddle.

"Is something the matter?" Lin asked.

"No. Why?" Denro licked his lips and brushed a hand over his beard as if flattening the peppered bush might make it more manageable.

"No reason," Lin lied. Perhaps the man was tired. They'd been on the road well over a handful of weeks. "Just wanted to ensure we were good before heading in there." Lin nodded toward Fentis on the horizon.

"We're perfectly fine." Denro touched his nose and stretched his back, glancing over his shoulder.

"I almost forgot to tell you," Lin said, noting Denro's movement. "There was a man in Lyre, the Alderman, he claimed, with a nose so flat you'd think he'd been hit by a shovel. Or that his pet goat had bitten out a piece of it. Claimed she could *smell* the magic." Lin waved his hands like a pauper show's magician might. He slapped the saddle horn and waited for Denro to laugh, but only the barest smile brushed his lips. "See, something is the matter."

Denro shifted in his saddle at Lin's words, creases forming in his brow. "Lindel," Denro started. His voice was smooth and low. "I've had time to think on this journey. It's a dangerous thing, as we both know. And while I chose not to fight, what you and those people have done... well, the more I consider it, the less it sits with me. You're like a son, but even family can be foolish and disagree."

"Denro," Lin whispered. "Why didn't you say something sooner?" He blinked twice, the towers in the distance blurring. "That's not fair."

"If we were to speak about fairness, about what is or isn't fair, I'm not sure I'd ever find silence or solace again. Many things aren't *fair*, like returning home from a round of evaluations and being woken in the night to learn that an assault on the Weavers is taking place. Then, finding not just untethered or rebel Binders but *traitors*? That isn't *fair*."

Lin blinked away tears. Denro spoke softly and stared at Lin the entire time. His beard had grown out, peppered with streaks graying entirely at the bottom during the time on the road.

"I'm not sorry for the part I played in all of that. But I am sorry we didn't have a chance to discuss how I felt before it happened. You taught me so much—"

"Your *feelings* would not have swayed mine!" Denro raised his voice. "An eye for an eye is not the way to right perceived wrongs. And now, the King will send *his* soldiers, send *his* Binders. The ones meant to keep our people in check. Far more than the few Noosemen sent to try to keep the peace. The Ferrucium was a pyre. Were things and histories burned that might be better kept untouched? Perhaps. But it kept the *shadows* at bay. And I don't simply mean the untethered!"

Denro's hands trembled, tugging at the reins lightly. The flood of words that finally broke was too much and shook him with each syllable.

Mellyr yanked harder at Lin's ear lobe, and Lin turned to look into the child's face. She was swaddled to his back, but the more she grew, the less she liked being restrained.

Lin nodded silently and pressed Nebra forward. Her hooves ate the road steadily, and Denro's mount kept three strides behind her. In his excitement to ride with Denro, he hadn't noticed how little the man had first opened up. How quick he'd been to leave Lin once seeing him at the Ferrucium. And now he knew why. If only their relationship could be mended with Bindings as easily as flesh was. He tried to swallow, but his throat felt tight, and he breathed ragged gasps.

Walls, more windbreaks than anything like what the Ferrucium had, looked carved from pure-white stone. And the towers appeared as if they were made of the same. Lin knew countless scholars studied within those towers and dedicated their lives to peace and searching out the truth of the unknowable. Hopefully, it also held people who knew Danica's actual history. And that they'd be willing to disclose it once they found out war was coming, even for them. Especially for them if Erias correctly anticipated King Lodram's retaliation. But Fentis was as far from the Northern border as you could get.

As Lin drew closer and the walls loomed higher, he blinked. His neck ached from craning to look at the towers, but every jolt on Nebra's back caused a strange blur of flashes around the buildings that were impossible to ignore. Mellyr grasped one of Lin's braids and held firm.

"Ow, stop it, Melly." Lin shook his head, but she didn't let go. "Denro," Lin asked, slowing Nebra. "Denro, do you see that?"

Denro didn't answer and pulled up alongside Lin. He stared up, eyes flicking from tower to tower and eventually resting on the tallest one that stabbed the horizon. "Mhmm."

Lin licked his lips and stood in his stirrups, sucking in a sharp breath as the air around the towers, or perhaps the white stone itself, shimmered with Bindings. If Tylle was correct and the color of the Binding reflected the caster's *spul* as they forced the magic into existence, what did these hues mean?

In shimmering swathes, like nets wrapped around the towers from base to tip, opaque blue and green Bindings floated around the stone. Lin squinted and tried to look from a separate angle. Maybe they didn't hover and were worked into the walls themselves, but that still didn't explain the color.

"What do you think it means that they're that color?" Lin asked.

A sigh that seemed to rattle Denro's lungs escaped him, and he shook his head. "I don't know."

Lin laughed and then saw how serious Denro's expression was as he spoke. "You come to be a scholar and don't care about the mysteries of Bindings?"

Denro's lips tightened into a line, and then he said, "My options were limited. The Ferrucium won't ever be the same. Lin, I was retired because of my connection to you. And Erias wanted all Evaluators replaced by his own men. So, my choices were to die fighting, join the forces that had stabbed the heart of the Ferrucium like a knife in the dark, or journey to Fentis and, when given a chance, encourage them. Beg them. Demand on old rites that they don't engage in the war to come. And demand I will."

Without a second look back, Denro rode past Lin through the ever-open gates of Fentis. Lin followed, hurt but unable to look away from the buildings. Lin would deliver his message and Denro his own, but maybe he could find common ground with his old mentor. The sooner he could give his message and convince them to aid the rebellion, the sooner Lin could return to Tylle. Not that she'd given him much reason to, but she had become his guidepost, and the time away from her had just proven that to him. There was an ache near his heart when he thought of how he traveled without her. But she'd chosen to stay and teach those willing to learn the old ways. That, and Tylle couldn't stand the sight of Mellyr. She hadn't even approved of the name. But Mellyr had seemed to smile at it. And it *felt* right compared to Azhalia.

Lin rubbed his eyes and urged Nebra forward through the gate behind Denro.

About the author

After a drunken game of D&D Greg DM'd ended rather splendidly, his closest friends told him he needed to write stories. A hobby that had always burned fiercely in his heart but that he set aside to handle the various hurdles of life. Greg took passion to pen (so to speak), and after many trials, errors, and learning spurts, he finally finished his first novel. When he's not writing, he's spending time with his amazingly supportive wife, playing pickleball or video games, and, of course, reading. Joe Abercrombie is one of his largest modern inspirations, and he wouldn't have started writing if not for the many amazing worlds created by so many other talented authors.

Other works:

Stones, Stars and the Storms Between

www.ingramcontent.com/pod-product-compliance
Lightning Source LLC
Chambersburg PA
CBHW022018310726
48972CB00006B/1708